WRONG PLACE WRONG TIME

OTHER COVENANT BOOKS

BY E. JAMES HARRISON:

Chariots to Jordan

The Cross Bearer

WRONG PLACE WRONG TIME

A SUSPENSE NOVEL

E. JAMES HARRISON

Covenant Communications, Inc.

For my wife, Debbie, who, more than anyone else in the world, deserves a heartfelt thank-you. She's tolerant of my adventures and is always—okay, usually—even a willing participant. Not only has she survived some of the stuff in this novel, but enough time has passed that we can talk about it without her palms getting sweaty. Which is a good thing because I like holding her hand, except when it's sweaty.

Cover image: *Foggy Empty Street At Night* © Gremlin. Courtesy of istockphoto.com

Published by Covenant Communications, Inc.
American Fork, Utah

Printed in the United States of America
First Printing: June 2019

26 25 24 23 22 21 20 19   10 9 8 7 6 5 4 3 2 1

ISBN: 978-1-52440-714-8

ACKNOWLEDGMENTS

I WANT TO THANK ALL of the people at Covenant Communications. It takes a lot of people to get a book into readers' hands, and they all do it with dedication. I'd especially like to thank Kami Hancock and Hannah Burr Bischoff. Kami is a gifted and precise editor with an amazing eye for detail. Hannah is probably the reason you picked up this book. She designed the cover and is a talented graphic designer. Thanks to both of you. This novel is much better because of your efforts.

There are several law-enforcement agencies that play important roles in this novel. To the real men and women of the United States Coast Guard Helicopter Interdiction Tactical Squadron (HITRON) as well as FBI agents and United States Department of Homeland Security officers who stand between us and violent people who would do us harm, I say thank you. Because you willingly risk your lives, we can sleep with both eyes closed.

Finally, and most sincerely, thanks to you, the reader. You are the reason I write. I hope you enjoy the time you spend within these pages.

PROLOGUE

It had become a ritual. United States Coast Guard Lieutenant Commander Matt Bidwell shoehorned himself into the copilot seat of the MH-65 Dolphin helicopter and carefully taped a small photograph to an uncluttered spot on the panel. With a smile, he kissed the tip of his index finger and lightly touched it to the image of the woman. He repeated the action twice more, lightly touching the two blanket-wrapped bundles nestled in the woman's arms.

Beside him in the pilot's seat, thirty-four-year-old Commander Jason Higgins barely noticed the process. It had happened so many times over the past two months that he'd come to expect it. Still, he couldn't stop himself from giving a slight jab. "Six months," he said as he pulled out a binder with the preflight checklist.

"Six months what?" Matt replied as he flipped a switch on the cluttered instrument panel.

"That's how long I give you before you stop the kissing routine whenever we head out on a mission," Higgins said with a nod toward the photograph.

"You're just jealous because you and Steph don't have any kids," Bidwill jabbed back.

"We have dogs, remember?"

"It's not the same, believe me."

"I know. We feed them once a day, they go to the bathroom by themselves, they don't get us up in the middle of the night, and if we want to go somewhere, we take them to a boarding kennel."

Bidwell shook his head as he pulled his own large binder from beside his seat and began flipping pages. "Someday, when you're an old man sitting alone in your rocking chair, you're going to wish you had kids."

"Maybe," Higgins replied as he began flipping switches, turning dials, and concentrating on the array of lights and instruments coming to life. Several minutes later, Higgins eased the bright-orange and white chopper off the rolling deck of the coast guard cutter *Diligence*. Clear of the ship's deck and superstructure, he pushed the helicopter's cyclic forward, causing the nose to dip slightly to allow the chopper's jet engines to push it through the night air.

While Higgins flew, Bidwell busied himself, entering frequencies into various communications radios and punching data into the onboard flight management system. For the next twenty minutes, except for an occasional exchange about the helicopter's performance and a little banter about babies and dogs, little was said as they sliced through the inky-black night. Bidwell repositioned the microphone attached to his helmet so it barely touched his lips and said, "Just once I'd like those weather guys to get it right." Pointing to the weather radar screen on the instrument panel, he said, "The storm looks bigger and angrier than their forecast."

Higgins cast a quick glance at the massive red blotch that covered much of the screen and swore. "Will we make the intercept before we hit that sucker?"

Bidwell punched numbers into the helicopter's flight management computer and compared the results to the weather radar's display. He gave his head half a shake. "It's too close to call. If anything, we'll probably catch the boat about the same time we hit the outer fringe of the thunderstorm." Swallowing, he added, "Are you sure you want to try this, boss?" Nodding toward the blotch on the radar screen, he added, "That's packing a lot of energy."

He had barely spoken the words when a little bubble of turbulence bounced the helicopter. It was a small jolt but enough to cause Bidwell to say, "At five hundred feet, I don't mind turbulence." Down at fifty, where they would be flying when they chased the boat, if they hit a strong downdraft, they were done. There was strain in his voice when he added, "I just got my twins; I'm not ready for them to be fatherless yet."

Higgins acknowledged the comment with a sideways glance. Then, into his microphone, he said, "Hey, Gunny, how you doing back there?"

Petty Officer Third Class Scott Robinson, "Gunny" to anyone who knew him, was strapped into a jump seat in the helicopter's main cabin. The tall, lanky West Texan was the third member of the helicopter's crew, and without his skill, the two men seated in the front of the helicopter would likely not be able to count this mission a success.

"Doin' jest fine, sir," Robinson drawled, giving his seatbelt and shoulder straps an extra tug.

"The radar is painting an ugly picture. Lots of red with only a little yellow and almost no green showing up," Higgins began. "The *Diligence* just radioed and wants to know if we're going to stay in pursuit or turn back. I think the bad guys are going to try to outrun us and hide in the storm."

For sixty seconds, anxious chatter flew back and forth as the three men haggled over the chance of success, their abilities, the helicopter's capabilities, and a dozen other issues. At the end of it, Higgins scrunched up his mouth and fell into silent thought. After a moment he looked at his copilot and said, "Radio the *Diligence*; tell them we're going to give it a shot." Then, almost as an afterthought, he added, "And we're getting close enough to the target we should go lights out."

Bidwell made a quick radio call to the ship and then said, "Lights out," as he reached up and flipped three small switches above his head. Instantly, every exterior light went out, and the helicopter was swallowed in the night's blackness.

As another small bounce of turbulence bobbled the helicopter, Gunny said, "This could shape up to be a li'l like ridin' a bull. But you know what? I'd rather be up here than down there."

"You got that right," Bidwell chimed in. "Six-foot seas and doing forty-five knots, they're probably barfing everywhere."

Higgins shot Bidwell a glance that said *Cut the chatter* as he manipulated the helicopter's controls to keep the machine flying straight and level.

A minute later, as Bidwell studied the icons on a radar screen, he said, "Hold back, Jason; they've slowed."

Higgins immediately slowed the helicopter and said, "Get HITRON control on the radio. We're going to catch up in a few minutes, and I want our intercept clearance before we do."

Bidwell leaned forward and selected the radio frequency for the coast guard's Helicopter Interdiction Tactical Squadron based in Jacksonville, Florida. "Mother Goose, Shark 947," Bidwell said into his microphone.

"Go ahead, 947."

"Shark 947 is approximately one to five minutes from target vessel, requesting initial intercept clearance."

After a brief pause, the radio crackled with, "Shark 947, you are cleared to identify subject vessel."

Bidwell acknowledged the clearance. Then, with a bit of apprehension in his voice, he said to Higgins, "You heard the man. Let's go."

"Gunny?" Higgins said into his microphone. "We're cleared to identify. Better get ready." At the same moment, both Higgins and Bidwell activated their night-vision goggles, transforming what had been pitch-blackness into eerie shades of green, gray, and white. Smiling at his newfound vision, Higgins put the helicopter into a shallow dive. In less than thirty seconds they were flying more than one hundred sixty-five miles an hour, barely fifty feet above the sea's white-capped waves.

Gunny's voice crackled through the intercom. "Remind me what it is we're looking for."

Bidwell keyed his mic and said, "Give me a sec; I've got a copy of the drug enforcement communiqué." Pulling a folded piece of paper from a zippered pocket in the leg of his flight suit, he scanned the lengthy paragraph for a description of the boat that was suspected of carrying two tons of cocaine with an estimated street value of twenty million dollars. "Lemme see. It says the suspect vessel is forty-eight feet; the manufacturer is Donzi; it's painted tangerine and white, with teal graphics. It has three outboard motors—"

"There she is!" Higgins interrupted as the ghostly image of the boat came into focus in his goggles. "One o'clock, two hundred yards."

Bidwell scanned the black ocean for only a second before saying, "Got it."

Manipulating the controls, Higgins guided the helicopter until it was fifty feet above and one hundred yards behind the boat. Then he slowed until he matched the boat's speed. With no exterior lights to betray their presence and the sound of their engines drowned out by the howling wind and the boat's own motors, they hung in the sky, stalking the boat's unsuspecting occupants.

Bidwell leaned forward until his goggles were almost touching the helicopter's windshield. "She's at least forty feet long. Appears to be a Donzi, but I can't tell for certain. She does have three big motors hanging off the back end. I'd say we've got a match."

From the back of the helicopter, Gunny said into his microphone, "I agree. Can't confirm the colors though."

"Call HITRON," Higgins ordered. "Tell them we have tentative ID."

A fraction of a minute later a voice burst into Bidwell's headset. "Shark 947, you are directed to intercept the suspect vessel, and the use of force is authorized."

"Gunny," Higgins said. "Game on."

"Yeees, sir," Gunny replied with a touch of glee in his voice. Sliding the side door of the helicopter open, Gunny did what he was very good at doing. Moving cautiously in the noisy blast of air caused by the helicopter's rotor, he installed an M240 machine gun into a turret. "Ready when you are, Commander."

Edging the helicopter forward until it was directly abeam the boat, Higgins made minute adjustments to the helicopter's controls and perfectly matched the boat's speed. "Begin intercept checklist," he ordered as he positioned the helicopter fifty feet above the tops of the waves and the length of a football field to the left of the boat.

"Law enforcement light on," Bidwell said as he flipped a switch that caused the intense bright-blue light to begin blinking under the belly of the helicopter.

"Identification light on," Bidwell called as he flipped a second switch. Bright lights instantly bathed the entire aircraft, perfectly illuminating the bright-orange helicopter with its distinctive U.S. Coast Guard emblem on the tail. The once-invisible helicopter suddenly gleamed bright orange in the black sky.

Switching a very high frequency marine radio to the emergency channel, Bidwell pressed a button and said, "This is U.S. Coast Guard helicopter hailing a forty-five-foot civilian boat with three outboard motors approximately . . . uh . . . 24' 14" North and 81' 49" West. Please respond."

Higgins and Bidwell watched through their night-vision goggles as the boat's driver craned his neck to look up at the helicopter then began stomping his feet madly on the deck of the boat.

Bidwell pressed the button of his microphone again and repeated the same message but added, "You are in U.S. waters and ordered by U.S. Coast Guard personnel to stop for boarding."

"You're not very persuasive, Matt. All they did was speed up," Higgins said as he increased the helicopter's speed slightly to match the suddenly quickened pace of the boat. "How far away is the intercept boat the *Diligence* sent out?" Higgins asked.

"About—"

"Doesn't matter," Higgins interrupted. "Look at them; they're going to try to make a run for it."

Bidwell looked down as the sleek boat again suddenly picked up speed, slamming headlong into the growing waves.

"Gunny," Higgins ordered into his microphone. "Stitch the sea."

"With pleasure, Commander," Gunny replied. With a huge grin on his face, Gunny began a routine he had performed countless times. Aiming the snout of the long-barreled machine gun, he said, "Guns hot!" and squeezed the trigger.

Like a man watering a garden with a hose, Gunny quickly raised and lowered the machine gun three times. Firing nearly a thousand rounds per minute, the gun laid down a lethal barrage of bullets, not into the boat, but fifty feet in front of it. With every fifth bullet glowing bright red as a phosphorous tracer, the stream of bullets appeared to be a solid red line that looked like an overgrown *Star Wars* lightsaber. Gunny had stitched the sea with bullets, and the message was clear: *Stop!*

But the boat didn't stop. Instead it began a series of sweeping S-turns. Gunny shook his head. "These guys are plain stupid," he said into his mic. "Do they really think I can't stop them?" Securing the machine gun, he hefted a Barrett M107 .50-caliber sniper rifle from its cradle and secured it in a set of canvas straps that would shield it from the helicopter's vibration. With the rifle secure, he shoved his night-vision goggles up onto his helmet and peered through the rifle's sophisticated scope. Even in the darkness the sight picture was as clear as day. Gunny first put the crosshairs on the man driving the boat then slowly shifted his aim to the nearest of the three massive outboard motors. Then he said into his mic, "Can't make the shot. Forward twenty."

Higgins responded by inching the helicopter forward twenty feet.

"Up ten," Gunny said, still peering through his scope. "Forward ten . . . forward five . . . HOLD!" Taking a deep breath and then letting it out, he gently squeezed the trigger. A fraction of a second later one of the boat motors exploded from the bullet's impact, sending hundreds of bits and pieces of metal and plastic hurtling through the air.

Still peering through the scope, Gunny shifted his sights to the driver and watched as he yanked the boat's throttle levers to neutral then instantly slumped forward over the steering wheel. It was then Gunny saw a chunk of metal protruding out the back of the driver's neck. "Target hit and they've stopped, but we have a casualty. The driver has shrapnel in the back of his neck," Gunny announced.

"Nice shot, Gunny," Bidwell said, ignoring the report of the casualty.

But Gunny didn't respond. Examining the boat through the rifle's scope, his eyes opened in horror as a man staggered up onto the deck with a shoulder-fired missile launcher in his hands. "Commander!" Gunny shouted into his microphone. "They've got a missile launcher!"

"What?" Higgins shouted.

Gunny pulled the rifle tighter to his shoulder for a better look through the scope. "It looks like one of those old British Blowpipe missiles terrorists use. Can I kill him?" Gunny screamed while staring into his scope.

"Is he pointing it at us?" Higgins replied frantically, holding the helicopter's position relative to the boat.

"Negative, but I'm sure he's gonna," Gunny drawled in alarm.

"You know the rules of engagement. If he aims at us, take him out, but only after he aims at us," Higgins ordered, holding the helicopter as steady as he could to give Gunny every advantage.

Gunny put the crosshairs of the scope solidly on the chest of the man standing on the deck, matching every movement of the rolling boat. As the man lifted the missile launcher to his shoulder and pointed it at the helicopter, Gunny squeezed the trigger.

At that exact moment, the helicopter hit a pocket of turbulence, sending it bouncing erratically upward and causing Gunny's bullet to fly harmlessly into the ocean a half mile from the man. In the same instant, the man on the deck pressed the trigger on the launcher, sending a rocket-propelled missile hurtling toward the helicopter at nearly a thousand miles per hour. The missile slammed into the tail, blowing the fan into a thousand pieces.

With nothing to counteract the massive torque the twin jet engines were sending to the main rotor, the helicopter began spinning like a merry-go-round on steroids. Through the first two rotations, Higgins and Bidwell instinctively did everything their training had preconditioned them to do. Midway through its third rotation, Higgins blacked out, his body unable to withstand the phenomenal centrifugal forces tearing at him. Bidwell lasted a fraction of a second longer, just enough to catch one final glimpse of the picture of his wife and twin babies.

Gunny was not so fortunate. Partway through the first rotation, he lost his death grip on the handhold beside the helicopter's open door. As his fingers slipped from around the metal, centrifugal force flung him into the machine gun, breaking his back and tossing both him and the machine gun out the door. The machine gun instantly tore loose from its restraints and whirled through the night air, sinking into the sea two hundred yards from the helicopter. Had Gunny's safety straps broken, he might have been tossed as well, but they didn't. Suspended outside the helicopter by his straps, he whirled in a circle like a ball at the end of a string.

In a little less than two seconds, the out-of-control helicopter made six complete rotations before it rolled onto its side. As it did, the first of the helicopter's four carbon-fiber rotor blades shattered as it struck the water, catapulting the machine sideways and slamming it into the sea so violently the cabin exploded as if a bomb had gone off inside. For a moment, most of the wreckage rode atop the churning sea. Then, slowly, the largest pieces of the mangled craft began slipping below the surface.

As the main cabin with its three dead crewmen began its three-hundred-foot descent to the blackness of the ocean floor, the man standing on the deck of the boat tossed the missile launcher into the sea and struggled in the wave-tossed boat to the driver's seat. Grabbing the injured-but-still-breathing driver under his armpits, the gunman dragged him to the side of the boat and hefted him into the ocean. Inching back to the driver's seat, he grasped the throttles of the two remaining outboard motors and shoved them forward, sending the boat leaping into the face of the storm and speeding away from the sinking helicopter.

CHAPTER ONE

The radical mastectomy had both taken and given something to Marena Walker. The taking had occurred four days after her fifty-seventh birthday and was over and done in two hours and forty-five minutes. The giving back had been longer and slower in coming.

For two years after her surgery, Marena had done daily battle with a host of emotional dragons. Some she had slain; others had simply refused to die. She'd spent hours with therapists and counselors, trying to sort out her thoughts and emotions, but salvation had come from a carrot, an egg, and a very old woman with a hunched back.

They had entered the reception area of the prosthetics lab at about the same time, Marena by herself and the old woman escorting a woman who could have been her daughter or, more likely, her granddaughter. The old woman had been sitting kitty-corner from Marena, their knees almost touching. Twenty minutes after their arrival, the old woman's young companion had been ushered to another room, leaving Marena and the old woman alone. After sitting quietly for several minutes and despite Marena's intense focus on her magazine, the old woman had said to her, "Dear, if you don't mind me saying, you don't seem so good. Are you all right?"

Marena had looked up briefly from the magazine, whose pages she'd been flipping fast enough to fan a fire, and snapped, "I'm fine." The words had come out with an edginess that was both apparent and intended.

The old woman had dismissed the retort with a gentle smile and said, "Are you sure?"

"Excuse me?" Marena had fired back.

The old woman had sat awkwardly in the chair, the bulge in her back making it impossible for her to sit straight, her hands resting on top of a small black purse on her lap. A thousand wrinkles had testified to at least eight decades of life. Her white hair had thinned to the point that, despite obviously careful brushing, her scalp was visible through the wisps of curls and waves. Her lips had worn a light coating of red lipstick and were pulled back in a slight smile, giving her face a kindly expression. Lifting an arthritic finger, she had pointed and said, "I can tell you're not fine by the way you're treating that poor magazine. You're not reading a word, and you're nearly ripping out the pages when you turn them."

It had been an awkward start to the conversation. Twice Marena had tried shutting it down with stinging responses, but the woman had persisted, brushing aside the rebuffs with her infuriating gentle smile and soft voice. Nearly fifteen minutes had passed before a pearl of wisdom emerged that was the beginning of what the mastectomy gave back to Marena.

"You see," the old woman had said, her hands still folded in her lap, "boiling water softens a carrot and hardens an egg. The water's the same; it's the way the carrot and the egg react that's different." Pointing to Marena's chest, she'd continued. "You can let this harden you and make you bitter, or you can let it soften you and turn you into something more than you think you are."

That night Marena had gone home and placed one carrot and one egg on the top shelf of her refrigerator. For a week, every time she'd opened the refrigerator door, she'd looked at them and asked herself the same question: "Am I a carrot or an egg?"

Marena had become a carrot. It wasn't an event; it had been a process, a two-year battle with its share of wounds. She'd slain the twin dragons of self-pity and anger in the first few months. Along the way, she'd surrendered her sometimes abrupt and prickly attitude and, for the most part, reined in her quick temper. Dealing with the changed appearance of her body had taken longer. That dragon hadn't fallen with one fatal blow; she'd beat it into submission by shifting her focus from equating womanhood with her physical appearance to a more holistic approach of having an overall healthy body. There had been no face-lift, tummy tuck, liposuction, or other surgical magic to enhance her 5'4", 118-pound body; she had just decided that part of being a carrot was taking care of her body—all of it. So Marena walked—her fifty-nine-year-old knees rebelled at running—for thirty minutes every morning and swam in the community pool at least twice each week.

Eighteen months into her effort, her husband had suggested that because she enjoyed swimming so much, perhaps they should try scuba diving. They did, and she had quit after her first ocean dive, terrified by a sense of claustrophobia. In the process, though, she had discovered she loved snorkeling, which was why she was now lying on a beach in the Dominican Republic.

Getting up from the chaise lounge, Marena did a deep back stretch and gazed out over the Caribbean's turquoise water. Smoothing back a few strands of her dark chestnut hair, she pulled a tube of sunscreen from her bag, squeezed long lines of the fragrant lotion onto her forearms and thighs, and then methodically spread the sunscreen onto every part of her body not protected by her swimming suit. Body glistening, she nudged the lounge with her toe until it was perfectly aligned with the sun's rays and lay down on her back.

Basking in the sun's skin-damaging rays was a chink in her health-conscious armor, but she reasoned that with her naturally dark hair and olive skin, she had a bit of added protection that blonde-haired, blue-eyed people didn't enjoy.

Ten minutes after dropping down on the chaise lounge, just as she was beginning to drift to sleep, she felt the coolness of a shadow fall over her. Rolling her head sideways and cracking her eyes open just enough to see her husband silhouetted in the sunlight, she waved her hand as if shooing him away and said, "You're blocking my sunshine."

"I intend to. But don't think of me as blocking your sunshine. Think of me as a shield between you and skin cancer."

Marena touched the oily coating on her arm and said, "No, Greg, this is my shield."

Greg smiled, dropped onto the chaise lounge next to Marena, and blew out a tired sigh.

Shielding her eyes from the sun, Marena asked, "So will the horse live?"

"There was never any question about that," Greg answered as he scanned the white sandy beach, giant palm trees, and brilliant turquoise ocean that stretched to the horizon.

"Then, what was the crisis? The way Mr. Blandenburg carried on when he called, I thought his horse was about to die."

"You spend a million bucks for a racehorse, even a hiccup makes you nervous," Greg replied.

"So what was the problem?"

"His trainer was concerned there was too much bleeding around the microfracture I repaired the day before we left. When he told Blandenburg about it, the old guy flew into a panic. You answered the phone when he was at the peak of his anxiety."

"Is it bad?"

Greg shook his head. "Everything's fine. After you left the room to come down here, I had them take some photos and email them to me. That took nearly thirty minutes. It only took ten seconds to see that everything is okay but nearly an hour to calm Blandenburg down and assure him his horse will race again."

Marena shook her head and said, "Why couldn't one of the other veterinarians in your clinic have handled it?"

Greg adjusted his sunglasses and replied, "With Blandenburg, it's me or nobody."

"That's the downside of being the best. So how long before he calls again?"

"Don't know, but it won't make any difference because I won't hear it; I turned off my phone. I even called the clinic and told them no calls or emails for two weeks. I'm officially off the grid, or whatever it is people say nowadays when they can't be reached." Greg leaned forward, tapped Marena's oil-coated arm as if checking a steak for doneness, and asked, "You going to lie here and bake for a while longer?"

"I don't have any plans; I've been waiting for you to finish. Why?"

Greg pointed toward a row of half a dozen wooden shacks that were scattered for a quarter mile along the beach. "I think I'll go talk with some of those guys; see what they have to offer."

"Don't bother," Marena said with a small shake of her head. "Just hang around here for a few minutes and they'll come to you. I've already been hit up three times this morning. Just kick back and soak up some sun or go for a swim. They'll spot you and start circling for the kill. The only way I got them to go away was to tell them to come back when they saw you."

"Did you get any prices?"

Marena gave a halfhearted shake of the head and, with her voice growing thicker with sleep, replied, "Not really. But they expect you to negotiate. I overheard one of the other guests talking with two different guys. There was a lot of back and forth. I couldn't hear everything, but it sounded like they settled for a lot less than where they started. Think Mexico."

Then she closed her eyes, letting herself succumb to the warmth of the sun's rays, and felt herself drifting off to sleep.

CHAPTER TWO

Greg adjusted his chaise lounge to a sitting position, kicked his feet together to knock off some of the sand, and sat quietly. Bored and restless after fifteen minutes of watching an endless parade of people walk along the beach, he took off his hat, T-shirt, and sunglasses, and walked into the turquoise water.

The first wave that hit him had the slightest chill. By the second, the chill was gone, and as the third approached, he dove in. Coming to the surface, he blew out a stream of air and licked the salty water from his lips. Plunging in, he started swimming parallel to the beach in long, easy strokes. When he had swum about fifty yards, he turned around, rolled onto his back, and backstroked to where he'd started. After floating on his back for a minute, he caught the crest of a wave, body surfed into waist-deep water, and stood up.

Although he was only three years older than his wife, time was taking its due measure from him. While his six-foot body was somewhere between the leanness of a marathon runner and the bulk of a weight lifter, his knees rebelled if they were forced to climb too many stairs. A bulging disc made him shift uncomfortably if he sat for too long or spent too many hours at his veterinary clinic repairing the blown-out joints of thoroughbred racehorses. The six-pack abs of younger days were gone, replaced with the slight paunch that showed he preferred a slice of cake after dinner to doing crunches in the gym. His once-thick hair was both receding and thinning, and tufts of gray flourished around his temples. By the end of the week in the sunshine, the light-brown color would bleach out to almost blond, which would help set off his bright-blue eyes. A dozen fine lines radiated from the corners of his eyes, and years of tending animals in the outdoors had given his skin a leathery appearance. Other than a nose that canted slightly to the left—the result of a bad tackle during a high school championship football game—his face was symmetrical, with a chiseled jawline and square chin. He was handsome in an earthy, rugged sort of way, Marena had told him on numerous occasions.

"Hey, mon, you lookin' fir to go divin'?"

Greg pushed his water-drenched hair off his forehead and looked at the ebony-skinned twenty-something-year-old man standing just at the water's edge. Even with his oversized ragged T-shirt, it was easy to tell the young man had a muscular body honed by physical labor. His English was decipherable but with a heavy Creole accent. "No, not diving; we're interested in snorkeling."

"Ah, mon, even better." Motioning rapidly with his arm, he added, "Come outta dat water, and we talk. I take you to da best snorkeling place in Punta Cana. Best in all Dominican Republic. Best in all Caribbean."

Greg sloshed out of the water and acted only moderately interested. "Really? What makes it the best?"

"Oh, it's beautiful, mon. Very, very beautiful. And secluded—only a few people ever go there. Beautiful reef there, mon—lots of fishes, sand sharks, and . . . how you say it . . . reys?"

"Rays? You mean stingrays?"

"Ya, ya, das it, mon," he said, breaking into a beaming smile that showed off amazingly straight and brilliantly white teeth. "Five hundred U.S. dollars, and I take you in my boat. Beautiful place. Lovely place. You will love it."

Greg choked. "Not for five hundred bucks you won't. I don't care how great it is; it's not worth that much," he said, starting toward his chaise lounge and shirt.

Matching Greg's pace step for step, the man said, "Aw, come on, mon, it's a great deal."

Lifting his shirt from the chaise lounge, Greg said, "Marena, you awake?"

The response was a sleep-clouded "Umm."

Slipping his shirt over his head, Greg said, "For five hundred bucks this guy says he'll take us snorkeling to a place nobody ever goes."

Marena raised her head slightly, eyed the man, and said groggily, "How about fifty bucks?"

"Ah, come on, lady. You tryin' to cheat po' Wiggy Wiggy."

"No more than you're trying to cheat us," Greg said.

"No, mon. Wiggy Wiggy, he don't cheat nobody. I tell you what. For you guys, I make a special deal. We go right now, and I'll take you for three fifty."

Greg shook his head. "Still too much; besides, we don't want to go right now."

"Okay, we don't go now. But, mon, it's worth a thousand bucks, maybe more. It's very, very pretty. Beautiful place. Very secluded. Excellent place. Lots of coral, wrecked boats, and feeshes. Perfect, perfect." Pausing only long enough to catch his breath, he continued. "Because I like you, I'm going to make you a special deal. Both of you for two fifty, and I'll even spear a fish and cook lunch for you. Coconut and bananas too. You love it. Good food. Wiggy Wiggy most excellent cook." Holding out his hand, he said, "Deal?"

Greg looked at the extended hand but made no motion to shake it. "Where is this place?"

"Secret place. Only Wiggy Wiggy goes there. But not far, mon. Not far. Two hours in Wiggy Wiggy's excellent boat. Look over there. See that great boat? Very safe boat. Good ride. See lots of pretty beaches along the way. Good place. No people. Come on; we go."

Greg slipped on his sunglasses and eyed the person standing in front of him. "Look, Wiggy Wiggy, I'll give you credit for your persistence, but that's too much money, and besides, we've got other things planned for the next few days. You got a business card or something? I'll call you."

Wiggy Wiggy shook his head and wagged his finger in front of Greg. "Oh no, mon. I can tell when you trying to get rid of Wiggy Wiggy. Let's make a deal now. I'll give you my best price ever. We'll go whenever you say. Tomorrow, two days from now, even next week."

Marena stood up, and in a tone that was more complimentary than critical, she said, "You don't take no for an answer, do you?"

"No, lady, not when I know what a great deal I'm making you. Believe me, you'll love this place. You'll have great time. Good food too. Let's make a deal."

Marena chuckled. "What's your real name? It can't be Wiggy Wiggy."

Wiggy Wiggy didn't hesitate. "Wiggains, lady. My name is Wiggains, but everybody call me Wiggy Wiggy. So what you say, lady, we go?"

Marena shot a quick glance at Greg, who shook his head. She said, "This secluded place of yours sounds great, but two hundred and fifty dollars is too much. How about a hundred dollars? And that includes lunch."

"Ah, lady, you breakin' Wiggy Wiggy's heart. Two hundred bucks and we go. You have best feesh dinner ever. You have a great, wonderful time."

Greg reached down and picked up Marena's bag. "Thanks, but we're going to pass."

Ignoring Greg's remark, Wiggy Wiggy turned to Marena, and said, "How about it, lady? One seventy-five and we go."

Marena shook her head. "Look, it sounds really nice." Nodding toward Greg, she said, "But we really want to check with some other people before we decide anything."

As Greg and Marena started to take a step, Wiggy Wiggy reached out and placed his hand on Greg's arm. "Look, I like you people, so Wiggy Wiggy, he goin' to be real honest." Pointing to the shacks along the beach, he said, "You can check wid dem guys if you want, but I tell you what gonna happen. Dem guys, they goin' charge you two hundred bucks and take you to some dumb place where a thousand tourists go. You be bumpin' into udder people. Den day give you a soggy sandwich and bottle of water and call it lunch. Dat's it. But . . . you agree to go with Wiggy Wiggy for *one fifty* and we go really special place."

Greg said, "One fifty?"

Wiggy Wiggy shoved out his hand, "Ya, mon, one-fifty. Best deal ever."

Greg looked at the proffered hand and hesitated. "We don't know when we'll go."

"Doesn't matter, mon. We go today, tomorrow, or whenever you say."

Greg gave a questioning look at Marena, who smiled and nodded. Then, looking at Wiggy Wiggy, he said, "Okay," and shook his hand. "Give me your phone number, and I'll call you in a couple days to set it up."

Wiggy Wiggy frowned. "No phone, mon. I'm here every morning about eight o'clock. You just come to this beach any day after eight o'clock, and I'll find you." Then he added, "Now look, mon, we have a deal. If udder guys come around and want to take you snorkeling, you tell 'em no deal; you goin' with Wiggy Wiggy. Okay?"

Greg raised his eyebrows and said, "Yeah, sure."

"Good, good. You'll have good time. You won't never forget it." And with a wave, he trotted down the beach toward another couple.

CHAPTER THREE

As William Lancaster—"Billy Joel," as he preferred to be called—approached the corner booth in the filthy, dimly lit bar, his $2,300 charcoal-gray suit made him stand out like a yellow dandelion in a field of green grass, which is exactly how he liked it.

At the insistence of a long-forgotten girlfriend, he'd spent time on a psychologist's couch spilling his guts. The sessions had ended when the man suggested his loud, foul-mouthed, deceitful, and brash personality was the result of Billy Joel never having come to grips with his drug-world wealth. He'd stormed out of the office and told one of his friends, who'd laughed and said the guy had it all wrong, that inside Billy Joel was just some big man trying to get out of his short, skinny body.

Raised in poverty by a drug-addict mother, he had no idea who his father was, and neither did his mother. He should have ended up with a bullet in his head at sixteen like other double-crossing, drug-dealing punks in his slummy Miami Gardens neighborhood, but he had one trait the others didn't have: intelligence. Not Rhodes Scholar intelligence—he could barely read—but street savvy. And he was amazingly gifted when it came to numbers. From his earliest days dealing drugs, he'd had no need for scraps of paper, notebooks, or computers to keep track of his drug deals. He stored everything with impressive accuracy in his clean-shaven head.

Harvard business professors would envy the mini-conglomerate he had amassed over the past eighteen years. If his business had been legal, they may have even held it up as the perfect example of a vertically integrated company—an undisputed success story. What had begun with small-time drug deals had grown into several legitimate businesses, all laundering gargantuan profits from the illegal drug trade. Billy Joel had fashioned himself as an important man. In truth, he was a very small fish in the world's pond of illicit drugs. Still, he was swimming with the biggest of them and was holding his own.

Pulling a paper napkin from a dented and rusting napkin holder on the table, Billy Joel carefully wiped the booth's dark-red vinyl cushion, crumpled the napkin, dropped it to the floor, and gingerly slid into the booth.

One of the two men who had trailed him into the bar stood a few feet from the booth, his right hand inside his own expensive suit jacket, gripping a concealed MAC-11 machine pistol. He stood unsmiling, scrutinizing the bar's four other patrons, all of whom either teetered on the edge of incapacitation from too much alcohol or who had already taken the plunge into unconsciousness and lay with their heads on a table. His second goon, smaller and more agile, took up a position at the bar where he could easily watch the seedy place's front and rear doors. They'd left a third man outside in an illegally parked black Ford Excursion, its windows tinted so dark it was impossible to tell anyone was inside. Billy Joel knew nobody, cop or otherwise, would say anything to his driver as he sat chain-smoking cigarettes and dropping the still-smoldering butts into the street.

Bavaro was a crime-riddled part of Punta Cana never featured in travel brochures, a place where making eye contact drew suspicion and unwanted conversation invited a bullet to the head or a knife to the belly. It was perfect for Billy Joel's purposes.

The bar's owner, a scraggly bearded, overweight *Dominicano* dressed in a dirty white T-shirt stretched tight over his protruding belly, shuffled up to the booth and asked, "*¿Qué quieres beber?*" When Billy Joel didn't immediately respond, he asked again, this time in English, "What do you want to drink?"

Billy Joel looked around the filthy bar and at the stains on the bar owner's T-shirt and said, "A bottle of water."

The man curled his lip at the cheap order and walked back to the bar and returned a moment later with Billy Joel's order. Setting the dripping bottle on the edge of the table, he said, "Two U.S. dollars."

Billy Joel made no effort to reach for a wallet or the wad of hundred dollar bills he had in a gold money clip in the front pocket of his trousers. Instead he nodded to the man standing near the booth, who pulled a money clip from his own pocket and sorted through the combination of

U.S. and Dominican money. Separating a Dominican ten-peso bill from the rest, he handed the owner the bill and said, "Keep the change. Don't come back unless we call you."

The bartender shrugged, mumbled something far too softly to be heard, and walked back behind the bar.

At precisely 10:30 P.M., the wooden entrance door of the bar opened, and a man who could have been a walking advertisement for Tommy Bahama clothing stepped in. Dressed in a coral-colored polo shirt—the collar turned up—and black jeans, the man stood motionless as he squinted against the garish lights of the bar. Looking around the room, he smiled ever so slightly when he spotted Billy Joel. With flip-flops slapping against his bare feet, he walked to the booth and said sarcastically, "Nice place. You come here often?"

Billy Joel set the bottle of water down on the table and broke into a toothy grin of his own. "It is nice, isn't it? Lovely lighting, charming décor, excellent service. But sadly, no, I don't come here often—only when I want to meet with really important people." Motioning to the cracked vinyl seat on the opposite side of the table, Billy Joel said, "Sit down, Scott. You want a drink?"

Scott Vaughn sat down without placing his hands on the red vinyl seat, the table, or anything else. Shaking his head at the offer of a drink, he said, "This place is disgusting. Why do you always pick such dumps for our meetings?"

"Because nobody will disturb us," Billy Joel answered. "Aside from the bartender, everyone else is so drunk they'll never know we were here."

Vaughn dismissed the comment with a shrug. Reaching up, he scratched at a small red bump in the middle of his cheek.

"Mosquito?" Billy Joel asked with a nod toward Vaughn's cheek.

Vaughn nodded as he continued to lightly scratch at the bump with his manicured fingernail.

"You gotta be careful, man; that Zika virus might get you. Wear some mosquito repellant or something."

Vaughn didn't smile as he looked at Billy Joel. "What can I do for you, Billy Joel?" he said coldly.

Billy Joel took a sip of water, wiped his lips with his fingers, and said, "You've made quite a name for yourself with that show you put on a few weeks ago, my friend."

"What show is that?" Vaughn asked.

"Shooting down that coast guard helicopter," Billy Joel said, placing the water bottle on the table.

Vaughn shrugged. "You paid me to safely deliver your merchandise. I did what was necessary. It arrived safely; I'd think that'd make you happy."

"Oh, I'm happy, man, very happy. Your trigger finger saved me some serious cash," Billy Joel said as he motioned to the man who had paid for the water.

Without saying a word, the man walked to the table, pulled a thick envelope from beneath his jacket, and placed it on the table. Then he returned to where he had been standing.

Billy Joel pushed the envelope toward Vaughn with the tips of his fingers.

Vaughn looked down at the envelope and then at Billy Joel but didn't move. "You've already paid me."

Billy Joel waved his hand in the air. "I know, I know. This is just a little something extra for your effort."

Vaughn picked up the envelope, slid open the flap, and thumbed the stack of bills. "Generous of you," he said.

"You take care of me; I take care of you," Billy Joel said with a smile.

Vaughn started to slide out of the booth, but Billy Joel lightly touched his arm and said, "Not yet. There's something else."

Vaughn hesitated slightly before easing back into the booth.

"There are some people who heard about your encounter with the coast guard," Billy Joel began. "They want to meet with you."

"What people?" Vaughn asked, as little lines of tension spread across his brow.

"People people," Billy Joel replied evasively with a shrug. "They want to do business with you."

Vaughn stared at Billy Joel for a long minute. Holding up his right hand, he extended two fingers and said, "There are only two people who know about the helicopter: you and me." Folding down a finger, he said, "I haven't said anything to anyone." Then, pointing his remaining extended finger at Billy Joel, he said, "That leaves you."

Billy Joel looked briefly at the finger and then at Vaughn. "Where've you been for the last two weeks, man? The moon?"

Vaughn shook his head. "Europe. Spain."

Billy Joel raised an eyebrow and nodded approvingly. "Nice." Then he said, "The word's on the street, man, and I mean everywhere—Miami, here, even the Bahamas. The drug cops have you pegged as the guy who did it."

Vaughn lowered his head slightly and glared at Billy Joe. "I wonder how they came to that conclusion."

Billy Joel shook his head. "Relax. They're just guessing, man. They don't know nothin'." Then, with a chuckle, he added, "They probably think you're the only guy crazy enough to do something like that." Glancing at his watch, he said, "But we're getting way off track here. The point is your gutsy move has come to the attention of some people who want to do business with you."

An uneasiness spread across Vaughn face. "How'd these people find out about you? And more importantly, how'd they make the connection between you and me?"

Billy Joel fidgeted slightly before he began. "Two nights ago, me and a couple of friends take some ladies to Club LIV in Miami. We're having a good time, but I need to go to the john. As I'm washing my hands, this guy—big Asian dude—steps up to the sink beside me and calls me by name. He says a friend of his wants to talk with me about the guy who shoots down helicopters with missiles. I told him he's confusing me with someone else because I don't know what he's talking about, and I turn to leave. Next thing I know, two other Asian dudes walk in. One blocks the door, and the other walks up and starts chatting me up, real friendly like. He tells me he needs something delivered to the States and wants to utilize the services of the man who shot down the helicopter."

"And you said?"

"I tell him to get out of my face, that I don't have a clue what he's talking about, and I start to push past him. I'm just about to the door when he tells me he can help me with a certain competitor of mine who has been hassling some of my dealers in Miami."

"So, naturally, you stop to listen," Vaughn interjected.

"Of course," Billy Joel said. "I'm a businessman. I have to take advantage of opportunities when they arise. Anyway, we have this little discussion right there in the john. He agrees to help me if I'll help him."

Vaughn stared at Billy Joel but said nothing.

"I'm told it's small—about the size of a suitcase and relatively light," Billy Joel said.

"Drugs?" Vaughn asked.

Billy Joel scowled and shook his head. "Of course not. Do you think I would help a competitor?"

"What is it?"

"Can't tell you," Billy Joel replied.

"Why?"

Billy Joel smiled and held out his hands. "Because I don't know. They didn't tell me. And why do you care anyway? Drugs, money, guns, body parts, even exotic animals—you do it all. You're a transporter. That's what you do. People pay, and you transport for a price—a very expensive price, I might add."

"Where is it, this little package?"

"Ah, that I know. It's here, in the Dominican Republic. I don't know exactly where, but it's here."

"Where does it need to be delivered?"

Billy Joel shook his head. "Don't know; they didn't tell me."

"And how much are these new friends of yours willing to pay for my services?"

"A hundred grand."

Vaughn laughed out loud. "Not interested."

Billy Joel looked at Vaughn with dismay and snorted. "Business must be good."

"Business is good enough I can pick and choose my work," Vaughn replied. "And I choose not to do this."

Billy Joel leaned forward. "How can you not be interested, man? We're talking a hundred grand for transporting some little package. It'll take you, what, maybe a couple of days? How can you not be interested?"

CHAPTER FOUR

Scott Vaughn had spent his adult life negotiating dirty deals with vile people. It had started innocently enough, when he was a college student on spring break in Cancun. Like thousands of other spring breakers, he and two dozen of his fellow Florida State University friends—male and female—had invaded a seedy little bar in search of cheap booze to lengthen their four-day binge. When a cadre of University of Florida Gator students flowed into the place, booze-induced insults had begun flying between the instate rivals. In no time, a brawl had broken out. When it had ended, there wasn't a table, mirror, piece of glass, or bit of bar that hadn't been broken, crushed, smashed, or damaged.

Nearly comatose on alcohol and hurting from the fight, but still alert enough to stumble when the sirens began wailing, Vaughn had managed to find what was left of the bar's rear door, pushed it open, and walked into the arms of a Cancun police department detective. Binding Vaughn's wrists behind his back with a plastic zip tie, the detective had forced him into the back seat of a plain white Honda Accord, along with two other drunken students, one of whom had passed out and the other who had retched all over the floor.

The cop drove the three of them to the police station and dumped them into a sweltering cell with five Mexican prisoners. Too drunk to make sense of any of it, the three students had passed out on the floor. Vaughn had awoken the next morning to see his two fellow students cowering in the cell corner, whimpering as the five men threatened and taunted them in broken English. As Vaughn pushed himself to a sitting position and rubbed his temples to ease the throbbing headache, two Mexicans had slowly started toward him.

The first one had sneered, hurled an insult about Vaughn's mother, and nudged him with the toe of his boot. In perfect Spanish, Vaughn had replied with a more graphic insult. The man had grabbed Vaughn by the collar and yanked him to his feet. As he did, Vaughn had head-butted the guy, breaking his nose. When the man slumped and clutched his bleeding nose, Vaughn had kicked him so hard in the side that he'd broke a rib. As the second man rushed forward, Vaughn had spread his arms out wide as if he was going to give the guy a big bear hug. Just as his attacker was about to slam into him, Vaughn had cupped his hands slightly and boxed the guy's ears so violently he'd perforated both of the man's eardrums. With one guy oozing blood from his nose and clutching his side and the other leaking trickles of blood from his ears, the other three Mexicans had backed away when Vaughn stepped toward them.

The jailers must have heard the scuffle from the next room, but it wasn't until they'd brought in some refried beans and tortillas for lunch that they realized what had happened. A flurry of Spanish had gone back and forth between the jailers and the Mexican prisoners. A few minutes later the Americans were moved to a separate cell.

Early the following day, the detective who had forced Vaughn into the car suddenly pushed through the door separating the cell from an outer office. Looking past Vaughn, he'd called to the other two students and said, "You are free to go." Then, looking at Vaughn, he'd said, "You are not."

Without so much as a glance at Vaughn, the other two had charged for the cell's door as the detective pulled it open. The detective had looked at them only long enough to say, "If you know what is good for you, you will leave Cancun and never come back."

The detective had closed and locked the cell door and then walked over and closed the thick wooden door to the outer office. When he'd turned back to Vaughn, he had a smile on his face, which grew warmer as he walked back to the cell. "They have wealthy parents," he'd said with a shrug. And, in near-perfect English, he'd continued. "You, on the other hand, are nothing more than . . . *basura blanca* . . . white trash."

Vaughn had glared at the man but said nothing.

With his smile morphing into a concerned look, the detective had begun, "You know, it doesn't look good for you. It was bad enough you were drunk and destroyed that wonderful little drinking establishment. Did you know that two girls were nearly killed in that brawl? It is bad, very bad." He'd shaken his head, and pointing to the adjacent cell, he'd said, "But what is more terrible is the way you injured those two fine Mexican citizens."

"They're lowlife creeps," Vaughn had hissed.

"Oh no, Mr. . . . How do you say your name? Va-ha-neh?" The detective had slaughtered the pronunciation, but Vaughn made no attempt to correct him.

"No, señor," the detective had said ominously. "The men you injured—they are two of our finest citizens. They just happened to be in jail because of a small thing—a traffic ticket, I think. I'm certain when a judge learns how you hurt them, he will be very unhappy. In my experience, you will probably be sentenced to five, maybe ten years in prison." His face had suddenly contorted into a very serious, worried expression. "Have you ever been inside a Mexican prison? No, I'm certain you haven't. Well, I have, Mr. Vaughn, and I can assure you it is not a pleasant place."

Vaughn had studied the detective's narrow eyes and asked, "What do you want from me?"

"Me? Want? Nothing, señor; I want nothing. I was simply explaining your . . . situation."

Vaughn had reached out and grasped two of the cell's bars at the exact height of the detective's neck. Leaning forward, he'd said, "What do you want?"

Smiling, and in a voice no louder than a whisper, the detective had said calmly, "Perhaps there is a way we can be of assistance to one another. I can help you out of your unpleasant circumstance, and you can deliver a few small packages to some associates of mine in Miami."

The next day Scott Vaughn had carried his first shipment of cocaine—four small latex balloons the size of unshelled pecans. They were inside his stomach. Standing at a sink inside a filthy house that was little more than a tin and cinderblock shack, the detective had forced him to swallow the balloons, making him wash each one down with glassfuls of microbe-laden tap water. As Vaughn gagged to get the balloons down, the detective had smiled sadistically and said, "This water is not the best in Cancun, but it will aid you in . . . expelling . . . the balloons." With Vaughn's stomach rumbling from too much water and the latex, the detective had escorted him to the airport. Standing at the terminal gate, he'd leaned toward Vaughn's ear and warned, "My associates will come to pick up the merchandise in two days.

Be sure you have all four of them, or they will be forced to recover them themselves." Pausing to smile the same sadistic smile, he'd added, "And the recovery will not be pleasant."

Vaughn had turned over the latex balloons two days later, spent weeks battling the effects of drinking the unpurified water, and learned that had a balloon burst in his stomach, he would have died a hideous death.

Two years later Vaughn was back in Cancun, not to swallow more drugs—he'd expanded far beyond that. He and two hired thugs had ambushed the blackmailing detective, taken him into the jungle, and forced him to swallow a small balloon filled with cocaine. This balloon, though, was made of Qualatex, not latex, and was easily digested. Then they'd staked him in the jungle and waited patiently until the detective's stomach acid ate through the balloon, releasing the cocaine into his stomach. As the detective had begun screaming in agony from the cocaine in his stomach, Vaughn had walked away.

Now Vaughn looked at Billy Joel without emotion. "You heard me. I'm not interested."

There was a tinge of anxiety in Billy Joel's voice when he said, "Come on, man. You're kidding, right? We're talking a hundred grand for doing next to nothing."

Vaughn began sliding out of the booth. "I have a rule: I don't do business with people I don't know, and I don't know your friends. I'm not interested."

Billy Joel threw up his hands and said, "So what am I supposed to tell these guys?"

Vaughn shrugged as he stood. "Anything you want, as long as you tell them I'm not interested."

Vaughn had only taken one step when Billy Joel let out a loud sigh and said, "You're forgetting one thing, Scott, something they felt might be necessary to remind you about."

Vaughn stopped and turned back but didn't say anything.

"You're forgetting they know you blew up the helicopter. Walk away, and they'll have drug agents on you like flies on stink. Do it, and you get a hundred grand, their silence, and maybe even more business. You don't want to mess this up, Scott. You really don't."

Vaughn felt his eyes grow hot with anger, and he took a step toward the little man seated in the booth. The slight glint of light off a gun barrel and the sound of a safety being clicked made him stop. He looked over to see the gun of one of Billy Joel's guard dogs pointed directly at his head.

"Sit down, Scott," Billy Joel said calmly while holding up his hand to the man with the machine pistol. "I need to make a phone call."

While Vaughn sat down, Billy Joel took a phone from his pocket, dialed a number, and put the phone to his ear. After a moment he said, "We have an agreement. He'll do it." Then, looking at Vaughn with a slight grin and a wink, he added, "But not for a hundred thousand like you wanted. He wants one fifty plus expenses. Half deposited into an account immediately."

Vaughn looked at Billy Joel in stunned surprise at how the drug dealer had played his hand with whomever was on the other end of the phone. Billy Joel didn't return the look; he was staring blankly into the darkness of the room. After a moment, he looked back at Vaughn with a grin. "Hang on," he said into the phone. Pulling a pen from his pocket and a napkin from the holder, he shoved them to Vaughn and said, "You know an account number where you want the money deposited?"

Vaughn nodded, took the pen, and wrote a number.

Billy Joel took the napkin and said into the phone, "You ready to write? It's the Royal Bank of Canada, Turks and Caicos branch." He read off the account number and said, "Got it?" There was a long moment of silence before Billy Joel said, "I'll tell him" and disconnected the call. Looking at the phone, he snarled, "Got you, you slimy . . ." but didn't finish. Then, looking at Vaughn, he said, "By tomorrow morning you'll have seventy-five thousand in that account. You'll be paid the remainder when the package is delivered."

Vaughn studied Billy Joel's face for a moment before saying, "Slimy what?"

Billy Joel shook his head to dismiss the question and said, "I gotcha fifty thousand more than they offered. That should take some of the pain out of this for you." Then, pulling an envelope from inside his suit jacket, he slid it across the table.

Vaughn slowly reached out and picked up the envelope. "What's this?"

"Don't know," Billy Joel replied. "It was sealed when they gave it to me, and I wasn't curious enough to open it. I was told to give it to you after you agreed to handle the transport."

Lifting the front of his shirt, Vaughn stuffed the envelope into the waistband of his pants next to the one Billy Joel had given him earlier.

Without saying anything more, he stood up and weaved his way to the door through the obstacle course of tables littered with empty bottles and drunks. When he stepped outside into the street, he flagged down a dented Datsun taxi.

***

Billy Joel watched Vaughn leave the bar, and only after the man had climbed in and the car had chugged away did Billy Joel reach into his pocket and pull out his phone once more. Dialing, he said, "It's me again. He just left with the envelope. I did exactly as you said. And now it's your turn. I want to know my woman is alive. Put her on the phone. I want to talk to her." A moment later he said, "Hey, baby, you okay? Have they hurt you?" There was a long pause as he listened to a stream of disjointed words laced with fear-riddled sobs. "Baby, look, ya gotta stop crying and keep calm, you hear me? Just calm down; everything's going to be okay. I did what they wanted, and they're gonna let you go. It's going to be fine. You'll be free in a few minutes. Trust me. Just hang in there." After listening to more crying, he calmly said, "Hand the phone back." A moment later Billy Joel curled his lip and spat into the phone, "Listen to me, you creep. You harm her, and I'm gonna hunt you down and kill you, you understand me? So drop her off exactly as we agreed. I'll be there in fifteen minutes, and she'd better be waiting for me—unharmed." Jamming the phone into his pocket, he turned to the two men who had come in with him and almost shouted, "We're going. Now!"

***

As Billy Joel and his two bodyguards filed toward the bar's exit, a shabbily dressed man with a shock of deep-black hair jerked from his sleep. Looking as though he hadn't had a bath in weeks and reeking of alcohol and tobacco, he made it only halfway to the door before he stopped to lean against a table to steady his wobbly legs. Looking through bloodshot eyes, he watched the three men climb into their waiting vehicle.

As the black Excursion pulled away from the curb, the drunk staggered out the door and, looking as if he would fall over any second, leaned against the bar's bright-green bricks. When the vehicle was fifty yards away, the drunk reached inside his tattered coat and pulled out a plastic object the size of a cigarette lighter. Extending a small antenna, he flipped open the cover and depressed a button. A fraction of a second later, a deafening blast echoed through the narrow street as the black Excursion exploded in a massive fireball.

Closing the lid, the man slipped the device into his pocket and stumbled his way in the opposite direction. When he had staggered for almost a block, he turned into a dark alley and began walking normally. Reaching inside his rumpled jacket, he pulled out a phone and dialed. In perfect Korean he said, "He has been eliminated. Kill the woman and dispose of her body."

CHAPTER FIVE

Vaughn waited until the taxi was almost back to his hotel before pulling the thinner of the two envelopes from the waistband of his jeans. He didn't open it; he simply turned it over and back, studying its texture. Peering out the window of the taxi at the seedy houses and stores that flashed by, he began tapping the envelope lightly on the leg of his jeans.

"Whatchu got, a love letter?" the driver said in broken English.

Vaughn slowly turned his preoccupied gaze from the scenes outside the car and looked into the rearview mirror. When he locked eyes with the smirking driver, he scowled.

The driver shrugged. "Hey, no beeg deel," he said as the gutless Datsun trundled past a lumbering truck belching thick black exhaust. "You don' wanna talk, we no talk."

With only the slightest movement, Vaughn lifted his shirt and slipped the envelope back into his waistband then stared out into the night.

As the taxi came to a stop under the hotel's portico, Vaughn leaned forward, dropped a twenty-dollar bill onto the front seat, and was out of the car before the driver had picked up the money.

Vaughn glanced at his watch—12:30 a.m.—as he stepped into the hotel's cavernous lobby. Six homes from any middle-class neighborhood could easily fit within its walls, and almost every foot of it was crammed with people. Thirty or forty were making fools of themselves trying to dance to the earsplitting music of a mediocre three-piece band. The rest were either huddled around an elaborate circular bar swilling liquor or standing next to the half-dozen tables overflowing with exotic finger foods from around the world. Nightlife was just getting under way at the Ocean Blue Resort.

Vaughn started walking across the polished marble floor to his room when a waitress carrying a tray of empty glasses asked, "Something to drink, señor?"

Vaughn looked at the waitress, checked his watch again, and hesitated only slightly before saying, "Yeah, sure. A piña colada."

Then, looking around the room, he pointed to an unoccupied bright-orange sofa in a secluded corner and said, "I'll be right over there."

Easing onto the sofa, Vaughn again pulled the envelope from his jeans. Glancing around to make sure nobody was watching, he tore open the envelope and gave it a gentle shake. A folded piece of paper the size of a business card floated out and dropped into his lap. He picked up the paper and unfolded it. In handwritten script so precise it looked as though it had been generated on a computer, Vaughn read, *El Gallo Azul, 1:30 P.M., tomorrow.*

"The Blue Rooster?" Vaughn said aloud.

As Vaughn concentrated on the note, the dark-haired waitress walked up and said, "Your piña colada."

"*Gracias,*" Vaughn said, accepting the drink.

"*De nada,*" the waitress replied. "Can I get you something else? Some shrimp or sushi, perhaps?"

"No, thanks." As the waitress turned to walk away, Vaughn called out, "Hey, just a minute. Are you from around here?"

"*Sí,*" she replied.

"You ever heard of a place called El Gallo Azul?"

There was a slight hesitancy but then a nod.

"You know where it is?"

Shaking her head, she answered, "I have never been there."

"You know anybody who has? Someone who can tell me where it is?"

The waitress eyed Vaughn suspiciously. "Why you want to go there? It's maybe not a good place for *gringos* to go."

Vaughn held up the paper and said, "A friend wants to meet there."

The waitress slowly shook her head. "There is maybe one man who knows. It will take me a few minutes." Then she turned and walked away.

Fifteen minutes later, thinking he'd been forgotten, Vaughn stood to leave, and a sapling thin Dominican man of thirty or thirty-five stepped in front of him. "You want go El Gallo Azul?" he asked in heavily accented English.

Vaughn stared down at the man. He was thin, with little more than almond-colored skin stretched taut over his bones. His gaunt face had deep-set black eyes and high cheekbones that gave his head a skull-like appearance and made him look more dead than alive. He wore a white silk shirt that was unbuttoned almost to his navel, revealing a chest that was so concaved it looked as if it might touch his backbone. Looped around his pencil-thin neck were half a dozen gold chains, the largest with an intricate gold cross dangling from it. His jet-black hair was pulled back into a ponytail and slicked down with so much oil it glistened even in the dim light. "Maybe," Vaughn said.

"Come on; I take you. We go now!"

Vaughn looked down at the skeletal man and asked, "Who are you?"

"Emesto," the man replied warmly. "Coleta, she say you want go to El Gallo Azul, so I here to take you. But we need to hurry, man. It's almost too late. You got money?"

Vaughn didn't move.

"Come on," Emesto said, placing his hand on Vaughn's arm and taking a step, "For fifty American dollars, I take you to El Gallo Azul."

Vaughn shoved Emesto's hand from his arm like it was diseased and said, "I don't want you to take me; I just want to know where it is."

Emesto frowned. "Coleta, she say you want to go, man. Fifty bucks too much? Come on; I take you for twenty-five bucks. But we must hurry."

Vaughn shook his head. "I don't want to go now. I just want to know where the restaurant is."

Emesto looked at Vaughn in confusion. "Restaurant? What you talking about? El Gallo Azul is no restaurant."

It was Vaughn's turn for confusion. "What is it?"

Emesto suddenly looked suspicious. "Why you want to go if you don't know what it is?"

"It's business; a meeting."

Emesto shook his head. "Meeting? There? That's crazy, man."

"So what is this place?"

"How you say in English . . . ?" Emesto paused, searching his memory for the word, but couldn't come up with it. Then he said, "Es cheekens!" Forming the fingers of his hands into claws, he said, "You know, cheekens that fight."

Vaughn narrowed his eyes then suddenly said, "The Blue Rooster is where chickens fight?"

Emesto shook his head. "Not cheekens—men!"

CHAPTER SIX

Vaughn idled the black Toyota Highlander up the dusty side street, tap-dancing on the brake as a flood of men and a trickle of women crowded ahead of him. The narrow street was clogged with beat-up cars, mopeds and bicycles, some parked helter-skelter along the sides of the road and others creeping forward at the same snail's pace at which he was moving. Pressing the button to lower the electric window, he yelled at a couple of teenage punks blocking his way. They looked up, mouthed a string of cuss words, and didn't move until he brushed the bumper of the Highlander against their legs. One of them balled up his fist and started back toward Vaughn's door but turned away when Vaughn placed a semiautomatic pistol on the dashboard. Easing alongside the punks, whose baggy jeans were slung so far below their waists they were in danger of falling off, he hissed, "Pull your pants up and get out of my way." They glared back and moved but didn't touch their jeans.

The houses lining the narrow street were a mixture of tin and cinderblock shacks, most painted a vibrant yellow, green, or light blue. Tall trees arched over the street, forming a canopy that allowed only an occasional thin shaft of sunlight to sneak through. When the congestion got so thick he could drive no farther, Vaughn angled the Highlander into a parking spot that partially blocked a driveway. Sliding the pistol into a holster in the small of his back, he rearranged his bulky T-shirt so the gun was totally concealed. Lifting the jeans on his right leg, he checked to make certain the thin stiletto knife was secured in the sheath strapped to his leg.

Easing from the vehicle, Vaughn joined the slow-moving gaggle of people walking toward a small chain-link arena at the end of the dead-end street—the only Anglo in a sea of Latinos and half an ocean of Asians.

The only sign announcing he had arrived at El Gallo Azul was a hand-lettered piece of plywood the size of a refrigerator door. The lopsided sign was hanging next to a small gate in the chain-link fence that surrounded the arena. Beside the gate, an Asian man the size of a mountain stood next to a petite girl who was sitting at a table. Showing no emotion whatsoever, the girl collected the two-dollar admission the sign proclaimed everyone must pay.

Vaughn angled away from the gate and stood in a conspicuous spot away from the flow of people. At exactly one-thirty a feminine voice from behind him softly said, "Mr. Vaughn?"

Surprised, Vaughn spun. "Yes?"

Another woman, a wispy, thin, twenty-something Asian woman with short black hair, black eyes, and dressed entirely in black from her blouse to her pants to her shoes gave a weak smile and said in perfect English, "Mr. Li Gun-no would like to meet with you in his car. Follow me, please."

Vaughn looked at the woman then scanned the area around her. He shook his head. "I don't meet strangers in their cars. Tell Mr. Li I will meet him here, out in the open, or, if he prefers, inside the arena."

The woman's faint smile melted to a frown. Without saying anything, she abruptly turned and walked away. Vaughn watched her as she threaded her way through the people and disappeared around the arena. Three minutes later she was back. "Mr. Li will meet you in the arena. Please follow me."

Vaughn smiled and said, "Lead on."

The arena was a dilapidated version of a Roman amphitheater, except that instead of being constructed of brick and mortar, it was cobbled together with used lumber, pipe, rope, and wire. It was slightly fewer than sixty feet in diameter. In the middle of the arena was a round cage. The seven-foot-high sides were constructed of rusty chain-link fencing, as was the top. The floor was made of plywood covered with a thin layer of sand. A small gate made of metal bars was the only way in or out.

A narrow walkway encircled the cage and separated it from the flimsy bleachers that surrounded it. The bleachers angled upward from the floor to almost the top of the twelve-foot-high chain-link fence surrounding the arena, providing seating for at least two hundred people to watch what happened inside the cage.

Vaughn followed the girl as she wormed her way to the far side of the arena. Stepping onto the bleachers, she climbed to the top row, where she pointed to a seat and said, "Wait here. Mr Li will arrive shortly." Vaughn remained standing.

Li arrived with two men at his side, both of whom he waved off as he stepped up near Vaughn. He was a small man, dressed like a Wall Street banker. He wore a dark-gray suit, starched white shirt, and paisley tie. On his nose were perched huge silver-rimmed sunglasses with bright-blue reflector lenses that covered much of his face and made it impossible to see his eyes.

"Mr. Vaughn," Li said. "Thank you for coming to meet with me." It was spoken in English, but the accent was so heavy Vaughn struggled to understand what was said.

Vaughn didn't exchange the pleasantry; he simply looked at the lenses in the glasses, seeing nothing but his own reflection looking back at him.

"You come very highly recommended," Li said, "from a mutual acquaintance."

Vaughn drew a breath to reply, but a roar of shouts and wild clapping filled the air. Turning away from Li's glasses, Vaughn looked down at an Asian man in tight boxing trunks who was stepping into the cage. Looking back at the glasses, Vaughn said with a touch of impatience, "Mr. Li, I'm very busy, and I assume you are as well. What is it I can do for you?"

Another roar of yelling, screaming, and foot-stomping broke out, and Vaughn and Li both looked down into the cage. Stepping into it was a thin but muscular Latino man dressed in bright red-and-green boxing trunks.

Li's lips cracked into a patronizing smile, and as the yelling died down, he said, "Forgive me. I forget you Americans like to get to the point."

Vaughn looked back at the glasses but didn't smile.

"Please, sit down," Li said, pointing to the dust-covered bleachers. As the two men sat, he said, "I am a businessman with a wide variety of interests. On occasion, associates of mine find it is necessary to ship certain items from one country to another as expeditiously as possible. Sometimes—for many different reasons—they prefer to use nontraditional methods to ship their items. This is—"

"Mr. Li," Vaughn interrupted. "Let me hurry this along. Billy Joel explained you have a small item you want transported from the Dominican Republic to the United States. Is that correct?"

Li offered a washed-out smile but said nothing.

Seeing Li's reaction, Vaughn plowed ahead. "My fee is one hundred and fifty thousand dollars plus expenses. I checked earlier this morning, and the initial deposit of seventy-five thousand has been wired into my account. The remainder is to be transferred at the time I make delivery. Is that your understanding?"

Li expelled a small breath of air before his attention was drawn by the sudden roar of the crowd. Turning to the cage to see what had distracted Li, Vaughn watched as the Latino man pummeled the Asian fighter with vicious martial arts kicks and hand strikes. As blood sprayed from the Asian's nose after the Latino landed a ferocious jab, Li said, "I have nothing to do with the financial arrangements. My responsibility is to see that the item is delivered to you; nothing more."

Vaughn nodded. "Fine. Then, all I need from you is to know where I am to pick up the shipment and where and when it is to be delivered."

"The package is here in the Dominican Republic," Li began. "It must be delivered to a small town in southeastern Idaho—Arco, to be precise. It is imperative it is delivered no later than one week from today."

Vaughn pulled back and shook his head. "Can't be done."

Except for a slight tilt of his head, Li sat unmoving, as if waiting for a more detailed explanation.

"I'm assuming whatever it is you want transported can't be handled through ordinary means, or you wouldn't be talking to me. That said, this isn't a matter of walking to the airport, climbing onto an airplane, and being there a day or two later. That means going by sea. Forget the specifics of getting it there without being detected. Do you realize the distance involved?"

"Yes, Mr. Vaughn," Li answered calmly. "Approximately six hundred miles of ocean and another two thousand seven hundred over land."

"And that combination is what makes it impossible. It would be easy to do in two weeks—maybe even a week and a half—but not in one week. At least, not if you want to do it without being discovered. What you're asking is impossible."

Li gave a patronizing smile and said, "Mr. Vaughn, that was a very nice performance you gave just now, but please do not attempt to renegotiate our agreement by claiming you can do the 'impossible' but it will cost more. In my world, we do not operate in that manner, and my associates would be very upset if they learned of your reaction."

Vaughn looked at Li and huffed. "Renegotiate? Hardly. I'm not attempting to change the terms. What I'm telling you is the reality of the situation. Trying to do this in so short a time carries significant risks."

Li's expression was calm. "I understand. But I also understand that you are being paid very well for your services, and you just told me you have already accepted seventy-five thousand dollars. It is apparent that we have overestimated your skills, and it sounds as if you are saying you are not capable of transporting our item. Therefore, simply return the money, and we will make other arrangements," Li said.

"My ability is not the issue." Vaughn bristled. "What's at issue is your desire for speed and avoiding detection. I am good at what I do because I don't do stupid things—things that draw unwanted attention. In my business, speed almost always attracts unwanted attention, and what you're asking for is speed. I'm prepared to move forward within your timeframe, but I want it perfectly clear that if it comes down to a choice between me getting caught or delivering your package, your package will lose. And I keep the money you've deposited. Is that clear?"

Li's lips tightened in the thinnest smile, and he tipped his head slightly forward. "As I was saying, the package must be delivered no later than one week from today."

Vaughn shrugged. "Now that we understand each other, you said the package is in the Dominican Republic. Where?"

Li smiled coyly and said, "It is in the Dominican Republic, Mr. Vaughn; that's all you need to know. I will be responsible for getting it to you."

"Fine, but it must be in my possession no later than this time tomorrow. If it isn't, our deal is off, and once again, there will be no refund of the seventy-five thousand dollars. Do you understand?" Without waiting for a reply, he stood and said, "I'm staying at the Ocean Blue Resort under the name of Larsen, Ronald Larsen. Call me by six o'clock this evening, and I'll give you detailed instructions about when and where you are to deliver the package to me."

"One more item, Mr. Vaughn," Li said, withdrawing an envelope from the inside pocket of his jacket and proffering it to Vaughn.

Vaughn looked at the envelope but made no effort to take it. "What's that?"

"Instructions and other information you will need. Read everything carefully."

As Vaughn took the envelope, another roar went up from the crowd, but not like before. Instead of shouts of encouragement, there were jeers and taunts. Vaughn looked down to see the Latino man lying facedown in the cage, unmoving. The Asian man wiped blood from his leaking nose with both hands and then wiped it on his already blood-smeared trunks. After waving a taunting fist at the crowd, who acted as though they had just watched their favorite cage fighter get knocked unconscious, the Asian man turned and looked up at Li Gun-no and bowed slightly.

Vaughn looked at the fighter and then at Li, who acknowledged the fighter's bow with a slight tip of his head. "Friend of yours?" Vaughn asked.

Li smiled. "My son."

CHAPTER SEVEN

VAUGHN SAT ON THE GROUND with his knees drawn almost to his chest. His elbows rested on his knees to steady the binoculars that were pressed against his eyes. "Hey, Manuel, you ever watch a TV show called *Miami Vice*?" he asked without lowering the binoculars.

The wiry man beside Vaughn looked over and skewed his eyebrows in confusion. "Huh?"

Vaughn twisted the little knob on the binoculars to sharpen the focus and said, "*Miami Vice*. You ever watch it?"

"I don't know what you're talking about, man. What's some TV show got to do with stealing a boat?"

Vaughn kept the binoculars pressed against his eyes. "Back in the mid-80s there was—"

"Mid-80s? Dude, I was three, maybe four years old back then. So no, I wasn't watchin' some lame TV show."

"Too bad. You probably would have gotten a kick out of it. It was about two undercover cops in Miami."

Manuel shook his head. "Yeah, so?"

Vaughn handed the binoculars to Manuel and pointed down the hill to the marina, where fifty or sixty boats were tied in neat little rows. "In the show, one of the cops—Sonny or Jimmy or something like that—raced around Miami on a thirty-nine-foot Chris-Craft Stinger. It was a tricked-out oceangoing race boat. Very fast." Then, nodding toward the marina, he said, "There's one tied up to the main dock down there."

Manuel raised the binoculars and spun the little knob to bring the boats into focus. Leaning forward, he scanned the main dock for the sleek, long-nosed boat. After a few seconds he softly chuckled. "Some people are just plain stupid. Why take a nice boat like that and put a hideous paint job on it?" He handed the binoculars back to Vaughn and said, "Either the owner or the guy who painted it was high on drugs."

Vaughn put the binoculars back up to his eyes and said, "Anybody who'll spend the kind of money that paint job cost is undoubtedly a fanatic about keeping his engines in perfect condition, and that's all I care about." Lowering the binoculars, Vaughn stood up and brushed bits of grass and dirt from his pants. "Can you get me into the marina at midnight?"

"Easy; no problem," Manuel replied as he stood up.

"I want a diversion of some kind too."

"Why?"

"When I fire up those twin engines in the middle of the night, the exhaust noise will be loud enough to raise your grandmother from her grave. I want something to distract people and camouflage the noise. Can you come up with something?"

Manuel looked down at the marina for a minute and then back at Vaughn. "Sure I can. Easy. But it's gonna cost you."

"It always does," Vaughn said. "How much?"

"For the diversion?"

Vaughn shook his head. "Everything."

"Ten grand."

Vaughn shook his head, but before he could say anything Manuel blurted, "It's the times, man." Holding out his hand and rubbing his thumb and finger together, he added, "Nobody takes a risk without expecting money—lots of it—in return. The marina manager and the night watchman are both going to want cash, and then your little diversion won't be cheap." After a short pause he nodded toward the boat and added, "You want it full of fuel?"

"Of course," Vaughn replied.

"That's another thousand."

"And I want four fifty-gallon drums of fuel loaded as well."

Looking through his binoculars, Vaughn studied the boat again. "*Offshore Account*! Who names a boat *Offshore Account*?"

Manuel shrugged. "Probably some corrupt banker from the Cayman Islands."

Vaughn didn't respond as he dropped the binoculars and lowered his sunglasses from the top of his head to his nose. Pulling a wad of money from his slacks, Vaughn shoved it into Manuel's shirt pocket. Patting the man on the cheek, he said, "I'll be down at the dock's main walkway at eleven thirty tonight. Make sure everything is ready."

Manuel pulled the cash from his pocket and quickly thumbed through the bills. "There's only three grand here."

Vaughn nodded. "You'll get the rest tonight when I climb onto the boat."

***

At exactly midnight, Vaughn stepped onto *Offshore Account*. "You ready with the diversion?" he asked.

"You ready to pay me?" Manuel replied.

Vaughn reached into the side pocket of the backpack he was carrying. Pulling out two stacks of bills, he handed them to Manuel. "It's all there, plus a little something extra."

Manuel took the money and shoved it into a small canvas bag.

"You going to count it?"

Manuel shook his head. "No time," he said as he untied the boat. "Give me sixty seconds and you'll be able to leave here without a worry."

Sixty seconds later, a horrific explosion ripped through an immaculately restored 1921 Thornycraft yacht. The explosion sent chunks of the million-dollar yacht's African mahogany hull and cabin hurtling through the air and raining down on every boat within a hundred feet.

As the fireball roared into the sky, Vaughn turned the keys of the Chris-Craft Stinger's twin engines. With the engines purring like kittens but the exhaust roaring like lions, Vaughn flipped on the lights, shifted the transmissions into gear, and eased away from the dock. Once clear of the breakwater, he shoved the throttles forward and *Offshore Account* leaped into the darkness.

An hour later Vaughn eased *Offshore Account* into a ramshackle boathouse that was barely wide and long enough to fit the vessel. After closing the boathouse's double doors, he walked up a rarely used path to an empty vacation home, climbed into his rental car, and drove to the Ocean Blue Resort.

It was two o'clock in the morning by the time Vaughn sat down on the edge of his bed and set the alarm for seven thirty. Five minutes later, he was asleep.

When the alarm buzzed him awake, he rolled out of bed; showered; dressed in faded jeans, polo shirt, and deck shoes; and hurriedly packed his suitcase and backpack. Walking around the room slowly, he checked every nook, corner, and desk drawer to be certain he hadn't dropped an important paper or left anything other than fingerprints. Satisfied the room was clean, he walked to the lobby and presented his electronic room keys. "I'd like to check out, please," he said with a smile to the young man standing behind the counter.

"Your name, please, señor?"

"Ronald Larsen."

Entering a few keystrokes into the computer, the young man looked at the screen and said, "You're leaving early, Mr. Larsen. I hope everything was satisfactory."

"Very," Vaughn replied.

A minute later a printer spit out three pages of paper. "There you go, Mr. Larsen. You're all checked out. Can I make any other arrangements for you?"

"No," Vaughn replied.

"Thank you for staying with us, and have a nice day."

"Thanks. I will," Vaughn replied as he folded the papers and stuffed them into his backpack.

An hour later he returned the rental car as Mr. Bob Stevenson. After paying in cash, he walked outside the car-rental building and hailed a cab. At 2:55 P.M., the driver dropped him off in front of the beachfront vacation home. Flinging his backpack over his shoulder, he picked up his suitcase and walked down to the ramshackle boathouse and climbed aboard *Offshore Account*. Dropping into one of the plush seats, he punched a number into his cell phone and listened for Mr. Li's heavily accented voice. "You on your way?"

"Yes," Li replied sharply.

"Where are you?" After listening to the response—the man was still a couple of hours away—Vaughn said, "I'll be waiting for you." He disconnected without waiting for a response and tossed the phone into his backpack. Rising, he untied the securing lines and started both engines. After backing out of the boathouse, he pointed the boat's nose toward open water and rammed the throttles as far forward as they would go.

CHAPTER EIGHT

Greg eased out of the bed and quietly padded his way across the hotel room's cool tile floor to a sliding-glass door going to the balcony. Silently moving the curtain aside, he pushed the door open and stepped into the early-morning sunshine. Two stories below him, maintenance workers in crisp white uniforms were arranging chairs and lounges around two massive swimming pools. A slight breeze blowing off the ocean gave the air a slightly salty taste and rustled the fronds of the palm trees. Above, cottony puffs of clouds floated in a blue sky.

"Ahh, another day in paradise," Marena said quietly as she stepped onto the balcony.

"I was trying to be quiet. Did I wake you?" Greg said, giving her a peck on the cheek.

"Not really. I've been halfway awake thinking about Wiggy Wiggy. I'm not sure what to expect today."

Greg chuckled. "Who knows? I keep telling myself if we don't expect too much, we won't be disappointed. I'm just hoping it's at least half what he claims. When I went down to the beach a couple of days ago to make arrangements, a couple of other guys approached me. When I told them we were going with Wiggy Wiggy, all they did was roll their eyes."

"That's not very reassuring."

"Exactly. But I figure when we meet up with him this morning, if we don't feel comfortable about it, we can cancel."

Marena yawned, did half a stretch, and said, "What time are we meeting him?"

"Ten o'clock. On the beach."

Breakfast in the hotel dining room was yogurt, fresh tropical fruit, and juice for Marena. Greg had two slices of French toast, some scrambled eggs, two slices of bacon, and guava juice.

At a few minutes before ten, they walked onto the beach with their snorkeling gear in hand to find Wiggy Wiggy smiling and waving at them.

"Come on, come on. We goin' to have a great fun day," he said. He grabbed their snorkeling gear, tossed it into the back of the boat, and extended his hand to Marena. "Come on, lady. Wiggy Wiggy will help you into da boat."

"Okay, once more," Greg began. "Where we going?"

Wiggy Wiggy shook his head as he took Marena by the arm and hoisted her into the boat. "Special place. Secret place. You gonna luv it, mon. Come on, get in. We go."

Greg and Marena exchanged glances and shrugs, and Greg climbed in.

With Greg and Marena seated on separate wooden benches, Wiggy Wiggy shoved the boat off the beach and jumped in. Scrambling to the back of the boat, he started the motor. Angling away from the beach, he revved the motor, and the boat began slicing through the water.

For over an hour the trio bounced and sliced their way through waves as they paralleled the shoreline, slowing or stopping every so often so Wiggy Wiggy could point out features in the coastline or tell them some historical fact. Then, unexpectedly, he turned the boat away from the palm tree-lined shoreline and headed toward open ocean.

"Where we going?" Greg yelled.

Wiggy Wiggy smiled. "Out to sea."

A bit of anxiety spread through Greg. "Why? I thought we were headed for a lagoon."

Wiggy Wiggy pointed into the distance at breakers crashing on a massive coral reef. "We gotta go through that reef, but only in da right place."

A few minutes later, a hundred yards outside the reef, Wiggy Wiggy slowed the boat. The waves crashed against the coral so violently that shockwaves reverberated through the air, causing Marena to cup her hands over her ears. With eyes as big as saucers, she swiveled in her seat from the front of the boat to look at Greg and Wiggy Wiggy.

Greg wrinkled his forehead. As she yelled something, he could see her lips moving and the anxiety on her face, but her words were lost in the roar of six-foot waves exploding as they slammed into the barely submerged reef. With each thunderous crash, the air filled with billions of foamy white droplets, creating a fine mist that hung perpetually in the air. Yelling to be heard over the crashing breakers, Greg turned to Wiggy Wiggy and shouted, "Please tell me we're not going in there!"

Wiggy Wiggy laughed out loud and shouted back, "Yes, mon, dat's exactly where we gonna go."

Greg glanced again at Marena, who uncovered her ears. She must have caught part of Wiggy Wiggy's response, because, squeezing the top rail of the boat in a death grip, she shouted, "We'll get killed."

"Ah, lady, you too much worry," Wiggy Wiggy yelled as he steered the boat parallel to the line of breakers. "Now looka here," he said, waving his arm across the expanse of violent waves to their left. "You try and go into the lagoon anywhere along here and you sure gonna die." Then, pointing to a rocky cliff that jutted out from the shoreline about a quarter mile ahead of them, he said, "But go in opposite ova dare, and you be safe as safe. You see, mon. Eveting be good. Jes hang on when Wiggy Wiggy tell you to hang on."

When the twenty-foot boat, with its small outboard motor, was directly opposite the rocky cliff, Wiggy Wiggy turned right, out to the ocean, rather than left, toward the shore. A few hundred yards away from the breakers, he reduced the throttle to an idle and let the boat bob up and down on the gently undulating two-foot swells.

Releasing her grip on the boat's railing and pushing the wild strands of hair out of her face, Marena breathed an obvious sign of relief. "It's almost quiet out here."

"And calm," Greg added.

"Okay, people, listen up. Now Wiggy Wiggy give you a lesson about goin' in and outta dat place." Turning the boat so its bow was pointed exactly toward the rocky cliff, he said, "Now looka straight ahead. Can you see dat da waves not breakin' so violently exactly ahead of us?"

Greg and Marena nodded.

"Da reason is because dare is a litta gap in the coral reef right tru dare. Instead of da water being only a couple feet deep like where all da breakers is, it's more like ten- or twelve-feet deep. We got plenty deep water to scoot in past the coral reef. Once inside da reef, is really smooth goin'. Only ting is, people, da waves, day gonna push us when we start goin' tru dat litta channel. We go fast, people." Then, letting out a gleeful laugh, he added, "Be way fun ride."

Greg looked at Marena, watching her expression carefully. Seeing slightly more calm than panic in her eyes, he turned to Wiggy Wiggy and asked, "What about coming out? You don't have a rocky cliff to aim for."

Wiggy Wiggy replied, "You right, mon, dare is no cliff ahead of you. *But*"—he smiled broadly—"dare is behind you. You just gotta get lined up good with the cliff at your back and go like crazy, straight out to the ocean. You get a little wet bustin' through waves comin' at cha, but not too bad. You see when we come out, mon—not so bad." Looking over at Marena, he said, "You ready, lady?"

Marena looked at Greg. He moved his head in a seesaw motion, giving her a less-than-enthusiastic nod. Swallowing, she wiped her hands on the shorts she was wearing over her swimsuit. Reaching out to grip the top rail of the boat once more in her left hand, she grasped the seat with her right and said, "I guess so."

With a gleeful laugh, Wiggy Wiggy goosed the throttle and yelled, "Hang on, people! We goin' for a ride."

The ride lasted less than a minute, but all three were drenched as the boat coasted into calmer water. "That wasn't nearly as bad as I thought it would be," Marena said with a relieved sigh.

"Dat cause Wiggy Wiggy such a good captain," he replied with a grin. Waving his hands frantically in the air and shaking his head with his mouth wide open, he said, "Udder guys, lady, day make you scream bloody murder when comin' into dis place. Den mos of dem die, churned into tiny pieces of fish food by da coral. Day not good captain like Wiggy Wiggy."

Greg exchanged grins with Marena as Wiggy Wiggy went through his antics and dialogue. Then Greg asked, "Where do we go from here?"

"We really close," Wiggy Wiggy replied. "Only quarter mile from here." Turning the boat sharply to the right so it was running parallel to the coastline, he added, "See dat litta jut of sand and da two really tall palm trees up ahead?"

"Yes," Greg answered, putting his hand up to his brows to shield his eyes from the sun's glare.

"Dat's da entrance to da lagoon. We goin' in right dare."

Two minutes later, as Wiggy Wiggy turned into the lagoon, Marena's mouth gaped open. "This is gorgeous!" she said as she scanned the crescent-shaped lagoon.

Greg peered into the water as they idled slowly forward. "It's like floating on air. The water is so clear you almost can't even tell it's there."

Marena pointed to a small structure extending over the water. "Are we going to the dock?"

"Aw, no, lady. Dat's a beat-up old ting. My dad, he built it long ago time. It's ready to fall down." Pointing to a spot where the water was as smooth as butter and the sand like powdered sugar, he said, "We goin' away over dare to da far side of the lagoon. We be closer to da good snorkeling and better spear feeshin'."

Fifty feet from the sugar sand beach, Wiggy Wiggy killed the motor and let the skiff float silently across the crystalline water. As the boat's keel scraped on the sandy beach, he jumped over the side and said, "We be here." Working his way to the bow, he pulled the boat onto the sand and held out his hand to Marena. "Let me help you, lady."

Marena took the outstretched hand and eased over the side of the boat. She scanned the half-moon bay ringed with giant palm trees and lush undergrowth as she sloshed the few feet to the powdery white-sand beach. "You didn't lie; this is paradise."

Wiggy Wiggy broke into a grin. "I told you, lady." Grabbing a large canvas bag with snorkeling gear, he added, "It's as pretty under the water as it is above." Looking at Greg, he said, "Mon, before you geet outta da boat, please to hand me da speargun. I gonna need it for lunch."

"What's on the menu?" Marena asked.

"We gonna have grilled parrotfish. But I am gonna boil sum green bananas in coconut milk. It be way good." Tossing the bag onto the sand, he reached out and took the speargun from Greg. "But we gotta feesh before we can eat," he said with a smile. "Come on. We get your snorkeling gear and go have some fun."

Kicking their fins, the trio glided back, forth, up, down, and around the lagoon's calm water. Hundreds of iridescent blue tang, yellow head wrasse, goatfish, and a dozen other varieties of fish swam within inches of them. Greg looked at his dive watch and shook his head. In what seemed like two minutes, more than two hours had whizzed past. After huffing out a mixture of water and air from his snorkel, he spit out the mouthpiece and pushed his dive mask onto his forehead. Taking a deep breath, he rolled over onto his back, extended his arms and legs, and floated on the surface of the lagoon's bathtub-warm water.

Two yards away, a steady stream of bubbles broke the surface of the turquoise water, followed a second later by Marena's head. "I've never seen so many fish in one place," she exclaimed.

"Especially when Wiggy Wiggy holds out a handful of tortilla pieces," Greg replied as he gently fanned his arms back and forth.

"Where is he, anyway?" Marena asked as she shoved her mask up onto her head.

Greg raised an arm slightly above the surface and pointed in the general direction of the dock. "He said he couldn't find a big enough parrotfish here, so he swam over there."

"I'm glad lunch is part of the deal; I'm starving."

Ten minutes later Wiggy Wiggy swam up with three speared parrotfish. "Thirty minutes," he said with a grin, "and you gonna have some good-tastin' feesh."

It wasn't thirty minutes—almost an hour passed before they ate. As Marena put the last forkful of grilled fish into her mouth, she said, "I'm not a big fish eater, but that was really good."

"Ah, lady, so the extra time it took Wiggy Wiggy was worth the wait?"

"It was." Looking at the lengthening shadows of the palm trees, she added, "Do we have time to snorkel some more?"

"You rest for a while first while Wiggy Wiggy clean up. Den you go snorkel. We got plenty time."

"No argument from me," Greg said as he lay in the shade of a palm tree. "I'm just going to catch a few winks." Pulling his cap down over his eyes, he folded his arms and was breathing deeply in less than a minute.

Greg sputtered to life when he felt the thinnest trickle of water on his chest. Seeing Marena standing above him smiling mischievously, he didn't hesitate. With a sweeping motion of his arm, he knocked her feet out from under her, and she crashed into the sand beside him.

Slapping him playfully on the chest, Marena pushed herself upright and with feigned annoyance said, "That was rude."

Greg chuckled and said, "And pouring water on me wasn't?"

"It's different when I do it," she said with a grin.

"Hey, you guys going snorkeling?" Wiggy Wiggy said as he walked up beside them.

Marena looked at Wiggy Wiggy and said, "What about the stingrays? You promised we'd see some."

"I know, I know," Wiggy Wiggy replied. "Too many things to see. We must come back another day."

Marena tilted her head and narrowed her eyes. "You did that on purpose, didn't you?"

"What? No way, lady," Wiggy Wiggy replied innocently.

Reinforcing his wife's suspicions, Greg agreed. "You purposely didn't show us any stingrays so we'd want to come back."

Wiggy Wiggy put both of his hands to his chest and said, "Oh no, mon. Wiggy Wiggy don't do dat ting. We jus ran outta time," he said, but the grin on his face belied his answer. "But if you wanna come back day afta tomorrow, Wiggy Wiggy will show you plenty stingrays. "Very good price. Same as today."

Marena shook her head but suppressed her smile as she pulled on her fins and mask. "You coming, Greg?"

"Right behind you." Looking at Wiggy Wiggy, he asked, "How long can we snorkel?"

Wiggy Wiggy shot a quick glance at the sun and then the shadows from the trees. "Be back in thirty minutes. Dat gives us plenty time to be back to Punta Cana before dark."

"Got it," Greg said as he slipped on his gear. Diving in, he kicked his way out into the lagoon, trailing behind Marena.

All too soon a shrill whistle caught Greg's attention as he broke the surface. Shoving his dive mask onto his forehead, he squinted his eyes against the glare of the sun and looked to the beach where Wiggy Wiggy was waving his arms and pointing to his wrist. "Dang," Greg muttered as he glanced at his watch. Pulling his mask back on, he searched below the water for Marena, who was kicking about ten feet below in pursuit of a school of brilliant blue tang. Sucking in a lungful of air, he dove below the surface. Kicking powerfully, he caught up to her and tapped her on the shoulder. When she looked at him, he pointed to his watch and then the surface. As they broke the surface, Greg spit out his snorkel and said, "We're late. We've got to go."

Marena looked over toward Wiggy Wiggy standing beside the skiff waving his arms and said, "How long have we been out here?"

"An hour. I should have been looking at my watch. We'd better hustle."

Without another word, the two of them began rapidly swimming toward the skiff.

"You guys havin' too much fun," Wiggy Wiggy said as they swam up beside the boat.

"Sorry, Wiggy Wiggy," Greg said. "It's my fault. I wasn't paying attention to the time."

Wiggy Wiggy shrugged. "It's no problem, mon. It took me a little longer to clean up, so I didn't bother you. We gonna be in fine shape, but we gotta go now."

Greg and Marena quickly removed their gear and dropped it into the skiff. "That was a lot of fun," Marena said as she squeezed water from her hair. Accepting a towel Wiggy Wiggy held out to her, she dried her face and arms, dropped the towel onto the skiff's seat, and in one fluid motion pulled herself up into the boat.

Greg walked to the bow of the skiff and said, "Climb in, Wiggy Wiggy. I'll push us off."

"T'anks, mon," Wiggy Wiggy replied as he climbed into the skiff and maneuvered his way past Marena to the outboard motor. "Okay, mon," he called out as he positioned himself to pull on the starting rope. "Push."

Pushing hard for several steps, Greg hauled himself into the skiff at the last second as the skiff coasted backward, away from the beach.

Wiggy Wiggy leaned back and yanked on the starting rope. The motor turned over but made no effort to start. Setting the choke and adjusting the throttle, Wiggy Wiggy gave another powerful pull on the starting rope. When nothing happened, he tried three more times in rapid succession.

"Did you remember to open the tank's vent?" Greg asked as the skiff drifted farther away from the beach.

Wiggy Wiggy nodded but said nothing.

"Did you prime it?"

Another nod.

"Does it have a kill switch?"

"Yeah, mon, but I already close it. Should be no problem."

"I don't want to ask a stupid question," Marena said. "But are we out of gas?"

Wiggy Wiggy shook his head, "Shouldn't be."

"Should you check?" Marena asked when he made no effort to move.

Wiggy Wiggy curled his lip and was about to dismiss the suggestion when Greg said, "Can't hurt."

Wiggy Wiggy gave a doubtful shrug and leaned forward to where two bright-red gas tanks were sitting in the bottom of the skiff. Removing the filler cap on the first, he peered inside. "About one gallon," he said. Removing the cap from the second, he said, "Full."

After another dozen frantic pulls on the starter rope, Wiggy Wiggy looked up and said, “We be drifting a long way. I tink it best, mon, if we get back to da shore and figgir dis out rather dan float around in da lagoon.”

“Whatever you think,” Greg said. “You got an oar or a paddle?”

Wiggy Wiggy smiled as he shook his head. “No, mon, but we got arms and legs. And we got fins!”

The three of them tried using diving fins as oars but gave up after a few minutes of little progress. “What if we get in the water and try pulling the boat to shore?” Marena asked.

“What do you think, Wiggy Wiggy, can we act like a motor and push it?” Greg asked.

“I think we pull it, mon. Be easier.”

Putting on their fins, mask and snorkels, Wiggy Wiggy and Greg jumped into the water. “Hey, lady, toss me those ropes,” Wiggy Wiggy said as he swam to the front of the boat. “I’ll tie them to the bow ring.”

With two ropes tied to the metal ring protruding from the bow of the boat, Wiggy Wiggy and Greg played out a dozen feet of rope from the coil they held in their hands. Wiggy Wiggy tied the rope around his waist, placing the knot in the middle of his back, and swam about ten feet ahead of Greg. Greg gripped his rope in both hands, rolled onto his back and said, “You ready, Wiggy Wiggy?”

“Ya, mon.”

“What should I do?” Marena asked.

“Sit there,” Greg replied. “Your hundred pounds isn’t going to make or break us. Okay, Wiggy Wiggy, let’s do this.”

With water frothing from the frantic kicking of the fins, the skiff slowly began following Greg and Wiggy Wiggy like a whale on a leash. Three minutes into the towing operation they stopped at almost the same time. Gasping a breath of air, Greg said, “This is tougher than I thought it would be.”

Looking around, Wiggy Wiggy said, “Ya, mon. It gonna be too far to get back to where we ate lunch. Let’s try to go ova dare by those thick trees.”

“Not much of a beach,” Greg said, “but it’s a lot closer.”

Turning at a right angle to where they had been headed, the two men resumed kicking. Three stops and ten minutes later they struggled onto the narrow beach and collapsed in exhaustion. Marena jumped out of the skiff and took the rope from Greg's hands. "Not that I think it's going to go anywhere, but I'm going to tie the rope around a tree."

While Marena tied, Greg looked over at Wiggy Wiggy and said, "What now?"

CHAPTER NINE

An hour later Marena watched as Wiggy Wiggy slumped beside the outboard motor and wiped his greasy hands on a rag that was already caked with dirt and grime. Shaking his head, their guide looked at Greg and said, "Dats all I know to do, mon. I don't know why da dumb ting won't start."

The trio exchanged disheartened glances, and an awkward minute of silence passed before Marena said, "Okay, well, if we can't get the thing to start, how about hiking out of here, is that a possibility?"

Wiggy Wiggy blew a snort out his nose and pointed to Marena's feet. "In dose flip-flops, you not gonna make it very far." Pointing to the tangled vegetation that was thick with trees, brush, vines, and grass, he said, "Pretty hard walkin'. Take you six, maybe seven hours." Then, pointing to the lowering sun, he said, "Besides, gettin' dark soon. Don't wanna be out tromping around in de dark in dat stuff."

Greg looked at his watch. "Six o'clock. What do we have—maybe an hour before sunset?"

Wiggy Wiggy gave a dejected nod. "About. Maybe a litta longer."

Greg and Marena looked at each other and shrugged while Wiggy Wiggy stared at the silent motor. Several minutes passed in silence before Greg finally spoke. "We can spend the night here."

Marena and Wiggy Wiggy both looked at him as if he'd lost his mind. "What? You're joking," Marena said, recoiling at the suggestion.

Greg shook his head. "Not at all." Pointing to a cooler in the back of the boat, he said, "We've got a dozen bottles of water, matches to build a fire, all the cooking utensils we need, and"—he pointed to the lagoon—"more fish than we can possibly eat. Tomorrow morning we can try and get the motor started or hike out." Pointing across the lagoon to the dock, he said, “It looks like there’s a road or at least a jeep trail leading away from the dock over there. How hard can it be to follow it out of here?”

There was another bout of silence as Marena and Wiggy Wiggy considered the idea. She looked at Wiggy Wiggy and said, “He’s got a point. Do you have a better idea?”

Wiggy Wiggy slowly shook his head. Then the corners of his mouth turned up in the faintest smile. “You good people,” he said sincerely. “T’anks.” And then, with a huge grin on his face, he said, “I tell you what. Wiggy Wiggy goin’ to make you the very finest dinner you ever ate.” Looking at Marena, he said, “We gonna have eel in coconut milk, plus some way good surprise food. You gonna really like dinna tonight.”

Marena’s head sagged, and she curled her lip. “Eel?”

Wiggy Wiggy nodded. “Yeah, lady. Way good. You liked lunch, didn’t ya?”

Marena nodded, albeit warily.

“Den, trus’ me, lady, you gonna love dinna.”

The sense of foreboding that had enveloped the trio only a few minutes before gave way to cautious enthusiasm. Greg said, “Eel it is. What can we do to help?”

Wiggy Wiggy jumped up from his seat and said, “Wiggy Wiggy goin’ to go swim over to dat dock. Der was a great perfect eel der dis mornin’. You know how to build a fire?”

“Absolutely,” Greg replied.

“Okay den, you guys build da fire while I spear an eel.” Then, opening the lid to a storage locker crammed with an assortment of rusty tools, oily rags, pieces of wire and an odd collection of broken motor parts, he pulled out a rusty machete. “Ova der on the ground is a bunch o’ coconuts. You split them open and poor the milk in dat pan. Save da coconut meat though. I gonna make someting way good with it.”

Greg nodded then pointed across the lagoon to the dock. “That’s quite a swim, Wiggy Wiggy. Are you sure you don’t want to just get a couple fish right around here?”

“No, mon. Not dat far for Wiggy Wiggy. No problem. You build fire and get coconut milk. I’ll get eel and be back fast.”

In less time than it took Greg and Marena to start carrying the pans, grill, and matches from the skiff to the beach, Wiggy Wiggy had donned his fins, mask, and snorkel. Grabbing the speargun, he dove into the water and started rapidly kicking toward the dock.

Fifteen minutes later, with the warm orange and yellow flames of a small fire licking at her cheeks, Marena tossed in two small pieces of driftwood and stood up. Stretching her back, she walked over to the boat and picked up an old pair of binoculars that had been mixed in with all the old engine parts. After looping the leather strap around her neck, she raised them to her eyes and looked across the cove at the dock.

"I'm not sure I'm excited about it, but dinner's coming," she called over her shoulder as she focused on Wiggy Wiggy, who was bobbing in the water near the dock, waving a four-foot-long eel from the tip of a spear. "I can't believe it's going to taste very good," she said as he began swimming quickly toward her.

She looked back at her husband, who whacked the top from his third coconut, and as he poured the milk into the pot, he looked over at the dock. "I agree, but he's been right about everything so far, so who knows?"

As Greg squatted down and picked up the fourth coconut, Marena shifted the binoculars to the entrance of the lagoon and exclaimed, "Unbelievable!" Calling over her shoulder, she said, "There's a boat coming in. We're about to be rescued."

Greg joined her and looked across the two hundred yards of flat, calm water to the lagoon's entrance. Marena took in the forty-foot teal, purple, blue, and white boat and glanced at Greg. He shook his head and said, "Crazy paint scheme, but I'd ride in a bathtub as long as they can help us."

As the low rumble of the boat's twin engines bounced around the cove, Marena followed Greg's gaze as he shifted it from the boat to the ebony body that had stopped swimming and was now looking at the boat. They watched as Wiggy Wiggy suddenly abandoned the spear gun and eel and began waving his arms frantically.

"What's he doing?" Marena asked, looking at Wiggy Wiggy. "Why's he waving at us and not the boat?"

They stared at Wiggy Wiggy's arm movements. Instead of facing the boat with his arms extended high above his head and waving side-to-side as if trying to draw the attention of the driver, he was moving them back and forth as if he was trying to tell them to back away or hide. "He's not waving at the boat, Marena," Greg said, his voice tinged with worry. "He's motioning for us to get off the beach."

Marena focused the binoculars on Wiggy Wiggy for a second and then lowered them again. "That doesn't make sense."

Greg seemed to ignore her comment as he looked first at Wiggy Wiggy and then over at the man standing at the helm of the boat. Dropping the coconut, he said, “Maybe not, but something’s not right. Let’s do what he wants.”

“Why?” Marena questioned as Greg began kicking sand onto the fire.

“Now!” Greg commanded. “Grab your jacket; let’s go.”

“Why?” Marena again demanded as she hurriedly grabbed the lightweight linen jacket from the skiff.

The sharp crack of a pistol shot shattered the air and made Greg and Marena abruptly look up in time to see Wiggy Wiggy dive below the water’s surface.

“Marena!” Greg screamed. “Come on!”

Curling her toes so her flip-flops wouldn’t come off, Marena ran to where Greg was standing. Pushing her ahead, Greg pointed to the sparsest part of the thick undergrowth and said, “Through there.” Bending over as he ran, he plunged into the jungle after her. They had gone only a dozen feet when another gunshot shattered the evening calm. “Wait,” Greg huffed out.

Marena stopped and looked over as Greg parted some of the foliage for an unobstructed view of the lagoon. Marena again raised the binoculars. Swimming madly toward the skiff with long, powerful strokes, Wiggy Wiggy had made it twenty-five yards from the dock when the boat turned and headed straight for him. The boat didn’t increase its speed; it bore down on him slowly and steadily.

“Swim, Wiggy Wiggy, swim,” Marena urged through her rising panic as she watched him frantically stroke to outpace the oncoming boat. But Wiggy Wiggy’s arms and legs were no match for the boat’s speed. The perfectly aimed boat rode up his back and over him. Marena gasped and clutched Greg’s arm.

The boat idled as the driver scanned the water. When Wiggy Wiggy’s unconscious body floated up behind the boat, the driver reversed the vessel and aimed the stern at the unmoving form. Letting the boat glide away from the red cloud that now tinged the water, the driver waited until the body bobbed back to the surface before continuing toward the dock.

Marena bent over and vomited.

“Come on,” Greg said, grabbing Marena by the arm. “We’re going.”

Marena shook off Greg’s hand, wiped bile from her lips on her forearm, and stared at Greg in stunned silence.

"Marena!" he said forcefully, gripping her by the arm, "Come on, we've got to go."

"Is he dead?" she mumbled without moving.

"I don't know. Maybe. Probably," Greg answered. Tugging Marena's arm, he said again, "We can't stay here. We've got to go!"

Marena swallowed, ran her hand over her face, and asked, "Where?"

"The road. If we can work our way around to it, we can follow it out of here. It has to lead somewhere."

They had struggled over less than a hundred feet when the sound of a car's engine and the blare of a horn made them stop in their tracks. "What's that?" Marena asked.

"Sounds like a car horn, but I can't tell where it came from."

"The dock—it sounded like it came from over by the dock."

A second later they heard the rumble of the boat's motors intensify. Dropping Marena's hand, Greg said, "Wait here. I'm going back for a look."

"No way!" Marena exclaimed, clamping onto Greg's hand. "I'm going wherever you're going."

Back where they'd watched Wiggy Wiggy's murder, Greg and Marena each parted the foliage and watched the boat accelerate toward the dock.

Parked in the small clearing at the end of the dock was a black Cadillac Escalade with three men standing beside it—one dressed in a black suit, the other two wearing black jeans and white T-shirts.

Marena's voice trembled. "Who are these people?"

Greg ignored the question as he watched the boat pull up to the dock and the driver toss securing lines to the two men in T-shirts. "Let me see those binoculars."

But Marena already had them up to her eyes with her shaking hands. "It looks like there are three men from the car, but I can only see one guy in the boat." She leaned slightly forward and watched as the boat driver climbed onto the dock.

"Can you tell what they're doing?" Greg asked.

"They've all walked to the back of the SUV, and one of them has pulled out a large suitcase. It's one of those aluminum jobs with the hard sides. The three guys in the SUV are Asian." Then, focusing more sharply, she continued. "The other guy is white. Deep tan, short dark hair . . ." She was just about to hand Greg the binoculars when the boat driver turned and looked straight at where she and Greg were hiding. Marena refocused the binoculars and studied the man. When he suddenly pointed to exactly where they were hiding, Marena lowered the binoculars from her eyes and dropped down, grabbing Greg by the arm to pull him down with her.

"What?" Greg said; he crouched next to her.

"The guy from the boat pointed right at us," she said.

"Did he see us?"

"I don't know. It looked like he could see us. I panicked."

"Let me see those," Greg said, reaching for the binoculars. Slowly rising, he parted the underbrush and focused on the dock.

"What's happening?"

"The guy in the suit and the boat driver must be arguing because the boat driver keeps pointing to the skiff. The man in the suit is shaking his head and pointing at the sun."

Marena stood slowly and again parted the foliage. A moment later the two men in jeans pulled guns from the waistbands of their pants and jumped from the dock to the beach. In an odd mixture of a fast walk and a trot, they began hurrying the quarter mile to the skiff. They had only covered about fifty feet when the boat driver hurried down the dock. Putting the suitcase into the boat, he untied the ropes and started the boat's engines, which instantly revved up, shattering the quiet of the lagoon, and the boat shot away from the dock. Marena watched the boat speed toward the lagoon's entrance. "He's in a hurry," she said.

"Darkness," Greg said. "He's got to make it through the breakers before it's too dark to see."

Marena cast a quick glance at the two men hurrying along the beach, and Greg grabbed her by the hand. "Come on," he said again. Together they charged into the tangled foliage.

CHAPTER TEN

Greg clamped his hand over Marena's mouth to stifle her scream when the first bullet slammed into a palm tree fifty feet from where they were sitting. The second bullet tore through the foliage, snapping thin branches and punching holes in leaves until its momentum was sapped and it tumbled harmlessly to the ground. Easing his hand from Marena's mouth, he whispered softly in her ear, "They don't know where we are; they're just shooting at noises."

Marena nodded in agreement, feeling only marginally comforted, and whispered back, "What do we do now?"

"Stay here," Greg whispered. "Can you hang on for a few more minutes?"

"Do I have a choice?"

Greg shook his head and put a finger to his lips.

Hang on was the right choice of words. They were perched thirty feet above the ground in a catalpa tree. Sitting precariously on a thick limb with their feet dangling in the air, they balanced themselves by clinging to a flimsy branch just above their heads. A minute later the two men had stumbled through the undergrowth and were standing directly below them.

The larger of the two men wiped sweat from his face and said, "This is pointless; we should go back."

"It wouldn't have been so pointless if you hadn't started shooting at shadows," the smaller of the two groused.

"I heard something; what was I supposed to do?"

"You didn't need to shoot. If there is anyone out here, your stupidity has told them exactly where we are."

The larger man ignored the comment. "It's getting too dark. I can barely see my feet. Let's go back. It's going to be hard enough just getting to the beach."

Blowing out a sigh, the smaller man shoved his pistol into his waistband and said, "We'll go back, but you must explain it to Father."

The larger man shrugged and swatted at the mosquitoes swarming above his head. "Fine. Let's just get out of here." Then, pointing with the gun to where they had just come from, he said, "You go first."

"Just don't shoot me," the smaller man snarled as he began clawing his way through the brush.

The two men had gone only half a dozen paces when panic spread through Marena. The nervous, unconscious wiggling of her feet had dislodged the flip-flop from between the toes on her right foot. Rapidly lifting her leg so it was straight out in front of her to keep the flip-flop from falling, she began wiggling her toes to work it back onto her foot. She'd almost succeeded when a cramp surged through her hamstring muscle with enough force it caused her leg to contract. The dark-brown flip-flop bobbled on her toes for the briefest second and fell.

As the flip-flop floated through the air, it tumbled over and over until it struck a small branch, which caused it to enter a flat spin. Rotating around and around, the sole down, it hit a bare spot of dirt with a distinct slap. A fraction of a second later, four rapid gunshots shattered the air, followed by a voice screaming, "Stop shooting, you idiot!"

"I heard something."

"Shut up and put that gun away. You're going to kill me."

"I heard something back there. Honest. It sounded like—"

"Shut up."

Greg looked over, his face shocked, as Marena suddenly clambered up from the limb. Balancing with one leg on the limb and holding onto a branch with one hand, she began rapidly massaging her hamstring. Looking over at Greg, she mouthed, "Charley horse."

Greg put his finger to his mouth and sat motionless, listening. When the thrashing and stumbling of the two men grew dimmer and finally subsided, he shook his head. "That was close," he whispered. "You okay?"

Marena nodded her head and grimaced in pain from the leg cramp. "Can we get down from here?" she whispered.

Greg shook his head. "Can you hang on for another couple of minutes?"

Marena massaged her leg more furiously. "Maybe."

Several minutes later the sound of a car starting made Greg stand up on the limb. "Now we can get down."

Five minutes later they were both kneeling on the ground in the dark, feeling with their hands for Marena's flip-flop. "Got it," Marena said. Then, after a short pause, she exclaimed, "It's got a hole in it! He shot my flip-flop!"

"We're lucky that's all he shot," Greg replied. "Your leg okay? Can you walk?"

"It's fine," Marena said.

It took an hour of stumbling over fallen trees, getting slapped in the face with unseen branches, Marena's flip-flop falling off, and swatting at hordes of riled-up mosquitoes before their roundabout route let them spill out onto the sandy beach. Fifteen minutes later, totally exhausted, they dropped down to a protected little spot of bare ground a hundred feet from the boat.

Sitting in the darkness, Marena asked, "How do you think Wiggy Wiggy knew to warn us?"

Greg shook his head. "Who knows?"

"Do you think he messed around with drugs and drug runners?"

Greg considered the question. "Maybe," he finally said. "He never told us why his father built the dock here. Maybe his dad was a drug runner. Whatever it was, when he saw the boat coming in, I think he just figured something was wrong."

"What do you mean?"

"Well, we're out here in a lagoon so remote and dangerous to get to that virtually nobody comes here. He probably saw the kind of boat drug runners use working its way into the lagoon and figured it couldn't be good."

"But why kill him? It's not like we saw him do anything illegal."

"I don't know, Marena. I have no idea how those people think."

Marena went quiet for a minute before softly asking, "How are we going to get out of here?"

Greg looked at her face silhouetted in the darkness. After a moment he said, "Tomorrow morning I think we should stick to our original plan. We can give the boat another try, and if we can't get it running, then we'll walk. I've been thinking about the motor on the skiff. We didn't check the fuel filter. I'm wondering if it's plugged."

"Do you know how to fix it if it is?"

"I've never tried on an outboard motor before, but it can't be that tough to figure out. I only wish I'd thought of it before now; then maybe this nightmare wouldn't have happened."

Marena shifted so their faces were only a couple of inches apart. Gripping his arm, she said, "Listen to me, Greg. This isn't your fault. Even if it is a stupid fuel filter issue, you couldn't have known. You're not to blame."

Greg looked at her, his lips tightening into a forced smile, but said nothing.

"Look," she said. "If the filter isn't the problem, at least we know that if that Escalade made it in here, there's got to be another way out. But remember earlier when Wiggy Wiggy said it would take six or seven hours to walk out? Who knows where we'll end up, but once we hit a highway or house, we can find a phone or someone to take us to a police station."

After several minutes of silence and just as Greg was surrendering to sleep, Marena said, "Greg, you awake?"

"Umm, barely."

"Do you think those guys will come back in the morning to try to find us?"

Greg opened his eyes slightly and mumbled, "Don't know."

"If we're going to try getting out of here in the boat, maybe we should be down there before the sun comes up. If we can get it started, don't you think we should be out of the lagoon at daylight in case they do show up?"

"Uh huh," Greg said groggily.

"Greg?"

"Yeah?"

"How much longer until daylight?"

Greg stirred, lifted his hands, and pressed the button on his dive watch to illuminate the dials. "It's just after midnight, so maybe another six hours." Dropping his hands, he muttered, "Now, try to get some sleep."

Marena snuggled closer, rested her head against his shoulder, and closed her eyes.

***

Not many hours later, when the sky was still utterly dark and filled with countless stars, Greg gently nudged Marena and said, "Wake up."

Marena opened her eyes, rubbed them, and asked, “What time is it?”

“Five,” Greg replied as he rolled his shoulders to try to work out some of the stiffness. Slowly rising, he made a halfhearted attempt to stretch and said, “I feel like I’ve been run over with a steamroller.”

Marena stretched her legs out in front of her and rolled her head from side to side. “I ache everywhere. I’m not sure I can move.”

“Don’t try. I’m going over to the skiff to see what I can figure out. I don’t know how long it will take me, but if you hear it start, get over there in a hurry.”

“It’s still dark,” Marena protested. “We can’t leave in the dark.”

Greg nodded. “I know, but I’d rather have it started and be doing donuts in the lagoon while waiting for daylight than wait for daylight and run the risk of those guys showing up.”

“Okay,” Marena said and laid her head back against the clump of grass she was using for a pillow.

Walking from the dense foliage onto the sandy beach, Greg had covered half the distance to the skiff when he dove onto his belly. A fraction of a second later a bright beam of light emanating from the dock swept past him, missing his body by less than a foot. Lifting his head barely enough to see, he watched the beam slowly pan around the perimeter of the lagoon. Frantically crawling on his knees and elbows, he made his way off the beach and rolled into the protection of a clump of tall grass. A second later, the beam again burst through the early-morning darkness, sweeping back and forth across the black water of the lagoon, the white sandy beach, and finally the thick green foliage that ringed the beach.

The beam swept past where Greg had first dropped to his belly, focused briefly on the skiff, and then panned back to the trail his crawling had left in the sand. Very slowly, the bright beam traced his trail from the beach to the clump of grass and stopped. Moving first an arm, then a leg, and then the other arm and leg, Greg pushed himself backward into the foliage and away from the brightness of the light. Once beyond the circle of light, he stood up and began running, crawling, stumbling, and thrashing his way through the undergrowth until he dove headfirst into the small protected clearing where Marena lay. Shaking her forcefully on her shoulder, he said, “Get up. We gotta go now!”

“What happened?” Marena said groggily as Greg yanked her to her feet.

“They’re still here. Put on your flip-flops; we don’t have much time.”

Marena wiggled her feet into the flip-flops, and Greg pulled Marena by the arm and headed into the jungle.

Marena struggled to keep up, and Greg cast a quick glance over his shoulder in time to see flashlight beams sweeping back and forth as two men began running along the beach.

In less than a hundred yards, Marena hissed, "Greg, you need to stop. I've lost one of my flip-flops."

Turning back, Greg dropped to his knees and began pawing through the damp grass and branches. Finding the flip-flop, he held it out to Marena. "You doing okay?"

"No! I'm scared," Marena said in a breathless sob that was far too loud.

Greg jumped up, gave her a tight hug, and said, "It's going to be okay. We're going to be just fine, but we need to keep moving."

"What makes you think we're going to be fine?" Marena choked out.

"Because those guys have no idea where we are or where we're headed. Besides, in another fifteen minutes, the sun will be up. All we need to do is find our way to that road, and we'll be okay."

Marena shook her head and said, "I'm so tired. Can't we just hide somewhere until daylight? My legs and feet hurt so badly I can hardly walk. You're lucky you have your dive booties; these flip-flops are falling apart."

Greg relaxed his hug and looked down at her feet and up at her dirty, scratched face. "I don't think it's safe to try hiding. Can you make it up this little hill? We can rest up there for a few minutes. If we're going to stop, I'd rather be on higher ground. We'd stand a better chance of seeing anyone coming toward us."

They struggled to a fallen palm tree and plunked down side by side. "What happened back there? Did they see you?" Marena asked.

"Who knows?" Greg answered. "But one thing is for certain: we're not getting out of here by boat."

They sat in silence, their backs tight against the tree's rough bark, and strained their ears for any manmade sounds. For nearly fifteen minutes they sat motionless, hearing nothing but endless buzzing of mosquitoes swarming around their sweaty bodies. Fifteen minutes after that the eastern sky began taking on the slightest hint of yellow. As the black of night slowly surrendered to a new day, Greg looked at Marena and said, "I know this is going to be tough on you, but if you're ready, I think we need to pick our way out of here."

CHAPTER ELEVEN

Marena braced herself next to Greg in the back of the dented Isuzu pickup truck as it swerved from the flow of traffic hurtling along the busy highway. As the driver skidded to a stop in the loose gravel on the side of the road, he poked his head out the window and shouted, *"Policia, policia,"* while pointing to a nondescript two-story stucco building fifty feet away.

Struggling to their feet and easing their aching and stiff bodies over the tailgate, Greg and Marina stepped into a cloud of blue exhaust. Taking a breath of the blue air, Marena nodded to the four squealing piglets they had shared the back of the truck with for two hours and said, "Smells better than them."

"Makes me glad I work with horses," Greg replied. Then, turning toward the truck's driver, he waved and called out, *"Gracias. Muchas gracias."*

The driver flashed a huge smile of rotting teeth, gave a little wave, and sped away, leaving a smoke screen of blue exhaust as the truck raced back onto the highway.

Marina turned and looked at the faded black letters emblazoned across the building. *"Policía Nacional Dominican,"* Greg mumbled.

"You think anyone speaks English?" Marena asked, pulling the torn and dirty linen jacket a little tighter around her equally dirty swimsuit and body.

"We can hope."

Greg pulled open the heavy glass door, and they stepped from the oppressive heat into the coolness of an air-conditioned lobby. The room was smaller than the living rooms of most homes, and while it wasn't exactly dirty, it wasn't clean. The trash can in the corner was overflowing with empty plastic water bottles, crumpled paper, and a white fast food sack. Three stark metal chairs lined one wall, and five more were arranged in a crude circle in the far corner. A trail of dried blood led from the entrance to a solid metal door in the opposite wall. Immediately beside the metal door was a small waist-high counter with a thick window of bulletproof glass, behind which sat an unsmiling thirty-something man in black army fatigues. The man looked up from his magazine and studied Greg and Marena as they approached.

Greg leaned forward to a small metal grate in the thick glass and asked in Spanish, *"¿Habla inglés?"*

The man shook his head.

Greg expelled a dejected sigh as he turned toward Marena.

The corners of her mouth dropped into a frown, and she was about to say something when the man stood and said, *"Un minuto"* and disappeared around a corner.

A minute later he returned, followed closely by a rotund little man with a balding head and sagging jowls. He was dressed in a wrinkled white shirt saturated with sweat stains that reached nearly to his waist. His tie was undone and askew, and his trousers sagged below his protruding belly. Muscling the first man aside, he leaned toward the metal grate and in heavily accented English asked brusquely, "What do you want?"

Greg took a breath, swallowed, and said, "I . . . we . . . want to report a murder."

"I see. And who are you?"

"My name is Greg Walker, and this is my wife, Marena. We're from the United States. We were—"

"Let me see your passports," the man bluntly interrupted. Pointing to a small opening at the bottom of the glass he said, "Push them through there."

Greg shook his head. "We don't have them with us."

"Why?"

"We were out snorkeling and—"

"Where are your papers?" He didn't say it angrily but with a definite sharp air of authority.

"Back at our hotel, locked in a safe," Greg replied. "We were out snorkeling and—"

In the almost three years since Marena's surgery, in her struggles to become a carrot, she had mostly succeeded in lengthening the fuse on her temper. But watching Wiggy Wiggy get brutally killed, fleeing for her life from men with guns, struggling for hours through the jungle, riding in the back of a pickup truck with squealing piglets, and now facing a cop who was more interested in their passports than in a murder, she exploded. "Look. We'll get you passports later. Right now we want to report a murder. Do you understand? Murder! We want to report a murder!"

The non-English-speaking man behind the glass may not have understood her words, but Marena knew there was no mistaking the anger and frustration in her voice. Both men pulled back at the sudden outburst and stared at Marena with wide eyes and mouths slightly agape. Before either of them could move, a third man strode up behind them. Well over six feet tall with broad shoulders and a narrow waist, thick black hair, and a perfectly trimmed moustache, he put a hand on the shoulder of each man and said, "Let them enter."

Without hesitating, the white-shirted man reached under the desk and pushed a button that buzzed the electronic lock in the door.

Pointing toward the door, the third man looked at Greg and said, "Push the door."

Greg pushed open the door and stepped aside so Marena could enter. In a hushed voice he said, "Wow, I haven't seen that in a while."

Through gritted teeth, Marena replied, "Sorry. I couldn't help myself," as she eased passed him.

"Don't apologize. They deserved it," Greg said as he followed her through the door.

"My name is Colonel Miguel Roman," the taller man said. "I am in charge of this and several other offices of the National Police Force. And you are?"

"Greg Walker, and this is my wife, Marena. We're on a vacation from the United States."

"Where in the United States, may I ask?"

"St. George, Utah," Marena replied only slightly more calmly. "It's a city in the southwest corner of the state."

"I see," he said with a slight nod of his head. "Please, follow me." Walking halfway down a dimly lit corridor, he said, "We'll go in here," and stepped aside to allow Greg and Marena to enter the room ahead of him.

As Marena brushed past Roman, the white-shirted man walked up and spoke to the colonel in Spanish.

Roman looked at the man and then at the Walkers. Shaking his head, he pointed back toward the outer office and gave a terse command.

The white-shirted man scowled at the apparent rebuff but turned and walked away.

Roman entered the cramped room and pulled the door partially closed behind him. As he walked past Marena, she said, "You speak English very well."

"Thank you," Roman replied matter-of-factly. "I spent a year in the United States working with your FBI and Drug Enforcement Agency. Please, sit down," he added, pointing to two gray metal folding chairs beside one of the two cluttered desks. "You look tired and thirsty; can I get you some water?"

"Yes, thank you," Marena said. "I'm dying of thirst."

As Roman walked out the door, Marena studied his perfectly laundered and pressed black fatigues and the mirrorlike shine on his combat boots. She leaned over to comment to Greg about it but stopped when Roman reappeared, two bottles of water in hand.

"If you need more, just ask."

Greg and Marena each unscrewed the caps and gulped down half the water without taking a breath. "Thank you," Greg replied. "Water has never tasted so good."

Roman smiled blandly. "Now," he said as Marena set her bottle down on the corner of desk. "I heard you say you want to report a murder. Can you give me some details?"

It took Greg and Marena, each jumping in from time to time to add details the other forgot, thirty minutes to relate their experience. At no time did Roman ask a question or make a note of any kind. His only movement was to repeatedly snap the cap of a pen on and off. When they finished, Roman snapped the cap on a final time and tossed the pen onto the desk. "Is that all?"

"Pretty much," Greg replied. "I can't think of anything else, can you?" he asked Marena.

Marena shook her head.

With an earnest expression on his face, Roman leaned forward and said, "The man who ran over this Wiggy Wiggy—can you describe him?"

Greg pointed to Marena and said, "She got a better look at him than I did."

Marena began slowly. "He has a dark complexion but probably isn't Hispanic; his hair is too light—more brown than black and cut short on the sides. No beard or mustache. I can't tell you the exact color of his eyes, but they were dark, maybe brown or black. Definitely not blue or gray; I'm sure of that. He was trim and looked to be in good physical shape. Not big with muscles, but solid, you know what I mean? Kind of like your build." Running a quick eye over Roman, she said, "Maybe a little smaller."

"How tall?" Roman asked.

"I don't know. Shorter than my husband, so maybe 5'10". Shorter than six feet, for sure, but he was taller than the three Asian men."

"How old?

Marena shrugged and shook her head. Her response came out as more of a question than an answer. "Late thirties? Maybe early forties. I don't know. Maybe even older."

Roman leaned back in his chair, obviously contemplating Marena's description. After a moment of silence, he leaned forward and said, "I'm afraid you really haven't given us much to go on."

Marena's jaw dropped, and her already-shortened fuse shrunk just a little more. "Excuse me?" she said in bewilderment. "We've told you all kinds of details. All you need to do is get in a boat or in a truck and go out to the lagoon, and you'll see everything."

Roman shook his head. "Let me explain it to you. First of all, this Wiggy Wiggy"—he hesitated—"Do you even know his real name?"

"Wiggains," Marena answered quickly.

"And?" Roman replied without emotion. "His last name—what is that?"

Marena looked at Greg for help. Seeing a blank face and a shallow headshake, she replied, "I don't know; he never said."

"Exactly," Roman replied evenly. "Even if we did know his name, it would make little difference. Based on what you've told me, I am almost certain he is Haitian, not Dominicano."

"How can you know that, and why does it matter?" Marena asked.

"His name alone is the most obvious clue. Because of early British influence in Haiti, Wiggains is a very common Haitian name, but not here. We Dominicanos are proud of our Spanish heritage. It is difficult to believe any Dominicano would name a child Wiggains. And as for why it matters, I don't need to remind you that Haiti is an impoverished country. Since the earthquake, there are virtually no records. Finding who he was, where he lived, or any relatives would be extremely difficult, most likely impossible."

"You must have some record of him entering the Dominican Republic. A visa or work permit or something like that," Greg interjected.

Roman shook his head and replied as if he was talking to a child. "Haiti and the Dominican Republic share the same island, and we have a common border. But, like your border with Mexico, it is like a sieve. When Haitians enter this country, they do not stop at our immigration office and apply for a visa because they know it would be refused. They sneak into the country illegally and hope to earn money to send back to their families. Based on what you've told me, I would be surprised if he *wasn't* here illegally."

"What about the murderer's boat? Can you check on that?" Marena asked.

"Perhaps, if we had something more to go on than the colors you told me—a registration number, the make or model, even a name would help."

"*Offshore Account*," Marena said bluntly.

Greg's head swiveled around to Marena in surprise. "How do you know that?"

"I saw it yesterday when I looked through the binoculars. It was painted in big gold letters on the back end."

Greg and Marena looked at Roman expectantly.

Marena's hope evaporated when Roman instantly replied with, "Stolen, we think. Yesterday afternoon we received a report that it was missing during a fire at a marina south of here," Roman answered.

"Well, you can at least go out to the lagoon and get Wiggy Wiggy's boat and retrieve his body," Marena said sharply.

"That we will attempt to do," Roman replied with a nod. "But, truthfully, I don't expect to find the boat or the body. Both will undoubtedly be gone by now."

The three of them sat in silence for a moment. Then Greg said, "So you're really not going to do anything, then, are you?"

Roman paused, exchanged eye contact with both of them, and then drew his mouth into a frown. "I've spent nearly twenty years in the National Police. During that time, I've dealt with countless drug-related murders. A few months ago a man, a woman, and their children were shot because the man got drunk one night and accidently mentioned to the wrong person that he helped load drugs onto a boat. The drug runners killed the man and his family as a warning to others who may have helped. Just recently, seven little children were killed in Bavaro when a car carrying drug traffickers exploded. We find bodies washed up on the beaches with bullet holes in their heads or people staked in the jungles, their stomachs cut open. But one thing we never find is enough evidence to lead us to the people who commit the crimes. So, while I will dispatch men to the lagoon, I suspect the boat will be gone and the body will be fish food at the bottom of the ocean."

"I see," Greg said slowly. "Where are we, then?"

"You've given me an accurate description of where the lagoon is, so it won't be difficult to find. We will thoroughly search the area for something that may lead us to the man in the boat or the Asian men in the car. In the meantime, I am requiring you to remain in the Dominican Republic, at least for a few more days. We may have additional questions for you."

Greg looked at Roman quizzically. "Requiring?"

"Yes. You are not free to leave just now."

"But we've done nothing wrong," Marena objected.

Roman shook his head. "You are not under arrest, but you are part of an investigation—a key part. You must remain in the Dominican Republic. I am not restricting where you may travel within the country, but I am requiring that you contact me whenever you travel outside Punta Cana." Picking up the pen he had been fiddling with earlier, Roman wrote on a piece of paper. "This is my mobile number. You are to call me every morning and every evening, letting me know your whereabouts."

"Why?" Marena asked.

Roman hesitated for a moment. "It is for your personal security."

Marena cocked her head slightly. "Are you suggesting we're in some kind of danger?"

Roman leaned slightly forward and said, "You witnessed what I suspect is a drug-related murder, Mrs. Walker, and you have provided me with a very accurate description of the murderer. You are the kind of—how shall I phrase this—loose end a drug runner would not like to leave untied. It is possible, perhaps even likely, that these men are still very much interested in finding you." Extending the paper to Greg, he added, "Of course, if you notice anyone or anything suspicious, you should call me immediately."

"They have no idea where to look for us," Greg said without reaching for the paper. "There are thousands of hotels in the Dominican Republic, and they don't know where we're staying."

"Agreed," Roman said. "Still, as remote as the possibility is, it is a possibility."

Marena looked at Greg in disbelief. Then, letting out a faint sigh, Greg reached out and took the paper. "Yeah, okay. We'll do whatever we can to cooperate."

"Excellent," Roman said, tossing the pen aside and standing. "Thank you for your assistance. Now I will have someone drive you to your hotel." Turning toward the door, he shouted, "Raul, come in here."

Almost instantly, the white-shirted man pushed open the door. "Yes?"

Before Raul had even stepped completely into the room, Colonel Roman began speaking in rapid-fire Spanish, repeatedly gesturing at the Walkers. After a lot of head-nodding and short responses by Raul, Colonel Roman turned to the Walkers and said, "This is Sergeant Raul Lopez. He will drive you to your hotel." Then, pulling his lips into a tight smile, he nodded to the paper in Greg's hand. "I will expect to hear from you at least twice each day, beginning as soon as you arrive back at your room."

Greg and Marena didn't respond as they turned and followed Raul into the hall. "We will go this way," Raul said and led them down a hall toward the rear door of the building. Once outside, he suddenly stopped and said, "I almost forgot. Before you leave, there is one final thing we must do."

"What's that?" Greg asked.

"I need a picture of each of you."

"Why?" Marena asked.

"Colonel Roman asked me to do it. It's completely routine. We do it whenever anyone is involved in a crime."

"But we've committed no crime," Greg objected.

"No, but you have witnessed one. Therefore, as part of our investigation, I must take your photograph."

Greg looked at Marena with a raised eyebrow and asked, "Where do we go? Back inside?"

"Right here is fine," Raul said, reaching into the pocket of his rumpled pants and pulling out a cell phone. "Just stand with your backs to the wall."

"You're going to take our picture with a cell phone?" Marena asked incredulously.

Raul nodded as he raised the phone. "It is more convenient this way. I will send the pictures by text message to our headquarters in Santo Domingo as part of the report. Electronics are marvelous, no?" Without hesitating, he took Greg's photograph and then Marena's. Examining the images, he said, "Perfect." Pointing to a small white car with a single blue light on top, he said, "We'll take that one."

It was a thirty-minute drive from the National Police building to their hotel. For twenty of those minutes, other than an occasional whisper back and forth between Greg and Marena, who were sharing the back seat, nothing was said. As they bounced through an almost-deserted intersection under construction, Raul looked in the rearview mirror and asked, "How did your discussion go with Colonel Roman?"

Greg looked at Raul's reflection in the mirror and said, "Not quite like we'd hoped."

"Frankly, I think it was a waste of time," Marena interjected bluntly. "I don't think he intends to do anything about the murder."

Raul responded with, "You are aware he wants you to remain in our country."

"Completely," Greg replied with a hint of annoyance. "He made that very clear."

Raul suddenly stomped on the accelerator and swung out to pass a bus loaded with tourists. Scooting around the bus, he eased back into his lane and once again looked back at Marena and her husband in the mirror. "Would you like some advice?"

"Advice?" Greg said.

"Go back to your hotel, pack your bags as quickly as you can, and get out of the Dominican Republic."

Marena jerked her head around so she was also looking at Raul's reflection in the mirror. "What?" Marena said. "Roman told us not to leave."

"How much do you value your lives?" Raul asked, swerving to avoid a small motorcycle loaded with three people that had cut into his lane.

"What are you saying?" Greg asked.

Raul let off the gas and eased the car into a small gravel turnout beside the highway. Shoving the gear selector into park, he turned around and said, "I listened through the door to your story, especially your description of the man who killed your friend. The colonel lied to you. Both he and I know very well the man you described." With his eyes darting back and forth between Greg and Marena, he said, "His name is Scott Vaughn, and he is someone whom the people in my government and your government would very much like to arrest. We come close to catching him, but he somehow always manages to slip away."

Marena studied Raul for moment before cautiously asking, "Why are you telling us this?"

Raul didn't hesitate. "Because you are innocent bystanders, and you don't deserve to die."

"What do you mean?" Marena asked nervously.

The expression on Raul's face was serious, and the tone of his voice bordered on ominous. "I suspect that, unless you leave the country tonight, by this time tomorrow we will be informing the U.S. Embassy in Santo Domingo of an unfortunate accident that claimed the lives of Mr. and Mrs. Greg Walker of St. George, Utah. Either that or you will simply disappear. Regardless, you will be dead." Raul paused, letting his gaze pass slowly between Greg and Marena. When he seemed satisfied their brains had registered the impact of what he had just said, he continued. "Do you recall the conversation Colonel Roman and I had just before he told you I would drive you to your hotel?"

Greg replied, "We don't speak Spanish, so we don't know what was said."

"He told me I was to put you under surveillance, that I was to assign two policemen to discreetly follow you wherever you went."

"Why?" Marena asked. "He already wants us to call him every morning and night."

"Officially, it is for your protection. He said he is concerned that someone, perhaps the man in the boat or maybe the Asian men you mentioned, would try to harm you."

"And is there an unofficial reason?" Greg asked.

Raul hesitated slightly, studying Greg. "There are some of us who believe Colonel Roman is more loyal to certain drug people than he is to the police or our government. Personally, I suspect he wants to know where you are so he can inform the drug dealers or Asians where to find you."

"So they can kill us too?" Marena asked, her heart pounding.

"Partly. Without you, there aren't any witnesses and we can officially dismiss the murder as another unsolved drug crime. But more than that, it is the money he will be paid for informing on you. It will be a generous amount—probably several thousand dollars."

Raul continued to watch Greg and Marena as they sank deeper into their seats. After a moment, he turned back around, shifted the car into gear, and began driving. A few minutes later, without another word being said, he turned the police car into the hotel's driveway and pulled under the hotel's portico. When he again put the car in park, Raul twisted around so he was looking at Greg and Marena. "I can delay making arrangements for the two policemen to follow you until tomorrow morning at eight o'clock—no later. Call Colonel Roman in an hour or two as he instructed, but then you must be gone tonight. Do you understand?"

They exchanged glances. Then Greg said, "Yes."

Greg opened the door, and he and Marena slid out of the car. He stepped up beside the driver's window and extended his hand. "Thank you. Sincerely, we truly thank you."

Marena nodded silently, still shocked from Raul's warning.

Raul smiled as he reached up and pumped Greg's hand. "You're welcome, Mr. Walker." Then, after a slight hesitation, he added, "Leave tonight, go back to St. George, Utah, and never come back."

CHAPTER TWELVE

THE BOEING 757 TOUCHED DOWN hard as it landed on the runway, jostling Greg and Marena in their seats. Greg relaxed and blew out a sigh. "I *looove* the USA," he exclaimed as he caught sight of the big blue sign showing *Miami International Airport* on the terminal building.

"So are you ever going to tell me how much you had to pay those two kids to let us take their standby seats?"

"You don't want to know."

"Sure I do; how much?" Marena pressed.

"Three hundred bucks and"—Greg held up his left arm—"my dive watch."

Marena laughed out loud. "Did you tell them it was a knockoff?"

"They didn't ask, and I didn't volunteer the information."

Their conversation was cut short when an aging flight attendant's voice crackled over the loud speaker, reminding passengers to remain in their seats until the airplane had come to a complete stop.

Greg leaned his head back on his seat and let out a sigh. "It's been an ugly few days. Getting back to doing surgery on horses will be a relief."

Marena was silent for a moment. Then she said, "As happy as I am to be back here, I feel like we've abandoned Wiggy Wiggy. He's dead, and nobody cares."

"We care, and I think, in his own way, that policeman who warned us cares," Greg said.

"I know. But we can't do anything about it, and neither can he," Marena replied as she watched a spindly old man rise from the row ahead of them and pull his suitcase from the overhead bin. Nodding toward the man, she added, "Looks like it's about our turn."

Fifteen minutes later they inched their way through roped lanes crammed with hundreds of people from dozens of arriving flights. Greg glanced at the sign in the distance that read *Passport Control* and said, "I feel like a rat in a maze."

Fifteen minutes after that, they finally worked their way to the front of the line, where a uniformed man stood on a raised platform, directing people to forty different processing booths. "Are you United States citizens?"

"Yes," Marena replied.

"Go to your left, down to station twenty-seven."

Marena looked down the long room and said, "That's half a football field away, and there are at least a dozen people already standing in line. How about station eight? There are only three people in that line," Marena said, pointing to a booth with a large numeral eight above it.

"Lady, I said twenty-seven. Go."

As they approached station eight, Marena glanced back at the guy who was directing people to various stations. Greg followed her gaze and saw the man look the other way. Marena turned to Greg and said, "I like station eight. How about you?"

Greg didn't respond; he simply grabbed Marena's arm and angled off the main walkway to stand behind the two people already standing in line at station eight.

A fraction of a second later, two more couples dropped in behind them. One of the ladies turned to Marena and said, "That guy's a jerk. He told us to walk down to station thirty-five, and there are probably twenty people standing in line down there. It makes no sense."

"Next," the man at station eight called out, motioning at one of the people ahead of them.

"They apparently aren't paid to make sense; they're paid to make our lives miserable," Marena replied sarcastically.

"It's this way every time we come through here. Total chaos," the woman said.

"This is the first time we've cleared customs in Miami, and we're getting a little nervous about making a connecting flight. Any suggestions?" Greg asked.

"Yeah, for sure," she said. "Is it just the two of you?"

Marena nodded and started to say something, but her words were cut off by a bellowed, "Next."

"Go up to the booth together. As long as you're traveling together, they'll check both of you at the same time. Hand the guy both of your passports at the same time. I don't know if it's a lot faster, but you'll save a little time."

"Next," a voice called.

Greg and Marena walked up to the man and smiled. He was young enough to be their son and was dressed in a dark-blue uniform with a bright gold nametag pinned over his left breast. The tag read *Walker.*

"Hey, maybe we're related," Greg joked as he placed his and Marena's passports on the counter. "That's our name."

"I don't think so," the homeland security agent replied dryly as he opened Greg's passport. "We're not the same color."

Greg recoiled slightly at the remark. The guy was ebony. "I hadn't noticed," Greg said.

Holding Greg's passport up to compare the picture with his face, the agent asked, "Where have you been?"

"The Dominican Republic."

"What was the purpose of your trip?"

"Vacation." *Some vacation,* Greg thought.

"How long were you there?"

"Seven days."

At that point the questions stopped, and the agent placed the passport on what looked like a scanner and then began tapping on a computer keyboard. A minute later he began carefully reading whatever information had popped onto his computer screen. Removing Greg's passport from the scanner, he placed it on another counter, away from Greg. Next he picked up Marena's passport and carefully examined it, comparing the picture to her face.

"Where have you been?"

Marena looked at Greg in surprise and then said, "We're traveling together."

"Where have you been?" the agent repeated brusquely.

"The Dominican Republic."

"What was the purpose of your trip?"

Marena shook her head at the redundancy of the questions. "Vacation."

"How long were you there?"

"Seven days."

Placing her passport on the scanner, he tapped his keyboard and read what appeared on his screen. Frowning slightly, he removed the passport from the scanner and picked up Greg's. Holding them both high above his head, he began waving them and said, "It will be just a moment."

A half minute later, a Department of Homeland Security guard strode up, his uniform perfectly pressed and his boots polished. He could have been a duplicate of Colonel Roman of the Dominican National Police, except Roman hadn't been wearing a 9-mm pistol on his right hip and two ammunition clips on his left. Roman also hadn't had a pouch with handcuffs on his belt, nor had he worn a bulletproof vest. Greg glanced at Marena, who eyed the man and in a hushed voice turned to Greg and said, "You're sure this is the United States and not some third-world country run by a dictator?"

Greg raised his eyebrows but said nothing.

Without acknowledging Greg or Marena, the man walked into the booth. The agent and the guard exchanged a few hushed words, and then Agent Walker pointed to the screen and said, "What about this?"

The guard bent forward and studied the screen. Shaking his head, the two of them exchanged a couple more words in hushed voices. Suddenly, he picked up the passports and walked out of the booth, striding quickly down a long corridor and disappearing inside a door.

"Something wrong?" Greg asked.

Agent Walker gave Greg a blank look and replied, "It will be just a minute."

Marena turned and looked at the lady who had offered her some advice about how to quickly get through passport control and shrugged as if to say she had no idea what was wrong. The woman shrugged in return.

Two minutes later the DHS guard returned with a third man, this one also dressed as a Colonel Roman lookalike, with fatigues, gun, and handcuffs. Entering the booth, the three of them looked at the computer screen. Puzzled, Greg leaned as far over the counter as he could and attempted to read the screen. As he did, one of them reached up and turned the screen so it was impossible for Greg to read anything. "What's the problem?" Greg asked.

The third DHS agent looked at Greg and Marena and said, "We'd like to ask you a few questions. Follow me." There was no *please*, and it wasn't spoken as a request.

"May we have our passports back?" Greg asked.

"No," the third DHS agent answered sharply. "This way."

CHAPTER THIRTEEN

VAUGHN PULLED BACK THE THROTTLES on *Offshore Account* and blew out an audible sigh as the multicolored boat slowed to a pace that was only slightly faster than a walk. Reaching into his backpack, he pulled out a handheld GPS and switched it on. "Only six miles," he mumbled to himself as he waited for the little device to come to life. A minute later the screen glowed bright, showing a trail that first twisted and turned through a congested mass of thousands of postage-stamp-sized islands and then moved in a straight line across Florida's wide-open Chokoloskee Bay.

Turning the boat so it was exactly centered on the trail shown on the GPS, Vaughn eased the throttles slightly forward and began slowly threading his way through the maze of islands with their moss-draped mangrove trees. He'd been awake for nearly twenty-four hours, fourteen since he'd burst out of the isolated lagoon in the Dominican Republic. In those fourteen hours, he had stopped his sixty-miles-per-hour run only once to transfer gasoline from barrels to the boat's fuel tank. Now, muscles aching, his shirt sticky with sweat and salt spray, he wanted off the hunk of floating fiberglass.

The quiet rumble of *Offshore Account*'s twin engines combined with the gentle slosh of water against the sides of the boat had a lulling effect on Vaughn's sleep-deprived body. Ten minutes after he'd started weaving through the fractured spits of land, the device suddenly squealed a high-pitched tone, and a synthesized voice blared, "Warning! You are no longer on your intended course. Turn left immediately." Jarred by the noise, Vaughn instinctively slammed the boat into reverse to stop the forward momentum. As the boat came to a standstill, he shifted into neutral and stared at the screen. The boat's gentle pace had lulled him to sleep, causing him to miss two turns depicted on the screen. Another thirty feet and he would have run the boat onto an island made of nothing but mangrove trees.

He could have avoided the maze of tree-clumped islands by doing what nearly every other boater did when coming or going to the backwater town of Everglades City, Florida, using a deep, wide channel the U.S. Army Corps of Engineers had dredged several years earlier. But that meant joining the flow of fishing and pleasure boats in the channel, and the fewer people who saw the distinctively painted boat, the better.

Like a pimple on an elephant, Everglades City, Florida, sat on the western edge of Florida's massive Everglades swamp. While the swamp covered an area larger than the state of Maryland, the little city of Everglades covered an area only ten square blocks, two of which were covered with water during storms. With a population of fewer than five hundred, there were more alligators and snakes swimming in its canals and ponds than people roaming its streets. That, along with its isolation, was why Vaughn relished the town.

Maneuvering around the last of the mangrove islands, Vaughn punched off the GPS and shoved the throttles to their stops, sending the boat in a seventy-mile-per-hour run across the three miles of Chokoloskee Bay. After that, it was only a quarter mile up a little-used canal, and he would be home—at least for the night.

Home was a metal-sided warehouse that salt air had turned rusty brown. It was small, not much larger than a starter home, and from the outside looked neglected. The inside was far different; it was spotless, including the painted cement floor. A partitioned area in one corner had a small kitchen, bed, sofa, TV, and bathroom with shower. Along one wall were two commercial-sized freezers, and along another were rows of empty shelves. All of it served a single purpose: to provide a place for Vaughn to transfer his customers' merchandise from boats to trucks or airplanes.

The building sat at the end of a dead-end street in a corner of the town that progress had long since skipped over. High school kids came to the area because neither the street nor the building had any lights. At night, they could make out, drink beer, and smoke pot with little fear of being caught. When he first bought the building, Vaughn had installed four exterior lights with motion detectors, but they had been shot out the first weekend and he hadn't bothered to report the incident or replace the lights.

The building backed onto a narrow canal barely deep enough to allow *Offshore Account* to sneak in. Access from the front was down a short gravel drive. The building had no windows and only two doors. The back door opened onto the dock and was fitted with three locks. The front door was an oversized garage door not quite large enough for a semitruck but large enough for just about anything else.

Vaughn guided *Offshore Account* against the dock behind a smaller boat with *Angler Too* painted on its stern. Switching off the keys, he closed his eyes and slumped in the seat, relieved to be free of the constant rumble of the engines and their noisy exhaust. For the first time in more than fourteen hours, the muscles in his neck and shoulders relaxed. Climbing from the boat, he tied it tightly to the dock and stretched. Just as he dropped his arms to his side, his satellite phone chirped. After glancing at the number on the display, he repositioned the antenna and held the phone to his ear. "Yeah?"

"You have a problem."

Vaughn was in the midst of a yawn, so he said nothing.

"Two people saw you kill that man in the lagoon."

Vaughn forced his yawning mouth closed and said, "I know that. But they were taken care of."

"No, unfortunately, they weren't, and that's why you have a problem."

Vaughn straightened. "How do you know they weren't killed?"

"Because they were very much alive when they were here a few hours ago. They gave a statement of what happened."

Vaughn rubbed his cheek and the back of his neck and uttered a curse at the Koreans. "Can they identify me?"

"They weren't shown any photographs, but they gave a description of you—a very detailed description."

"How detailed?"

There was a slight chuckle. "Detailed enough I could have drawn a very accurate picture of you, and I'm no artist. There is no question it was you. They are eyewitnesses to the murder."

Vaughn shook his head and cursed again. "Who are they?"

"A man and a woman from the States. The man you ran over was Haitian. He had taken them snorkeling."

There was a pause as Vaughn began pacing along the dock. "Where are they staying? Can I get to them or have someone else get to them?"

"They are no longer in the Dominican Republic."

"Where are they?"

"On their way home. They left the country last night."

Vaughn spat out a curse and said, "You should have contacted me sooner. It would have been much easier to deal with them there."

"Maybe, maybe not. They were to be under protective surveillance. You wouldn't have been able to get close to them."

Reaching the end of the dock, Vaughn turned around and started back. "Do you know their names?"

Vaughn could hear paper being shuffled. "Greg and Marena Walker."

"Where do they live?"

"St. George, Utah."

Vaughn frowned. "You got an address?"

There was a pause, and Vaughn could hear more paper shuffling. "Yes, it is—"

"Just a minute," Vaughn interrupted. "I need to get some paper." Cradling the phone on his shoulder, Vaughn pawed through his backpack, pulled out a crumpled napkin, and wrote the address. "Okay, I got it," Vaughn said, examining the napkin.

"Do you have your cell phone nearby?"

Vaughn pulled his cell from his pocket. "Yeah, why?"

"Just a minute. You should be receiving a message about . . . now."

Vaughn's cell chirped, announcing a new message. Cradling the satellite phone on his shoulder, Vaughn tapped the screen of his cell a couple of times and watched two crystal-clear images appear on his screen.

"Did you receive it?"

Vaughn nodded his head as though the man on the phone could see him as he eyed the photographs. "Greg and Marena Walker of St. George, Utah, I assume."

"Taken only a few hours ago."

A broad smile formed on Vaughn's lips. "You've done well, my friend."

"I assume you will show your gratitude for my help in the usual way? Perhaps with an added measure of appreciation for the pictures?"

Still staring at the screen, it took Vaughn a couple of seconds to respond. "Of course," he said and disconnected the call.

CHAPTER FOURTEEN

Vaughn set the aluminum suitcase by the door and pulled keys from a side pocket of his backpack. Unlocking the three locks securing the heavy steel door in its frame, he nudged the door open with his toe, picked up the suitcase, and stepped inside the warehouse. After punching a code into a keypad to disarm the alarm system, he flipped four switches, flooding the room with bright light.

The room was empty except for an old white Ford delivery van parked nearly in the center. The windowless vehicle was in decent condition for its age, with good paint, no noticeable dents, and no identifying words or letters painted on the side. It was the kind of vehicle a plumber or deliveryman would drive—the kind people saw and almost instantly disregarded because it had no exterior markings.

Vaughn unlocked the van's rear doors and pushed a tall stack of heavy moving blankets aside. Gently placing the suitcase on the floor of the van, he covered it with several blankets and then neatly arranged several more blankets around it, making it appear that the van was loaded with nothing but blankets.

A few moments later Vaughn had locked the van, reset the alarm, turned off the lights, and closed and locked the door. Soon he had *Offshore Account* and *Angler Too* tied together and was motoring along the canal.

Like a baby elephant gripping its mother's tail with its trunk, the much smaller *Angler Too* obediently followed *Offshore Account* as Vaughn retraced his route through the maze of mangrove-covered islands to the open waters of the Gulf of Mexico.

One hour later and twenty miles offshore, Vaughn switched off *Offshore Account*'s engines. The depth finder on the instrument panel showed the ocean's bottom to be one hundred and twenty feet below.

Securing the two boats side by side, Vaughn stepped down into the larger boat's cabin and opened the windows and roof hatch. Then he placed a small package the size of a deck of cards on the floor and stepped back out into the bright sunlight. Lifting the engine hatch cover, he eased down between the two engines and removed an exhaust hose. Water began pouring through the four-inch opening, soaking his feet. He repeated the action three more times for the remaining hoses. By the time he undid the last hose, he was standing in water above his ankles. Smiling at his handiwork, Vaughn climbed out of the engine compartment, jumped into *Angler Too*, and untied the ropes holding the two boats together. He pulled a small device from his backpack and, starting the boat's engine, he idled fifty feet away and pressed the button on the device. A muffled blast reverberated through the air, and *Offshore Account* bucked, rising slightly above the water. Smiling, Vaughn dropped into a seat and watched.

With water pouring into a four-foot hole in the bottom of the boat as well as the four exhaust openings, it took an hour and a package of Twinkies washed down by a bottle of lukewarm water before the brightly colored *Offshore Account* had settled deep enough into the water for the waves to break over its shiny topside. Fifteen minutes later the boat had slipped completely below the surface and was beginning a slow but steady descent to its final resting place.

Stuffing a Twinkie wrapper inside the empty water bottle, Vaughn tossed it into the ocean, turned up the collar of his shirt to protect his neck from the rays of the scorching sun, and restarted *Angler Too*'s engine. An hour later he joined the flow of pleasure boats headed to Everglades City, not by the circuitous route around trees and islands but through the main channel. Smiling at passing boaters and appearing as if he was just returning from a day of fishing, he worked his way back to the rusty warehouse.

Inside the building, with all the doors locked and the alarm set, Vaughn showered, ate a microwave dinner, and dropped into bed. Ten hours later, just as the early-morning sun was turning the sky from black to purple, Vaughn set the alarm, secured the warehouse, and locked the chain-link gates. By the time he climbed into the van and drove out of the warehouse, the sun was sending the first streaks of orange across the sky.

Obeying every traffic law, Vaughn drove to Main Street, worked his way around the town's only roundabout, and headed south to the gravel road leading to the airport. By airline standards, the Everglades City Airport was so small it might as well not exist. But anyone flying a small general aviation airplane would find the airport very inviting; for Vaughn, it was perfect.

The airport sat on a narrow spit of land surrounded on three sides by ocean. Both ends of the single runway almost had water lapping on the tarmac, and only a row of low trees separated one side from the Gulf of Mexico's waves. Three buildings were spaced along the taxiway. Passing the first building, the airport office, Vaughn waved to a twenty-something woman who poked her head out the door at the rare sound of a car. Adjacent to the office was a much larger building with a weathered sign that read *Everglades Air Services*. Its big doors were wide open, and inside, two airplanes were parked, both in a state of disrepair and looking as if they hadn't been touched in months. The third building, much newer and three times the combined size of the other two, sat at the far end of the taxiway. It was a condominium for airplanes. An enterprising pilot/developer had constructed the building and divided it into eight hangar sections with the idea of keeping one for himself and selling off seven to other pilots. Only two had sold in five years, both to Vaughn. One housed a twin-engine Piper Aztec airplane, a workhorse into which Vaughn could stuff nearly a ton of drugs and still fly in and out of remote airstrips or major metropolitan areas. The second housed a single-engine amphibious float plane he sometimes used when a boat didn't meet a client's needs.

Vaughn drove to his hangar, punched a code into a keypad beside the hangar door, and waited as the huge door opened, revealing a gleaming tan and white twin-engine airplane. In a move he'd done dozens of times before, he carefully eased the van around the airplane's wing and parked in a corner of the hangar. In less than five minutes, he stowed his backpack, a small leather bag with a change of clothes, and the silver suitcase inside the Aztec. Five minutes after that, he had the airplane out of the hangar and the door closed. Soon he was skimming a hundred feet above the Gulf of Mexico at a hundred fifty miles per hour.

CHAPTER FIFTEEN

THE SIGN HANGING ABOVE THE doorway of the building read *Las Cruses, New Mexico*. A second, smaller, sign hung below it proclaimed the elevation to be 4,456 feet. Stenciled on the door itself in sloppy black paint was *Pilot Lounge*.

Lounge was too generous a word. The walls were mustard yellow and lime green that clashed hideously with the old black-flecked orange linoleum floor tile. Half the ceiling tile had brown water stains, compliments of a once-leaking roof, and the blue leather couch and matching recliner were castoffs from a thrift store.

"Man, I hate this weather," a jean-clad man steamed as he burst through the door and stomped his cowboy boots on a greasy piece of old carpet. Peeling off his rain-soaked jacket, he shook it rapidly, sending a cascade of water drops onto the linoleum floor. "It sucks," he said, tossing the jacket onto the arm of the couch and walking over to a simmering coffee pot.

Vaughn looked up from the dog-eared magazine he was reading but didn't say anything.

"The weather's almost as bad as this place," the man said as he poured the black liquid into a Styrofoam cup.

Vaughn looked around the pilot lounge and said, "At least it's dry."

The lanky man chuckled as he opened a package of creamer and poured it into the cup. "It is that, but I've been stuck here almost twenty-four hours, and the walls are starting to close in, you know what I mean? Landed last night for fuel and then had a mechanical issue and couldn't get out ahead of the storm."

Vaughn tossed the three-month-old magazine onto a scratched and chipped table and asked, "Where'd you fly in from?"

"Reno, Nevada," the man replied, gently blowing at the now caramel-colored liquid in the cup. "I've been dodging one storm system after another for two days."

"Where you headed?"

"South Texas—a place called Victoria," the pilot said, sitting on the couch and stretching his legs out in front of him. Jerking his head toward the rain-splattered plate glass window, he said, "I'm ferrying that decrepit old Cessna Centurion to its new owner. I just need it to hang together for a few more hours, and then it's someone else's worry."

Vaughn smiled as he looked at the Cessna through the window. "I've logged a few hours in a Centurion. Not a bad airplane," he said.

The pilot shrugged, sipped his coffee, and said, "How about you? What made you choose this garden spot to land in?"

"Ice," Vaughn said. "I was picking up too much on the wings. It forced me down."

"Better to be on the ground wishing you were flying than to be flying and wishing you were on the ground."

"Mmm," Vaughn said. Pointing out the window, he added, "Looks like the rain is slowing down and the clouds are getting a little lighter. This might be over."

"Maybe," the pilot said, rising from the couch and walking to where Vaughn stood. "But I don't think so." Nodding to a computer sitting in the corner of the room, he said, "I checked the forecast a few minutes ago, and this storm system has stalled on top of us. The forecasters think it'll be at least midnight before things improve."

Vaughn looked at his watch and frowned at the idea of being delayed for another six hours. "I guess I'll go grab a burger at the grill next door and then find a quiet corner and get some sleep. Have a good flight to Texas," he said and walked out the door.

A greasy hamburger, oil-saturated French fries, and a soda in his stomach, Vaughn dodged sleet and puddles as he loped back to the pilot's lounge. With the Texas-bound pilot nowhere to be found, he stretched out on the couch and closed his eyes.

Two hours later the soft chirping of his cell phone pulled him from a fitful sleep. Vaughn looked at the caller ID but didn't recognize the number, so he silenced the phone and laid his head back down. Fifteen seconds later his phone chirped again, this time alerting him to a new voicemail message. He dialed the voicemail number, and as he listened to the message, he became annoyed. A moment later his phone rang again; this time he answered it. "Hello?"

"Mr. Vaughn, I'm glad you answered your phone."

Vaughn instantly recognized Li Gun-no's heavily accented voice. Rubbing sleep from his eyes, he said, "What do you want, Mr. Li?"

"Where are you?"

Vaughn worked his tongue around his mouth to rid it of the taste of greasy hamburger. "Las Cruces, New Mexico."

There was a brief pause and then, "Las Cruces? That isn't on the route I was expecting you to take. Why are you there?"

Vaughn cleared his throat and answered bluntly, "To clean up a mess you created for me."

"Oh?" Li asked.

"You were supposed to eliminate the two people who saw me run over that guy in the lagoon. You didn't do it."

Li hesitated for only half a second before saying, "*Yet,* Mr. Vaughn. We haven't taken care of them *yet*. We will handle it. In fact, I have people searching for them as we speak."

"You're too late; they left the Dominican Republic. They're back in the States."

"How do you know that?"

"I just do," Vaughn replied.

"That they are in the States isn't a problem for us, Mr. Vaughn," Li said confidently. "We can handle it as easily there as here."

Vaughn laughed derisively. "You couldn't handle it on a small island overrun with corrupt cops; you think you can do it here?"

There was a brief silence before Li said, "I assure you, Mr. Vaughn, the fact that they are in the States is not a problem. We have assets we can call upon to solve this problem. Trust me. We will handle it."

Vaughn shook his head as he said, "The problem is, I don't trust you. And that means you don't get a second chance. Those people can positively identify me; they are a liability that puts me in jeopardy. I'll take care of this myself."

Vaughn heard Li let out a short sigh. "If that is your wish, but I remind you, Mr. Vaughn, that you agreed and assured us that you would deliver our package by the required date."

"Your package and its delivery aren't nearly as important to me as my future," Vaughn shot back. "Standing on the dock, you assured me you would eliminate them. 'Easy,' you said. 'Their bodies will never be found,' you bragged. Well, not only are they not dead, but they have given a very accurate description of me to the Dominican Republic police, who by now have probably transmitted it to every law enforcement agency in the world. Until now, no one has been able to connect me directly to any crime. You've messed up, and now I have to take time to clean up your mess."

There was another long silence during which Vaughn could hear muffled chatter in the background. Finally, Li said, "I have been instructed to tell you that if you deliver our package ahead of schedule, you will be rewarded with an additional fifty thousand dollars."

Vaughn took a breath to respond, but Li continued. "However, failure to deliver our package as agreed will have unfortunate personal consequences for you." There was a pause and then, "You should not forget about the coast guard helicopter." Then another pause, this one longer. In a much sterner voice, Li said, "Make our delivery first, Mr. Vaughn. I assure you, after you have done what we ask, you will not need to worry about your other problem; we will take care of it for you."

"I don't need or want your help," Vaughn snapped.

"Suit yourself, Mr. Vaughn, but our business must come first. Now, do you still have the sealed envelope I gave you when we gave you the suitcase?"

"Yes," Vaughn said cautiously.

"Have you opened it?"

"No."

"Please open the envelope and read the contents. From this point forward, you will follow the instructions it contains. Is that clear, Mr. Vaughn?"

Vaughn didn't reply. He couldn't; the connection was gone.

He sucked in a deep breath, cursed, and angrily threw the phone onto the dilapidated sofa. "I don't want your extra fifty thousand," he mumbled. Running his hands over his short-cropped hair, he began walking in circles around the room. He walked to the computer and coaxed it out of its sleep mode. After a few keystrokes, he examined the National Oceanic and Atmospheric Administration's weather forecast, which predicted icing conditions exactly where he wanted to go.

Walking into the small bathroom, Vaughn splashed water onto his face, dried himself off, picked up his phone and coat, and hurried out the door of the lounge. Putting on his coat as he trotted across the tarmac, he dodged an obstacle course of puddles until he reached his airplane.

CHAPTER SIXTEEN

"Sit anywhere you can find a chair," the Department of Homeland Security agent said gruffly as Greg and Marena followed him into the waiting room.

The room was the size of three living rooms. Its floor was covered with a drab, unpadded gray carpet, and its walls were painted a sterile white. There were two doors. The main one, through which they had entered, was made of thick glass and controlled by an electronic lock. Seated at a desk beside the door was an armed guard wearing black combat fatigues. The second door was in the far corner and made of dull gray metal. Forty chairs made of chrome and black vinyl ringed three of the four walls. Twenty more ran down the middle of the room, their backs to each other. Most of the chairs were occupied. A television was mounted on each wall, and all the screens showed the same manicured news anchorwoman blathering about Afghan rebels. Beside each television was a bright red sign with bold white letters that said *No use of cell phones, cameras, or computers allowed.*

Greg scanned the room and then looked over at Marena, who was still eyeing the mishmash of people sprawled on the chairs. "Half the countries in the world are probably represented here," Marena said softly.

Greg nodded and pointed to the only two unoccupied chairs that were side by side.

As they sat down, the guard who had escorted them into the room walked over to the gray door. Punching a code into an electronic lock, he waited until he heard a soft buzz, pushed the door open, and disappeared into a dimly lit hallway.

Marena swiveled slightly in her chair to look around.

Greg marveled that two days ago they had been surrounded by people who were laughing, joking, and completely relaxed. Now not a single person smiled, and two dozen of them had lines of worry etched so deeply in their faces they looked like dried mud that was ready to crack. No one made eye contact.

Greg nudged Marena softly in the ribs and inclined his head slightly toward a young Latino man, who looked to be about thirty, sitting directly across from them. He had the thick neck and barrel chest of a weight lifter and, Greg thought, easily tipped the scales at two hundred and fifty pounds. He was dressed in designer jeans and a tropical print shirt and had sunglasses perched on top of his head. He could have stepped out of a photo shoot for *Esquire* magazine, except for one thing: he was crying. He was doing his best to hide the tears leaking from his eyes and the clear liquid dripping from the tip of his nose, but the almost inaudible sobs and shaking of his shoulders gave him away.

He sat hunched over, his elbows resting on his knees with the tips of his fingers pressed to his forehead. Unexpectedly, he leaned back, wiped his eyes with the heels of his hands, and looked around the room. Acting as though he was trying to be as inconspicuous as possible, he pulled a cell phone from his shirt pocket. Doing his best to hide the phone from two guards who were chatting beside the main door, he punched in a number and then cradled the small device in the palm of his hand. He used his hand as a shield as he held it to his ear. He spoke far too softly to be heard and had turned his head so it was impossible for the guards to see him, but within ten seconds the door near Greg and Marena flew open and an armed guard stormed into the room.

Every head turned toward the guard as he strode up to the crying man and demanded, "Put that phone away, *now*!"

The Latino man looked up at the guard, hurriedly spoke a few words in Spanish into the phone, and then, in halting English, said to the guard, "Please. My wife and two young children are waiting in the airport. They don't know what's happened to me."

The guard shook his head and said, "I don't care who's waiting for you or where they are. No phones are allowed; put it away—now!"

Looking as if a dam of tears was about to break, the young man slowly lowered the phone and put it back into his shirt pocket.

Marena leaned closer to Greg and whispered, "Those two guards by the entrance couldn't even see the phone. How'd they know he was talking?"

Greg raised his eyebrows and pointed to a black object the size of a tennis ball hanging innocently from the ceiling in a corner of the room. "Smile," he said dryly. "You're on *Candid Camera*."

Marena looked up at the object and replied, "Oh, I didn't see them."

Greg nodded. "I count five more. I'm sure they can see every inch of this room."

Marena looked at each of the six black spheres in turn. "This isn't right," she said. "We're being treated like criminals." She took a breath to say something more but stopped when a clipboard-carrying middle-aged woman sat down beside her.

"Mrs. Walker?" the woman asked.

"Yes?" Marena responded cautiously.

The woman was dressed in a uniform, but it was unlike the guard's. She wore dark-blue slacks, a matching blue vest, and a long-sleeved white shirt with thin red strips. Her mousy-brown hair was slightly disheveled, and she looked tired. "Are you traveling with luggage?"

"Yes," Marena answered.

"Will you please show me your luggage-claim tickets? I need to write down the numbers."

"Why?" Greg asked suspiciously, exchanging a wary glance with Marena.

"I don't know. I've simply been asked to obtain your luggage-claim numbers."

"Why are we here?" Greg asked.

"I don't have any idea," the woman replied with a shrug.

"Then why do you want our luggage-claim numbers?" Marena asked.

"I suspect it's because *they*"—she nodded toward the guards—"want to inspect your luggage and don't want it to go on ahead before you do."

Greg shifted his gaze from the woman to Marena and back to the woman. "What do you mean, go on ahead of us? How long are we going to be here?"

"I really don't have any idea," the woman replied with the slightest tinge of impatience. "I work for the airline, not them. I've been asked to get your baggage-claim numbers so your baggage can be pulled from your scheduled flight."

"Our flight leaves for Las Vegas in less than two hours," Marena said, looking at her watch. "We can't miss it."

The woman placed the clipboard she had been holding on her lap and said, "I really don't know how long you're going to be here. Are you Americans?"

"Yes," Greg answered.

"That's good. Based on my experience, that will help. They tend to deal with Americans more quickly than foreigners."

"Great," Marena huffed.

The woman drew her lips back in a partial smile. "When you're finally allowed to leave, if you've missed your flight, simply go to any of our ticket counters and explain to the agent that you were detained in passport control. You'll be booked on the next available flight without any additional charge. Now, may I see your baggage-claim tickets so I can write down the numbers?"

Greg shook his head in confusion but unzipped an inside pocket in his computer case and pulled out the paper ticket envelope. "Here."

Greg and Marena watched as the woman copied the numbers from the claim tickets to the paper on her clipboard. After checking to make certain she hadn't made a mistake, she turned to Marena and said, "I hope your day turns out better than it has apparently begun." Giving an almost sincere smile, she stood up, walked to the main entrance, and waited for a guard to open the electronic lock so she could exit the room.

Greg gave Marena's hand a squeeze. "You doing okay?"

Marena shook her head. "I don't understand what's happening, and I'm scared. Aren't you?"

"Not so much scared as confused." Then, with more confidence than he felt, he added, "Look, it's going to be okay. Just try and relax."

"That's a little hard to do right now," Marena said. "We've witnessed a murder, snuck out of a country, and now we're sitting in some, some"—her voice quivered nervously—"some detention cell, and nobody will even tell us why."

At that exact moment the door opened and a guard stepped partially into view. "Harazim?" he said loudly enough for his voice to carry through the room. "Vaclav Harazim?"

A seventy-something man with curly salt-and-pepper hair stood up in the middle of the room.

"Bring any items you have, and follow me," the guard ordered.

Hesitantly, the man picked up the small suitcase and overcoat and shuffled his way to the door.

"He looks worried," Greg said out the side of mouth to Marena.

She nodded, but she wasn't looking at Greg or the man. She was looking at the Latino man sitting across from her. Greg followed her gaze, watching as the man folded his arms across his chest and once again inconspicuously reached into his shirt to remove his cell phone. Placing his phone by his leg so it was partially hidden, he tapped repeatedly on the keypad. Nudging Greg, Marena smirked as she nodded her head toward the man. "He's sending a text."

An hour later Greg shook his head and slapped his hands on his knees. "This is ridiculous," he said. "In the past hour they've only called five people from the room. If we have to wait for everyone who was sitting in the room when we got here, we'll be here a week. The next time that door opens and they call for someone, I think I'm going to make a bit of a stink."

Two minutes later a guard in the ever-present black fatigues opened the door. As Greg stood up, the guard called out, "Walker. Marena Walker."

"Finally." Greg huffed as he grabbed his computer bag and helped Marena stand up.

As Greg walked toward the door, the guard held up his hand and shook his head. "*Marena* Walker," he growled. "Not you."

"He's my husband," Marena said nervously. "We're traveling together. Is there a reason he can't come with me?"

The guard looked at Greg as he considered Marena's question. Without saying anything, he stepped aside barely enough to allow Greg to enter. Then, looking at Marena, he said, "Follow me."

They followed the guard down a long, brightly lit corridor, passing three closed doors with frosted glass windows. They stopped at the fourth door and waited while the guard pushed it and stepped aside, motioning for them to enter. "Wait here."

"We're really getting close to missing our connecting flight," Greg said as the man started to leave. "Do you know how long we're going to be here?"

"No idea," the guard answered and closed the door.

They could have been in an interrogation room transported straight out of a television cop show, except for one thing: there wasn't the typical bare lightbulb dangling from a wire. Instead, bright fluorescent lights flickered overhead, bathing the room in an almost garish light. The room was small, probably twelve feet square, and had a black metal table tucked against one wall. Except for two cheap folding chairs, one on either side of the table, there was no other furniture. Hanging in the middle of one wall was a picture of an American flag in a cheap metal frame. Three walls were painted the same stark white as the room they had just left. The bottom half of the fourth wall was painted the same white as the other three, but the top half was a mirror, or at least that's what it appeared to be.

CHAPTER SEVENTEEN

A FORTY-SOMETHING-YEAR-OLD MAN WITH SUN-BLEACHED blond hair startled Greg and Marena as he noisily pulled open the door. He was dressed like every other guard they had seen, black fatigues, shined combat boots, and a leather belt with a gun, handcuffs, and other paraphernalia attached. The only difference was the laptop computer he held in his hand. Behind him came a second man, probably in his mid-fifties, with short-cropped hair and dressed in a business suit. He stepped into the room just far enough that he could partially close the door, making the room virtually escape-proof.

Placing the laptop on the table, the guard sat down with his back to the mirror and looked at Marena. Pointing to the folding chair that was facing the mirror, he said, "Have a seat."

Marena shifted her gaze from the guard to the chair, then gave Greg a quick glance and the man standing in the doorway an even quicker glance, and then slowly slid onto the chair. Greg stayed standing by her side.

"Which country did you arrive from?"

Marena removed her purse straps from her shoulder and placed the purse on her lap as she answered, "The Dominican Republic."

"How long were you there?"

"About a week," Marena replied.

"Please be more specific."

"Okay, seven days and six nights," Marena said.

"What was the purpose of your trip?"

Greg leaned forward slightly and said, "Look, I don't mean to be rude, but we've been through this twice already. Why do we need to go through it again with you?"

The guard looked up at Greg, glared, and then looked at Marena. "What was the purpose of your trip?" he repeated.

Marena frowned, looking over at Greg, who was still peering down at the guard and shaking his head. “We were on vacation,” she said.

“You came back early. Why is that?”

Greg and Marena exchanged nervous glances. “How do you know we came back early?” Greg asked.

The guard pointed to the screen on his computer and said, “Your hotel and airline reservations. You weren’t supposed to return for five more days.”

“How’d you get them?” Greg demanded.

“I’ll ask the questions,” the guard responded. “You answer them. Why did you return early?”

Growing more nervous, Marena said, “We witnessed a murder. A policeman in Punta Cana interviewed us and then advised us to leave.”

“A murder?” the guard asked skeptically.

“Yes,” she said, annoyed at the guard’s doubtful expression.

“Tell me about this alleged murder.”

Marena stared blankly at the guard and hesitantly began describing Wiggy Wiggy waving his arms as a warning to seek cover. When she reached the part about his frantic swim as the boat was bearing down on him, her voice caught with emotion. She faltered so completely when she tried to describe the scene that Greg had to finish the grisly details.

“What happened next?” the guard asked.

While Marena pawed through her purse for a tissue, Greg gave a brief but accurate summation of everything that had occurred.

“The suitcase—can you describe it?”

Greg shrugged. “It wasn’t anything fancy—just one of those aluminum suitcases.”

“What size was it?”

“I don’t know exactly. Too big to go in the overhead bin on an airplane but probably not the great big size with wheels you sometimes see people pulling in airports.” Then, looking at Marena as if for confirmation, he gestured with his arms and added, “More like a medium size.”

Marena nodded in agreement.

The guard tapped a flurry of keystrokes and then looked at Marena. “Can you describe the man driving the boat?”

Marena dabbed at a tear in the corner of her eye and then choked out the same detailed description she had given Colonel Roman less than twenty-four hours earlier.

More tapping on the keyboard, and then, "That's a pretty accurate description for a guy who was several hundred feet away from you and who was sitting in a boat at the time of the alleged murder," the guard replied.

"Binoculars," Greg interjected.

Marena blew her nose with the tissue and scowled at the guard. "You keep saying, 'alleged murder.' There is nothing *alleged* about it. The man was murdered. We saw it."

The guard looked at Marena and said, "Just one more question."

"Yes?" Marena replied with relief.

"Have you ever lived in . . . Arizona?"

Marena looked at the guard in bewilderment. "What?"

"Arizona. Have you ever lived there?"

Marena shook her head. "No," she replied. "Never."

After a short pause, the guard reached up and closed his laptop. "You're free to go," he said as he leaned back in his chair.

Greg and Marena looked at each other in surprise. "That's it?" Greg asked.

"Yes. You can leave."

"Wait a minute," Greg said. "We've been sitting here for nearly two hours and just told you about a murder, and now you tell us we can leave, and that's it? Don't you think we deserve more of an explanation?"

The guard stood up, gave a halfhearted shrug as he looked at Marena, and said, "You have a very common surname." Then, stepping around the desk, he motioned to the door. The man in the suit was no longer there, and the door was completely open. "The guard by the entrance will instruct you on where you can retrieve your luggage." Looking at his watch, he added, "If I were you, I'd hurry. There is a chance you can still make your scheduled flight."

When it was obvious the man had no intentions of saying anything more, Marena looked at Greg, who grabbed her by the elbow and said, "Let's get going."

Marena pulled her arm free of Greg's grasp. Staring at the guard, she asked, "Are you going to do something about Wiggy Wiggy's murder?"

The guard looked at her and shook his head. "Can't," he said. "We have no authority in the Dominican Republic. The cops there can handle it."

"But they're not going to do anything; they already told us that," Marena said in exasperation.

The guard shrugged. "Then, I guess nobody's going to do anything."

Marena felt angry heat overtake her face, and she sucked in a breath of air to explode.

"Marena," Greg said, retaking her arm. "This is going nowhere." Giving her a gentle nudge, he said forcefully, "Let's go! We're going to miss our flight."

Marena shot a quick glance at Greg and glared at the guard. Flinging her purse over her shoulder, she walked from the room.

***

The guard tucked the laptop under his arm and followed the Walkers as they hurried along the corridor leading to the main waiting area. After they had disappeared through an exit door on the left, he turned right and walked through an unmarked steel door. Walking down another corridor, he pushed open a door to a small, dimly lit room not much larger than a bathroom. As he walked inside and set the computer on a table, the man in the business suit who had stood guard at the door during his interview said, "You have a very common name? Is that the *best* you could come up with?"

The guard glared at the man. "No, Agent Hovey, that is not the best I could do." Then, making no attempt to conceal his annoyance, he added, "But it is the best I could do with such short notice. You didn't give us much time to help with your charade."

CHAPTER EIGHTEEN

Six hours later, FBI Special Agent Wayne Hovey dropped the telephone receiver into its cradle and blew out a sigh. Tipping back in his chair at the same time he ran his fingers through his hair, he looked at the two men entering his office and said, "I'm coming up empty."

Larry Nichols—lean and squared-jawed, with similar salt-and-pepper hair—dropped into a chair by the desk and said, "Likewise."

The other man, dressed in a neatly tailored three-piece gray suit, walked to a window and looked out at the overcast Miami sky. Hovey swiveled his chair slightly to look at him and asked, "What about you, Chris? Anything?"

Chris Pulsipher shook his head. "Nada."

"I've got one more possibility," Hovey said, looking down at a piece of paper that four hours earlier had been a neatly typed list of names and phone numbers but was now covered with doodles, illegible scribbles, and crossed-off names. "Some guy named Stuart Bringhurst. He works at the Department of Energy's office of Intelligence and Counterintelligence."

Pulsipher, who was exactly half Hovey's fifty-two years of age and sported the regulation FBI haircut, leaned against the window and asked, "What do they do?"

"All Washington told me is they gather information on all the nuclear weapons and weapons-grade material scattered around the world."

"Since when has the Department of Energy been in the intelligence business?" Larry asked.

"Who knows?" Hovey replied as he picked up the phone and punched in a series of numbers. Five minutes, four transfers, and a brief introduction later, he said, "Mr. Bringhurst, thank you for taking my call. Do you mind if I put you on speaker? I have two other agents in my office, and I'd like them to be part of this conversation."

After a short pause, Hovey pressed a button on his phone and asked, "Mr. Bringhurst, can you hear me?"

"Loud and clear," a soft-spoken voice answered.

"Great. I have Special Agents Larry Nichols and Chris Pulsipher here with me. We have a couple of questions, if you can spare us a few minutes."

"I'm due in a meeting soon, but I'm all yours for seven minutes."

Nichols shifted slightly in his chair as he suppressed a grin. "Get talking," he mouthed silently to Hovey.

Hovey launched in. "We're dealing with a situation that isn't quite making sense to us. We've been on the phone for several hours checking with other federal agencies and have come up empty, so we're hoping you can help."

"I'll do what I can," Bringhurst said.

"A couple of days ago we got a tip from a cop in the Dominican Republic about a guy we've been trying to apprehend for almost two years. The perp transports illegal drugs, money, and other stuff for anyone willing to pay his price. Long story short, the cop tipped us about a man and woman who witnessed our guy murder someone. We intercepted and interviewed them when they came back to the U.S. They told us about the murder, but they also told us they saw three Asian men give our guy a metal suitcase. The guy put the suitcase on a boat and took off for parts unknown. We're trying to sort out two things. First, it's unheard of for Asians to be involved in any kind of activity—drugs, human trafficking, money-laundering, whatever—via the Dominican Republic. They stick almost exclusively to cities along the west coast, like Seattle and Los Angles; it's closer to home and much easier for them. The second thing we're trying to get a grip on is what he's transporting. This guy is as elusive as the wind, but if we can figure out what he's transporting or for whom . . . well, we're hoping it will give us a lead on where he might surface. None of this fits the typical mold for either this guy or the people involved, so we're on a fishing expedition."

"We're down to about six minutes here; how can I help you catch your fish?"

Hovey looked at Pulsipher, who looked at his watch and raised his eyebrows. Then he said, "You deal with nuclear materials and such; could this guy be transporting some kind of small nuclear device for terrorist purposes?"

After a short pause, Bringhurst said, "Asians?"

Hovey answered, "Yes."

"That covers a pretty huge swath of humanity. Can you narrow it down a bit? I mean, were they Japanese, Chinese, Korean, or—"

"No idea," Hovey interrupted. "All we know is they're Asian."

"And you have absolutely no idea where he's headed? I don't mean specifically, but a region, such as Iraq, Afghanistan, or even the Philippines."

"None," Hovey replied impatiently. "The best I can tell you is for the two years we've been chasing this guy, we've never found his tracks outside the Western Hemisphere."

There was another pause, this one long enough that Hovey said, "Mr. Bringhurst?"

"Yeah, sorry," Bringhurst said. "I was just trying to figure out if there are any dots connecting your guy with a little something we're working on."

"What kind of dots?" Hovey asked.

"A small amount of weapons-grade plutonium disappeared from a facility in Russia twelve weeks ago. We tracked it through Uzbekistan and caught a sniff of it in Islamabad, but from there, the trail's gone cold."

"You think there might be a connection?" Hovey asked, sitting more upright in his chair.

"I was considering it. It's feasible Asians might be involved, particularly North Koreans, but I can't make sense of your guy only working in the Western Hemisphere. That's too big a jump—geographically, I mean. Your guy would need to know Central Asia."

"Okay," Hovey said, with a hint of dejection. "What about my original question. Could this guy be transporting a nuclear device, maybe intended for someplace here in the Western Hemisphere?"

"The short answer is no. You can't simply put a nuclear bomb in a container the size of a suitcase. That only happens in the movies."

"What about enriched uranium or plutonium or whatever the stuff is they make nuclear bombs out of?" Nichols asked.

"It's conceivable, but it would make absolutely no sense whatsoever. What would they do with it when they got it to its destination? Enriched uranium is essential, but it is only one part of a nuclear device. It would require half a dozen other components—very sophisticated components—to create a bomb, not to mention a facility capable of putting it all together. Other than the United States, there isn't a country in the Western

Hemisphere capable of making a nuclear device. Our office very carefully monitors not only the supply of weapons-grade uranium and plutonium throughout the world but also every company that has the technology to manufacture the other components of a device. Trust me, if some rogue country or terrorist organization was attempting to build a nuclear device, even a small one, there would be all sorts of clues popping up long before they ever got to the point of assembling a nuclear bomb. It would be impossible for us *not* to know about it."

Hovey gave Nichols and Pulsipher a discouraged head shake and then said to the speakerphone, "So we can cross nuclear bomb off our list of possible items in the suitcase, then?"

"Absolutely; it simply can't happen. Building a nuclear bomb takes tremendous sophistication." Then, after a short pause, the disembodied voice said, "If you're thinking there's something in that suitcase that can disrupt a country, specifically the United States, there are two possibilities that come to my mind. First, maybe it's a triggering device for explosives that are already here—not nuclear, but conventional explosives. Getting explosive material is a cinch. Any high school kid with access to the Internet can concoct a brew that will explode. The difficult part is initiating and controlling the explosion. Doing that requires a triggering device of some sort, which requires significantly more expertise. The reason you read about would-be bombers blowing themselves up while building a bomb isn't because the explosives malfunctioned but because their triggering device did."

"I see," Hovey said.

"The second and, in my opinion, more likely possibility is the suitcase contains toxins or microorganisms like bacteria, viruses, or even fungi of some sort. You can pack enough of certain deadly viruses into a suitcase to wipe out the population of an entire state. I deal with atoms, protons, and neutrons, which in the right form can be deadly, but the process to make them deadly, as I mentioned, requires tremendous sophistication. That isn't true about viruses and such. I think you should seriously consider living organisms."

"Like anthrax?"

"No, not really. You can create anthrax in a garden shed for twenty-five hundred dollars. There are many more deadly and virulent options out there. But really, Agent Hovey, I'm way out of my area of expertise. All I can tell you for certain is that that suitcase does not contain a nuclear bomb."

Hovey frowned and said, "Well, thanks for letting us pick your brain."

"You're welcome. I'm running late, so I have to end this conversation, but you said Asians, right?"

"Yes," Hovey answered.

"Have you spoken with Mike Phillips over at the Department of State's Bureau of Intelligence?"

Hovey raised his eyebrows and looked at Nichols and Pulsipher. "I didn't know the State Department had an intelligence unit," he said to Bringhurst.

"Yeah, they do. Phillips is a PhD—brilliant guy—but more than that, he probably knows the various Asian communities better than anyone. I've got to go, but I'm going to put you on hold and ask my assistant to get you his number. Goodbye."

A minute later Hovey was punching Michael D. Phillips's direct number into the phone. Halfway through the second ring, the speakerphone once again came alive. "Mike Phillips."

"Dr. Phillips, this is Wayne Hovey. I'm an FBI special agent in Miami. I have two other agents in my office; do you have a few minutes so we can speak with you?"

The speakerphone cracked out a hesitant, "I do."

Hovey told Phillips why he was calling, after which Phillips said, "Based on your explanation, I see three possibilities. First, these three men are simply doing something entirely on their own—acting as rogues, if you will. Second, Asian organized crime syndicates are looking to expand into the Caribbean or at least establish transshipment points to the U.S. via the Caribbean. Third, and perhaps less likely, this is a government-backed activity of some kind."

"It makes no sense for Asians to try and expand their drug trade or human trafficking through the Caribbean," Hovey replied. "They already have existing routes through the Canadian–U.S. border. And they certainly aren't going to try to expand their activities into the Caribbean; the Mexican and Central American cartels would attack them in a heartbeat. It would be a bloodbath; it's a fight they stand no chance of winning."

Pulsipher leaned toward the speakerphone and asked, "What about the notion of government-backed terrorism of some kind? Stuart Bringhurst suggested the idea of a triggering device or deadly toxins. What's your reaction to that?"

Phillips answer was immediate. "If you go down that road, there is only one possibility."

"What's that?" Hovey asked.

"North Korea."

"Why?" Pulsipher asked.

"It's a simple process of elimination. The governments of Thailand, Cambodia, Vietnam, Japan, etc. have no interest in destabilizing the U.S., nor do they have any terrorist organizations targeting the U.S. On the other hand, North Korea's new dictator is unbalanced enough to try such a scheme."

Hovey leaned back in his chair, rubbed the stubble on his chin, and traded glances with Nichols and Pulsipher. "Okay, any idea what they might be trying to do?" he asked.

"Oh, a thousand possibilities come to mind," Phillips said. "You said Stuart Bringhurst suggested the idea of toxins. If North Korea is behind it, I doubt that. They don't have a history of chemical warfare, nor is their collective psyche geared to that. With North Korea, you should be thinking more in terms of nuclear issues."

Hovey shook his head at the speakerphone. "Bringhurst says it can't be nuclear, that it's impossible."

"I can assure you, gentlemen, that if it is North Korea you're dealing with, you are not searching for deadly toxins. Its leader is a megalomaniac who would want to see major chaos in one fell swoop. He would not be content to wait for toxins to do their dirty work. With him, it's all about the show."

Hovey made no effort to hide the long, frustrated sigh he blew out. After a moment of nobody saying anything, he leaned forward and let his finger hover over the disconnect button on the speakerphone. "Thanks, Dr. Phillips. We appreciate your time. I *think* you've helped."

"Good luck, gentlemen," Phillips said. "Don't hesitate to call if I can be of further assistance."

Hovey didn't respond; he simply lowered his finger onto the button and cut off the connection.

Pulsipher walked over to a second chair by the desk and sat down. "So where are we now?" he asked. "We've got one expert telling us it can't be a bomb and must be toxins and another telling us just the opposite."

Hovey's response was to twirl his chair away from his agents so he was looking out the window. He leaned back, clasped his hands over his stomach and began rocking slowly back and forth. For two minutes the only sound in the room was the quiet hum of the air conditioner and the obnoxious squeak of Hovey's chair as he rocked.

The relative quiet in the office was interrupted when the buzzer on Hovey's phone sounded, followed immediately by a female voice over the speaker saying, "You have a call on line three: Colonel Roman from the Dominican Republic."

"Tell him I'm in a conference and I'll call him back," Hovey replied without turning from the window.

A moment later the buzzer went off again and the voice said, "He says it has to do with Scott Vaughn. He thinks you might want to talk with him. You still want me to tell him you'll call him back?"

Hovey didn't answer. He spun his chair around, punched the button on his phone, and lifted the receiver to his ear. "Hovey."

After a few moments of sitting motionless, Hovey grabbed a pen and scribbled notes on a pad. A moment later he said, "Thanks, Colonel. I'm not sure how much it helps, but it's more than we had a few minutes ago. I appreciate the call," and he plunked the receiver down.

"Well?" Nichols asked. "Good news?"

"I'm not sure. Roman's been running a sting operation for the past several months, and last night he snagged a couple of his cops." Looking at his notes, Hovey continued. "One of them, Raul Lopez, admitted he has been feeding Scott Vaughn information for more than two years."

"And?" Nichols said.

"This morning during an interrogation, he told Roman he sent photographs of the Walkers and their address to Vaughn."

Pulsipher looked at Hovey and asked, "So how does that help us?"

Hovey ignored the question and looked at Nichols. "Larry, you remember that snitch we arrested last year, the guy who said he could peg Vaughn as the one who transported the lungs and kidneys illegally removed from some peasants in Guatemala? A big black guy—what was his—?"

"Rodney Cavender?"

"Yup, that's him," Hovey said, shaking a finger at Nichols.

"He's dead; Vaughn killed him. Or at least we think he did," Nichols said.

"From the time word leaked that Cavender could lead us to Vaughn, how long was it before he was murdered?" Hovey asked.

"I don't remember for sure, but it was within a day or two. It was gruesome too. He had his tongue cut out and—"

Hovey cut him off with the wave of a hand. "What matters is that it took almost no time for Vaughn to target the guy."

Nichols leaned forward and said, "So you're thinking if we somehow get the word out that we have people who can positively identify Vaughn as a killer, he'll try getting to them?"

Hovey shook his head. "We don't need to get the word out. That Raul dude has already done it for us. Vaughn's going after the Walkers. Why else would he want their pictures and address?"

"And when he does, we'll be waiting?" Nichols asked.

Hovey said, "Exactly."

"So we forget the suitcase and concentrate on the Walkers?" Nichols said.

"We don't need to forget the suitcase entirely, but we do shift our focus to the Walkers."

"I like it," Nichols said.

Pulsipher leaned forward and said, "I don't. There are red flags everywhere. First, hanging the Walkers out as bait is not only risky—it's just wrong. You're playing with the lives of two innocent people. Second, we don't know for certain he'll go after them; we're just guessing. Third, don't forget he has a suitcase to deliver. It could take days, weeks, or even months before he goes after the Walkers. We can't watch them forever. And finally, there is the question of whether the Walkers will even agree to acting as bait."

Hovey looked over at Nichols and gave a smile that bordered on a smirk. Then he turned to Pulsipher and said, "Chris, welcome to your new world. You spent the last three years in New York chasing white-collar crooks using your computer and spreadsheets, but that's not how it works in the slime pit Larry and I wallow in here in Miami." Then, holding up his hand, he raised a finger. "First, I understand how you feel about using the Walkers as bait, as you call it. The fact is, though, whether or not we use them doesn't change their risk in the least."

"Sure it does," Pulsipher objected. "We're exposing them to unnecessary risk and painting huge targets on them."

Hovey shook his head. "The Walkers drew the targets on themselves when they reported the murder. Second," he said, holding up another finger, "is the suitcase. There are only two reasons people hire Vaughn: speed and secrecy. Whatever's in that suitcase needs to be delivered quickly. We won't be waiting weeks or months. He'll go after the Walkers quickly, either before or immediately after he makes the delivery."

"Okay, but the biggest question is the Walkers," Pulsipher said. "You don't know they'll go along with this. What happens when you tell them what we're going to do and they say no?"

Hovey dropped his hand to his desk and said, "I didn't say we're going to tell them."

CHAPTER NINETEEN

Greg opened his eyes, but in the darkness, it took his brain a confused minute to figure out he wasn't asleep in a jungle and the noise wasn't a gun-wielding man creeping up on him. He was home, and the noise was Marena as she eased off the bed and walked toward the door. "What's the matter?" he said, raising up on an elbow and looking at her silhouetted figure.

"Can't sleep," Marena answered.

Greg thought for a moment before saying, "Wiggy Wiggy?" In the dim light radiating from the red numbers on the clock, he saw her nodding her head. He didn't really want to talk—he wanted to sleep—but he said, "You want to talk about it?"

"You're tired; you should sleep."

Greg took a deep breath, forced his eyes to focus, and said, "I'm okay. Come sit down. We can talk."

Marena walked back to the bed and climbed in. As both of them adjusted the pillows against the bed's headboard, she said, "Every time I close my eyes, images of him come flooding in. I see it all over again. The boat, him swimming frantically, and . . ." She fell silent for a moment before saying, "And the blood." Pushing her hair off her forehead, she said, "I start thinking that if I hadn't negotiated with him, he wouldn't have taken us and he'd still be alive. I shouldn't have done it. It's my fault."

Greg shook his head. "It's not your fault."

"I've tried to tell myself that, but somehow I don't believe it. If only—"

Greg cut her off. "Marena, you can 'if only' this forever." He'd tried to say it reassuringly, but it came off more sternly than he'd intended. "If only we hadn't gone . . . if only the boat motor had started . . . if only we'd gone another day. There's no end to it. But none of that changes anything."

In the dark, Greg hadn't noticed the tears forming in Marena's eyes. He waited as she leaned over and quickly plucked two tissues from the box beside the bed. After she finished blotting her watery eyes, he said, "The only person who carries any fault for this is the guy who killed him. Nobody else. You can't blame yourself."

Marena looked over at him, the tears coming a little heavier, but she said nothing.

Greg put his arm around her shoulders and pulled her close. She leaned her head against him and cried, making no further effort to wipe away her tears. After a few minutes of silence, she said, "Greg?"

"Yes?"

"Let's go up to the ranch."

Greg pulled back slightly. "Why?"

"I'd just like to get away—go someplace different. I'm not ready to be home."

It was Greg's turn for silence. After a moment, he began a string of mild objections. "It's going to be cold and probably snowy."

"I know, and that's why I want to go—it will be different. Well, that and I have a thousand things to do up there. It will take my mind off . . ." Her voice faltered.

"We won't have much time. I need to be back at the clinic in five days, and we'll lose two just driving there and back."

Marena pushed away and said, "What if we fly? We can be there in two hours in the Bonanza."

Greg thought for a moment and then with his thumb wiped away a tear that was streaking down Marena's face. "When do you want to leave?"

Marena leaned over and looked at the clock on the nightstand. "In five hours."

At eight o'clock the next morning, Greg placed two small suitcases into the car's trunk and slid into the driver's seat. Glancing at his watch, he shook his head. "This must be some kind of a record. We only got home eleven hours ago."

Marena pulled her car door closed and said, "Thanks for doing this. I know it's kind of a hassle, but—"

Greg cut her off. "We needed to go up one more time to get the house winterized, so it's all good."

Greg started the engine and had backed halfway down the driveway when a faint "Marena, wait!" filtered through the air.

"Stop, Greg," Marena said. "Anita's waving at us." Lowering her window, Marena smiled at the neighbor and returned the wave.

A moment later eighty-year-old Anita Lorch tottered up to the car. "I thought you two weren't going to be back for a few more days," she said as she leaned against Marena's door.

Marena removed her sunglasses and said, "We weren't, but things changed, so we came home early."

"Well, it's nice to have you back. Your house always looks so dark and lonely when you're gone. The neighborhood isn't quite the same when you're away."

Greg leaned over so he could see Anita and said, "Actually, Anita, we're leaving again right now. Kind of in a hurry too."

"But you just got home," Anita protested.

Marena smiled and said, "We're headed up to our place in Idaho for a couple of days—going to check on things once more before winter locks us out."

Pointing her arthritic finger at Greg, Anita said, "You'd better drive safely, and I hope you don't get snowed in. I watched the weather last night, and there's a huge storm coming down from Canada. It's going to be cold and snowy for the next few days."

"We're flying up," Marena said. "It'll only take us two hours. We'll beat the storm and come back after it passes through."

"Well, be careful, dear," Anita said, patting Marena on the arm as she straightened up to her full five-foot stature.

"We will," Marena said with another smile. "Keep an eye on the house for us. If you see a moving van pull up and someone starts hauling furniture out, call the cops." Then, with a little finger wave, she added, "See you in a few days."

Greg shifted the car into gear as he said, "She's a great neighbor—a little overprotective, maybe, and sometimes too nosey, but a great neighbor."

The flight took exactly two hours and twelve minutes from wheels up to wheels down and covered 313 miles, but Preston, Idaho, and St. George, Utah, were worlds apart, or at least the weather was. "I forgot how cold it can be here in December," Marena said as she lifted a suitcase out of the airplane's baggage compartment and placed it inside the old Chevrolet Tahoe they kept in the hangar.

"Yeah, it's not quite the same as lying on a beach in Punta Cana," Greg said as he began guiding the Bonanza back into the empty hangar.

Marena shook her head. "I'm never going back; too many bad memories."

Greg nodded in agreement and said, "Get in the Tahoe. It won't be warm yet, but at least you'll be out of the wind. I'll close up the hangar."

Marena didn't hesitate. She jumped into the white SUV, and after securing the hangar, Greg climbed in and blew on his hands, grateful Marena had already cranked the heater to maximum. "Man, it's cold."

"I'm surprised how much snow there is already," Marena said as they pulled out onto the highway. "For the first of December, there's a lot of white out there."

Thirty minutes later Greg let off the accelerator and tapped the brakes a couple of times as they rounded the final shallow curve before reaching the drive leading to their house, where he slowed to a stop, looking at the half foot of snow and shaking his head. Engaging the four-wheel drive, he turned onto the short drive that wound its way through a grove of pine and aspen trees to the garage. After parking inside, Greg and Marena grabbed their bags and trudged up the steps and along the sidewalk to the house.

By 10:00 P.M., with the furnace running full blast, the thermometer inside the house had stubbornly inched from forty-five to sixty degrees. Uncertain when the house would grow warmer, Greg helped Marena pile thick blankets and quilts onto the bed. Burrowing under the covers, they snuggled together and almost instantly drifted to sleep.

CHAPTER TWENTY

Vaughn's eyes were little more than two narrow slits as the Aztec rolled to a stop on the transient airplane parking ramp at the St. George airport. The luminous dial on his watch said 3:14 A.M., and his body was lightyears beyond tired. Dodging storms, ice, and turbulence for the past several hours had left him mentally depleted and physically exhausted. Both his mind and his body begged for sleep. Setting the brakes and shutting down the airplane's engines, he dropped his hands to his lap, leaned his head back against the seat, and instantly fell asleep.

It was the heavy tapping on the airplane's window that caused him to jerk awake. A redheaded twenty-something kid stood beside the airplane, his jacket proclaiming he was an employee of the Above View Jet Center. "You okay?" the kid mouthed.

Vaughn blinked half a dozen times and looked at the kid and then at his watch. 3:45. He ran his tongue around the inside of his dry mouth and said groggily, "Yeah, fine."

Leaning closer to the airplane, the kid jerked his thumb toward the building and asked, "You want to go inside?"

Vaughn nodded and slowly began extracting his stiff and weary body from the airplane. As he stepped onto the ground, Vaughn said, "I just got in and wasn't sure you were open."

"Twenty-four-seven," the kid answered way too brightly for this hour. "I watched you taxi up and waited, thinking you'd come in. When you didn't, I thought I better make sure you were okay."

Vaughn nodded. "Thanks. I'm fine; just tired."

"You need fuel?"

"Yes," Vaughn said. "Top off the tanks. And do you have a pilot's lounge or someplace I can crash for a couple of hours?"

"Sure," the redhead replied. "We've got a really nice lounge with couches, recliners, and a TV. Heck, we've even got a room with a couple of cots you can sleep in. No windows, so the sunshine won't bother you. And we've got a room with exercise equipment and a shower."

"I'll pass on the exercise equipment but take you up on the cot and a shower a little later."

"Go for it, man. I'll get your plane fueled. I'll be goin' home in another hour, but I'll leave your fuel ticket on the front desk. You can pay when you wake up."

"Thanks," Vaughn said. He reached into his pocket and handed the kid a twenty-dollar bill. "I appreciate it. And where can I get a rental car? I'll need one after I get a few hours of sleep."

"By the time you wake up, our receptionist will be here. She'll make arrangements for you."

"Thanks," Vaughn said again and, reaching inside the airplane, grabbed his backpack and overnight bag. Then he locked the door and staggered into the building to the waiting cot.

Five hours later a muffled mixture of chatter and laughter from beyond the door pulled Vaughn from sleep. Glancing at his watch, he swung his legs off the cot and sat up. Elbows on his knees, he ran his fingers through his hair and tried to clear his mouth of the leftover taste of the greasy hamburger and fries from Las Cruces. Straightening his rumpled clothes, he grabbed his backpack and bag and walked out into the bright sunlit foyer.

"You must be Mr. Aztec," a bubbly blonde receptionist said on seeing Vaughn enter the spacious room. "How'd you sleep?"

Vaughn put on the best smile he could manage and said, "Pretty good. That cot's more comfortable than I thought it would be."

The receptionist chuckled. "You must have been *really* tired. Nobody has ever said that."

Vaughn smiled. "When I came in last night, the fuel guy said you have showers. Where are they?"

"Down the hall, second door on your left. You'll need your own towel and stuff though."

"Got it," he said, lifting his overnight bag slightly. "Oh, and the kid also said you could make arrangements for a rental car for me; is that right?"

"Sure. When do you want it?"

Vaughn looked at the huge clock made from an airplane propeller that was hanging on the wall behind the receptionist. "It's nine now; about nine forty-five?"

"Great. I'll call the rental agency and have someone here to pick you up. By the way, we have coffee, donuts, and fruit in the room next to the showers. Help yourself. Oh, and how long will you need the rental car?"

Vaughn smiled. "Not long. If everything goes right, I should be back in a couple of hours. My plane is fueled, right?"

The receptionist picked up a small sheet of paper and waved it in the air. "Fueled and ready to go."

An hour later Vaughn stood at the rental car counter and handed a VISA card bearing the name *Richard Jacobsen* to the woman at the counter. "Really, Mr. Jacobsen, we can upgrade you to a full-size car for the same price. It would be much more elegant and far more impressive."

Vaughn shook his head. "Thanks, but the little white Malibu will be fine for what I have to do."

The woman looked at the designer clothing Vaughn was wearing and raised her eyebrows. "Whatever you prefer," she said with a slight nod.

As the woman tapped on her computer keyboard, Vaughn fished through his backpack, pulled out a slip of paper, and entered an address into a map app on his phone. Almost instantly his screen displayed a map of St. George and a bright-blue line showing the streets he should take.

The woman placed a paper on the counter, handed Vaughn a pen, and said, "Please sign here, here, and here."

Vaughn smiled pleasantly, made three indecipherable scribbles on the paper, and pushed it back to her.

"You're ready to go," the woman said cheerfully. Handing the keys to Vaughn, she said, "Your car is out the sliding doors and to your right. It's in space nine. Drive safely."

Twenty minutes later Vaughn slowly drove past the Walkers' house. Then he drove past going the opposite direction and drove around the block. Circling the block a second time, he slowed only slightly as he approached the house. Had he been paying closer attention to the street than the house, he wouldn't have hit the arthritic old Basset Hound that had run out into the street doing its pitiful best to chase a cat. It was a glancing blow, not the kind that drew blood or did any permanent damage, but it was enough to cause its equally old owner to come racing out into the street.

"Stop! You hit my dog!"

Vaughn hit the brakes and jumped from the car. Hurrying around the front, he and the old woman reached the dazed hound at the same moment.

Looking at the unmoving dog lying on its side, she said, "You've killed him; you've killed my Harpo."

Vaughn squatted down just as the ancient dog struggled to its feet and shook its head. "I don't think so," he replied. "I barely clipped him. Actually, I think he hit me, not the other way around."

Tail wagging and tongue hanging out, Harpo looked up at the woman and let out a deep, playful bark. The woman leaned over and began running her hands over every inch of the dog, starting with its head and working to its tail. Panting and slobbering, the dog seemed delighted in the attention and responded by licking her cheek. After a moment, she slowly straightened up and said, "I think you're right. It doesn't feel like anything's broken, and he seems more excited than he's been in ages."

"A brush with death will do that to you," Vaughn said with a smile.

"I suppose so." Then, studying Vaughn's face, she said, "I don't recognize you. You don't live around here, do you?"

Vaughn shook his head. "No, I don't." Stammering slightly, he said, "I just came . . . to visit some friends."

"Who?"

"What?" Vaughn said in surprise.

"Who are you visiting?" she asked with the bluntness that came with old age. "I know everyone around here. Who are you visiting?"

Vaughn swallowed, looked at the short, aged woman, and considered lying but then said, "The Walkers. I was looking for the Walkers' house."

"You found it," she proclaimed as she pointed to the hacienda-style home. "But you missed them; they aren't home."

The corners of Vaughn mouth turned down in a disappointed frown. "Missed them?"

"Yup, they've gone. How do you know the Walkers?"

Vaughn spread his lips into his most engaging smile. "Well, actually, we just met a few days ago. They were on a trip to the Dominican Republic. I was there on business, and we got to know each other. It was one of those times when you meet someone and become instant friends. You ever had that happen to you? Anyway, they invited me to come see them. I am on my way to a business convention in Southern California—I sell vacuum cleaners—and decided on a whim to stop." Then, after a short pause, he said, "Do you know where they went or when they will be back? I'd really like to see them."

"Well, if you're just passing through, you won't be able to see them," she said, shaking her head of unruly gray hair. Then, turning to the dog that had wandered off and was sniffing around a rosebush, she yelled, "Harpo, come over here."

Vaughn watched as the dog completely ignored the command and went to another rosebush. Vaughn made a show of looking at his watch. "I really don't have much time. Do you know where I can find the Walkers?"

The woman nodded but studied Vaughn without saying anything.

"Well?" Vaughn said after an awkward moment.

"What did you say your name is?"

Vaughn beamed his warmest smile and in his most charming voice said, "Oh, I'm sorry. I should have introduced myself. I'm Dan Johnson, district sales manager for the Kirby Vacuum Cleaning company." Then, reaching into his back pocket, he pulled out his wallet and thumbed through some of the contents. "Oh, darn it. I was going to give you one of my business cards, but it looks like I'm out."

"Oh, that's all right," the woman said with a dismissive wave. "I'd just throw it away when I got into the house."

Vaughn chuckled. "Well, in that case, maybe it's a good thing I didn't have one. But you were about to tell me where I can find the Walkers."

"Oh, that's right. They're in Idaho."

"Excuse me?" Vaughn said in surprise.

"They have a ranch in a little place in Idaho. They've gone up there for a few days."

"I didn't know they had another home," Vaughn said smiling. "They didn't tell me that. Where is it?"

"It's in a little town in the mountains outside of Preston. A place called Mink Creek."

CHAPTER TWENTY-ONE

Vaughn returned the car, took a shuttle back to the Above View Jet Center, and walked into the lobby just in time to see an animated TV weatherman talking excitedly about the "perfect storm." Colorful graphics depicted a cold-air mass sweeping down from Canada and colliding with heavy moisture flowing in from the Pacific. The result, the weatherman said ominously, was a massive weather system that had stalled over the entire southern half of Idaho and would produce staggering amounts of snow before the storm slowly drifted east to the ski resorts in the Colorado Rockies.

A moment later Vaughn was on his phone with weather briefers at the FAA. Giving them a fictitious name and airplane registration number so he couldn't be tracked or identified, he asked for more details about the storm system. The man on the other end of the phone confirmed what Vaughn had just seen on the TV and added that flight was not recommended. Vaughn thanked the man, rushed out of the building, and sprinted to his airplane.

The first thirty minutes of Vaughn's flight from St. George to Preston had been nothing but billowy thick clouds. The last sixty minutes had been an ugly replay of the night before. Moisture-laden clouds coated his airplane in a slowly thickening layer of ice. Unseen turbulence slapped the airplane from the top, bottom, and sides, tossing him around with enough force that he became disoriented whenever he glanced from his instruments to the grayness outside. The scant five hours of sleep combined with the stress of flying in the horrendous weather left him white-knuckled, sweating, and totally exhausted as the Aztec landed with a poof in the blanket of snow coating Preston's single runway.

Tapping the brakes lightly to keep from skidding, Vaughn leaned as far forward as he could so he could see well enough to guide the airplane from the runway. Unfamiliar with the airport's layout and unable to distinguish anything in the heavily falling snow, he stopped the plane. Unexpectedly, a voice crackled in his headset. "Hey, twin engine Aztec, nice landing. You're crazy to be out in this stuff, but nice landing. You need help getting to the parking ramp?"

Vaughn let out a sigh and keyed his microphone. "I do," he replied. "I can't see a thing."

"You're one lucky pilot, that's all I've got to say," the voice replied. "Stay where you are. I'll be out with a snowplow in a couple of minutes to give you a trail to follow." Then, after a pause, he said again, "You're one lucky pilot. Crazy but lucky."

A few minutes later Vaughn could see the faint yellow light of a truck blinking at him through the white snowflakes. A few feet from the airplane, the truck made a U-turn and headed back the way it had come. Vaughn pushed the throttles forward and coaxed the airplane to move into the path the truck plowed. He followed it to a large parking area with only one other airplane and shut off the engines. A second later a bearded man was rapping on the airplane's door. "Come inside the building," he said, pointing to a small yellow house, and then the man disappeared in a blur of snowflakes.

Vaughn burst through the door of the building, blew out a loud "Phew," and stomped his feet on the floor, sending tiny snowballs flying from his shoes and pants. "That's the worst I've ever been in," he said, running his hands through his wet hair.

The bearded man slowly shook his head as he peeled off his heavy coat. "You're crazy, man," he said. Pointing out the window at the Aztec, he said, "You see how much ice you have on your airplane. It's amazing you could keep it in the air."

"I just about didn't," Vaughn replied. "You got a bathroom? I need to go really bad."

The man laughed loudly enough it reverberated off the room's walls. "Yeah, I bet you do," he replied. "Through that door," he said, pointing to the door on the opposite side of the room.

A few moments later, as Vaughn came back into the room, he felt only slightly more composed than when he'd landed. Walking up to the counter behind which the bearded man stood shuffling through a mound of papers he said, "Do you have a heated hangar I can put my airplane in overnight to get rid of the ice and keep it out of the snow?"

The man shook his head. "If it wasn't snowing so hard, you'd be able to see there are only a dozen hangars in the entire airport. All of them are stuffed full of airplanes, cars, motor homes, and other stuff. You couldn't fit an airplane in with a shoehorn."

"There's nothing?" Vaughn said incredulously as he walked over to a window. Peering through the falling snow, he pointed to the faint outline of a large hangar that was barely visible. "What about that one?" he asked.

The man looked to where Vaughn was pointing. "Umm, don't know," he said.

"Is there room? Will my airplane fit in there?"

"Oh, it'd fit okay. I just don't know if the people will want another airplane in with—"

Vaughn suddenly changed his demeanor. Smiling as he fished his wallet from his pants, he asked, "What's your name?"

"Littles. Craig Littles."

Extracting a fifty-dollar bill from his wallet, Vaughn extended it to Littles and said, "Craig, will you give the owners a call for me? Tell them it's just for tonight. I'll be leaving tomorrow."

Littles looked at the fifty and shook his head, making no effort to reach for the money.

"What's the matter? A phone call isn't worth fifty bucks?"

"It isn't that," Littles replied. "I'll make the phone call—for free. It's just that unless you're stupider than I think, and I think you're pretty stupid for flying in this, you're not going to be leaving here tomorrow or even the next day, at least not in that airplane." Shoving his hands into a pocket of his grease-stained coveralls, he said, "The latest weather report says this is just the beginning of a three-day storm."

"That's not what was forecast this morning when I checked."

Littles nodded. "Yeah, well, that's what it is now."

Vaughn went silent and turned away from Littles. After pacing to a large window and looking out at the swirling blizzard, he turned to Littles and said, "You ever heard of a little town in Idaho called Arco?"

Littles nodded again. "Yeah."

Vaughn raised his eyebrows at the remark. "How far is it from here?"

"By air or highway?"

"Highway," Vaughn said.

"Not sure exactly—about a hundred and fifty miles, more or less."

"Good roads?" Vaughn asked.

"Depends on how you go," Littles replied. "There are fifty miles of freeway, and the rest is two-lane county roads. There are other routes, but they're two-lane roads the whole way."

"So a little more than a couple of hours and I can be there, right?"

"Yeah, if the sun's shining and the roads are dry." Motioning out the window, Littles said, "Today you probably wouldn't make it."

Vaughn went quiet again as he put the money and wallet back into his pocket. "Will you make the call about the hangar? And is there a car rental place in Preston, someplace I can get a four-wheel drive vehicle?"

Littles laughed. "Car rental? In Preston?" Shaking his head, he said, "If you need wheels while you're here in town, the airport has a loaner car you can use. It ain't four-wheel drive; in fact, it ain't much of anything, but it gets around."

Vaughn swore. A moment later he reached back into his pocket, retrieved his wallet, and extracted eight fifty-dollar bills. "Call the people who own the hangar. Tell them I'll give them two hundred bucks a night if they'll let me put my airplane in there." Turning away, he said, "I gotta use the bathroom again."

As Vaughn emerged from the bathroom, he heard Littles say into the phone, " . . . two nights." Then, after a pause, he said, "I have the cash lying on the counter right here in front of me." After another pause he said, "Okay, I'll tell him. Talk to you later."

Littles hung up the old black phone and said, "It's a go. We'll need to shuffle their airplane so there's enough room, but you're set."

"Thanks," Vaughn said, putting on his coat. "Let's put it away, and then I'd like to make arrangements to use the loaner car. It looks like I'm going to be stuck here for at least tonight, so I might as well get a motel room. Preston does have a motel, doesn't it?"

"Oh yeah; pretty decent too; it's on the other end of town."

CHAPTER TWENTY-TWO

THE DULL THUMPS OF CAR doors slamming closed were just enough to drag Vaughn from a fitful sleep. He rolled over and cracked his eyelids open only wide enough to see 4:09 P.M. showing on the motel's cheap alarm clock. Although his brain told him to get out of bed, his exhausted body didn't move, begging to add just a few more minutes of sleep to the twelve hours he'd had. He had nearly drifted off again when muffled chatter from the room next door floated through the motel's thin walls. Pulling the blankets over his head and burrowing deeper into the pillow, Vaughn fought to keep his brain from coming to life. When the chatter got loud enough Vaughn could almost decipher the words, he cursed and flung off the blankets. Swinging his legs off the bed, he sat motionless for a moment, letting his brain take in the surroundings and remind him he was in Preston, Idaho.

Dressed in his underwear and a T-shirt, the coolness of the air in the room caused an involuntarily shiver to streak through his body as he stood up. He walked to the small heater and twisted the dial to the maximum setting and then padded across the worn and stained carpet to the window. Parting the dark-blue vinyl drapes just enough to peek outside, he gasped.

The airport's courtesy car was piled with nearly a foot of snow, making it look more like a deformed marshmallow than a car. The Volkswagen bug parked next to it resembled the top of a giant mushroom. The four-wheel drive pickup truck in which the people in the next room had arrived looked as if it had been through a war zone. It was coated in a thick layer of grimy brown slush, and the wheel wells were so thick with accumulated snow and ice there was hardly room for the tires. The windshield had two small half-moon circles that were somewhat free of snow, but it was obvious they had been unable to keep up with the onslaught.

Vaughn leaned forward until his nose was nearly touching the glass, straining to see the small motel office, the highway, or anything more than fifty feet away. It was impossible; the snow was falling so hard and in such big flakes everything was obscured in a blanket of gray and white. Shaking his head in dismay, he rubbed his hand over his stubble of a beard and cursed again. Closing the drapes, he walked to the bathroom.

Shaved, showered, and dressed, Vaughn walked to the window and drew open the drapes. He was hoping to see sunlight, but what came through the window was the steel-gray light of early evening. In the distance, he could barely make out the faint glow of the motel's sign announcing there was no vacancy. He walked to the small desk in the room, picked up the remote control, and called the television to life. It was already tuned to a news channel in Pocatello. On the screen was a thirty-something woman with a grave expression on her face. She was standing in front of a map of Idaho, giving a detailed explanation about the massive storm that had settled over all of central and southern Idaho and most of northern Utah. As she rattled on, a graphic flicked up on the screen, showing the major highways in Idaho that were either closed or listed as having treacherous driving conditions.

Vaughn scanned the image on the TV. Locating Preston and Arco, it took him only a few seconds to realize the roads between the two towns were either closed or treacherous. Turning up the volume, he listened carefully as the woman detailed that road crews were unable to keep up with the record-setting snowfall, so the Utah Highway Patrol and Idaho State Police had jointly decided to close I-15 from Brigham City, Utah, to Idaho Falls, Idaho.

The screen changed to a snow-covered reporter and Idaho State trooper standing beside a police cruiser. No, the trooper said, this was not the first time such a large section of the interstate had been closed. Yes, it was true that all snowplows had been instructed to return to their facilities and wait out the storm. Yes, they were aware that many people were stranded on the interstate, but there was little or nothing they could do at the present time. No, he had no idea how long the interstate would remain closed.

Vaughn tossed down the remote and opened an Idaho map he had taken from the courtesy car. He scoured every route he could find between Preston and Arco and compared the highway numbers to the list that was once again on the TV screen.

Clicking off the TV, he picked up his backpack and withdrew the envelope Li had given him at the cage fight and pulled out the three pages of instructions he'd read half a dozen times. He tossed the first two pages onto the bed and scanned down the third page until he found the phone number he needed.

Punching the number into his phone, he began pacing. On the fourth ring he mumbled, "Come on, answer the phone." On the sixth ring, a feminine voice came on instructing him to leave a message. Frowning, he said, "This is Scott Vaughn. We need to talk. Call me."

Dropping his phone onto the bed, he walked to the window. He'd barely parted the curtains for another look at the sea of white snow when his phone rang. "Hello?" he said cautiously.

"You called, Mr. Vaughn?"

Vaughn expected to hear Mr. Li's voice. Instead he heard a younger but stronger voice that spoke heavily accented English.

"Who is this?" Vaughn asked.

"That's unimportant. I am returning your call."

"Fine. Look, we've got a problem."

"What is the nature of *your* problem, Mr. Vaughn?" the voice said without emotion.

"*Our* problem is that I'm not going to meet your deadline."

There was a moment of silence and then, "Why is that, Mr. Vaughn?"

"I'm sitting in a motel room in Preston, Idaho, in a blizzard. There's nearly a foot of snow on the ground."

"So what is your problem, Mr. Vaughn?"

"The problem is most of the roads are closed."

"Find one that is open."

Vaughn shook his head and said, "You don't understand." Then, making no effort to conceal his frustration, he added, "Even if I could find an open road, I've only driven in snow twice. Both times ended in a wreck. So you can see *we* have a problem."

Suddenly another voice sounded in Vaughn's ear. It was older, raspy, and gruff. "Perhaps you do not understand the seriousness of the situation. It is imperative you deliver our package as agreed. Failure is not an option. You must do whatever is necessary to make the delivery." Then, in a very slow, threatening tone, he said, "There will be serious consequences if you do not deliver as agreed." The voice allowed the words to hang in the air for a moment. Then, in a more reconciliatory tone, he added, "At the same time, the reward for delivering as agreed will be twice what you were originally expecting."

Vaughn had been holding the small phone so tightly against his ear that its black plastic surface had a light coating of sweat. Standing up, he walked over to the window without saying anything into the phone.

"Mr. Vaughn, did I make myself clear? Do you understand?"

"Yeah, you're perfectly clear. I understand completely," he replied as he gazed at the hood of the courtesy car, which had accumulated another two inches of snow since he'd woken up.

"Excellent. Please remember the deadline is tomorrow morning at ten. You must not be late." Then the connection went dead.

CHAPTER TWENTY-THREE

Marena peered over her husband's shoulder at the wires, pipes, and valves as he shimmied deeper inside the nonworking machine.

"Why is it that a furnace quits working when you need it most?" Greg asked.

"Murphy's Law?" Marena replied. "What's wrong?"

"Fan motor."

"Can you fix it?"

"Nope, it's shot. We need a new one," Greg answered as he yanked a wrench to loosen a stuck bolt.

"Can we get a replacement in Preston, or will we need to go to Logan?"

"Don't know. I'm hoping Preston," Greg said as he extracted the last bolt and eased the motor out of the furnace. "While I check a couple of other things, will you call Wilson Heating and see if they have a replacement?" Pointing to a metal label on the motor, he said, "You'll need to write down those numbers."

Marena copied the numbers onto a piece of paper and hurried up the stairs from the small utility room in time to answer a ringing telephone. Returning a few minutes later, she said, "We're in luck. They have a motor in stock, and they'll hold it for us, but we have to be there no later than two o'clock, which means we need to leave now. This storm is causing grief for lots of people, and they need to go out on service calls. Also, that was Craig Littles on the phone. He says the guy who flew in last night and asked to put his airplane in our hangar paid him. He's got four hundred dollars in cash for us."

"Perfect. We'll pick up the money while we're out," Greg said as he pushed himself to his feet.

Fifteen minutes later, as Greg guided the Tahoe onto the highway amid mattress-size snowflakes, Marena turned on the radio as the beginning strains of a Mannheim Steamroller Christmas song started playing. Seconds into the song, a piercing, shrill, wobbling tone blocked out the music, and a disembodied, synthetic voice said, "The National Weather Service has issued a winter storm warning for the mountains of Northern Utah and the south, central, and eastern portions of Idaho. Extreme snowfall is expected, with depths ranging from twelve to eighteen inches at the lower elevations and twenty-four to forty-eight inches at higher mountain elevations. Driving conditions will be hazardous throughout the region, with whiteout conditions prevailing. Repeat, the National Weather Service has issued . . ."

Marena turned down the volume. Looking at the snowflakes pelting the windshield, she made no effort to disguise the anxiety in her voice. "Do we really need to go out in this mess this afternoon?"

Greg glanced over and returned his focus to the road. He must have seen the tension on her face, because he said, "It's going to be okay. We'll take it slow. We'll get the motor, scoot over and pick up some groceries, and stop at the airport to pick up the money on our way back. We'll be home in two or three hours."

"As long as it's before dark; I hate being on the road in a snowstorm when it's dark."

The snow-packed roads turned the normally thirty-minute drive into an hour venture. The stop to pick up the fan motor and groceries added another ninety minutes because of hordes of people stocking up on food. Nearly two-and-a-half hours after they'd left, Greg eased the Tahoe into the snow-covered parking lot at the airport as the first hint of darkness was falling.

"So much for a quick trip to town," Marena said as she looked out at the snowflakes swirling in the vehicle's headlights. "And we've got another hour drive home—in the dark. There are times when I hate snow. This is one of them."

"What a change from a week ago," he said, shifting the car into park. Nodding to the small building that housed the airport office, he said, "You want to wait here or come in?"

Marena had her seatbelt unbuckled before Greg had finished his sentence. "I have to go to the bathroom," she said, pulling on her thick woolen mittens.

In their brief thirty-foot walk from the Tahoe to the airport office door, Greg and Marena were covered with a layer of snow. Bursting through the door, they stomped their snow-covered feet on the black mat and shook snow from their coats like dogs. "Craig, you here?" Greg shouted as he closed the door and pulled off his brown leather gloves.

"In the back room," a nasally voice croaked.

"I'm going to the bathroom," Marena said.

"I'll wait," Greg said.

When Marena came back, she walked with Greg down a narrow, dimly lit hallway and turned into a small office that time had forgotten. An old wooden desk that was nicked, chipped, and scratched took up most of the space. It was piled high with old issues of newspapers, magazines, and an assortment of papers. On one corner of the desk an old airplane carburetor was sitting in pieces in a cardboard box, leaking an occasional drop of gasoline. Dozens of unframed pictures were stapled to two of the walls, each showing a grinning man or woman standing beside an airplane. Leaning in one corner was a six-foot-tall wooden propeller, its heavily varnished surface glistening in the light from the overhead fluorescent bulbs. The floor around the overflowing trash can was littered with wadded-up tissues.

Greg looked at Marena and then the bald, red-bearded man seated at the desk and said, "You don't look so good."

Craig Littles wasn't so much sitting at the desk as he was half sprawled over it, his head cradled in the crook of one arm and his other hand daubing at his red nose with a tissue. Pushing himself to a fully upright position, he wiped a small dribble from the tip of his nose and mumbled, "Miserable cold. It's hit me suddenly, like a ton of bricks. I feel awful." Pulling another tissue from a box, he eyed Greg and Marena's snow-covered coats and shook his head. "Man, you're either brave or crazy for coming out in this storm."

"More crazy than brave," Marena said as she sat down on the only chair that wasn't stacked with papers.

"We had to come to Preston for a furnace motor and some groceries. I thought as long as we were here, we'd pick up the money and take a peek in the hangar to check on things. You got the guy's airplane tucked in okay?" Greg asked, brushing water droplets from the sleeve of his coat.

"Yup," Craig replied through half-closed eyes. "But I'll bet there's an ocean of water on your hangar floor by now. You wouldn't believe how much ice he had on his wings and props," he added, taking a swipe at his nose with the tissue. "I'm sure the guy was only a few minutes away from falling out of the sky. It was bad."

"Flatland guy? Not used to flying in the mountains?" Greg asked.

Craig shrugged his shoulders. "I think so. We made small talk while putting his plane in your hangar, but he danced around my questions, especially about where he was from and what brought him to Preston."

"He was probably too embarrassed to admit anything," Marena chirped.

Craig shrugged again. "I got kind of curious, so this morning before this stinking cold hit me so hard, I got on my computer and checked one of those websites that track airplanes that file flight plans. I did a search of the last twenty-four hours for his airplane's registration number—666 SV. Nothing. So then I went out to the FAA's website and checked the registration. It's a Piper Aztec owned by some company in Delaware—I'm sure it's a shell company. I do know two things about him though."

"Which are?" Marena asked.

"His name and that he has plenty of cash," Craig answered.

Marena said, "What's his name?"

"John Smith."

"And his money?" Greg asked.

Craig slid his desk chair back a couple of inches and pulled open the top drawer, extracting a stack of fifty-dollar bills. Wiping his nose on the sleeve of his flannel shirt, he said, "It was pretty amazing. The guy opened his backpack and pulled out bills like they were Monopoly money," he said as he counted out eight of the bills and held them up to Greg.

Greg took the money and said, "Four hundred bucks for two nights?"

Craig smiled and held out his hands. "Hey, he's the one who offered to pay you two hundred bucks a night, and I didn't argue with him." Then, with the closest thing to a grin he could muster, he added, "I didn't tell him you'd probably let him put his plane in there for free."

Greg pointed to the stack of bills Craig still held in his hand and asked, "What's that for? Does he need work done on his airplane?"

Craig shook his head. "He wanted to use the airport's courtesy car. At first he only wanted it overnight, but then he decided he might need it for a few days."

"A few days?" Marena questioned, leaning forward slightly in her chair. "I didn't know you let people take it for that long."

"We don't normally, but with the ugly weather we're having, I was pretty sure nobody else would be flying in and needing it, so I told him he could use it if he paid a rental fee up front and left a deposit."

"How much did you tell him?" Greg asked as he eyed the stack of money.

"A hundred bucks a day—plus gas—and either a credit card or two thousand dollars as a cash deposit."

Greg laughed. "You serious? You could buy that old piece of junk for a thousand bucks."

Craig put the cash in his drawer and leaned back in his chair. "You know, I fully expected him to pull out a credit card and hand it to me, but he didn't. He put his wallet back into his pocket and opened his backpack. He pulled out two little bundles of fifties—a thousand bucks in each—for the deposit. Then he pulled out a wad of cash—not neat little stacks like before, but just a big roll of green. It was like watching Mary Poppins herself. Every time he reached into his backpack, he pulled out more cash. Anyway, he peeled off a couple hundred dollars for two days' rent. Then he counted out *another* hundred and told me it should cover the gasoline and whatever was left over was mine."

"Amazing," Marena said.

"For sure," Criag said. "I just wanted to have a peek inside his backpack to see how many more little bundles and rolls he had stashed inside."

"You think he's a drug mule?" Greg asked. "Hauling drugs in his airplane?"

"I don't know. Maybe," Craig answered with a shrug. "His airplane's really nice though. I thought those drug runners used beat-up old airplanes held together with baling wire and duct tape."

"What's this guy's name again?" Marena asked.

"Smith. John Smith," Craig said.

"Now you got me curious," Greg said. "Did you—?"

"Yes," Craig interrupted. "I checked the FAA pilot database for a pilot named John Smith."

"And?" Marena asked.

"The response came back that there were too many pilots with the same name, and I needed to narrow my search by adding a city and state to the search parameters."

"And you couldn't because, you said, you don't know where he's from," Marena finished for him.

Craig let out a gargantuan sneeze, grabbed a tissue, and nodded.

"That's strange," Marena said, sinking back in her chair and crossing her legs. "Huge wads of cash, won't tell you where he's from or where he's going—makes you wonder if John Smith is even his real name."

Craig blew his nose so loudly it sounded like a goose honking, and he said, "I'm pretty sure it isn't his name."

"Yeah? Why?" Greg asked as he slipped the four hundred bucks into his pocket.

"Nothing in particular; he was just kind of evasive about things, that's all."

"If he is carrying drugs, why would he be in this part of Idaho?" Marena asked.

"My guess is the weather forced him down," Craig offered.

"Sounds like it," Greg said. After a pause he added, "You know, the guy could be legit, but as long as we're here, I think we'll take a couple of minutes to check out his airplane. I'm willing to help some guy in trouble, but I'm a little nervous after hearing what you said about him. I'll just take a quick peek inside; maybe there's something that will tell us more."

"I watched him lock it," Craig said. "He wanted to make sure nobody could get in the hangar. He was all concerned about security, although I don't know why. Except for his overnight bag, the airplane was clean and neat as a pin inside. He asked me to give him my key to your hangar, but I told him no way. He got a little huffy about that, but I told him it was against airport policy. I told him if he came and got me, I would unlock the hangar whenever he wanted."

Marena stood up. "Come on, Greg. Let's just go home. After last week, I don't want to get involved in anything."

Greg looked at Marena and gave a sympathetic nod but said, "Five minutes, Marena; that's all it will take."

"Nothing takes five minutes, Greg," Marena retorted in frustration. "What's the point? Craig already said there's nothing in there. Besides, you don't have a key to his airplane."

Craig blew his nose, and as he wiped it, he said, "Marena, if you've got a key to one airplane, you've got a key to half the airplanes in the world. There's nothing sacred about airplane door locks. With a little work, one key fits almost all of them."

Greg zipped up his jacket and said, "You coming, Craig?"

Craig shook his head. "Not me. I feel more dead than alive. I'm already chilled to the bone. The last thing I want to do is go play in the cold and snow. I'm taking some cold medicine and heading to bed."

CHAPTER TWENTY-FOUR

Greg was lying on his belly across the airplane's two front seats, his legs protruding out the door. His head was nearly beneath the pilot's seat as he strained to see if anything was hidden while Marena perched in the back seat, flipping through page after page of the contents from a large brown manila envelope she had found.

Until that moment, other than an occasional comment from one or the other about something they had discovered—or not discovered—the only noise in the heated hangar had been the slow but steady drip of water as the snow and ice melted and dripped from the airplane's wings onto the polished concrete floor.

"Mr. and Mrs. Walker?"

Under the circumstances, Greg and Marena's reactions were predictable. Startled by the voice, Greg raised up so quickly he slammed the back of his head into the control wheel and grunted at the pain. Marena's reaction was more dramatic; she yelped and flung the sheets of paper she'd been holding through the air, one of them landing on Greg's hand he had splayed on the pilot's seat. Greg looked to where the voice had come from.

"Of St. George, Utah?" the voice's owner said almost pleasantly. Then, as the two of them stared at him in shock, he added, "This is an amazing coincidence. I came to check on my airplane, and who should I find searching through it but the very people I'm searching for."

Working his way up to a kneeling position so he could face the man, Greg rubbed the back of his head with his hand and asked, "Do we know you?"

"We've never met, but you've seen me, at least from a distance, and I've seen pictures of you."

"Look," Greg said. "I don't know who you are, but we own this hangar. Someone put this airplane in here last night, and we're just trying to find out who the owner is. If it's your airplane, then great; we don't need to look any further."

Marena gasped. Greg looked over to see her mouth sag open. Slowly she said, "You're the man from the lagoon! You're Scott Vaughn. You killed . . ." She didn't finish the sentence.

Greg whirled his attention back to the man. Vaughn's lips drew back in a tight smile as he moved around the wing and pointed the 9-mm pistol at Greg's chest. "I think it would be a good idea for you both to climb out of my airplane." Motioning with the pistol, he added sternly, "Do it now, and do it very, very slowly. You first," he said, pointing at Greg.

Greg looked at the handgun, then at Marena, and then at Vaughn again. With his eyes focused on the gun, he eased out of the airplane, standing as close to the airplane and as far away from Vaughn as possible. Behind him he heard the sound of paper and the manila envelope fall to the floor of the airplane as Marena slowly contorted her way out of the airplane. Then she stood beside Greg.

"How did you find out who we are?" Greg asked.

Vaughn chuckled. "It was almost too easy. As the airport manager and I were putting my airplane in the hangar, he mentioned you by name."

"I don't mean here," Greg said, shaking his head. "Before. How did you find out about us?"

"Ah, you mean in the Dominican Republic?" Vaughn asked. "That was my good friend Raul. He gave me your name, told me where you live, when you left Punta Cana, and even sent me your pictures. I wouldn't ordinarily admit all that to anyone, but seeing as both of you are going to die very shortly, it won't make any difference."

Greg's stomach dropped. "Raul? You mean the short little cop?"

Vaughn smiled. "That's the one."

"You won't get away with it," Marena spit out.

Vaughn gave a condescending look. "Mrs. Walker—or should I call you Marena?—that's exactly what I'll get away with."

"Just like you think you'll get away with running over Wiggy Wiggy with your boat?" Marena shot back.

"Wiggy Wiggy? Was that the kid's name?"

"You'll never get away with it because we've already told the police what you did, and we've given them your description."

Vaughn laughed. "You seem to have already forgotten how well connected I am with the police in the Dominican Republic. Raul has seen to it that your report has been altered significantly. The person who ran over your friend is several inches shorter than me and has blond hair and blue eyes."

Greg took a breath and said, "What do you want from us?"

"Help," Vaughn answered quickly. "Is that your SUV parked outside?"

Greg and Marena looked at each other, but neither of them replied.

"Of course it's yours," Vaughn said. "I want you to drive me to Arco."

"Drive yourself," Greg replied defiantly.

"I can't. You see, I am a Southern boy and don't know how to drive in snow. I can fly airplanes and drive any boat ever made, but I don't have any experience driving in snow, and, well, it is imperative I get to Arco by ten o'clock tomorrow morning." Pointing the gun directly at Greg's head, he said, "And you're going to drive me there. After which the two of you will have a terrible accident—the victims of a robbery gone bad."

"I won't do it," Greg said.

Vaughn smiled and very calmly replied, "Oh, I'm positive you will."

Greg shook his head. "I wouldn't drive you to the hangar next door, let alone to Arco. You might as well shoot me here and now."

Vaughn tipped his head slightly and said, "Oh, I'm not going to shoot you—at least not yet. And I'm not going to shoot her," he said, motioning toward Marena with the gun. "At least not yet," he repeated. Reaching into his coat pocket, he pulled out a black-handled switchblade knife and depressed a button, causing a six-inch blade to instantly swing out and glisten in the overhead lights. Turning the knife side to side as if to admire its razor-sharp blade, he said, "No, I'm not going to kill her. What I will do is start carving. First I'm going to cut off the little finger on her right hand just to show you I'm serious. Then, if you're still unwilling, the little finger on her left hand. By then I'm pretty sure you'll be willing to drive because, you see, she has a lot of other body parts I can slice away to help motivate you. For every delay you cause, your wife will lose another part of her body. So, you see, Greg, I'm quite sure you'll drive me to Arco."

"You're a sadistic creep," Greg hissed.

Vaughn shrugged and rotated the knife. "Sadistic, yes, but not a creep," he said and walked toward them, aiming the gun at Greg's chest and flicking the knife back and forth toward Marena.

CHAPTER TWENTY-FIVE

Greg waited until Vaughn was only a few feet away then quickly reached up and placed his hand on top of Marena's head. He shoved forcefully downward and backward, causing her to crumple to the floor under the belly of the airplane. "Run!" he shouted.

Vaughn looked down at Marena and, stooping slightly, shifted his aim from Greg's chest to Marena, who was scampering under the airplane on her hands and knees. Greg kicked out with his foot, barely grazing Vaughn's shooting hand just as he'd pulled the trigger. The bullet punched through the soft aluminum of the airplane and slammed into the steel frame of a seat.

The gun's roar inside the confined metal building was as deafening as if Greg's head was in a bucket someone was beating with a pipe. Vaughn raised his forearms to his ears to muffle the noise, and in that brief second, Greg glanced back to see Marena scoot out from beneath the airplane and run toward a dark corner of the hangar. With echoes of the gunshot still reverberating, Greg whipped his head back to Vaughn, who again aimed the pistol at the fleeing Marena. As he did, Greg kicked again, this time with more force and accuracy. The kick caught Vaughn squarely in his right wrist, sending the pistol clattering across the top of the airplane's wing and falling to the floor.

Vaughn shifted the knife from his left to his right hand and sneered. "I can kill you as easily with a knife as with a gun."

"Try," Greg snarled and lunged, but his jacket snagged on the wing and stopped him short.

Vaughn sidestepped the lunge, ducked under the wing, and scooped up the gun in an almost fluid motion. "Stop!" he yelled, pointing the gun at Greg's chest. With his eyes carefully trained on Greg, Vaughn retracted the knife's blade and put it into his pocket. Then, aiming the gun at Greg's left arm, he squeezed the trigger.

The reverberation of the second gunshot was as deafening as the first. It drowned out Greg's scream as the hollow-point bullet grazed his left bicep and shattered the Aztec's side window.

"Don't move!" Vaughn shouted as Greg clutched his arm. "That bullet hit exactly where I was aiming. If you move, the next one goes in your left leg."

Greg gritted his teeth together as he looked down at the thin trickle of blood oozing from between his fingers. "You should have killed me when you had the chance," he said, lowering his hand and wiping the blood on the airplane's white-painted wing. "You may not get another."

Vaughn laughed. "I don't want you dead, Mr. Walker. I need you to drive me to Arco, remember? After that, I'll have plenty of time to kill you both." Then, looking toward the corner of the hangar where Marena had run to, he yelled, "Mrs. Walker, I've shot your husband. Now, do the sensible thing, and come out here. You have my word I won't harm you."

"Don't do it, Marena," Greg screamed. "Run!"

"Shut up," Vaughn shouted at Greg. Then, motioning with the gun, he said quietly, "You and I are going to walk slowly over to the door. Don't make any quick moves, or I'll shoot you in the leg. Do you understand?"

Greg glared at Vaughn but said nothing.

Vaughn faced Greg and slowly backed his way toward the door, keeping the gun trained on Greg's chest the entire time. When they were ten feet from the door, Greg caught a quick movement out the corner of his eye, and the slightest smile spread across his face. A fraction of a second later, the lights went out.

"What the . . . ?" Vaughn said as the hangar was suddenly plunged into total darkness.

Greg didn't hesitate. He squatted low, dashed beneath Vaughn's airplane, and slid to the floor behind the main landing gear of his own plane. Robbed of sight by the darkness, he cautiously stood up and ran his hands along the airplane's cold metal skin until he felt the door latch and yanked it open. Reaching inside with his uninjured arm, he shoved aside two small blankets and a pillow before wrapping his fingers around the handles of a small travel bag.

"Give it up," Vaughn called out.

Greg yanked the bag from the airplane and set it on the floor beside him. Undoing the zipper barely enough to slip his hand inside, he fingered aside packages of bandages, gauze, ointment, and other first-aid supplies until he felt the barrel of a .357 magnum revolver.

"Now!" Vaughn shouted. "Give it up now!"

As Greg pulled the revolver from the bag, he heard a distinct swooshing noise, followed a fraction of a second later by Vaughn's intense scream, which was followed by the blinding muzzle flash and earsplitting sound of two gunshots.

It took Greg's ears a moment to stop ringing. When they did, he could hear Marena's muffled sobs and Vaughn's pain-filled groans.

Greg dropped to the floor and began crawling toward the sobs. He'd covered only a few feet when he heard Marena yelp in pain and Vaughn growl, "Where's the light switch?"

There were the sounds of a slight scuffle, and just as Greg crawled behind a stack of plywood, the lights came on, momentarily causing him to shut his eyes to the unexpected brightness. Opening his eyes, he peered over the plywood, and his mouth gaped open.

Marena was on her knees, a very thin trickle of blood dripping from her hand. Vaughn was standing behind her. In one hand he held his gun, the barrel pressed against her head. In the other he had a fistful of her hair, which he yanked viciously, pulling her to her feet and causing her to scream.

Greg studied Vaughn, who stood with all his weight on one leg. The other was slightly bent at the knee, and there was a dark smudge on the leg of his trousers. On the ground a few feet from him was a metal pipe about the length of a baseball bat.

"You hear her screaming, Walker?" Vaughn yelled, filling the hangar with his angry, pain-laden voice. "That's nothing compared to what you're going hear if you don't come out right now."

Greg watched as Marena reached up to try to pry Vaughn's hand from her hair. As she did, Vaughn yanked back hard, forcing her head back so violently she was looking up at the roof as she let out another ear-splitting scream.

"You got five seconds," Vaughn shouted. "And then I'm blowing a hole in her knee as payback for hitting mine with a pipe. One . . . two . . . three . . ."

"Stop," Greg said, slowly standing, his arms at his side and the revolver clasped gingerly between his thumb and index finger. "I'm right here."

"Drop the gun!" Vaughn shouted as he stepped closer to Marena. "Now, or I kill her."

Greg let the gun slip from his fingers.

Pointing his own gun at Greg, Vaughn shouted, "Kick it over here."

Greg kicked the gun, sending it skidding almost to Vaughn's feet.

Vaughn shoved Marena so forcefully she tumbled forward onto the cement floor. Then he pick up the revolver and tucked it inside his coat pocket.

Greg rushed to Marena, lifted her to her feet, and hugged her. She broke free from the hug and held out her right hand. A few drops of blood dripped from a small surface wound. "You shot me!" she shouted.

"Shut up," Vaughn hissed angrily, his face still contorted in pain while he rubbed his knee.

Clutching her bullet-grazed hand to her chest, Marena nodded with her head toward the short length of pipe on the floor and said to Greg, "I hit him in the knee with the pipe." Then she looked back at Vaughn and said hotly, "I wish I'd hit you in the head!"

"I said shut up!" Vaughn said. Sucking in a deep breath against the searing pain in his knee, he said, "Listen very carefully because I'm only going to say this one time. In a concealed compartment behind the back seat of my airplane is an aluminum suitcase. Walker, you're going to climb in there and get it while I keep my gun aimed at your wife. Make even the slightest wrong move, and I'll put bullets in both of her legs. Then we're all going to get in your SUV and go for a ride. The two of you will get in the front seat, and I'm going to ride in the back. The first time I sense anything out of the ordinary," Vaughn said, pointing the gun at Marena, "I put a bullet in her. Is that clear?"

CHAPTER TWENTY-SIX

"I don't think they're here," Chris Pulsipher said from the back seat of the black SUV. Hovey glanced over his shoulder to glance at Pulsipher, who picked the last bit of lunch from his teeth with a toothpick.

The three FBI agents—Pulsipher, Wayne Hovey, and Larry Nichols—sat staring at the same empty house. "I agree," Nichols finally said. "Nothing's changed since last night when we got here. The gates are closed, the blinds are the same, and the outside lights are burning bright in the middle of the day. They might as well have put a sign in the front yard advertising that nobody's home."

Hovey blew out a sigh. "Drive around the block. I want to see the house from the back again."

Nichols started the SUV and did as he was told. As they passed the back of the house, all three craned their necks to see between houses and trees and over fences to the back of the house. "It's all the same," Pulsipher said. "Nothing's changed."

Hovey ran his hand over the early-afternoon stubble on his chin and cleared his throat. "Drive back to the neighbor's house and park."

"Why?" Nichols asked in surprise.

"Because I'm going to go talk to them," Hovey said.

"Isn't that being a little obvious?" Nichols said.

"We need more information," Hovey replied.

The SUV had barely stopped rolling before he jumped out and walked in long strides across the lawn to the front door. The chime of the doorbell brought an instantaneous howl from inside the house, followed almost immediately by a woman shouting, "Harpo, be quiet." A second later the door swung open.

"Hi! Mrs. Walker, my name is Arnold Palmer, and my company said you called asking to see an agent about our new life insurance policy. Is now—"

The elderly woman looked at Hovey and said, "Excuse me, young man, but you've got the wrong house and the wrong person. I'm not Mrs. Walker." Then looking down at the basset hound that had wormed its way out the partially open door, she hollered, "Harpo! Come back in here."

Acting completely confused, Hovey said, "Isn't this 543—"

"No, you have the wrong house. This is 561, and my name is Anita Lorcher."

"Oh, I am so sorry," Hovey said. "Can you point me to the Walkers' house?"

Anita gestured to the Walkers' place. "They live there."

"Oh, thanks," Hovey said, looking to where Anita pointed.

"But I can save you some footsteps," Anita said.

"How's that?" Hovey asked.

"They aren't home. They left on another trip."

"Dang," Hovey said, making a show of swinging his fist in disappointment. "I was looking forward to talking with them about our new life-insurance plans. Do you have any idea where they went or when they will be back?"

Anita scrunched up her forehead. "You're the second person who has asked me that in two days."

"Oh, really?" Hovey said, leaning slightly forward. "Somebody else stopped by?" Then, scowling, he said, "Oh man, I bet it was Jack Nicholas. He's a new sales guy who's always trying to cut in on my business." Holding out his arms, he said, "Short guy, about this tall, bald, and wears glasses?"

"Oh, heavens no," Anita replied. Looking past Hovey, she yelled, "Harpo, get out of those flowers." Then to Hovey she said, "I love that dog, I truly do, but sometimes—"

"What did this other guy look like?" Hovey pressed.

"What?" Anita asked, looking over Hovey's shoulder. He glanced to where she was looking and saw Harpo mashing flowers with each step.

"The other guy, what'd he look like?" Hovey repeated as he turned back to Anita.

"Can you imagine? He ran into Harpo with his car."

Hovey gritted his teeth, forced a thin slit of a smile, and said, "That's terrible. But can you describe him for me? It would sure help me."

Anita paused, looked at Hovey, and said, "Well, he's about your height, has a really good suntan—but he would, of course, because he said he was down in the Dominican Republic on vacation and that's where he met the Walkers. He said they became friends, and that's why he was here. He wanted to say hello to them. Harpo! Get back here," Anita screamed as the dog began trotting down the driveway.

"This other fellow," Hovey said. "When was he here?"

"Excuse me," Anita said, brushing past Hovey, "but I need to go get my dog before he wanders off to who knows where."

As Anita moved past him, Hovey asked again, "This other guy, when was he here?"

Anita paused and shook her head. "Yesterday morning . . . no, afternoon . . . yes, he was here yesterday afternoon because the Walkers had already left for their home in Mink Creek, Idaho."

"Mink Creek?" Hovey asked.

"Yes, they own a ranch there and said they were going to get away for a few days. Harpo! Come back here," Anita said again and tottered off down the sidewalk, leaving her front door wide open.

Hovey ran across the lawn and yanked the SUV's door open so forcefully it startled Pulsipher and Nichols. "Vaughn's been here. Get driving," he said to Nichols. Turning to Pulsipher, he said, "Find out where Mink Creek, Idaho, is."

"Where am I driving to?" Nichols asked as he shifted the car into gear.

"The airport," Hovey said. Turning back to Pulsipher, who was busy tapping on his cell phone, he said, "You got it yet, Pulsipher?"

"Give me a minute," Pulsipher answered, tapping and sliding his finger on the phone's screen. After a pause he said, "Which one do you want? There are two of them in Idaho."

"Two? No way," Hovey exclaimed. "Where are they?"

"Umm, one is just south of Pocatello, and the other is just north of Preston."

"That doesn't help me. I don't know where Pocatello and Preston are. Which one is closer?"

Pulsipher tapped his screen a few times and replied, "Unreal. They're both about three hundred miles from here. Different roads but about the same distance."

Hovey slammed his fist into the seat. "Go back," he commanded Nichols. "Go back to that lady's house."

Nichols spun the SUV around and raced back down the block. Before he'd brought the vehicle to a stop, Hovey was out the door and trotting across the lawn to where Anita was pulling a weed from among her flowers. "Uh, excuse me, I have another question for you."

Anita straightened up and looked at Hovey. "Yes?" she said.

"You told me the Walkers were going to Mink Creek, Idaho. I happen to know there are two Mink Creeks. You don't know which one they were going to, do you?"

Anita stared at Hovey suspiciously. "Who are you again?"

"Palmer, Arnold Palmer," Hovey said.

Anita shook her head. "No, you're not. Arnold Palmer is much older, and he's a golfer, not an insurance salesman."

"You don't think there can be two Arnold Palmers in the world?"

"Harpo, come over here," Anita shouted. Surprisingly, the dog walked over to where they were standing and sat down next to the woman. "Good dog," Anita said, patting him on the head. Then, looking at Hovey, she said, "I'd like to see some identification. Show me your business card."

Hovey let out a sigh. "Look, Mrs., Mrs.—"

"Lorcher, Anita Lorcher."

Reaching into his coat pocket, Hovey pulled out his leather-bound FBI credentials and flipped it open. "Look, Mrs. Lorcher, you're right. I'm not Arnold Palmer. My name is Wayne Hovey. I'm a special agent with the Federal Bureau of Investigation, and it's important I speak with the Walkers."

Anita didn't bother to look at the badge and credentials Hovey was dangling in front of her. Instead, she took a step back and said, "Why should I believe you? You lied to me once; how do I know you aren't lying to me again?"

Hovey shoved the credentials out until they almost touched Anita's face. "Because of this," he exclaimed. "Look at it. It will prove I'm an FBI agent."

"You think I haven't watched enough TV to know you could easily forge something like that?"

In exasperation, Hovey turned to the SUV and shouted, "Nichols, Pulsipher, come here." Turning to Anita, he said, "There are two more FBI agents. They'll vouch for me."

"Really, Mr. Palmer or Hovey or whoever you are, do you think I'm going to accept their word? They'll probably lie to me just like you did. No, what I'm going to do is call the police and have them come out and investigate this." And with that, she spun on her heels and walked to the house with Harpo bouncing along behind her.

As Nichols and Pulsipher strode up, Hovey said, "The woman won't tell me which Mink Creek it is, and she doesn't believe we're FBI. She's gone to call the local cops."

"You're serious?" Nichols said incredulously.

"Serious as a heart attack," Hovey said. Turning to Pulsipher, he said, "This woman said the Walkers went to their ranch. Any idea if both of those Mink Creeks are rural ranching communities?"

"Based on the map in my phone, the one by Preston definitely is. It's in the mountains in the middle of nowhere. The other one is about fifteen miles south of Pocatello. It looks more recreational than ranching."

"But it's still rural, right?"

"Yup."

Hovey shoved his credentials back into his pocket just as Anita reappeared. "I called the police. They said they would have someone here within fifteen minutes."

"Look, Mrs. Lorcher," Hovey began. "I'm sorry I wasn't totally honest with you the first time, but you've got to believe me now. I'm a federal agent. It's very important we speak to the Walkers. I can't do that if I don't know where they are. Just tell me where their ranch is, and we'll be gone."

Anita crossed her arms across her chest and said, "We'll wait for the police to arrive. And you should know my husband is watching us out the window and is on the phone with the police right now in case we need them."

It was only ten minutes until a police car rolled up and an officer climbed out. After two minutes of quick conversation, he turned to Anita and said, "Mrs. Lorcher, these are legitimate credentials. These men really are FBI agents. You should tell them what they need to know."

Looking at Hovey, Anita said, "I'm sorry. But you can't be too careful nowadays."

"It's okay," Hovey said. "Just tell me which Mink Creek they went to: the one by Preston or the one by Pocatello?"

Anita looked from Hovey to Nichols to Pulsipher to the policeman and then back to Hovey. "I don't know," she said. "I didn't know there were two Mink Creeks, and they've never mentioned any town besides Mink Creek."

Hovey's shoulders slumped and his mouth opened. "You don't know?"

Anita shook her head. "I don't have any idea."

"They never talked about roads they traveled, landmarks around their ranch . . . anything?"

Anita shook her head. "Nothing. All I know is they were going to fly their airplane there."

Hovey eyes widened at the possibility of a lead. "They were going to fly there? In their own airplane?"

Anita nodded. "Yes, and I told the other man that as well."

Hovey turned to Pulsipher and asked, "Either of the Mink Creeks have an airport?" but Pulsipher had anticipated the question and was already tapping away on his phone.

Shaking his head, Pulsipher said, "Neither one. There's an airport in Preston, which is about twenty miles from Mink Creek number one, and there's one in Pocatello, which is about fifteen miles from number two."

"Where are you trying to get to?" the uniformed police officer asked. "I'm originally from Malad, which is about halfway between Preston and Pocatello."

Four pairs of eyes instantly focused on the cop. Hovey said, "We're looking for a small ranching community called Mink Creek that has a nearby airport."

"The Mink Creek just south of Pocatello is a recreation area—bunch of campgrounds, cabins, and such. There aren't any ranches, at least that I know of. I've never been to the one by Preston, but I played football in high school, and Preston was in our division. It's a farming community, so my guess is Mink Creek is as well."

"Thanks," Hovey said. Then, as he grabbed Pulsipher and Nichols each by an arm and shoved them toward the SUV, he said to Pulsipher, "Find the nearest major airport to Preston, Idaho."

As the SUV lurched away from the curb, Pulsipher said, "Salt Lake is the closest we're going to get."

The drive to the St. George airport should have taken twenty minutes. Blowing through stop signs and red lights, Nichols did it in fifteen. As they drew up to the main entrance to the airport, Hovey bailed out, shouting, "You check in the rental car; I'll get seats on the next flight," and disappeared through the sliding-glass doors. Three minutes later Hovey stood looking at the smiling reservation agent in disbelief.

Pointing out the huge array of windows to the small silver regional jet just lifting from the runway, she said, "I'm sorry, sir; if you'd have been here fifteen minutes earlier, we probably could have gotten you on that flight."

Hovey leaned over the small counter and said, "Look, I'm an FBI agent, and it's critical I get to Salt Lake. Can you call the airplane back?"

The agent almost laughed. "Maybe if you were the president of the United States," she said.

Hovey cursed and slammed his hand on the counter, causing the reservation agent to jump back. "When's the next flight to Salt Lake?"

The reservation agent shook her head and pointed to the electronic display on the wall behind her. In bright red letters, the word *Cancelled* flashed next to every flight scheduled for Salt Lake. "Snow storm," she said. "The flight that just departed was the last one out. Our dispatch department has been notified that the Salt Lake International Airport will close in about one hour. It's apparently snowing so heavily there they can't keep the runways open."

"How long?" Hovey said.

"Sir?"

"How long until you'll have a flight to Salt Lake?"

The agent forced a smile and said, "I don't have any idea."

Hovey shook his head in frustration, reached inside his coat pocket, and pulled out his FBI credentials. Looking at the reservation agent's name badge pinned to her blouse, he said, "Hailey, I am Special Agent Wayne Hovey. It is critical I get to Salt Lake City as soon as possible. Is there someone you can call—those dispatchers you mentioned—and find out when you will have a flight going to Salt Lake?"

Hailey looked at the ID and then at Hovey. "I can call, Mr. Hovey," she said patiently, "but it is highly unlikely anyone will be able to tell me anything more than I've just told you."

Hovey put his ID back into his coat and snapped, "Make the call."

The call took less than thirty seconds, and as Hovey listened to the one-sided conversation, a deeper frown spread over his face. As Hailey hung up the phone, she said, "I'm sorry, Mr. Hovey, but the earliest any flights will be going to Salt Lake will probably be late tomorrow afternoon, but even that is uncertain. It may well be much longer. This is a major storm, and it's creating havoc everywhere. There are no flights into or out of Salt Lake."

Hovey shook his head in frustration. "How far is Salt Lake? Do you know?" he asked.

"Um, about three hundred miles," Hailey said. "Give or take a little."

"Thanks," Hovey said and abruptly turned from the counter. Walking up to Nichols and Pulsipher, who were just coming in the door, he said, "No flights. Salt Lake airport is closed." Before either of them could respond, he turned to Nichols and said, "Did that SUV we've been driving have four-wheel drive?"

Nichols said, "Yeah, why?"

"Go back and re-rent it. We're driving to Idaho." Nichols nodded and hurried back out the doors he'd just entered through. Then, turning to Pulsipher, Hovey said, "Where'd you say you were from?"

"Montana."

"You know how to drive in snow?"

"Of course I know how to drive in snow."

"Good. You drive."

"It's snowing up there?"

"Blizzard," Hovey replied. "How far is Mink Creek from Salt Lake?"

"Just checked," Pulsipher answered, holding out his phone. "Google Maps says one hundred twenty-seven miles."

Hovey went silent for a minute and then said, "So about four hundred fifty miles from here. At seventy miles per hour, we should be there in six or seven hours."

Pulsipher looked at Hovey and laughed. "Wayne, you just told me there's a blizzard up there. There's no way we'll be driving seventy miles an hour. If there really is a blizzard, we'll be lucky to get there at all."

Hovey chewed on his lower lip and cursed as he ran his fingers through his hair. He furrowed his eyebrows as he concentrated on trying to determine their next course of action.

Pulsipher looked at him and said, "So are we going to call them?"

"Who?" Hovey answered.

"The Walkers. Should we warn them?"

Hovey looked at Pulsipher for a moment, ran his hands across his mouth, and frowned. "No," he said flatly.

"Are you kidding me?" Pulsipher said incredulously. "They've got a known killer stalking them."

Hovey snapped, "We don't know that. All we know is that the neighbor lady told someone where they are."

"Come on, Wayne," Pulsipher said. "Vaughn is after them, and you know it. He tracked them this far, and he isn't going to give up now."

Hovey shook his head and said, "We're not calling them."

Pulsipher was incredulous. "Okay, if you're not going to call them, at least call the local cops and tell them to provide some protection."

Hovey glared at Pulsipher and fired back, “What, and run the risk of having them screw this up? No way. They’d go charging in like the cavalry, lights flashing and sirens blaring. Vaughn would know in a heartbeat we’re onto him, and he’d vanish just like he’s done before. This is the closest we’ve ever come, and I’m not letting some backwater country-bumpkin sheriff mess it up. I’ll involve the local cops when we get there, but not until then.”

Pulsipher shook his head, disbelief etched into every feature of his face. “You’re screwed up. You’re playing with people’s lives.”

The screeching of the SUV’s tires as Nichols pulled up caused both men to look toward the curb. “Get in,” Hovey commanded.

CHAPTER TWENTY-SEVEN

"Sheriff Koford?" Wayne Hovey asked as he peered inside the small office.

Koford rose from the chair and said, "That's me."

Walking to where Koford stood, Hovey extended his hand and said, "I'm Wayne Hovey, and these are Special Agents Larry Nichols and Chris Pulsipher. Thanks for seeing us."

"No problem," Koford replied, shaking hands with each of the agents. "Have a seat," he said, pointing to a cracked and worn brown-leather sofa that took up an entire wall of the small office. Pulling a wooden chair from beside his desk, Koford positioned it so he could sit opposite the couch and look at all three men. "It isn't often the FBI makes it way to Franklin County. I'd offer you some coffee, but we don't have any. We do have some hot chocolate, though, or I can get you a soda."

Hovey shook his head and said, "Thanks. We just finished breakfast."

Koford looked at his watch. "Kind of a late breakfast, wasn't it? It's getting close to dinnertime."

"Long night," Hovey replied. "The roads were crummy between here and Salt Lake. We got stuck once, and, well, it was just slow going."

Koford nodded. "Frankly, I'm kind of surprised you even made it. Most roads are impassable because of the snow."

"Yeah, we know. We went around a few barricades," Pulsipher chimed in.

Koford looked at the young agent and raised his eyebrows. "Gutsy," he said. Then, after a short pause, he added, "And a little stupid." Leaning back in his chair, he said, "On the phone you said you had a few things to discuss. What can I do for you?"

"Are you familiar with a couple named Greg and Marena Walker? They live in a little town called Mink Creek."

"Sure am. I know them really well. He's a great veterinarian. My wife and I used to go out to dinner with them," Koford replied, shifting in his seat. "Nice people. They lived here for several years before they moved south and he started treating expensive race horses. They still own a ranch in the mountains up one of the canyons."

Hovey nodded. "That's them."

"Are they in trouble?" Koford asked.

"Not in the sense that they've broken any laws," Hovey said.

"Why are you interested in them?"

Hovey blew out a short breath and said, "Well . . . we're not really interested in them."

Koford wrinkled his brow. "Then, why are you asking about them?"

"We're interested in someone they might know."

"Who is that?" Koford pressed.

"You wouldn't know him," Hovey replied, eyeing the sheriff.

Evan Koford was tall, had a full head of silver hair, and was in far better physical shape than probably any other sixty-some-odd-year-old man in the county—or surrounding counties.

Koford pushed himself out of his chair. "Mr. Hovey," he said, looking down at him, "It was nice meeting you. But I'm a little too busy to sit here and play twenty questions. You've danced around every question I've asked. If you want to tell me what's going on and how I can be of assistance, great. Otherwise, there's the door. I've got work to do."

Hovey glanced at his fellow agents in surprise. Pulsipher bit his lip in an obvious effort to stifle a smirk while Nichols looked up at Koford in surprise. Turning back to the sheriff, Hovey said, "Whoa, Sheriff. I'm not trying to play games here—just the opposite. It's just that"—he hesitated—"there's a very real chance it may be nothing. Truthfully, what we're trying to do is a longshot, but it's about the only thing we've got."

"Okay," Koford said, sitting down. "Tell me what you've got, and I'll see if I can help."

"We're really not interested in the Walkers. The FBI's interest is in a person named Scott Vaughn. In his sleazebag world, he's what is known as a transporter, someone who transports illicit commodities."

"Like drugs," Koford said.

Hovey nodded. "Yeah, sure, drugs. But he's also been linked to transporting everything from black-market human livers, kidneys, and lungs to large amounts of currency. And we know he's dabbled in transporting illegal military equipment and arms. The only thing we're pretty certain he doesn't transport is people—for some unknown reason, he stays away from the slave trade."

"Sweet guy," Koford drawled.

"Yeah, the kind you'd want your daughter to date," Hovey deadpanned. "He's also been linked to the murders of a couple of U.S. Drug Enforcement agents in Nicaragua."

"And some local cops in Honduras and Mexico," Nichols inserted.

Hovey cast a side glance at Nichols and nodded. Looking back at Koford, he continued. "We also think he's responsible for blowing up a coast guard helicopter with a missile, although that's a little uncertain."

"So where do the Walkers fit into all this?" Koford asked.

Hovey sighed. "Several days ago we got a tip from one of the few honest cops in the Dominican Republic, a guy I worked with a few years ago. He told me the Walkers witnessed Vaughn murder a man while they were on vacation down there."

"They were in the wrong place at the wrong time and saw a drug deal go down?" Koford conjectured.

"They were definitely in the wrong place at the wrong time," Hovey replied. "But we're not sure it was a drug deal. Based on the description they gave the cops down there, we think it was something else."

"Like what?" Koford queried.

"Not sure," Hovey admitted.

"Any ideas?" Koford asked.

"We've considered everything from diamonds to a nuclear bomb." Then, waving his hand in the air as if to shoo away the discussion, Hovey continued. "But that really isn't the point. We're after Vaughn, not what he's transporting."

Koford scratched his head. "Okay, I'm totally confused. You're chasing some guy who committed a crime in a country where you have absolutely no jurisdiction, who is transporting something you don't care about, and this all ties into the Walkers?" Koford said, shaking his head. "Come on, guys; you're back to wasting time here."

"We think Vaughn may be targeting the Walkers for a hit," Pulsipher blurted in frustration. "We're following them because we think Vaughn will come after them because they witnessed the murder."

Koford looked at Pulsipher and then shifted his gaze back to Hovey. After a minute he raised his eyebrows and said, "Pretty gutsy of the Walkers to be willing to be your bait."

Hovey felt some of the color seep from his face and little stress lines form around his eyes. He shifted uncomfortably, swallowed, exhaled, and said, "They don't know."

The shock on Koford's face was obvious. He leaned forward in his chair and said, "They have no idea you're playing them?"

Hovey shook his head. "Not yet. That's one reason we're here in the middle of this crummy weather you're having. If you can explain to us where their ranch is and how to get there, we're going to talk with them."

"I don't think so," Koford said.

"Why?" Hovey asked.

"Unless you've got a snowmobile or a dogsled, you don't stand a chance of getting up to their house. They live in the mountains. The highway department closed the road up that canyon several hours ago. By now there's more than a foot of snow on the highway between here and there."

Hovey blew out a long sigh and leaned his head back on the couch. A second later he raised his head and said, "Well, there's at least one consolation. If we can't get there, neither can Vaughn."

"Unless he has a snowmobile," Koford said. After a moment of silence, he nodded toward the phone on his desk and added, "You want to call them?"

Hovey shook his head, "Naw, that's the kind of conversation you want to have face-to-face, if you know what I mean."

Koford studied the three agents and shook his head. "No, Agent Hovey, I don't know what you mean. You have a serial murderer chasing two innocent people who have no idea someone is after them." Pulling a phone directory from his desk drawer, Koford extended it to Hovey and said, "Are you going to call them, or am I? I'm not going to have my friends be unwitting pawns in your game."

Hovey stared at the proffered book and scrunched his lips tightly together. Grabbing the directory, he angrily flipped to the correct page, tapped the number into his cell phone, and glared at Koford while he listened to one unanswered ring after another. After the sixth ring, a feminine voice came on the line and told him to leave a message. "No answer," he said, slipping the phone into his pocket. "You have a cell phone number for them, by chance?"

Koford shook his head. "Nope, but it wouldn't make any difference anyway; up where they live, there isn't any cell reception. Too many mountains. Everybody up there has a landline."

After a moment of silence, with each of the men exchanging uncertain glances, Koford picked up the phone on his desk and punched in a number. After a brief pause he said into the phone, "Lynn, I need some help from your search and rescue people. I need to get three guys up to Mink Creek. Yeah, I know the road is closed. Can you get them up there on snowmobiles? They need to go immediately, as soon as you can arrange it; this is an emergency. I need to get them to the Walkers' place. Huh? I'll ask." Lowering the phone slightly away from his mouth, Koford looked at the three agents and asked, "You guys ever ridden a snowmobile?"

Hovey and Nichols shook their heads while Pulsipher nodded.

"One has; two haven't," Koford said into the phone. Eyeing each of the agents, he added, "Oh, and they're all going to need outfits—boots, gloves, helmets, the works—can you scrounge something up?" Then, almost as an afterthought, he said, "Hey, Lynn, make it four snowmobiles. I'm going too." Listening for half a second, he said, "Okay, we'll meet you in thirty minutes at the *S* and *R* building."

Koford had barely replaced the phone when Hovey asked, "How far is it?"

"Twenty-three, maybe twenty-four miles from here."

"How long will it take us? An hour or two?"

Koford laughed. "These sleds will do ninety miles an hour. An hour from now you'll be standing at their front door. For two of you, the hardest part will be hanging on."

It took a little longer to get everyone outfitted than expected, but ninety minutes later the four men were standing on the Walkers' porch in snow-covered garb.

"Knock again," Hovey said. "Louder this time."

When after a minute there was no result, Koford said, "I'm going around back. Most people around here leave their doors unlocked. In fact, I'm surprised this door is locked." Stepping off the porch, he disappeared into the swirling storm. A minute later he opened the front door from inside the house. "The back door was unlocked, but there's nobody here; the house is empty."

Hovey peeked around Koford into the small living room. "Any signs of a struggle or anything out of place?"

Koford shook his head. "The only thing that looks unusual is in the basement. The furnace is torn apart."

"Let's check out the garage—see if their car is there," Hovey said.

A moment later, after peering through the garage windows at the empty space, Koford said, "I've no idea where they are, but they aren't here. In another five minutes it's going to be getting dark. What do you guys want to do?"

Hovey, Nichols, and Pulsipher exchanged looks. Hovey shrugged and said, "I guess we'd better get back to Preston and rethink this."

CHAPTER TWENTY-EIGHT

Craig Littles rolled onto his back, wheezed, sneezed, and reached for a tissue, all without lifting his head from his pillow. Wiping his watery eyes and dripping nose, he crumpled the damp tissue and let it drop. It landed on the floor beside his bed, missing the trash can by six inches and joining a dozen other wadded tissues. "Stinking cold," he grumbled, massaging his aching temples with his fingertips. Rolling onto his side, he tossed off the thick layer of covers he'd been buried under to stave off the chills that racked his body. Free of the covers, he sat on the edge of the bed and slipped his stocking-covered feet into a pair of large bunny slippers his nephew had given him as a practical joke.

Padding his way to the bathroom in an antihistamine-induced stupor, he rifled through his medicine cabinet until he found a bottle of aspirin. Fishing two of the small white tablets from the nearly empty bottle, he shuffled to his kitchen counter and picked up an oversized mug that was half full of flat soda. He took a swallow, popped in a tablet, and washed it down with a couple of gulps of the tepid liquid. He raised his hand to put the second pill into his mouth but abruptly stopped. Placing the pill and the mug on the counter, he leaned over the sink and peered out the window.

Craig Littles loved his part-time job as Preston's airport manager for a long list of reasons, but near the top was the small yellow house he was provided as part of his monthly salary. It had a small living room, a cramped kitchen, a matchbox-size bathroom, and two bedrooms, one not much larger than the walk-in closets in most modern houses. It was small and cozy, the perfect size for a confirmed bachelor. A pilot himself, he especially enjoyed its location. It was perched in line with the row of hangars that lined one side of the runway and gave him an unobstructed view of not only the hangars but the runway, parking lot, and just about every inch of the airport property. From the small kitchen window or the slightly larger window in the living room, he could watch people come and go in the parking lot, pull and push their airplanes in and out of the hangars, or watch them land and take off. For Craig, it was idyllic.

"What the . . . ?" he muttered to himself as he strained to see through the wind-swirled snowflakes that fell by the millions.

Turning from the window, he walked into the living room, picked up his binoculars, and walked to its larger window. Putting them to his eyes, he twirled the knob until the barely distinguishable silhouettes of three people came into his snowflake-clouded vision. The deluge of snowflakes falling through the magnified lenses made him sway with dizziness, so he leaned his elbows against the window to steady himself. A thin sliver of yellow light flooded from the Walkers' hangar door, giving just enough brightness for him to watch one person put a suitcase into the back of a vehicle. Blinking his eyes several times to clear his vision, Craig watched two people get into the front seats as a third got into the back seat. Craig kept the binoculars plastered to his eyes as the vehicle slowly made its way toward him. Focusing as the Walkers' Tahoe passed in front of his house, Craig stood with his mouth gaping open as the glow of the vehicle's interior lights illuminated its occupants.

Lowering the binoculars, Craig watched in stunned silence as the familiar Tahoe turned onto the main highway—not turning right toward Mink Creek, but left, to Idaho Falls and beyond.

Raising the binoculars again, Craig aimed them at the hangar where the sliver of light still shone through the hangar door. Only then did he see the two almost invisible dots of the courtesy car's red tail lights.

Craig dropped the binoculars onto the couch and walked back to his bedroom. He kicked off his bunny slippers, took off his flannel pajamas, and put on a thick wool shirt and insulated coveralls. Sitting on his bed, he had to stop twice while lacing up his heavy work boots to daub a tissue to his dripping nose. Walking into a tiny alcove off the kitchen, he pulled on big rubber galoshes, wrapped a thick red scarf around his neck, yanked a knit stocking hat down over his ears and worked his way into a billowy down-filled coat and heavy leather mittens. Then he stepped out into a blizzard.

It was nearly one hundred yards from his kitchen door to the courtesy car, and by the time he got there his coat was white. He thought he probably looked like a walking snowman.

Wiping his leaking nose with the tip of his mitten, he slogged the last fifty feet to the car and brushed snow away from the window, stooping down to look inside. Seeing the keys dangling from the ignition, he turned and walked to the hangar door. Stepping inside, he brushed snow from the sleeves of his jacket, pulled off his knit hat, and yelled, "Hello?"

Stomping snow from his boots, he shook his hat free of snow and walked farther into the hangar. "Anybody here?" he shouted. He walked around the nose of the Aztec and stopped in his tracks. The streak of red blood on the wing's white paint made him gasp.

Pulling off his mittens, he briskly walked around the wing and looked at the airplane's bullet-shattered window and open door. Looking inside the cabin and seeing no one, he spun around. As he did, his eye caught the slightest glint of light reflecting off a metal object on the floor. Cautiously walking to where he saw the reflection, he bent over and picked up the empty brass bullet casing then instantly placed it back where it was. Looking quickly around him, he pulled his stocking cap back on and raced for the door.

In spite of his stuffy nose, pounding headache, and aching body, Craig Littles ran. His huge galoshes sent up poofs of fluffy white snow as each foot struck the ground as he raced toward the dim yellow light coming from his kitchen window. With his chest heaving, he bounded up the four steps and slammed into the kitchen door so hard the glass rattled. Not bothering to close the door behind him, he pulled off his hat and dropped it and his mittens onto the floor. He picked up the phone and dialed 9-1-1.

"Sheriff's office; what is your emergency?" a calm feminine voice said.

"Yeah, this is Craig Littles at the airport. Is the sheriff there?"

"Hello, Craig. It's Helen Rogers. What's your emergency?"

"Helen, I gotta talk to the sheriff; is he there?"

"He's in the building but not in his—"

"Where is he?"

"Upstairs in the lunchroom. He and three FBI agents just got back from a snowmobile trip to Mink Creek. They're drinking hot chocolate and trying to get warm."

"Run up and get him for me, Helen. Now!" Craig barked.

"I'll get him, Craig, but it's going to take a minute. Please remain calm."

"I'm calm, Helen, I'm calm. Just get Koford."

"Hold on."

"Come on, come on," Craig said impatiently into the silent phone as he paced back and forth across the linoleum tile of his kitchen, leaving a trail of snow and water drops with each step.

Thirty seconds later Craig heard a voice in his outdated black phone say, "Yeah, Craig, what's up?"

"You gotta get to the airport right now. I just came from the Walkers' hangar, and there's blood and bullet shells in there."

Silence and then, "Is there anyone else around there, Craig?"

"Nobody. But I just saw three people leave in the Walkers' SUV, and the courtesy car is parked outside the hangar door. Nobody's in it."

"Don't touch anything, Craig. I'm on my way."

Craig dropped the receiver back into its cradle and walked to the bathroom, pulled off a long stream of toilet paper, and blew his nose. Dropping the toilet paper into the toilet, he walked back to the kitchen and peered out the window into the dark night. After ten minutes of tromping back and forth between the bathroom to blow his nose and the kitchen to look out the window to make certain the car hadn't suddenly moved, he finally saw the faint flashing of blue and red lights, causing a psychedelic lightshow as they reflected off the white snowflakes.

Pulling on his hat and zipping up his coat, Craig hurried down the stairs as the sheriff's car pulled up beside his house. Opening the passenger door, he jumped in, showering snow and water all over the seat, floor, and computer console. "It doesn't look good," Craig said, shaking his head. "Turn around, and drive through that gate over there."

"We need to wait for just a minute," Koford said, shifting the car into park. "I'm expecting someone."

"Who?"

"The FBI."

Confused, Craig said, "Why the FBI?"

"It's a long story," Koford said as the headlights of a black Suburban blazed through the car's rear window as the large vehicle came to a stop behind them. Koford rolled down his window and stuck his arm out, motioning for the Suburban to follow him, then dropped his car into gear and followed Craig's directions.

While quick introductions were made, all five men stepped into the hangar far enough to be out of the falling snow but not so far they would disturb any potential evidence or clues. Craig pushed his way to the front of the group and pointed to the far wing of the Aztec. "There's blood on that wing, and the window is shattered," he said. "And over there are a couple of bullet casings. Come on, I'll show you."

"No," Hovey said forcefully enough to stop Craig in his tracks. Moving so he was standing beside Craig, he said, "Without walking over there, will you describe exactly where you went and what you did?"

"Sure," Craig replied and explained where he had gone.

Hovey pressed him. "Are you sure that's all you did? You didn't walk around the planes or go to the back of the hangar to see if anyone was back there?"

Craig shook his head. "No. To be honest, the whole thing was creepy, and I booked it out of here."

"So you didn't pick anything up or move anything?" Hovey questioned.

"Oh," Craig said. "I did pick up one of the bullet casings, but I put it back exactly where I found it."

Hovey raised his eyebrows. "How about that pipe? Did you put it there or move it?" he asked, pointing to the length of pipe that was lying on the floor.

"No, and I can tell you one thing for certain: it wasn't there when we put the airplane in the hangar yesterday because I would have stepped on it."

Hovey looked at Craig and asked, "You helped put this airplane in here? Don't both of these airplanes belong to the Walkers?" he asked.

Craig looked at Hovey like he was from outer space. "No," he exclaimed. "Why would they need two airplanes? The Bonanza back there is the Walkers', and this Aztec belongs to some guy named John Smith. He flew in last night just before the storm closed us down."

Hovey, Nichols, and Pulsipher exchanged nervous glances. "Pulsipher," Hovey said, "do you have that photo of Vaughn with you?"

Pulsipher didn't answer as he shoved his hand into the inside breast pocket of his suit coat. Pulling out a photo, he handed it to Hovey.

"Is this the guy who flew in?" Hovey asked, holding out the photograph.

Craig looked, not bothering to hold the photo. "Yup, that's him—no question about it."

A worried look spread over Hovey's face. "His name is Scott Vaughn, not John Smith," Hovey said matter-of-factly, handing the photo back to Pulsipher.

Sheriff Koford stepped in. "Craig, let's take this one step at a time, from the beginning."

Craig rehearsed everything he'd seen and done from the moment he got up to get his aspirin until he'd placed the 9-1-1 call. When he was finished, he said, "That's it."

"So you definitely saw Greg and Marena in the front seat of the Tahoe?" Koford asked.

"Absolutely—no mistaking them."

"And this other guy, Vaughn—he was in the backseat?" Koford's brows were knit as he focused on Craig's responses.

Craig nodded.

"And they turned up the highway toward Idaho Falls?" Pulsipher asked.

Craig nodded again.

Hovey interjected, "And you definitely saw one of them put a metal suitcase in the Tahoe?"

"I did."

Hovey shook his head and said to the other agents, "I understand Vaughn taking the Walkers somewhere to kill them and dispose of their bodies. What I don't understand is why he would take the suitcase with him."

Over the next fifteen minutes, after the agents and Koford gave Craig a brief rundown of what they knew of Vaughn and his suitcase, the five men stood in the hangar tossing out one idea after another. Each was ultimately discounted. Finally, it was Craig who said, "Maybe he needs the Walkers. Maybe he needs to get somewhere to make a delivery and he can't drive in snow."

"What makes you say that?" Hovey asked.

"Well . . ." Craig stopped mid-sentence and sneezed three times in rapid succession, coating Hovey and Koford with a fine layer of spray. Nichols jumped back, away from Craig. "When he asked to use the courtesy car, he asked how far it was to Arco."

"Arco?" Hovey said. "Where is Arco?"

"It's a small community about a hundred fifty miles northwest of here," Koford answered.

"Anything of any importance ever happen in Arco?" Hovey asked Koford. "What's its claim to fame?"

"The nearest thing is the INL," Koford said. "It's not far from Arco."

"What's that?" Pulsipher asked.

"Idaho National Laboratory," Craig and Koford said in unison.

"Laboratory?" Hovey asked, his face suddenly creased with worry lines. "What kind of laboratory? Somewhere out west here there's a biological warfare place. Is that this INL?"

Koford shook his head. "That's the Tooele Army Depot west of Salt Lake. They've got huge stockpiles of bombs filled with deadly toxins."

"Okay, what's at this INL place?" Hovey asked.

Koford's face was somber. "Nuclear."

"What do you mean?" Hovey asked.

"It's the largest nuclear-testing facility in the world. There's probably more nuclear material at Arco, Idaho, than anywhere else."

CHAPTER TWENTY-NINE

Kelli Latimore was engaged once, but the idea of "till death do we part" had gone up in a puff of smoke in the midst of a soul-searching heart-to-heart discussion with her fiancé. She'd awkwardly revealed a "little habit." It had been a poor choice of words, or at least a poor way of saying it, but that coupled with her coy evasiveness to his questions had quickly led down a dark path. No, it wasn't alcohol or prescription drugs, she'd told him, and with an emphatic headshake she'd insisted it wasn't cocaine, meth, or marijuana that had its claws in her.

"What then?" he'd asked, clearly bracing himself for her response.

It had taken her a minute, but she'd quietly said, "Horseracing."

His jaw had dropped, and for a second, he'd stared at her with a dumbfounded expression. Then he'd roared with a relieved laugh. "You're kidding. That's it? I was expecting something terrible. Lots of people play the ponies every now and again." After twenty minutes of revealing how often and how much money she'd "invested" in her habit, his relief had turned to anxiety. "You're addicted to betting on horses," he'd stated flatly.

"No," she'd shot back, she wasn't "addicted" because she could stop any time she wanted.

"Great," he'd fired. "Quit right now. I'm a diesel mechanic; I can't afford to be married to a gambler."

She'd quit for exactly eleven days. On the evening of the twelfth day, during another soul-searching discussion with the love of her life, she'd confessed to betting—and losing—a thousand dollars earlier that morning. That was when the ultimatum had come: Either she got counseling or it was over. She'd blown up, insisting she didn't have the problem—he did. He was oppressive, domineering, and chauvinistic. Three days later, with only a few more words between them, he'd walked away.

In reality, Kelli's father shouldered some of the blame for his daughter's addiction. Marc Latimore had been a semi-successful quarter horse trainer until California racing authorities had discovered he had a penchant for betting on horses as well as training them. And when it was discovered he and a jockey had thrown a race at Santa Anita so they could score on a bet, he'd been barred from the industry for life. While his career had died a sudden death, his addiction to betting had lingered on. Much to the anger and frustration of Kelli's emotionally abused mother, Marc had taught their only child the ropes of horse betting. And now, despite her insistence, Kelli was as hopelessly addicted to it as a street junkie was to heroin.

Unlike her father, who was a habitual loser, Kelli seemed to have a knack for picking winners, at least in the early days. She'd tasted victory often enough she'd started to believe the myth her father had hoisted on her: "Girl, you're truly gifted. You have a sixth sense." Her "gift" had served her well for the first year—her wins had easily galloped ahead of her losses. Midway through the second year, her "gift" threw a shoe and things began unraveling until her wins and losses had been running nose and nose. During the past twelve months, the losses had lunged out of the starting gate and galloped ahead of the wins.

Parry Dugay, the cowboy-boot-wearing bookie from the Fort Hall Indian Reservation who had financed her habit and taken half of her meager winnings, had demanded the ten thousand dollars she owed him. His threats about what he'd do to her for not paying had been graphic enough that she'd offered him her car and leftover diamond engagement ring, but he hadn't wanted stuff; he'd wanted his cash—all of it. And Kelli didn't have it.

Two days after Parry Dugay had demanded his money, Kelli had raced home from work, run into her apartment, and locked all three locks. Ensconced in her semi-secure space, she'd changed her clothes and eaten leftover pizza washed down with diet soda. As she was tossing the empty pizza box into the trash, a timid *tap tap tap* on her door had made her jump. She'd pulled out her cell phone and pressed the 9 and the 1 and hesitated. With her thumb poised over the 1 on the keypad, she'd quietly walked to the door and said, "Who is it?"

"Open up, girl," a feminine voice had replied. "It's Carrie and Lacey."

Kelli had lowered the phone to her side and cautiously asked, "Just the two of you?"

"Of course. Who else would be with us?"

Kelli had undone the locks and twisted the knob. The door had barely cracked open when the two girls pushed past her, knocking her back. At nearly six feet tall, Carrie Jacobs dwarfed Kelli. "Get your coat; we're going to Howie's," she'd said.

Kelli had looked at the two girls, confused.

"Yogurt, Kelli. We're hungry for frozen yogurt," a slightly plump Lacey Adams had said. Then, holding up her hands and wiggling her fingers, she'd added, "With nuts and all those little sprinkle things loaded on top."

Kelli had closed the door, set all three locks again, and walked past the two girls. Dropping down onto her worn sofa, she'd said, "I don't feel like it; not tonight."

In unison the girls' lower jaws had sagged. "What?" Carrie asked in dismay. "When has there ever been a time you didn't want frozen yogurt?"

"You sick?" Lacey had asked.

Kelli had shaken her head. "No, I'm just not in the mood to go out."

After fifteen minutes of cajoling and a ten-minute drive, the three girls had stood in Howie's Frozen Yogurt Emporium. Kelli had loaded her paper bowl with butter brickle, cinnamon bun, and two especially large portions of salted caramel yogurt from the self-serve machines. She'd added two huge spoonfuls of Georgia peach preserves and a thick coating of melted milk chocolate and topped it all off with a spoonful of crushed macadamia nuts, another of shredded coconut, and an extra-large spoonful of colorful chocolate sprinkles.

Lacey had looked over at Kelli's almost overflowing bowl and said with more than a little envy, "I don't know how you do it."

"Do what?" Kelli had asked.

"Eat as much as you do and stay so trim. If I ate that, I'd have to spend three days in the gym on a treadmill."

"High metabolism," Kelli had said and quickly turned around.

The impact had been as unexpected as it was disastrous. Kelli had slammed into a man, splattering the entire contents of her bowl down the front of his dark-blue sport coat.

The man, aghast, had shouted an expletive; Kelli had been mortified and stood speechless. Carrie and Lacey had looked on with their mouths gaping open. As Howie's employees had scurried to clean frozen yogurt from the floor, Kelli had mumbled apologies and awkwardly dabbed at the gooey mess dripping from the man's jacket, making things worse.

The man had stood unsmiling and rigid as Kelli stopped swiping at the jacket and stammered out an awkward introduction. After apologizing for the tenth or twelfth time, and not knowing what else to do, she had offered to have the jacket cleaned. Without hesitating, the man had removed it and held it out to her. Dumbfounded that he had accepted her offer, Kelli had taken the jacket, along with a business card from Mr. Li Gun-no. After a quick conversation about when and where he could retrieve his cleaned jacket, the upset man had stormed out of Howie's without ordering any frozen yogurt.

Two days later, when Mr. Li had stopped at Kelli's apartment to pick up his jacket, he was a different man. A beaming smile had lit up his face, and he'd been gracious—almost deferential. As Kelli handed him the plastic-wrapped jacket, she had once again apologized profusely for the accident. Mr. Li had accepted the apology with a slight bow and then suggested that perhaps he may have been at fault and should bear some of the blame. He had then insisted on reimbursing Kelli for the cost of dry cleaning the jacket, to which Kelli mildly protested but ultimately agreed. As Mr. Li handed Kelli the money, he had suggested that perhaps there was a way the two of them could be mutually helpful to each other. Kelli had smiled and told him she didn't see how. It was then that Mr. Li's smile had faded, and his voice had taken on a more serious tone. He had slowly explained that he knew where Kelli worked and described some of her habits. Then, after a short pause, he'd told her he was also aware of Kelli's indebtedness to a certain cowboy-boot-wearing bookie from Fort Hall.

Kellie had listened, dumbfounded, horrified, at what Mr. Li knew about her. She had told him to leave, but instead of moving, he made a proposal. In return for a little information, he would see that the betting debt was eliminated forever. No, she didn't need to do anything illegal; he just needed a few specific details about where she worked. Once she helped him, she would never see him again. After nearly an hour of questions and answers, Kelli had reluctantly agreed to help Mr. Li.

"And I won't owe you any money?" she'd asked for the fourth or fifth time.

"Not a penny," Mr. Li had replied with an engaging smile.

True to his word, when Kelli had arrived home from work on the day Parry Dugay was expected, Mr. Li was sitting in his car in front of her apartment. Inside the apartment, Mr. Li had opened a small canvas bag and counted out ten thousand dollars in hundred-dollar bills. After a smile, bow, and handshake, Mr. Li had returned to his car and driven away.

An hour later Dugay had banged on the door. "Kelli, girl," he'd called through the door. "It's me, Parry; it's pay-up time."

Kelli had stood with one hand pressing against the triple-locked door and the other holding her cell phone, on which she had already dialed a 9 and a 1. Through the door she'd said, "There's a cardboard box beside the door; you see it?"

There had been a slightly confused, "Yeah, so?"

"Your money's in there."

"Huh?"

"Open the box. The money's in there—all ten thousand."

Through the door Kelli had heard Parry pick up the box and cut the tape that sealed it shut. Two minutes had passed without a sound. Then, suddenly, "Well, well, well, Kelli girl. I don't know how you did it, but it's all here."

"Get out of here, Dugay, and never come back," Kelli had snarled. "If I ever see you again—anywhere—I'm calling the cops. You hear me?"

"Hey," Parry had said through the door in a syrupy-sweet voice, "It's been a pleasure doing business with you. If you ever want anything, just let me know."

***

An hour later, when Parry Dugay had walked in the front door of his isolated doublewide mobile home on the edge of the reservation, Mr. Li was waiting for him. Startled, Parry had reached to his belt for what Mr. Li could see was a .32-caliber pistol the man had hidden in a holster in his belt. Parry's hand had barely gripped the gun when Li landed a violent kick to the side of his head. Dugay had crumpled to the ground, unconscious. Li had opened the box to check that the cash was still inside and then walked to an old propane wall heater and turned it on without lighting the flame. Sniffing a couple of times to make certain the propane gas was streaming into the trailer, he had made his way to the door. Pulling a long, thin candle from his pocket, he'd lit the wick, let a few drops of melted wax puddle onto the floor, and then stood the candle in the puddle and held it until the wax solidified. With the candle burning brightly, he'd carefully closed the door and walked to his car. He'd driven a quarter of a mile to a clump of cottonwood trees and parked. Fifteen minutes later a thunderous explosion had blown the trailer into a thousand pieces. A few minutes later, as the first faint sounds of sirens had filtered through the air, Mr. Li started his car and drove in the opposite direction of the oncoming fire trucks.

That had been three months, a hundred lies, and a dozen secrets ago.

CHAPTER THIRTY

Kelli Latimore smiled broadly at the group of seventeen people standing in a loosely formed semicircle in front of her. "Welcome and thank you for joining us on our tour of the facility today. My name is Kelli Latimore, and for the next forty-five minutes, I get to be your guide." Facing the crowd but walking backward, she motioned for the group to follow. Even backward she walked at a pace that was fast enough to cause an overweight man to grumble to his wife that he wished Kelli would slow down. Kelli heard the comment but ignored it.

Coming to an abrupt stop beside a large photograph that occupied most of a wall, she motioned with her arms for the group to crowd around her. "Once again, on behalf of all of us at the Idaho National Laboratory, I want to welcome you on our tour today." With a broad smile and a head bob, she continued. "Behind me is an aerial photograph of the installation." Using a small laser pointer, she aimed the red beam at a small building and said, "We are in this building. As you can see, we are on the extreme eastern edge of the complex."

Standing in about the middle of the group and acting as if he were hanging on every word Kelli spoke was Mr. Li. Kelli was only mildly fazed by his presence. In the months since the frozen yogurt accident and his ten-thousand-dollar payment, this was the eighth time he had been in one of her tour groups.

Kelli's official title at the Idaho National Laboratory was Guest Representative, but she and those she worked with were almost always referred to as tour guides. It was their job to escort the constant flow of curious visitors to see a few of the sights at America's premier nuclear-testing facility.

"The Idaho National Laboratory sits almost midway between Arco, Idaho, to the west and Idaho Falls and Blackfoot to the east," Kelli explained, pointing out each of the communities with her laser pointer. "The facility encompasses nearly nine hundred square miles and is spread over parts of Butte, Bingham, Bonneville, and Jefferson counties. To give you some perspective, that is almost the same size as the state of Rhode Island. More than four thousand people are pleased to be employees of this remarkable facility."

Kelli, still smiling, cleared her throat and continued. "The federal research facility was established in 1949 as the National Reactor Testing Station. In 1975 it became known as the Energy Research and Development Administration, and for two years it was nicknamed ERDA. In 1977 it was renamed the Idaho National Engineering Laboratory and was known by that moniker for nearly two decades. Two years ago it became known as the Idaho National Laboratory, or as we like to call it, INL."

She took a breath to continue with her memorized speech, but a bald-headed man at the very back of the group asked, "So what really goes on in this place? Some super-secret nuclear stuff?"

Kelli beamed a huge smile and replied enthusiastically, "Glad you asked." Then, in a response that had been carefully scripted by attorneys, public relations spin doctors, and scientists, she proceeded to answer the question without really answering it. "Yes, we do work with nuclear material—quite a bit of it, actually. While some of our projects are government-related and require that we maintain certain levels of confidence, much of what we do is aimed at harnessing the vast power of nuclear energy and developing safe ways of handling nuclear waste." Then, to steer the dialogue back to her memorized message, she said, "Throughout its lifetime, there have been more than fifty one-of-a-kind nuclear reactors built by various organizations here at the facility, all of them aimed at harnessing the power of the atom and making our world a better place."

What Kelli said was true. What she didn't say, because it wasn't part of her approved dialogue, was that during the same time those fifty nuclear reactors were being built to make the world a better place, three times that many projects were being completed within the complex that made the world a far deadlier place.

A large woman in bright-green capri pants and a yellow tank top that strained to contain her ample girth raised her hand. "Excuse me, miss, but you just mentioned that this place deals with a lot of nuclear material. Are we in danger of radiation just by being here?"

Kelli smiled. "Another great question," she replied as if the woman had just asked a question worthy of the Pulitzer Prize. "No, you have absolutely nothing to fear. You are in no danger whatsoever of radioactive contamination." Removing a small black plastic badge the size of a quarter that was clipped to the lapel of her stylish red blouse, Kelli held it out for everyone to see. "This is a dosimeter badge I am required to wear at all times while I'm at the facility. It is sensitive to many different radioactive isotopes, including X-rays, gammas, betas, and neutrons. I am required to turn this badge in and get a new one every week. The old one is tested to see if during the week I have been exposed to any radioactive isotopes. In all the years I've been working here, never once has it shown any exposure whatsoever. In fact, you receive more X-rays from an afternoon stroll in the sunshine than from anything here at INL."

Kelli's answer wasn't completely true, at least that's what a lab assistant once told her. Every week her badge tested positive for several radioactive isotopes far in excess of what someone working away from the facility would encounter. But some government employee somewhere had determined that based on current research, the level of radiation did not pose a serious threat to her health, so each week she was told everything was within "allowable limits."

"So where is all this radioactive stuff, and how do you keep it from harming people?" the same bald guy who had asked the first question said.

"Wow, I'm impressed. You're asking some very pertinent questions," Kelli said. "I'll answer your question as we walk to our next exhibit." She immediately began leading the group down the hallway toward a large, open room that was flooded with sunlight.

"Over the years, as the world's needs have changed, the mission of INL has changed. In the early days, emphasis was placed on developing nuclear reactors as a way to provide electricity for our homes and cities, something at which we were very successful. In fact, on the afternoon of December 20, 1951, in a small building not far from where we are standing, a row of four lightbulbs was lit using nuclear energy. That was the first time nuclear energy had been used in such a fashion." Taking a quick breath, she deftly bounced over the military applications. "For a brief period during the late '50s and '60s, a portion of our facility was devoted to expanding the

United States military's nuclear warfare capabilities." Then, using her most upbeat voice, Kelli continued. "Today, besides all the scientific research we do, a part of the INL facility has a far more peaceful mission than nuclear warfare. The lab's engineers are developing technology, shaping policy, and leading initiatives to secure the nuclear fuel cycle and prevent the proliferation of weapons of mass destruction."

Having worked at INL for some time now, Kelli knew that most people were more concerned with keeping up with her pace than listening to what she said, but upon hearing "weapons of mass destruction," several suddenly perked up. The bald man shouted out, "You mean bombs? There are nuclear bombs here?"

Kelli brought the group to a halt beside a large table the size of most living rooms. It was a scale model of the INL's massive facility, complete with tiny buildings, roads, and even miniature cars, trucks, and people. "Please," she said, "spread out around the table, and we'll continue."

From the far side of the table, a high-school-aged kid with short-cropped hair and dark-rimmed glasses said, "What about the bombs? Where are they?"

Kelli looked over at the kid and nodded, acknowledging his repeat of the bald man's question. After the group stopped shuffling and jockeying for positions around the table, she said, "Back to the question about bombs. As you know, a weapon of mass destruction depends upon nuclear material as the means of destruction. Typically, this is highly enriched uranium. INL scientists are leading a global initiative to secure foreign stockpiles of fresh and spent highly enriched uranium. As we acquire this material, our scientists are able to modify it so it becomes low-enriched uranium. This low-enriched material is safer and far more stable. Once altered, we place it in secure storage areas beneath the ground . . . here." Pointing the beam of her laser at the model, she identified several patches of desert that looked as barren and untouched as any other place on the model.

With each group she took on a tour, Kelli pointed to a different place on the map as the location of where the low-grade uranium was buried. In truth, she had no idea and didn't really care where the stuff was buried. She did know, however, exactly where the highly enriched uranium was stored before it was altered, not because her job entitled her to know such things but because Mr. Li had demanded she find out. When she had at first refused, saying it would be a breach of security, Mr. Li reminded her that she was in his debt to the amount of thirteen thousand dollars—the original ten plus three more he had provided for her gambling habit. She could pay him right then and he would go away, or she could obtain the information he'd needed, and he'd needed it within the week. Three days later she'd handed Li a tourist brochure produced by INL's public relations department that showed a reduced version of the scale model by which she was standing. She had circled in blue ink each of the buildings where the enriched uranium was housed.

"Have there ever been any mishaps or accidents here?" asked an elderly man with a full head of snow-white hair.

This question came up in some form or another during every tour Kelli had ever conducted. Her scripted answer was always the same, and because they were standing beside the model right then, she aimed her laser at a small building and said, "On November 8, 2011, a worker in this building discovered an open container of plutonium-related material. All seventeen workers in the building were taken to hospitals. None were found to be contaminated with dangerous levels of radiation nor were investigators able to determine how the container had become open."

Kelli's scripted answer was truthful, just not completely so. Six of the seventeen people in the building had proved to have been exposed to low-level radiation that had required close observation and monitoring for months. But more ominously, and completely left out of Kelli's script, was an accident that had occurred several years earlier at Stationary Low Power Plant Number One, a small reactor in the middle of the complex. The reactor had been destroyed when a control rod was pulled too far out of the reactor, leading to core meltdown. The explosion that followed had caused the reactor to break free from its cement encasement and jump nine feet into the air. The concussion from the blast had killed three military maintenance personnel working on the reactor. Their bodies had been so saturated with radioactive isotopes they were quickly—and quietly—buried in coffins made of several inches of pure lead. While the three lay practically glowing in their coffins, the desert winds had carried some of the radiation that had escaped from the reactor to the east, directly to the people of Idaho Falls and Blackfoot. Hundreds were eventually stricken with cancer from the downwind fallout, and dozens died, but nobody could pin the sickness and death to the incident.

***

As other tourists were listening to Kelli and studying the model where she pointed the laser beam, Mr. Li removed a camera from the pocket of his jacket and snapped a dozen pictures of the model. He wasn't aiming where the laser's red dot pointed, like other tourists. His pictures were of a small building almost in the center of the nine hundred square mile complex, as well as the roads leading to it. His country didn't have a single satellite capable of taking images of the facility from space, but they didn't need it. Over the past several months, with Kelli's help and that of his hundred-dollar digital camera, he had obtained all but one last piece of information.

CHAPTER THIRTY-ONE

Kelli watched as the dark-green car slowly rounded the corner and crunched its way along the snow-covered street toward her. When it was exactly opposite her, it glided to a stop, and the rear window rolled down three inches. From inside, Mr. Li's voice called out, "Kelli, thank you for agreeing to meet me. Please, get in so you are out of the snow."

Obediently, Kelli opened the rear door and slid in. Pulling the hood off her head and shaking snowflakes onto the seat, she glanced over to Mr. Li and then to the two other Asian men in the front seat. The driver was thin-faced, with sunken cheeks and protruding cheekbones. The man in the passenger seat was heavier, with a round face and short hair. Kelli looked back at Mr. Li and then slowly reached for the door handle.

Mr. Li shook his head slightly and smiled warmly. "Please, Kelli. There is no cause for concern." Nodding to the front seat, he said, "I'd like you to meet two of my associates." Pointing to the man seated behind the wheel, he said, "This is Mr. Li." Extending his arm toward the other man in the front passenger seat, he said, "And this is also Mr. Li. They are brothers."

Kelli looked at the two men warily and said, "And your sons?"

Li gave the slightest smile but said nothing.

As the driver eased the car away from the curb, Mr. Li said, "We would like to talk with you for a few minutes and thought it would be easiest if we took a short drive."

"What do we have to talk about?" Kelli asked with a slight tremble in her voice as the car glided across the soft cushion of snow.

"Your job," Mr. Li replied. "And also the money you owe me."

Kelli shook her head and said, "I don't owe you any money. I've done everything you asked and more. And the last time we talked, you told me we were finished, that you didn't need anything more from me."

Mr. Li nodded. "That is true; I did tell you that. Unfortunately, sometimes things change. I can assure you, though, after you complete one more very small request, I will be gone from your life forever."

Kelli studied Li's black eyes in the fading daylight. "No," she said defiantly. "I'm finished. I'm not going to help you anymore."

Li smiled patiently. "I'm sorry you feel that way, Kelli, because I'm afraid I must insist."

Kelli shook her head. "No, I won't do it anymore. Stop the car. I want to get out!"

Li looked at Kelli for a moment and gave her a forced smile. Then, to the driver, he said, "Please stop the car."

The driver pulled into the parking lot of a closed-down gas station and stopped the car. He then reached inside his coat pocket, extracted a folded sheet of paper, and handed it back to Li.

Li took the paper, unfolded it, looked at it briefly, and passed it over to Kelli without saying a word.

"What . . . ?" Kelli muttered in confusion as she looked at the photo. "That's my father!" she exclaimed, looking briefly at Li and then back at the photo, her heart pounding with fear. "Why . . . where . . . how . . . ?" she stammered, pulling the photo closer to examine it.

The photo was printed on a sheet of plain white paper, giving it a slightly grainy quality, but it was clear enough. It depicted a small rundown motel room with linoleum tile, orange walls, a sagging bed, and white plastic drapes that were barely open. Near the foot of the bed was a single wooden chair with Kelli's father seated in it, his hands tied behind his back and each ankle tied to a leg of the chair. A white rope encircled his chest, forcing him to sit upright. His head lolled down, his chin resting on his chest. The distance from which the photograph was taken made it difficult to see details, but there was no mistaking the cuts and bruises on his face—he had been beaten.

Kelli looked at the photo, then at Li, and again at the photo. Her jaw was clenched tight when she looked back at Li. "You savages!" she screamed and lunged across the seat at Li, the long, manicured fingernails of her left hand aimed at his eyes and those of her right hand aimed at his throat.

Her attack was so sudden Li's only reaction was to scrunch his eyes closed tightly. The thin skin of his eyelids did nothing to protect his left eye. The manicurist who had trimmed and painted Kelli's fingernails only an hour earlier had cut the tips so they were square, not pointed. Much to Kelli's earlier annoyance, the woman had left the edge of the fingernail on her ring finger unfiled and the corner wickedly sharp. Sitting in the car as she was, the angle was perfect for her attack. Li screamed with enraged pain. By the time the car's other two other occupants turned around and reached over the high-backed seats to grab Kelli, the damage had been done.

Clutching his bleeding eye and screaming in pain, Li kicked at Kelli as the other men pulled her away. In a pain-clouded effort to escape Kelli's still-clawing fingers, Li lifted the door handle, spilling him and Kelli onto the ground. Struggling to her feet, Kelli charged out into the snow-covered street and began running for her life.

Li struggled to his knees as the brothers jumped from the car. The driver pulled Li to his feet, but before he could say anything, Li screamed, "Get her!"

Despite Kelli's head start, her short legs were no match for the two men. Within fifty yards the slenderer of the two had shortened her lead to only a few strides. Kelli could hear his heavy breathing and cast a quick glance over her shoulder just as he lunged for her. If he had taken one more step, he would have tackled her around the knees with both arms. As it was, his outstretched hands grabbed her ankle and only for a split second. Knocked off-balance in the snow, Kelli tumbled to the ground and rolled. She glimpsed the man as he skidded through the snow on his belly. Dazed, Kelli was almost to her feet when the second man slammed into her with so much force it knocked the air from her lungs and sent her careening through the snow. She could do nothing more. She was lying facedown in the snow, crying, when both men grabbed her by the arms and jerked her to her feet. She made an exhausted attempt to break free of their grip as they half-dragged her back toward Li and the car, but her small stature was no match for their grip.

Li was sitting in the back seat of the car, the door open and his feet on the ground. Three bright-red ribbons of blood streaked down from beneath the hand he had cupped over his eye. "You witch," he hissed as the trio drew up beside the car. "You will pay for this."

CHAPTER THIRTY-TWO

Rexene Gilger knew her children shuddered every time she slid behind the wheel of her copper-colored 1967 Chevrolet Impala. Bicyclists and pedestrians were generally safe from her feistiness, lead foot, and diminishing vision, but other motorists were fair game. Get in her way and she'd flash her lights or lay on the horn; cut her off and she'd issue a horn blast and an obscene gesture.

Twice in the past three years her son and three daughters had ganged up on her as they'd sat around her kitchen table, intent on taking the keys to the aging Impala away from her. They were short conversations and didn't go as her children had planned. On both occasions Rexene had curtly asked her children to leave and told them, "You can have the keys to my car after they place me in a coffin, and not one second before."

Away from the car, others seemed to delight in Rexene's company. With a feisty, razor-sharp wit belying her innocent short and slightly overweight frame and frosty white hair, and only occasionally given to cussing, Rexene was almost always the life of the party, which made her a hit with not only her octogenarian friends but her grandkids and their friends.

Rexene told everyone it was her job that gave her vitality for life and kept her mind alert and her body mostly free of aches and pains. For three hours every school day, Rexene was at Bonneville High School in Idaho Falls. She was a cashier. She sat on a stool at the end of the cafeteria line, charging kids for the pizza, soda, and other more nutritious food. She'd been trading barbs, scolding poor behavior, talking trash, and laughing at and with high schoolers for thirty years. The same kids who were once trying to sneak extra drinks without paying or starting food fights were now the judges, dentists, mechanics, and plumbers of Idaho Falls, and Rexene was on a first-name basis with all of them. She had more connections than any politician.

On her eightieth birthday her driver's license was due for renewal and required her to take a driving test. After the test, the examiner—a former high school football jock named Dayne—leaned over and told her he was sorry but she had failed. She had made an improper lane change and hadn't come to a complete stop at any of the three stop signs. Rexene listened politely as he explained that her driving days were over. Grinning at Dayne, she reminded him of the time she had watched him and a cheerleader—now his wife's best friend—engage in some unbecoming activity under the bleachers after a football game. It would be most unfortunate, she said, if his wife were to learn about the activity. Her license was renewed.

If her children shuddered at her driving, they would be aghast if they knew Rexene packed a .32-caliber semiautomatic pistol in her purse. On a sultry summer evening four years earlier, she and her best friend, Luciene Whitney, had been walking to Luciene's car after attending a women's meeting at their church. It had been dark and the parking lot poorly lit, and as Luciene and Rexene walked up to their doors, a man had run up behind Rexene. Slamming into her with almost enough force to knock her to the pavement, he'd grabbed the straps of Rexene's purse and tugged. Rather than let him have the purse, she'd started beating him with the cane she'd been using while her newly replaced hip finished healing.

Never one to back down from helping someone in need, Luciene had hurried around the car to aid Rexene. Swinging her own purse by the straps, Luciene had clobbered the attacker in the side of the head. Enraged, the man had spun around and drove his fist into Luciene's chin, knocking out three teeth and sending her flying onto the hood of the car with a dislocated jaw. Releasing the grip on her purse, Rexene had rushed to Luciene's side. As the attacker ran away with both purses, Rexene had vowed no one would ever hurt her or her friends like that again.

The next day, after visiting Luciene in the hospital, Rexene had gone to a gun shop owned by a former high school student, bought a pistol, and enrolled in a class to get a concealed-weapon permit. Two weeks later the permit had arrived in the mail. The next day she'd called yet another former high school student, this one now a sergeant in the Idaho Falls police department, and said she wanted lessons in shooting her new pistol. Off to the gun range they went. Any attacker more than fifteen feet away had little to fear for his safety—she couldn't hit a thing. But at ten feet or less, she could double-tap two shots into the silhouette target's chest with surprising accuracy. Rexene Gilger was a pistol-packing great-grandma.

But it wasn't a pistol that occupied Rexene's thoughts now; it was snow. Even though she would never admit it to her children or anyone else, Rexene didn't like driving in snow. Truth be told, it was one of the few things that genuinely frightened her. The big old Impala was a tried-and-true tank on dry payment or rain; snow was a different matter. The rear-wheel-drive car would fishtail and skid without the slightest provocation, and Rexene's tendency to drive with one foot on the gas pedal and one foot on the brake created plenty of provocation, even with the studded snow tires she'd made sure to have installed before the first snowfall of the season.

Twice on the drive to the hospital in the heavy snowstorm she had tried to stop at stop signs. Twice the Impala had skidded right through them without slowing, the wheels locking up. The second time it was only the quick action of another driver that had kept her from broadsiding the poor guy. Somewhat frazzled, she now walked into Luciene's dimly lit hospital room, shook melting snow from her coat, and placed it over the arm of a chair. Sitting gently on the edge of Luciene's bed, she began a one-sided conversation. "Luciene," she said, patting the clammy, almost lifeless hand of her friend. "Do you remember the time that punk attacked us in the parking lot and stole our purses?"

The frail woman lying in the bed, with auburn hair and sunken cheeks, didn't open her eyes, move her mouth, or lift a finger in response. She couldn't. The drugs coursing through her body made sure of it. She was in a drug-induced coma and had been for nearly two weeks. The paramedics theorized that she had tripped on a small rug she kept in front of her kitchen sink and had fallen, striking her head on the way down and breaking her hip when she landed. Luciene's physicians had induced the coma in an effort to give her brain a chance to heal.

For fifteen minutes Rexene prattled on, touching lightly on half a dozen topics that under more pleasant circumstances would have brought a laugh or warm smile to Luciene's normally radiant face. Looking out the window at the dark night and the increasingly heavy snowstorm, Rexene eased off the side of the bed and said in her most upbeat voice, "I'd love to stay here and swap lies with you, but those big white snowflakes are calling my name, and I'd better scoot home before things get too bad." Putting on her coat, she said to her peacefully sleeping best friend, "Look, girl, I'll be back tomorrow. Until then, don't be chasing any of those young doctors around the halls. Leave that to me."

Drawing her coat snugly around her, Rexene smiled, leaned over, and lightly kissed her friend on the forehead before walking out the hospital door. Three minutes and a short elevator ride later, Rexene traded the sterile but warm hospital room for pitch-black night, biting wind, and blowing snow as she shuffled her snow-boot-encased feet through almost eight inches of fluffy powder. Retrieving a long-handled brush from the Impala's trunk, she carefully and methodically brushed the accumulated snow from her windows. Brushing the huge flakes from her shoulders with her gloved hands, she opened the door and slid behind the wheel. Expelling a nervous sigh, she started the car and very slowly began working her way out of the hospital parking lot.

It had taken her nearly thirty minutes to crawl her way to the hospital for her daily visit with Luciene. That was in daylight, and she had managed to get behind a snowplow. Going home would take much longer. The dark night, swirling snowflakes, and occasional glare from the headlights of oncoming cars would each take their toll. "Just take it easy," Rexene told herself. "Don't hurry and don't do anything stupid, and you'll be just fine." Gripping the wheel with both hands and leaning so far forward her nose was almost touching the steering wheel, Rexene crawled the car out of the parking lot and onto the street for the long drive home.

CHAPTER THIRTY-THREE

Kelli whimpered as she knelt in the snow beside the car, her head in her hands. The brothers stood on either side of her, each with a hand gripping her shoulder so tightly that even through the thickness of her coat she cringed in pain. Except for a single vocal outburst from Li, the animated exchange in Korean going on between Li and her two guards was too muffled to hear.

Just as her body heat began melting snow and the knees in her jeans grew wet, the two men yanked her to her feet and shoved her to the rear of the car. As one man held her so tightly in a bear hug she could barely breathe, the other opened the trunk, reached inside a black leather bag, and extracted a roll of silver duct tape. Tearing off a four-inch piece, he gripped her tightly by the jaw and slapped the tape over her mouth, turning her frightened screams into little more than muffled noises. Pulling her arms in front of her, he squeezed her wrists together and wrapped them several times with the tape. Gripping her tightly around her calves with one arm to force her ankles together, he wrapped her ankles several times.

Kelli's nearly silent screams only drew smiles from the men as they lifted her off the ground and dropped her into the trunk, banging her head on the metal edge, causing an instant headache. The trunk went dark as he hurriedly slammed the lid closed.

***

The brothers climbed into the front seats as Li slowly swung his legs into the back seat of the car and pulled the door closed. Sliding down in the seat and leaning his head back so he was nearly reclining, he moaned, "Take me to a hospital."

"Yes, of course," the driver said. After a short pause he asked, "Where is it?"

Li swore and said derisively, "Did you not study a map of the city before they sent you here?" He didn't wait for a reply. "Turn around," he hissed. "Drive to Sunnyside Road; it is two or three miles behind us. When you get there, turn right. In one or two miles you will see the hospital."

Li watched as the driver put the car into gear and heard the man stomp on the gas pedal at the same time he cranked the wheel hard left, putting the car in a wild fishtail that sent Li flinging against the door. "Be careful, you idiot!" he screamed.

After nearly two minutes of silence, the driver looked into the rearview mirror and said, "We can't leave her in there for too long; she will freeze."

"Let her freeze." Li groaned.

The driver raised his eyebrows at the response but said nothing for nearly two more minutes. As he made a hasty lane change, cutting off a lumbering semitruck, which resulted in a sustained blast of an air horn, he said, "We need her tomorrow, alive and well. If she is dead, all that has been planned and worked for is wasted."

Li closed his good eye and gritted his teeth, the pain in his damaged eye excruciating. Taking a breath, he said, "Oh, we will keep her alive, but when this is all finished, she is mine to deal with, do you understand?" He opened his good eyes to ensure they did.

Both men nodded, but neither said anything.

"Take me to the hospital, and then take the girl back to the motel where you are staying. Assure her that no harm will come to her or her father and that I will talk with her when I return from the hospital. Do not remove the tape; is that clear?" Turning his head to the man in the passenger seat, he said, "Seok, you are to stay with her." Rolling his head back to the driver, he instructed, "Hwan, after you drop them off, come back to the hospital and wait for me. Do you understand?"

Each of the men again nodded, and Li again closed his good eye.

Fifteen minutes later the car pulled alongside the curb and stopped by a sign pointing the way to the hospital's emergency room. Without saying a word, Li got out of the car and walked toward the sliding-glass doors, not turning back to look at the car.

***

Two times during the fifteen minutes she had been trapped in the trunk, Kelli had succumbed to a wave of claustrophobic panic. When the Koreans had slammed the trunk closed, anxiety had flooded over her and she'd instantly started screaming and breathing through her nose in such short breaths she'd hyperventilated, blacking out. As her unconscious body had taken control and her breathing returned to normal, she'd jerked awake with a start, only to let the confined blackness overcome her and cause her to pass out again. The third time, as fear washed over her, she'd curled into the fetal position and instinctively tried to hide her face with her hands. That's when she had realized the stupidity of her captors. They had taped her wrists securely, but they had left her arms in front of her rather than placed them behind her back.

Now, as the car pulled away from wherever it had stopped, Kelli forced herself to take a deep breath and fight off a fresh wave of panic. Using her numb fingers, she gripped a small corner of the duct tape and slowly peeled it from her mouth. For a long moment she laid still, her eyes closed against the darkness, simply licking her lips and breathing through her mouth. As fear again welled up within her, she began frantically twisting her arms and hands, trying to work her wrists free of the silver tape. In desperation, she began gnawing at the thick layers of tape with her teeth. A fraction of an inch at a time, she managed to slide a single tooth between her skin and the tape and sever it. Soon her hands were free. In the confines of the trunk, unraveling the tape from her ankles took only a little longer.

Desperate to be free of the coffin-like space, she began feeling around the sides of the trunk in search of the small emergency safety latch that would release the trunk. "Come on," she said softly, "I know it's here somewhere." And then her cold fingers touched the tiny plastic handle, and she closed her eyes and sighed in relief. The next time they stopped, she would get out.

As the forward movement of the car began slowing, Kelli grasped the plastic handle firmly in both hands and waited. The instant the car came to a complete stop, she yanked the handle. There was a dull pop as the locking mechanism released, but the lid didn't spring open as she'd expected. Panicked, she tugged again on the handle with one hand and pressed against the lid with the other. The lid rose just enough that Kelli could see out. As the car again began moving forward, Kelli gave the lid an adrenaline-charged shove, and in a half-roll, half-leap, pushed herself up and out of the trunk, landing on her knees on the road. Grimacing, she struggled to her feet and forced her stiff, cold legs to begin moving toward two dim headlights that were very slowly approaching her.

With snow pelting her face, Kelli ran toward the lights, her nearly numb feet stinging with pain every time they struck the ground. Still less than half the distance to the oncoming car lights, her lungs began burning, rebelling at having to suck in gasps of the bitter-cold air. Fifty steps later her legs and lungs gave out completely, and she crumpled to the ground, sending up a plume of snow as she slid to the side of the road. Wiping snow from her face, Kelli pushed herself to her knees as the slow-moving car's headlights swept past her. Screaming for help, she struggled to her feet and began chasing the car. It was an easy chase. The car was moving only slightly faster than a rapid walk.

Grabbing the door handle with her right hand, Kelli began pounding on the passenger window with her left as she chased beside the moving car. "Please help me," she screamed. "Please, please, let me in the car. You must help me."

It took the driver only a split second to react. Even though the snow-frosted figure trotting beside the car looked more like a snowman than a woman, her eyes instantly lit with recognition.

Slamming on the brakes and skidding the Impala to a stop, the driver shifted the car into park, unfastened her seatbelt, reached across the seat, and popped up the door lock. Instantly, Kelli was inside the car, and in a single motion, she yanked the door closed and punched down the lock.

Looking over at the driver, Kelli recognized Rexene Gilger, who wrinkled her forehead as she quickly studied the snow-covered person beside her, as if she was trying to dredge from memory the name of the former high school student. Suddenly her eyes popped wider open. "Kell—" she started to say, but that was as far as she got.

A gloved fist hammered against Rexene's window, and a man's voice yelled, "Open the door! Now!" Simultaneously, another person began yanking on the passenger-door handle and screaming, "Open the door! Open the door!"

Inside the car, Kelli screamed hysterically and, motioning with her arms, yelled, "Drive! Drive! Drive! They're trying to kill me!"

For an eighty-someodd-year-old grandma caught in a blizzard with two men yelling and pounding on the outside of her car while a hysterical girl was screaming on the inside, Rexene Gilger reacted with surprising calmness. Looking quickly at the two men outside and back at Kelli, she shifted the car into gear and mashed the gas pedal. The result surprised everyone. The car went nowhere. The studded snow tires spun wildly, churning through the snow as quickly as a hot knife sliced through butter, but the car didn't move an inch. Shifting the car into reverse, Rexene again stomped the gas pedal to the floor. As the engine raced, the tires spun, coating the two men outside in a shower of snow. But not finding anything but slippery snow for traction, the old car remained motionless.

A grin formed on the man's face who had been banging on Rexene's window. Stepping closer to the window, he screamed, "Give us the girl and we'll let you go. Do you understand? Just give us the girl; that's all we want."

Rexene looked over at Kelli, who stared back with eyes the size of saucers. "Please, no. Please, no," she screamed, shaking her head wildly. "They kidnapped me and want to kill me."

Then Rexene did something she had presumably never done before. Reaching inside her purse, she pulled out a pistol and cranked her window down less than an inch. Leaning back lest the man try and reach through to grab her, she hollered, "What did you say?"

When the man leaned down to look inside, she raised the pistol and squeezed the trigger a single time. Inside the car, the pistol's bark was deafening. The bullet did its work.

Dropping the pistol beside her onto her seat, Rexene shifted the car into drive and pressed on the gas pedal. This time she pressed gently, allowing the steel studs and deep lugs in the tires to bite into the snow. Kelly looked at the men outside as, slowly, the heavy Impala crept forward, leaving one man lying in snow that was turning crimson and the second man standing over him.

Shaking, Kelli looked over at her rescuer in relieved awe. Rexene didn't look back as she guided the car along what wasn't quite the middle of the street. A long moment later she eased off the gas pedal as two dim red tail lights came into view. Without stopping, she eased around the car with its trunk and both front doors wide open. Instead of turning right toward her home, Rexene turned left.

CHAPTER THIRTY-FOUR

KELLI SHIFTED IN THE METAL chair, pulling the thin gray blanket more tightly around her shoulders with one hand while cradling a cup of steaming hot chocolate in the other. With the blanket arranged, she held the cup in both hands and savored the heat of the cup as it warmed her icy-cold fingers. Blowing gently, she put the cup to her lips and took a tentative sip. Satisfied it wouldn't scald her mouth, she took a mouthful of the liquid. As the hot chocolate worked its way down her throat, the tenseness in her body began to melt, and her shoulders relaxed.

"Feeling better?" the uniformed policewoman asked empathetically.

Kelli nodded. "Yes, thanks," she replied barely loud enough to be heard. "Where's Rexene?"

"She's safe," the policewoman replied. "She's in another part of the building giving a statement about what happened."

Kelli gave a quick smile and then took another sip of hot chocolate. "She saved my life."

The policewoman nodded. "From what you've told me, it sounds that way."

"Can I see her? I want to thank her again."

The policewoman shook her head. "Not tonight. She's a bit rattled. When she's finished talking with our detectives, we'll take her home. I'll try to get a phone number for her so you can call her tomorrow."

A thirty-something-year-old man with brown hair, steel-gray eyes, and a body-builder physique eased along a row of desks and walked to where Kelli was sitting.

Holding out a not-so-fluffy white towel, he said, "I'll hold your hot chocolate, and you can use this to dry your hair. I've seen wet cats that look better than you do right now."

Kelli looked at the proffered towel and then up at the man's neutral expression. After a moment's hesitation, she exchanged the cup for the towel. Putting the towel over her head, she vigorously rubbed her short hair, shook her head a couple of times, and then wiped her face and neck. "Thanks," she said, holding out the now-damp towel.

"I'm Detective Steve Gwilliam," he said calmly, accepting the towel and handing Kelli the cup of hot chocolate.

"Thanks," Kelli repeated and took another sip.

"You feeling good enough to talk for a few minutes?" the detective said.

Kelli nodded but said nothing.

"Good," Gwilliam said, rolling a desk chair across the floor and plopping down so they were sitting almost knee to knee. "Let's start with how you came to be riding around in the trunk of a car on snowy night."

Kelli nodded toward the policewoman and said, "I explained that to her a few minutes ago."

Gwilliam nodded. "I know, but I want to get it firsthand."

Kelli placed the cup of hot chocolate on the nearby desk and pulled the blanket more tightly around her. Speaking almost hesitantly, she began, "The man's name is Li, or at least that's what he told me."

Forty-five minutes and two dozen questions later, Gwilliam leaned back in his chair, ran his fingers through his gel-streaked hair, and said simply, "That's quite a story."

"You don't believe me, do you?"

Gwilliam looked into Kelli's eyes and hesitated. "It isn't that I don't believe you; it's that I'm having a difficult time sorting out why Li targeted you. No offense, Kelli, but there are a lot of people at INL in more"—he paused as if searching for the right word—"in more *delicate* positions than you. Trust me; I've had to deal with a few of the people out there in my professional capacity. They may be brilliant, but some of them have serious behavioral issues they would not want publicized. Why blackmail you rather than one of them?"

"I'm not sure," Kelli said, shaking her head.

"Not sure?" Gwilliam asked, furrowing his brow. "Does that mean you have an idea?"

Kelli shrugged. "When it comes down to it, I'm a pretty low-level nobody there. I know that. There are all these brainy people walking around in starched white coats, their pockets filled with pens and their eyeglasses perched on the ends of their noses. Every day they go to the same building, to the same office, and to the same laboratory. But with me, it's different. Even though I'm an inconsequential nobody, my security pass allows me to go lots of places without raising suspicion about why I'm there. All those important people see me without really seeing me, if you know what I mean. Think about the person who empties your trashcan every day. You see him but don't really pay much attention to him. The security people see me and wave, never questioning why I'm there. The brainy people dismiss me with a condescending smile and go about their important stuff. I'm so low on the totem pole I don't even warrant a second glance, let alone suspicion."

Gwilliam folded his arms across his chest and thought for a minute. "So you think this Li guy wants you to escort him someplace or do something you wouldn't be suspected of doing?"

Kelli suddenly grew tense with worry. "Maybe I shouldn't be telling you all this. Are you going to arrest me?"

Still leaning back in his chair, Gwilliam shrugged his shoulders and said, "I don't know. Up to this point, you haven't told me you've done anything illegal. Unethical, maybe, but not illegal."

Kelli returned Gwilliam's gaze, carefully considering what he had just said. After a long pause she finally said, "I've thought a lot about it the past several days. The fact is I don't really know what they want."

"No ideas?" Gwilliam prodded.

Kelli hesitated. "I don't think it's Li who needs to get somewhere. I think it's someone or something they need to get access to."

"What makes you think that?"

"Li is Asian, but I'm not sure of his specific nationality. The day after tomorrow we have a large delegation of people coming to tour the facility."

"Asian?" Gwilliam guessed.

Kelli shook her head. "The schedule says they're from all over the world—China, Korea, India, Russia, Japan, Canada, Australia, Mexico, England—just about everywhere. They're nuclear scientists; supposedly, they are touring several different facilities in the United States and other countries."

"Why?" Gwilliam asked.

Kelli shook her head. "I don't know." Shrugging her shoulders, she said, "That's not something I'm entitled to know; again, it's above my height on the totem pole."

"Got ya," Gwilliam said with a knowing smile.

"All Li told me is that he had one simple task for me to perform. Once I did it, he said I would never hear from him again."

"Simple task?" Gwilliam said. "What simple task could you do better than anyone else?"

Kelli didn't have a chance to answer. From across the room an overweight policeman called out, "Gwilliam?"

"Over here, Jerry," Gwilliam said, raising his hand in the air.

Jerry forded his way across the sea of vacant desks in more of a waddle than a walk. Coming to a stop beside Gwilliam, he said, "No luck. We broadcast an alert to all the patrol cars, but it's a zoo out there. There are so many accidents and stuck cars we're running from one crisis to the next. It'll be pure luck if we happened to see the car she was riding in. Besides, the only description we have is that it was a car with two Asian guys in it. It's not much to go on," he said with a shrug.

Gwilliam frowned and said, "Thanks. I appreciate the effort."

"What about hospitals?" Kelli interrupted. "Li's eye was injured. I'm sure he needed medical help," she said, rubbing the sharp edge of her fingernail. "And the guy Rexene shot is either dead or wounded."

The rotund officer shook his head. "The emergency rooms are flooded with people from car wrecks, so it's a little difficult, but so far nobody named Li has turned up, and definitely no gunshot victims. It would help if we had a license number or the make, model, and color of the car."

Gwilliam looked at Kelli and raised his eyebrows. "Can you give us anything more? Color, make, or model? Name or emblem? Anything?" he asked.

"I don't know cars," she answered. "But I do know it was dark green."

"License plate?" Gwilliam asked. "Did you see it?"

Kelli frowned. "Sort of," Kelli answered. "It wasn't an Idaho plate; I know that."

"How?"

"Idaho plates are red and begin with a number followed by a letter, like *1F* or *2B*, and then a series of numbers. When they shoved me into the trunk, I remember seeing the plate was light-colored and had two groups of letters and numbers. The first three were numbers, and the last three were letters. Like *123 ABC*."

Jerry perked up slightly. "Could be a Utah plate," he said. "How about letters or numbers? Do you remember any?"

Kelli wrinkled her forehead. "Only two," she said. "There was a *K* and an *M*."

"How do you remember that?" Gwilliam asked as though simultaneously impressed and surprised.

"When I rolled out of the trunk, my hand brushed the back of the car and knocked some snow off the plate. I remember thinking the *K* was for Kelli and the *M* was for Marc."

"Marc?" Gwilliam asked.

"My dad's name."

Jerry inclined his head, nodding. "Well, at least that's something—not much, but it's more than we had five minutes ago. I'll see what I can do."

Gwilliam nodded. "Thanks, Jerry. Let me know."

"Sure, but don't expect too much," Jerry called over his shoulder as he walked toward a candy-dispensing machine.

After Jerry was out of earshot, Kelli asked, "What about my father?"

Gwilliam sighed, rubbed his hand over his short stubble of a beard and said candidly, echoing Jerry's words, "We don't have much to go on. Based on the description you gave from the photograph, that seedy motel room—if that's what it was—could be in any of a couple dozen motels in the city. And that's only in Idaho Falls. He might be in Blackfoot, Pocatello, Arco, or a dozen other small towns around here."

"You've got to get people checking them," Kelli demanded.

Gwilliam huffed. "Take a peek out that window," he said. "We don't have the manpower. Every guy we've got is out dealing with stupid motorists who won't stay off the snowy streets. You heard Jerry; our guys are running from wreck to wreck."

Up until that moment Kelli had managed to keep her emotions in check, but the reality of Gwilliam's statement crashed down on her like an avalanche, and she suddenly lost it. She didn't begin wailing uncontrollably or fly into a hysterical rage. Instead, her chin dropped, her shoulders sagged, and the arms that had kept the blanket pulled tightly around her dropped to her lap. As the blanket slipped from her shoulders, tears rolled down her cheeks and dripped onto her lap.

Gwilliam watched Kelli sob almost silently for a moment before he stood up and walked to a nearby desk. Picking up a box of tissues, he returned to where Kelli sat and held it out to her.

Kelli pulled out three tissues and mumbled, "Thanks."

Gwilliam set the box of tissues on the desk beside Kelli and watched as she daubed at her eyes with the tissue, trying to avoid streaking what was left of her makeup. Considering her frizzy hair, dirt-streaked cheeks, and wet clothes, the gesture was absurd, but it was a habit.

"Look," Gwilliam said with a certain amount of finality. "I'm not sure there's much more you can tell us or that we can do at this point. Do you have someplace safe you can go? Someplace besides your apartment?"

Kelli looked up through watery eyes but didn't nod or shake her head; she just looked.

"Your parents' place? A friend's? A boyfriend's?" Gwilliam asked. "Any place?"

After a long moment, she finally nodded. "I have two close friends; they share an apartment. They'd probably let me crash at their place for a couple of days," she choked out between sobs.

Gwilliam slid a desk phone to her and said, "Call them." Then, looking at the policewoman standing near Kelli, he said, "Get an officer to take her to her apartment for some clothes and then take her to her friends' place."

The policewoman pointed outside and said, "It's going to be a while before we can shake somebody loose to do it; how about you take her?"

Gwilliam shook his head. "Can't. I've been told I have to attend a late-night meeting, and I won't have time." Then, looking at Kelli, he said, "I'll be in touch."

CHAPTER THIRTY-FIVE

Hovey looked at the 12:45 a.m. displayed on his digital watch. He, Nichols, and Pulsipher had made the trip from Preston to the INL general office on Fremont Street in Idaho Falls in six hours. On a snow-free night, the drive would have taken them less than two. As Pulsipher guided the black Suburban into a space between an unmarked police car and an SUV with the INL logo on the door, he blew out an exhausted sigh of relief and leaned his head back against the headrest. "I'm beat," he said.

Hovey again glanced at his watch and said, "Buck up, Pulsipher; we're fifteen minutes late, and they're waiting for us."

"Give the guy a break," Nichols said as he reached for his door handle. "You've been back there snoozing for hours, and he's been up here doing battle with the snow."

Hovey ignored the comment and grabbed the leather computer bag beside him. Shoving his door open, he sucked in a quick gasp of air when the stinging wind and blowing snow assaulted him. "I hate snow," he grumbled.

Three minutes after being hustled through the security area, the three men were led down a brightly lit corridor to a glass-enclosed conference room. Ten people were already seated around the table; some were chatting, a few were sitting with their eyes closed, and a couple of people were using their phones. Everybody was dressed casually, some of them a bit disheveled.

As the three agents entered the conference room, a trim man with graying hair stood up and extended his hand to Hovey. "I'm David Sweeny, manager of security here at INL."

Hovey pumped the extended hand and said, "Wayne Hovey. And this is Larry Nichols and Chris Pulsipher."

"How was the drive?" Sweeny asked.

"Delightful," Pulsipher replied. "Really wonderful weather you have here in Idaho."

Sweeny chuckled. "Yeah, sometimes we get a real snowstorm—not just these little squalls." Then, turning to Hovey, he said, "Well, this is everyone you asked for plus a couple more. It's your show."

Nichols and Pulsipher each found vacant chairs on the far side of the table while Hovey laid his bag on the table next to Sweeny. He didn't need to ask people to be quiet; nobody was speaking, and everyone was looking at him. "I'm Wayne Hovey, Special Agent from the FBI's Miami office." He pointed to Nichols and Pulsipher and introduced them. "Although you might all know each other, it would be helpful if we can take a minute to go around the table so you can introduce yourselves and the organizations you're with. Let's start here," he said, pointing to the man seated on Sweeny's left.

Virtually every law enforcement agency in southeastern Idaho was represented, from the FBI office in Idaho Falls to the tribal police of the Shoshone-Bannock tribe, and not one of them was wearing a happy expression.

"Well," Hovey said after the introductions were finished, "I guess I need to begin by thanking you for being here. There's no uncomplicated way to explain why we're here and what we're concerned about, so I'll dive in."

Pulling his laptop computer from the leather bag, he powered it on and connected it to a projector sitting on the table. A couple of keystrokes later, a very clear image of Scott Vaughn appeared on a large screen. "This is Scott Vaughn. For the past eighteen months he has been the number one priority of the Miami office, and he's the reason we're here tonight." Reaching into his bag, he pulled out a thick folder and dropped it onto the table. "This is a complete psychological profile the FBI has worked up on him. You're welcome to read it later, but I want to emphasize that this man is extremely dangerous; he kills without remorse. If you encounter him, you should assume he will not hesitate to try to kill you."

Certain he now had everyone's attention, Hovey took a quick breath and launched into a brief synopsis about Vaughn, the Walkers, and the suitcase. He finished with, "So, without knowing anything for certain, we think it's possible, maybe even probable, that the suitcase contains something intended for someone or something within INL."

With that, the questions started. Maggie Tuller, an agent in the FBI's Idaho Falls office, asked, "Could it be a nuclear bomb?"

Hovey shook his head. "Impossible."

"A conventional bomb, then?" she said. "PETN, HMX, or RDX?"

"Sure, any of those are possible," Hovey said.

Tuller immediately turned to the INL's associate director, John Lewellen, and asked, "Is it possible a bomb could blow up radioactive materials stored here, and they would in turn cause a nuclear explosion?"

"No, it isn't," Lewellen replied matter-of-factly.

"Well, then, could a bomb explode the radioactive stuff you keep here and cause massive radioactive fallout?" she said.

Lewellen scrunch his face into a scowl and replied cautiously, "*Massive* is a relative expression."

"Wait a minute, wait a minute," the portly sheriff from Bonneville County interrupted. "Don't you store that stuff underground in bombproof bunkers?"

Lewellen gave an exhausted look, cleared his throat, and slowly said, "There aren't any bombproof bunkers at INL. Quite frankly, we've never considered the need for such a thing." Looking quickly around the table, he continued. "We do store some of the more unstable material in underground bunkers, but the majority—the vast majority—is stored aboveground in large metal warehouse-type buildings."

Agent Tuller jumped back in with, "Okay, so if a bomb of sufficient capacity destroyed one of the storage buildings, could radioactive material escape and contaminate people in Idaho Falls, Blackfoot, and the surrounding areas?"

Lewellen stared at Tuller for a long moment, chewed the inside of his lip, and finally said, "The bomb wouldn't need to *destroy* the building. It would only need to be powerful enough to cause the roof or walls to collapse. The steel girders would almost certainly puncture the containers, releasing—"

"How many buildings would they need to blow up to release the radiation? Ten? Twenty? Fifty?" the Bonneville sheriff asked.

Lewellen looked at the sheriff and softly replied, "One."

"One?" Tuller said incredulously.

Lewellen gave a single nod but said nothing more.

For about ten seconds the room was quiet. Then more questions began flying as rapidly as bullets from a machine gun.

"Why INL? Why not New York or Los Angeles, where they could kill more people?"

"Why not a nuclear power plant?"

"INL encompasses thousands of acres, with hundreds of buildings? What are the most likely targets?"

"Who would want to detonate a bomb, and what's the motive?"

"What security measures does INL have in place?"

"What is the FBI doing on a national level?"

"Have other federal agencies been briefed?"

In less than a minute the room was in total confusion.

When there was a brief pause in the barrage of questions, from the far corner of the room, Denny Long Standing Bear, with the tribal police, raised his hand. In a soft-spoken, measured voice he said, "Agent Hovey, you told us Vaughn picked up the suitcase in the Dominican Republic."

Hovey nodded. "That's right."

"How did it get there? Do you know?"

Hovey shook his head. "All we know is it was given to him by some men Asian men. We're assuming it has a Far East connection, but that's only an assumption."

Steve Gwilliam hadn't said a single word during the entire meeting. Suddenly, he leaned forward and said, "Asians?"

Hovey nodded.

"Earlier tonight we picked up a girl who works here at INL—Kelli Latimore. She had been abducted by three Asian men but managed to escape."

Suddenly, every eye turned to Gwilliam. He shifted slightly in his chair and said, "From what she says, over the past six months she has been blackmailed to provide information about some of the facilities here."

Associate Director Lewellen practically flew out of his chair. "Which facilities? If we know which ones they're interested in, I can tell you if their plan will succeed. And we can also be better prepared."

Gwilliam shook his head. "No idea," he said.

Hovey looked at Gwilliam and asked, "Do you know where this girl is? Can we meet with her?"

"I know where she was a few hours ago."

CHAPTER THIRTY-SIX

MARENA'S HAND THROBBED FROM HER wound, but she was far more concerned about the murderer in the middle of the back seat. Greg sat rigidly in the driver's seat, his knuckles white as he gripped the steering wheel and strained to see through the avalanche of snowflakes that pelted the windshield. "I've gotta stop and clean the wipers off," he said, looking in the rearview mirror at Vaughn.

"No," Vaughn replied. "Keep driving."

"Are you crazy?" Marena exclaimed, only half turning around. "The wipers are crusted with ice and doing virtually nothing. Look out there. We need to stop and clean them off."

Leaning forward and squinting to see through the snow-streaked windshield, Greg said, "You're the guy with the gun and you're calling the shots, but in another two or three minutes, I won't be able see well enough to drive."

In her half-turned position, Marena could see Vaughn studying the back of her husband's head before looking out the windows into the totally black night. "Okay, you can stop," Vaughn said, leaning forward and placing the barrel of the gun at the base of Marena's skull. She tensed and gripped the door handle. "But if you're not back inside this truck in thirty seconds, some part of your wife is going to get shot."

Greg said nothing as he let off the gas pedal and allowed the Tahoe to slow on its own. Marena looked over at him, gave a weak smile, and said, "Hurry."

The Tahoe had barely coasted to a stop before Greg shoved open the door and bailed out. With bare hands, he brushed the ice-crusted snow from the windshield and cleaned one wiper blade. Scurrying around to

Marena's side, he repeated the actions and started back to his own door, stopping briefly to chip away a thin layer of ice that coated the headlights. Climbing back into the Tahoe, he brushed snow from his shoulders and head.

"How much farther?" Vaughn asked as he lowered the gun.

Marena looked at him and felt a small measure of satisfaction when he saw him flinch in pain. "How do I know?" Greg retorted. "I don't have the faintest idea how far we've come." Shifting the Tahoe into gear, he added, "I'm not sure we're even still on the road."

"I've been watching," Vaughn said. "You've been averaging about twenty miles per hour. We've been going for almost four hours, so we should be almost to Blackfoot."

"Yeah, well, that would be fine if we were on the freeway, but we're not. We're wandering these county roads, and it's a lot farther. We're lucky we've made it this far without getting stuck on the side of the road."

Marena abruptly turned to look at Vaughn fully. "Why are you doing this?"

"Doing what?" Vaughn replied.

"This!" Marena said, trembling. "All of it. Why Wiggy Wiggy? Why are you making us drive you to Arco? Why are going to kill us? What's so important in that suitcase?"

Vaughn seemed to consider her questions. After a short pause, he answered with a single word, "Money."

"How much are you getting paid?" she asked, filled with disgust.

"Enough," Vaughn answered.

Marena looked briefly at Greg before saying, "Let us go, and we'll give you more. We're not rich, but we have money."

Vaughn burst out a loud laugh. "Lady, you don't have enough money."

"How much is enough?" she asked.

"Shut up and turn around," Vaughn answered testily. "This conversation isn't going anywhere."

She obeyed but only turned back partially so she could still watch him out of the corners of her eyes. Vaughn reached inside his jacket pocket and pulled out his cell phone. He frowned as he looked at the display. Greg must have caught sight of him in the mirror because he said, "There isn't going to be any phone reception out here, so you might as well stop checking your phone."

Vaughn looked up at Greg's reflection in the mirror and said, "I'm not trying to make a call; I was checking to see if my GPS works." Then, in frustration, he said, "Why don't you have a GPS in this outfit?"

Greg shook his head. "Don't need one. The only time I drive this is when I know where I'm going."

"Yeah, well, smart guy, this is one time when you don't know, isn't it?"

"Oh, I know where I'm going; I just don't know if we'll get there," Greg replied.

"Just shut up and drive, will ya?" Vaughn half shouted, shoving his phone back into his pocket and rubbing his knee.

A couple of minutes passed in silence, and then Marena said again, "How much?"

"How much what?" Vaughn said.

"How much does someone pay you to kill people and deliver a suitcase?"

"You ask too many questions," Vaughn snarled.

"It must bother you—killing people and always looking over your shoulder, wondering if someone is going to come after you," she pressed.

Vaughn looked at Marena and replied, "I stopped being bothered by killing people a very long time ago."

"You won't get away with it. You know that, don't you?" she said.

"With what?"

"Killing us," Marena said.

Vaughn again broke out in laughter. "Lady, there isn't the slightest doubt in my mind I'll get away with it. That's the easy part."

"What if we promise not to tell anyone about you or what happened in the Dominican Republic? Will you let us go?"

Greg and Vaughn both stared over at Marena with a look that said they could hardly believe what she had just asked. Then Greg returned his focus to the road.

"Now, that's a novel idea," Vaughn said sardonically. Then, with even more sarcasm, he added, "I'm really surprised I didn't think of that myself." Shaking his head, he continued. "For some reason, I have a really difficult time believing you'd keep your word."

"You're both right," Greg said. "You'll never get away with killing us, and we'd never keep our word. You're pure slime, Vaughn; you deserve a firing squad or to rot in prison somewhere."

Vaughn leaned forward and viciously slammed the pistol's butt into the back of Greg's head. The blow knocked Greg unconscious, and as his body went slack, he slumped forward against the steering wheel, his right foot jamming down on the gas pedal. The sudden surge of power caused the Tahoe's wheels to lose what little traction they had in the snow, and the SUV instantly began fishtailing erratically.

Marena and Vaughn reacted in the same way, both reaching to pull Greg's slumped body away from the steering wheel.

"Get his foot off the gas pedal!" Vaughn shouted as the Tahoe careened right and then left in ever-larger arcs.

Marena reached out to pull on Greg's leg, but the erratic movement of the vehicle caused her seatbelt to lock up, stopping her three inches shy of his leg. Vaughn instantly realized Marena's predicament and shouted, "Undo your seatbelt!"

Marena looked from Vaughn to Greg and then down at the seatbelt buckle. In the split second between her decision to punch the button on her seatbelt and actually doing it, the Tahoe left the road, slid sideways down a slight embankment, and came to an abrupt stop, pinned against a scrubby cedar tree. With the motor still racing and the tires spinning, Marena shouted at Vaughn, "You idiot!" Straining against her still-fastened seatbelt, she grasped the ignition key and turned it, silencing the engine.

While Vaughn sank back in his seat and heaved a sigh, Marena frantically undid her seatbelt and took Greg's face in her hands. "Greg. Greg, can you hear me?" Not waiting for a response, she picked up his wrist and felt for a pulse, heaving a sigh of her own. "Well, at least you didn't kill him," she snarled at Vaughn as she felt the flow of blood in his wrist. Tapping Greg's cheek lightly with her fingers, she said, "Greg, honey, come on, wake up."

Greg let out a groggy moan and moved his head slightly. "Come on, Greg," Marena encouraged softly, using her fingers to raise his head.

Slowly, Greg opened his eyes, and even more slowly, he placed his hand on the back of his head. Gently rubbing the lump that was forming, he closed his eyes and slumped forward.

CHAPTER THIRTY-SEVEN

LI LAY ON THE SMALL examination table in the emergency room, no doubt looking like a war casualty. A huge pad of white gauze covered his right eye, and the petite physician was taping over the gauze what looked like a plastic bubble. "You must leave this protective plastic cover in place for the next twenty-four hours," the woman said as she taped it to his face. Pulling another piece of bright-yellow tape from the dispenser, she said, "You're a very lucky man. Just five millimeters higher, and you would be permanently blind. As it is, your condition is temporary. You said it was metal from a car wreck?"

Li nodded.

"Well, there aren't any metal fragments or slivers still in your eye, so again, you're very lucky. The anesthetic I used on your eye will wear off in an hour or so, and you may feel some discomfort. This cover will prevent you from rubbing it, especially when you sleep. I'll prescribe some eye drops you'll need to use. Do you understand?"

Li managed a soft, "Yes," and gave a weak smile.

"Okay, then. It looks like I'm finished here. A nurse will be in shortly to give you further instructions and a prescription for pain. After that, you'll have a visit from someone from the billing office who will discuss payment options. Once they're finished, you're free to go. Please be certain to check with your personal doctor as soon as possible. He or she will advise you on further treatment options. Of course, if you experience any bleeding or extreme pain in the next twenty-four hours, do not hesitate to return here."

Li smiled again, said, "Thank you for your services," and sat up.

Just as the physician had predicted, a nurse and the billing clerk showed up, but in reverse order. The billing clerk stuck her head through the partially opened door and said, "Mr. Jones?"

Li gave her a confused look and said, "Huh?"

"Are you Mr. Lee Jones?"

It took Li a moment to recall that Jones was the fictitious name he had used when he'd registered. "Oh, sorry," he said. "Yes, I'm Mr. Jones."

The clerk methodically reviewed each of the charges shown on her computer printout and asked Li if he had any questions. When Li replied that he did not, she asked, "How would you like to pay for these charges today?"

"Will you accept cash?" Li asked in a subdued voice.

The clerk looked at Li as if he had three eyes and stammered, "Uh, sure, I guess so. You're the first person who's ever offered to pay with cash." Then, wrinkling her forehead slightly, she said, "You do understand your bill is slightly over twelve hundred dollars, don't you?"

Li gave a condescending smile and replied, "Twelve hundred and two to be exact, you said." Pulling a money clip from the front pocket of his trousers, he counted out the exact amount and handed the clerk the cash.

The clerk was leaving as the nurse appeared—her clipboard in hand—and reviewed the doctor's orders in detail. Li scribbled a completely indecipherable signature on each of the three pages of instructions the nurse reviewed with him. "Do you have someone coming to pick you up?" she asked politely. "Because of the medicines you have been given, you should not drive for the next twelve hours."

"Yes, someone will be here shortly," Li replied.

"Great. You're welcome to wait in the lobby, but we need this room. We're swamped with patients. I'll get you a wheelchair."

"That won't be necessary. I'm able to walk."

The nurse frowned and said, "Really, I think a wheelchair would be best."

Li shook his head and snapped, "No. That isn't necessary. I can walk."

The nurse recoiled slightly and said, "Okay, then. Would you like help putting on your coat?"

"No, I can manage," Li replied.

The nurse raised her eyebrows and said almost formally, "Then, I'll just escort you to the lobby."

Li walked into the lobby, and the nurse finally left as he scanned the faces of the dozens of people sitting and standing in the crowded waiting room. He frowned. Wanting fresh air to help clear his head, he walked out the emergency-room doors and stood under an awning, hunching his shoulders against the cold. A few seconds later his cell phone chirped.

"Where are you?" Li demanded as he put the phone to his ear.

"There has been a problem," the voice on the other end of the phone said.

Li paused, swallowed, and asked, "What kind of problem?"

There was a long silence before the voice said, "Seok is dead. The girl has escaped."

Li closed his one good eye and shook his head as he tipped it slightly upward. After a moment he asked, "How?"

"Shot," the voice answered.

"What?" Li exclaimed loudly, startling a woman who was rushing past with a baby in her arms.

"She had an accomplice," the voice said defensively.

Li shook his head, trying to clear the light covering of drug-induced fog that still floated around in his brain. "Impossible," he muttered. Taking a deep breath, he asked, "Where are you, and where is Seok's body?"

"Look straight ahead, and you will see me pulling up toward the curb."

Li looked up, saw the car, and disconnected the call. Pulling his coat up around his neck, he walked out from under the awning and into the swirling snow. The blast of crisp, cold air was like a slap in the face and shook some of the grogginess from his brain. Yanking open the car door, he cautiously lowered himself into the seat and said, "Explain everything."

Li sat almost immobile for ten minutes, listening carefully to each word as it poured from Hwan's mouth. When the man was finished, Li took another deep breath. Looking at his watch, he calculated the time difference between Idaho Falls and North Korea and shook his head. He would wait for at least two hours before placing the call. Getting the general out of bed to report bad news was never a good idea.

"Where is the girl's father?"

"At the same motel where we left him," Hwan replied.

"And Seok?" Li asked.

The driver jerked his head toward the back of the car. "In the trunk."

Li nodded. "Take me to the girl's father. Someone must pay for this. Then we will dispose of both bodies."

It took nearly thirty minutes for Hwan and Li to make their way from the hospital to the sleazy motel. As they rounded the final corner, Li hissed out a Korean profanity. "Keep driving—slowly! Do not stop."

Two Idaho Falls police cars were parked helter-skelter in front of the forest-green door of the motel. A third car, its flashing blue lights making the falling snowflakes sparkle like a mirror ball, was parked in front of the office door. As Li and the driver slowly eased along the street, a fourth car pulled in beside the first two, and a man stepped out of the driver's-side door while a young girl jumped out of the passenger door and ran to room seven.

Li swore, this time in English and Korean. "It's the girl!" he exclaimed. "It's Kelli."

"How did they . . . ?" Hwan asked, his voice trailing off before he finished his sentence.

Li looked over at Hwan and hissed, "What difference does it make? They found him. And now they have the girl." Rubbing his good eye, Li sighed very deeply. "What else could possibly go wrong?" he muttered. Looking at his watch, he again mentally calculated what time it was in Korea. Only thirty minutes had passed since the last time he'd made the calculations. He would need to make the call, but perhaps he could put it off until tomorrow. Shaking his head, he looked out his window at the scene in the motel parking lot and said, "Drive to Arco."

CHAPTER THIRTY-EIGHT

The bright headlights materialized so suddenly it was like they fell from the sky in a snowflake. One minute there was nothing but black night filled with wind-driven snowflakes, and the next, white headlights glowed brightly. Only a few seconds after that, flashing red and blue strobe lights lit up the sky. Li pulled the collar of his jacket around his neck as he said, "Remain silent. I will do all the talking."

Hwan nodded as he backed slightly away from the car.

A moment later an overweight Idaho State Trooper emerged from his pickup and slipped and slid his way to where Li and Hwan were standing beside their car. "You hurt?" the trooper asked anxiously, pointing at Li's bandaged eye.

Li raised his hand to the plastic bubble shielding his eye and said, "I had eye surgery for cataracts earlier today. I am fine." Then, pointing to the car, he added, "But we are stuck."

"What happened?" the trooper asked, although it was obvious.

"We lost control and skidded off the side of the road."

The trooper looked Li and Hwan over hurriedly and pulled his coat tighter around himself.

"Can you help us?" Li asked. "I think a slight pull is all it will take."

The trooper shook his head. "I'm not allowed to pull you—too much liability if I damage your car. But I can use my radio to call a wrecker for you."

Li gave an involuntary shiver against the cold. "Where is the nearest wrecker?"

"Arco," the trooper replied.

Li frowned. "How long will it take to get here?"

"Depends," the trooper said, raising his shoulders and hunching his back against the blowing snow assaulting his pudgy neck. "There's only one wrecker in town, and on a night like this, I image he's got more business than he can handle."

Li hunched his shoulders against the snow and cold as he looked at the trooper. "What if we agree you will not be responsible for any damage? Will you then pull us out?"

The trooper shook his head. "Sorry. Can't do it."

Li shook his head. "Well, then, is there any way you can check to see how long it will be before the wrecker can pull us out?" Li asked.

"That I can do," the trooper replied. "But there's no sense in you standing out in the snow. If you want to turn your car off to save gas, you can wait in my truck."

Li shook his head. "No, that isn't necessary. We will wait in our car. It's very warm, and we have plenty of fuel."

The trooper shrugged, turned around, and worked his way toward his truck. When he was out of earshot, Li turned to Hwan and said sternly, "Get in the car."

Five long minutes later the trooper opened the door of his pickup, but instead of walking toward Li's car, he walked to the back of his pickup truck. Watching in the rearview mirror, Li saw him return from the back of his truck with a long length of heavy tow chain and walk toward Li and Hwan.

"I think he's going to pull us out," Hwan said as the trooper slowly approached the car.

"Stay in here; I will talk to him," Li said, quickly opening the door and stepping into the storm.

"This is your lucky day," the trooper said as he neared Li and the front of the car. "It'll be at least three hours before the wrecker can get to you, and I'm not allowed to leave you until assistance arrives. There's just been a car rollover with serious injuries back toward Idaho Falls, and I'm the only person who's available to respond." Extending the end of the chain to Li, he said, "I won't hook this to your car because I don't want to be responsible for damages, but if you want to hook it up, I'll pull you out."

Li didn't hesitate. Taking the end of the chain, he walked to the front of the car and dropped to his knees. Behind him the trooper said, "Don't tell me you guys drove all the way up from Utah in this storm."

Li lay on the ground, trying to find a sturdy part of the car's frame to attach the chain to. "No," he replied honestly. "It is a rental car. My friend drove up from Salt Lake a few days ago." Then, after a pause, he said, "There. I think that will work," and stood up, brushing snow from his pants and coat.

Five minutes later Hwan and Li were back on the road, headed to Arco, and the trooper was headed in the opposite direction toward Idaho Falls. Two hours after that, Hwan and Li pulled into a nearly deserted motel in Arco.

***

Jerry Thompson of the Idaho Falls Police Department had issued an all-points bulletin for a dark-green Ford Taurus registered to the Hertz Corporation, with its Utah license plate number. The occupants, two Asian males, one possibly wearing a heavy bandage over his eye, were wanted for questioning in connection with a kidnapping and were to be considered armed and dangerous.

It had taken a total of four hours before the accident was cleaned up and the trooper who had towed a stuck rental car two hours before was back in his pickup truck. Three hours after that, while sitting in his pickup eating a ham and cheese sandwich and swilling a soda, the trooper scanned the messages on his computer. Tossing the partially eaten sandwich onto the dashboard, he picked up his phone and placed a call.

***

Li punched a small button on his wristwatch to silence an alarm. He had had a fitful few hours of sleep. Hwan lay in one bed, snoring loudly, while Li lay in the other, his mind jumping back and forth between the pain in his eye and the contingency plan his masters in Korea had engineered months ago. Everything would have been so easy if only Kelli had cooperated. But all was not lost. The contingency plan was more complicated and would require more of Li and Hwan, but success was at their fingertips. All that remained was taking the suitcase delivery, and as long as that happened by no later than ten o'clock in the morning, success was assured.

Hwan stirred and groaned. "I am not well," he said.

Li rolled over, momentarily forgetting his injured eye until the plastic bubble snagged on the pillow. Raising his head from the pillow, he asked without sympathy, "What's wrong?"

Hwan slowly lowered the blankets from around his head. Reaching up, he began massaging his temples with the tips of his fingers. "My head aches, and I have chills," Hwan replied, closing his eyes.

"You're coming down with a cold," Li replied dismissively. "It's nothing."

Hwan rose from his bed and shuffled into the bathroom, noisily closing the door behind him. Twenty minutes later he emerged, freshly bathed but with a sniffling nose and watery eyes. He said nothing to Li as he walked to where his clothes laid, draped over the back of a chair. He shuddered as he slipped his leg into the slightly damp jeans and put on his shirt and socks.

Forty-five minutes later the two men were sitting in their room at a scratched and wobbly table, a dozen papers and photos scattered before them. Hwan wiped his dripping nose with a piece of toilet tissue and asked, "Do you believe the girl has told them of our plans?"

Li shook his head without looking up from the satellite photo he held in his hand. "She doesn't know our plan," he replied.

"She knows enough," Hwan said.

Li let the satellite image of the INL facility drop from his hand. "All she knows is we wanted access to a certain building. She has no idea why or when. And she knows absolutely nothing about our contingency plan."

"Still, I think it prudent to assume they know something will happen."

"If you want something to concern yourself about," Li snipped, "rehearse how you are going to wire the triggering device to the explosives now that Seok is dead."

Hwan was silent for a moment before asking, "Are you worried?"

Li reached up and pulled the cheap curtains away from the window, exposing the still blackness of the early morning. A single light shone from the top of a light pole in the small parking lot, sending out a triangular cone of light that illuminated thousands of snowflakes as they fell from the sky. "Look out there; of course I'm worried," he replied, letting the curtain fall back into place.

CHAPTER THIRTY-NINE

It took Greg nearly fifteen minutes of slipping in and out of consciousness before he finally managed to keep his eyes open and stop his head from imitating a bobblehead doll. The entire time, Vaughn and Marena had traded a flurry of hostile words, increasing the pounding that raged inside Greg's head.

"Come on, Walker," Vaughn finally spat at Greg. "We're wasting time. Start driving."

Greg rubbed his aching head and said, "You're really something, Vaughn. Look outside. We've slid sideways into a tree, there's a foot of snow on the ground, and we need to somehow claw our way back up the embankment. You think it's as easy as starting this thing up and driving out of here?"

"I think you're going to try," Vaughn replied, pointing the pistol at Marena. "Really hard."

Greg closed his eyes and sighed and then leaned forward and turned the key. The Tahoe's engine sparked to life, and Greg shifted it into gear. Then, pretending to adjust his sitting position, he surreptitiously turned the dial on the four-wheel drive control, disengaging the four-wheel drive. The Tahoe moved forward a quarter of an inch and stopped, the tires spinning in the deep snow. Greg frowned, shifted into reverse, and repeated his actions. Except for the spinning tires, the Tahoe sat motionless. "We're not going anywhere," Greg said, slamming the Tahoe into park.

"You didn't try very hard, Walker," Vaughn shot back. Placing the pistol inches from Marena's skull, he said, "Try harder."

Greg blew out an exasperated breath, gritted his teeth, and dropped the Tahoe into gear. Mashing the gas pedal to the floorboard, the Tahoe's wheels whined furiously, digging deeper into the snow and wedging the vehicle tighter against the cedar tree. Shifting into reverse, he did the same thing and got the same results. "Happy?" Greg exclaimed. "I can sit here and do this all night, but we're still not going anywhere."

Greg watched Vaughn in the rearview mirror as the man worked his jaw. After a moment he said, "Get out and dig."

"With what?" Greg spat back.

"Your hands, your feet—your teeth, for all I care. Just dig us out."

"You really are a southern boy, aren't you?" Greg replied. "Right now we have two choices. We find someone to tow us out, or we sit here. That's it. Those are our only choices," he said with finality. As his words hung in the air, Greg glanced over at Marena and tipped his head ever so slightly toward the instrument panel.

Greg watched Marena's face as she scanned the panel. When her eyes locked on the unlit icon showing the four-wheel drive was not engaged, her eyebrows raised ever so slightly and she barely ticked the corners of her mouth upward.

Vaughn suddenly bolted forward and extended his gun so it was nearly touching Marena's ear and said, "What was that for?"

"What?"

"You looked at him and grinned."

Marena pulled back from the gun and shook her head, "I did not. You're seeing things."

Vaughn grabbed a handful of Marena's hair and yanked her head against the barrel of the gun. "Lady, I stay alive by watching people, and you just flashed him a hint of a smile. But you don't have anything to smile about, do you, so why'd you do it?" He answered his own question a heartbeat later when he looked at the instrument panel. "Why isn't that little four-wheel drive light on?" Then, as if a light went on in his mind, he let go of Marena's hair and slapped Greg's head with the palm of his hand. "Nice try," he hissed. "That light's been on ever since we started." Then, pointing at the fourwheel drive control knob, he said, "Stomp on it."

"If I do, we'll get stuck for sure," Greg replied.

Vaughn leaned forward until his mouth was nearly touching Greg's ear and growled, "No more games. I said, stomp on it. Get this thing moving!"

Greg did as commanded, but the Tahoe didn't. Instead of climbing up the slight embankment, all the sudden burst of power did was make the back end slide sideways. In only a few seconds, the vehicle had spun ninety degrees so that instead of being able to traverse up the embankment at a shallow angle, it was sitting perpendicular to the road, its tires whirling in commotion but getting nowhere.

After another ten seconds of the engine screaming at nearly full throttle and the Tahoe doing nothing but digging itself deeper into the snow, Greg let off the gas and dropped his hands to his side. "Satisfied?" he said in disgust, slamming the gear selector into park.

For a long moment nobody said anything. Greg was lost in thought. Vaughn broke the silence. "Get out and dig," he said again.

Greg didn't move. "You haven't listened to anything I've said so far, so I don't know why you'll listen now, but digging isn't going to cut it. We either need to be pulled or pushed out of here—end of story." He glared at Vaughn in the rearview mirror.

Vaughn rubbed the stubble on his face, apparently thinking. After a minute he repeated angrily, "Get out and dig."

Greg sighed, reached down and zipped up his coat, pulled the hood over his head, and slipped on his gloves. A second later Marena began doing the same.

"Where are you going?" Vaughn asked Marena.

"To help dig," she replied.

"Oh no, you're not," Vaughn said. "You're staying right here with me. You're insurance. If he decides to try something stupid, like run off, I'll shoot you."

Greg looked at Vaughn and said, "It'll go a lot faster if she helps."

Vaughn scowled. "Do you really think I'm that stupid?" Shaking his head, he said, "One out there, and one in here." Then, waving the pistol at Greg, he said, "Dig."

Greg shoved open the door, allowing a blast of cold, snow-laden air to rush into the warm but stuffy Tahoe. Climbing out and slamming the door closed, he walked to the front of the vehicle and began trying to clear two paths, each just a tire-width wide, with his hands and feet.

With a snow shovel and his head not pounding so severely he was nauseous, Greg probably could have dug the twin trails in an hour. After three hours and endless tongue lashings from Vaughn whenever he climbed into the Tahoe to warm his nearly frozen feet and hands, Vaughn finally said, "It's taking too long. We're gonna try it."

Greg used every snow-driving trick he had mastered over the years to coax the Tahoe up the embankment, but his best efforts yielded only half of the thirty feet necessary to get back to the road. Cold, wet, and exhausted, he turned around to Vaughn and said, "I'm done. I can't feel my fingers or toes, my coat is soaking wet from sweat and snow, and I'm so tired I can't see straight. That's it. If you want out, you can get out and dig for a while."

Vaughn smiled and said, "Not me; her! Get out there," he said to Marena.

Greg looked over at the startled expression on Marena's face and shook his head. "Stay here, Marena. I'll go."

"No, she goes," Vaughn said, motioning with the pistol. "Get out there, and hurry."

"You know, we're never going to make it to Arco by ten o'clock," Marena said bluntly. Looking at her watch, she said, "It's almost six in the morning now, and we've been at this stupid venture all night. Even if we get back on the road in another hour, it's still going to be noon before we're in Arco."

Vaughn's countenance immediately turned dark. "Shut up," he said. "Just get out there and dig."

"Oh, I'll go dig, but there isn't any way you're going to make it."

Greg looked down at the gas gauge. Letting the Tahoe idle for hours while they had been stuck had taken its toll. "We've got another problem," he said.

"Yeah, what's that?" Vaughn snarled.

"We've got less than a quarter of a tank of gas left. The odds of getting to Arco are stacked against us. Just give it up."

Vaughn leaned forward, looked at the gauge, and then shouted at Marena, "Get out. Now!"

Marena bundled up and got out of the vehicle. Staggering to where Greg had left off digging the trail, she started pushing snow away with her foot. Greg watched as snowflakes began coating her deep-red jacket with a layer of white. An hour later, just as the sky was beginning to show the first hint of daylight, she staggered back to the Tahoe and climbed inside. "I'm frozen," she stammered, barely able to make her mouth and face contort to form the words.

"This is insane," Greg hissed at Vaughn.

Vaughn was silent for a minute and then said, "This is what we're going to do. I'm going to drive." Looking at Greg, he said, "And you're going to push. And, for your wife's sake, don't try running away or doing anything heroic. I can kill her as easily now as a few hours from now."

As Greg grunted and pushed and Vaughn stomped on the gas pedal, the Tahoe spun, spit, and churned its way back onto the snow-packed road. Switching back to their original seats, Greg began driving and looked over at Marena. "At least it's beginning to get light."

Hours later and with the gas gauge pegged solidly on empty, Greg guided the Tahoe past a small, faded sign welcoming visitors to Arco, Idaho. "We need gasoline," Greg said, his speech slightly slurred from lack of sleep.

Vaughn leaned forward, looked at the gas gauge and asked, "How long has the little warning light been on?"

Greg shook his head. "I don't know—twenty, maybe thirty minutes."

"We've got enough. We're not going far."

Greg shrugged, too tired to care. "Okay, then. Where to now?"

"What street are we on?" Vaughn asked.

Greg made no effort to look at the street sign as they passed an intersection. "I don't know. You know everything; you tell me."

Vaughn jabbed the gun's barrel into Greg's shoulder and said, "What does that sign say?"

"Stop it!" Marena screamed. Wiping condensation from her side window she said, "Front Street and . . . it looks like Park Road."

"Stay on Front Street until you come to a road going to our left called Sunset," Vaughn replied. "It shouldn't be far."

"You been here before?" Marena asked.

"No, but I have good directions," Vaughn said. Greg glanced into the mirror to see Vaughn patting an envelope that was sitting on top of his backpack. "When you get to Sunset, turn left."

"We really ought to get some gasoline," Greg repeated, returning his attention to the road.

Vaughn looked at his watch. "No time," he replied.

Marena said, "You're already two-and-a-half hours late. Do you think a few more minutes is going to matter? If we run out of gas, you're going to be a lot later."

"Shut up, will you?" Vaughn said, pulling his cell phone from his pocket.

A blinking yellow light hanging over an intersection caused Greg to slow the Tahoe to a crawl. "I can't read the sign," he said, leaning over the steering wheel and peering through the white blur of snowflakes.

"It's Sunset," Marena said.

Vaughn said, "About a mile ahead, we'll come to a road veering to our right. If there's a sign, it'll say *3300 West*."

A few minutes later Vaughn commanded, "Turn here. Look at your odometer. When you've gone seven-tenths of a mile, there will be a side road. Turn right."

"Where we going?" Marena asked.

"Your final resting place," Vaughn replied. "An abandoned farm."

Finding the narrow road was easy. A set of tire tracks—almost filled in with fresh-fallen snow—were clearly visible. "Follow the tracks," Vaughn said.

The four-wheel drive Tahoe had no trouble pushing through the snow-covered road, but whatever vehicle had driven in earlier clearly had. The tracks fishtailed from side to side, and in two places, they looked as though the vehicle had gone entirely off the road.

On a beautiful summer morning with a clear blue sky and meadowlarks singing, someone with a vivid imagination may have found the abandoned farm livable. At just past noon with wind-driven snowflakes coming down in chaotic swirls, the house, outbuildings, and corrals looked like an abandoned Arctic outpost. The only thing that wasn't decaying, rusting, or falling down was a green sedan parked in front of the house.

"Drive up and park beside that car," Vaughn commanded.

Greg eased the Tahoe forward until it was beside the car. "Now what?" he asked, shifting the Tahoe into park.

"Get out. Very slowly."

CHAPTER FORTY

Agent Hovey rose from his chair at the table as Kelli and Gwilliam entered the small conference room. Extending his hand to Kelli, he said, "Thank you for coming to meet with us, Miss Latimore."

Kelli accepted the proffered hand and gave a strained smile. "I told you on the phone I'd do whatever I can to help."

Hovey pointed to the two other agents in the room. "These are Agents Nichols and Pulsipher." Pointing to a chair beside his, Hovey said, "Please, sit down." When everyone was seated, Hovey said, "May I call you Kelli?"

Kelli nodded nervously but didn't reply.

Trying to put her at ease, Hovey said, "First of all, Kelli, we're not here to discuss anything you may have done for Mr. Li. It's obvious from what we've been told that he coerced you into helping him. That's unfortunate. Our interest is finding a man named Scott Vaughn. Ever heard that name?"

Kelli shook her head.

"Mr. Vaughn is wanted by the FBI and several other law-enforcement agencies. He's also wanted by some foreign governments. He's involved in numerous illegal activities and suspected in the murders of several people. We have reason to believe he is either on his way to this area or is already here."

Kelli studied Hovey's graying hair and wrinkled face for a moment before saying, "I'm a little confused. I don't see how this Vaughn person and what happened to me are connected."

"Truthfully," Hovey replied, "We're not sure they are, but there are several things that may be more than coincidental, and that's why we want to talk with you." Leaning forward and resting his hands on the table he said, "When did you first meet this man Li that you've told Gwilliam about?"

For the next ninety minutes, Hovey asked question after question, and Nichols and Pulsipher scribbled notes on yellow legal pads about Kelli's answers. Finally, Hovey leaned back in his chair and said, "So you really don't have any idea why Li was trying to get access to the INL facility?"

Kelli shook her head.

"Did he ever mention Arco?"

Kelli shook her head and shrugged her shoulders. "Never."

As Hovey folded his arms across his chest and shook his own head, Pulsipher leaned slightly forward, cleared his throat, and said, "Kelli, would you mind just theorizing for a minute?"

"Sure, I guess so," Kelli replied.

"If you wanted to create a major problem at INL, what would you do?"

"What kind of problem?" Kelli asked.

"I don't know," Pulsipher replied, raising his arms in the air. "Something really disruptive—something that would cause a lot of chaos."

"I don't know—maybe pull a fire alarm when there really wasn't a fire."

Pulsipher smiled patiently and said, "No, no, I mean something *really* big—something that would affect a lot of people."

"I guess I'd blow something up," Kelli said with slight hesitation.

"Okay," Pulsipher said, nodding his head. "But what? What would you blow up?"

"A reactor, I guess," Kelli answered.

"Do you have access to any reactors?" Nichols chimed in.

"No," Kelli replied.

Hovey unfolded his arms, leaned forward, and asked, "None? You can't get to any reactor?"

"No," Kelli replied, shaking her head. "Not even close to one."

Hovey, Pulsipher, and Nichols all exchanged confused glances. "Where, exactly, does your security badge allow you to go?" Hovey asked.

Kelli opened her mouth to answer but stopped when Gwilliam's cell phone announced an incoming call by playing a rap tune. Gwilliam fumbled through his coat pocket, grabbed the phone, and looked at the display. Without hesitating, he tapped the screen and put the phone to his ear. "Gwilliam," he said, standing up and walking toward the conference room door.

As Gwilliam walked, Kelli softly said, "I have access to lots of—"

Gwilliam stopped in mid-stride, turned toward the conference table, and waved his arm, causing the four people seated around the table to look at him. The expression on his face caused their muted conversation to stop. "Thanks for the information," Gwilliam said, taking the phone from his ear and tapping the screen to disconnect the call. "We may have something," he said, walking back toward the table. "That was our dispatcher. A state trooper says he pulled a car matching the APB out of a snowbank late last night."

"Where?" Hovey asked anxiously.

"About thirty miles outside of Arco," Gwilliam answered.

Hovey, Nichols, and Pulsipher were on their feet and stuffing notepads into their bags in seconds. "Does Arco have a police department?" Hovey asked, pulling his coat from the back of his chair.

"Nope," Gwilliam answered. "Too small. The nearest to Arco is in Butte County. The sheriff's office handles law enforcement."

Hovey nodded. "Got a number for them?" he asked, slipping his arms inside his coat sleeves.

"No, but I can have one for you in about thirty seconds," Gwilliam answered, lifting his phone again. He cradled his phone on his shoulder as he talked, scribbling a number on a piece of paper that Pulsipher had pushed across the table to him. Hanging up, he said, "There you go."

"Call 'em," Hovey said, pointing to Nichols, "and put it on speaker." Then, looking at Gwilliam, he asked, "What's the sheriff's name?"

"Dan Bowler," Gwilliam said. "Good guy."

Nichols leaned over the table and placed the call. On the third ring a mature female voice answered. "Butte County Sheriff's Office."

"This is Special Agent Wayne Hovey with the FBI. May I speak with Sheriff Bowler?"

"I'm sorry, he's out ill today. Is there something I can help you with?"

"Who are you?" Hovey asked.

"Helen Kruger. I'm the secretary here."

Hovey frowned. "Who's in charge when Bowler's not there?"

"Well, that depends on what you're talking about. I'm in charge of the office, Bruce Belmont's in charge of the jail, and—"

"Is there a chief deputy in your county?" Hovey asked, his voice becoming more and more impatient with each syllable.

"There is," Helen replied. "His name is Jim Clark, but he's out west of town helping with a car wreck."

Hovey took a big breath and quickly expelled it through his nose. "Can you get him on the radio? It's important."

"I can try," Helen replied, "but reception is spotty where he is."

"Will you please try? And when you contact him, please ask him to call me immediately." Hovey spat out a series of numbers and asked, "Did you get that?"

"Of course."

"Thanks." Turning to Gwilliam, he said, "Will you make sure Kelli gets home okay?"

"Sure, but I don't think you understand. Arco may be just a little backwater town of a few hundred people, but there are thousands and thousands of acres surrounding it. You won't have a clue where to look."

CHAPTER FORTY-ONE

The Walkers climbed out of the Tahoe and Vaughn eased out more slowly behind them, supporting his damaged knee with one hand while keeping the gun aimed at Greg with the other. Once outside, he was instantly lashed by wind and blowing snow. Pulling his collar up, Vaughn scanned the decrepit-looking house. The roof of what had been a covered porch was mostly gone, leaving the upright supports looking like forlorn sentinels guarding the house's front door. The large plate-glass window that overlooked the porch had long since surrendered to kids practicing their shooting skills, as had every other window in the brown clapboard house. The front door was splintered from the riddling of hundreds of bullets, but unlike the glass, it had not surrendered; it was tightly closed in the frame.

"Walk to the front door," Vaughn commanded, motioning with the gun.

Greg and Marena made their way to the front of the Tahoe, joined hands, and began trudging side by side. "It's too deep," Marena said, struggling to move her short legs through the deep snow.

"I'll break a trail," Greg replied. "Walk behind me. It'll be easier."

Marena paused while Greg took a couple of steps forward, and as she did Vaughn yelled, "No. I want you to walk side by side. I want to see both of you."

Greg looked at Vaughn and, over the howl of the wind, said, "Give us a break, Vaughn. Do you really think we're going to run away through all this snow?"

"Walk," Vaughn commanded. "Side by side."

"You're sick, you know that, Vaughn?" Greg spat back angrily.

Vaughn's answer was to point the gun at Greg's head.

"You can't shoot me," Greg said. "You need me. You'll never be able to drive out of here by yourself."

"But I don't need her," Vaughn said, pointing the gun at Marena. "Now, walk."

Still two dozen feet from the house, Vaughn was struggling to keep up. His damaged knee had swollen to twice its normal size, and sitting for hours in the Tahoe had made it stiff. It wouldn't flex enough for him to lift it above the deep snow, so he had no choice but to do an awkward step, drag, step, drag. With each step, the polished leather soles of his stylish loafers absorbed tiny bits of moisture, slowly making the leather as slippery as ice on a hot skillet.

A sudden gust of wind-driven snow slammed into Vaughn's face, causing him to involuntarily close his eyes and lower his head just as he shifted his weight onto his damaged knee. His closed eyes, his swollen and nearly useless knee, and the slippery leather of his shoes were too much, and he began to fall.

Looking like a circus clown on ice, Vaughn worked his legs and flailed his arms to keep from crashing to the ground, but the leather soles were too slick, and his feet went out from under him, sending him over backward. What should have been a soft landing in fluffy white snow was transformed into a back-wrenching blow by a football-size rock hidden beneath the powder.

Landing on his back, his spine just above his hips took the blunt force of the rock, causing him to scream as a searing jolt of pain coursed through his back. Writhing in agony, he lost his grip on the gun, and it slipped from his hand, sinking into the snow.

Greg's reaction was instantaneous. "Run," he shouted at Marena as he pushed through the snow toward where Vaughn lay, struggling against the pain and blindly feeling through the snow for his gun with his hand.

Marena didn't move. "Where?" she shouted. "Where do I go?"

Greg paused in midstride only long enough to shout, "There!" Through the haze of pain, Vaughn saw Greg point to the ramshackle barn.

As Marena began plowing through the snow, Greg lunged at Vaughn, slamming into him just as he'd managed to sit up. Vaughn again screamed in pain and half-rolled away as Greg began frantically pawing through the snow for the gun. Looking like a dog digging for a bone, Greg sent handfuls of snow flying. But he didn't find the gun; Vaughn did.

The first bullet whizzed through the air, grazing Greg's neck. The second caught him in the shoulder, spinning him around like a top and showering the white snow with bright-red drops of blood. Greg dropped face-first into the powdery snow with enough force he was almost completely buried. Vaughn struggled to his feet, gun in hand, and stood over Greg's still body. Gritting his teeth against the pain in his knee and back, he steadied his swaying body and aimed the gun at Greg's outline in the snow. Squeezing the trigger, he sent a third bullet ripping into Greg's back, the impact driving Greg's blood-stained body deeper into the snow. Grimacing in pain, Vaughn turned and began awkwardly following the trail of footprints toward the barn.

CHAPTER FORTY-TWO

Li sat on a chair in the basement of the farmhouse holding a ridiculously small phone to his ear. It was one of two truly outstanding technological creations his country had developed. While most of the people in North Korea teetered on the edge of starvation, countless resources—human and monetary—had been spent developing the miniature marvel. Half the size of his smartphone, its plastic body held enough encryption software to make any conversation it transmitted virtually indecipherable. Like every other satellite phone, however, it had a bulky antenna, and it was rubbing against the bandages that held the plastic bubble protecting his eye in place.

The call would be detected by snooping U.S. government satellites that constantly monitored the airwaves for every cellular call, but unlike the other calls, Li's words would be transformed into a series of digital data that was impossible for even the largest supercomputer to untangle.

As the first delicate buzz sounded in his ear, Li's mouth went dry as cotton. By the second tone, his stomach had formed a knot. Halfway through the third tone, a Korean voice said simply, "Yes?"

Taking a quick breath and blowing it out through his nose, Li adjusted the plastic bubble over his eye to relieve the annoying pressure and said, "General Jung?"

"What is it?" Jung asked curtly.

Li took another slight breath, ran his tongue around the inside of his mouth to spread the little saliva that had accumulated, and said, "We have encountered a number of unexpected obstacles."

There was a long silence before Jung commanded, "Continue."

Li again adjusted the plastic bubble and said, "It has not arrived as scheduled. Our window of opportunity to move forward with both our original and backup plans has passed."

A long moment of silence filled the airwaves between Arco, Idaho, and Pyongyang, North Korea. "Where is it?" Jung asked, his voice barely in control.

Li shook his head as he said, "I do not know." Looking at the 12:15 on his watch, he added, "I have not heard from our contact."

"Why?" Jung asked.

Li moved the phone slightly so the antenna would be less irritating to his wound. "I do not know," he said. "It is snowing very hard here, and I do not have cellular coverage. It may be that the cellular towers are inoperative."

There was a very long silence, long enough that Li took the phone away from his ear and checked the display to be certain the call was still connected. Returning the phone to his ear, he caught the sound of muffled voices. He strained to hear, but they were far too faint. Suddenly Jung's voice blasted into this ear. "You are to recover it at all costs, do you understand?"

Li nodded as he replied, "Yes."

"You are to be certain the man who is transporting it is eliminated."

"You want him killed?" Li asked bluntly.

"Of course, you idiot," Jung shouted back. "And be certain there is nothing in his possession that can be traced back to us."

"I understand," Li replied. Expecting more to be said, he continued holding the phone to his ear. After a moment of silence, he took the phone away and looked at the display. The connection had been severed.

Collapsing the antenna, he looked at Hwan. "We are to make a recovery and kill the man who is transporting it," he said.

"And then what?" Hwan asked, wiping his runny nose with the back of his hand and wiping it on his pants.

Li gave Hwan a blank stare. "I don't know. I wasn't told."

"Are we to get it out of the country?" Hwan pressed.

Li shrugged. "I told you; I don't know."

It was at that moment the first of the three muffled gunshots echoed from outside into the basement. Li jumped to his feet so quickly he sent his wooden chair skidding across the room. Hwan's reaction was only slightly less dramatic. He was on his feet and had pulled a pistol from his shoulder holster before Li's chair came to a stop. The second shot sounded before either of them had taken a step and the third as they were halfway across the basement's dirt floor.

Racing up the rickety stairway two stairs at a time, Li and Hwan stooped over and crept to the opening that had once been a large picture window. Crouching on either side of the opening, they peered out into the blinding snowstorm.

"Who is that?" Hwan whispered.

Li didn't answer immediately; he was concentrating on the man standing in the blinding snowstorm. As the man turned away from them and began awkwardly gimping toward the barn, Li said, "Scott Vaughn."

Hwan looked at Li in confusion. "Then, who is lying in the snow, and why is Vaughn going to the barn?"

"I don't know," Li replied, shaking his head.

Li and Hwan watched Vaughn struggle toward the barn until Vaughn's outline was lost in the blizzard. "Come," Li said, rising from his crouched position. "I will follow him. I want you to go around to the back of the barn and find a way to get inside."

"And then what?" Hwan asked, rising to his feet.

"We will wait and see. Unless he attacks me, do not let him know you are there."

Li and Hwan opened the door and stepped onto the porch, pausing only long enough to raise their collars against the wind. Stepping from the porch, they began struggling through the deepening snow.

CHAPTER FORTY-THREE

The two-story barn was made of rough-sawn lumber that looked like it had been painted bright white fifty years earlier but hadn't seen a coat of paint since. Time, wind, rain, and snow had not been kind. The boards of the once-white walls were now a dull brown and streaked with rust where they had been nailed to the framework. One of the two large doors that should have been covering the massive opening was gone completely; the other was lying cockeyed in the opening, its upper hinge broken and its lower hinge bent almost to the breaking point. The roof was made of corrugated metal and was intact except for two or three small pieces. It looked as though neighborhood boys had trained their rifles skyward and riddled the metal with hundreds of holes over the years.

The building was a combination hay barn and milk parlor, a throwback to the days when farming families milked a dozen cows, raised a few chickens, and grew enough hay to feed the cows and horses during the winter months. One entire wall had stanchions, where cows were once restrained while being milked. Along the other wall was a greasy and dusty workbench littered with mice droppings, pieces of rusty metal, and broken bottles that had once held peaches, pears, and other produce a farm wife had likely canned. Anything of any value had long since grown legs and walked away. A ladder made from pieces of rotting lumber led to a loft that still had a thick layer of loose hay and straw on its floor. Even with the wind that blew through the barn, it had a musty smell of dirt, mice urine, moldy hay, and used oil and grease.

"Mrs. Walker," Vaughn called loudly from just inside the door. "I know you're in here." Looking down at the trail of little chunks of snow that littered the dirt floor, he shouted, "Your husband is dead. I shot him three times. That'll make it a little more difficult for me to drive out of here, but I'll manage." Vaughn took a couple of steps into the barn and smiled. The snow that had accumulated on Marena's boots and pants as she'd run through the snow had left a perfect trail across the floor that lead directly to the ladder.

Vaughn began slowly limping, following the trail of snow that littered the floor. Gripping the rickety ladder, he worked his way from rung to rung until he was high enough to hoist himself onto the loft. Standing up, he smiled again. More chunks of snow left a perfect trail to the back of the loft, where they disappeared into a deep pile of straw.

Walking with deliberate steps that made the ancient boards creak and moan, he slowly made his way forward. "Mrs. Walker, did you really think you could hide under that pile of straw?" he said in a nasally and condescending voice, as if he was talking to a child who was playing hide and seek.

The straw pile took up less than half the loft and covered an area about the size of a large living room in a house. It was mounded in the middle to a depth of about four feet and gradually tapered to the edges. Stopping just short of the edge of the pile, a sadistic smile spread across Vaughn's lips.

Except for a series of indentations that led to the deepest part of the pile, the straw was covered with a heavy layer of gray dust and dirt the wind had deposited over the years. There, in an area the size of a kitchen table, the dirt and dust were completely gone, and the straw looked as if it had been fluffed up. "Mrs. Walker," Vaughn said softly, looking at the disturbed straw. "We can do this the easy way or the hard way; it really makes no difference to me. But you must die; there is simply no alternative." Shifting his weight to take pressure off his injured knee, he continued. "You have become a liability. I wish it didn't have to be like this—I really do—but you realize this is your fault. If you hadn't gone to the police in the Dominican Republic, none of this would have happened. So you have no one to blame but you and your dead husband."

Studying the straw, Vaughn saw the slightest movement in some of the strands. "It's really too bad I'm in such a hurry. I would have enjoyed making you suffer a little for the damage you did to my knee. Goodbye, Mrs. Walker." Raising the pistol, he aimed it at the movement and squeezed the trigger twice, paused very briefly, and shot twice more.

The reverberation of the gunshots inside the barn was enough to cause an avalanche of snow to tumble from the roof. It hit the ground with a thunderous roar, startling Vaughn and causing him to look away. When he looked back at the straw, a smiled spread across his lips; a dozen unmistakable bright-red drops of blood stained the yellow straw.

CHAPTER FORTY-FOUR

Special Agent Larry Nichols leaned his shoulder against the Suburban's passenger door and pushed, forcing it open against the howling wind and blowing snow. Stepping outside, he tried to ease the door closed, but the wind caught it and slammed it shut, eliciting a grumble from Hovey about being careful. Nichols lifted his feet high and placed them gingerly in the snow, trying to avoid getting too much up the insides of his pant legs.

By just about every standard, the M-M Motel in Arco, Idaho, was small. Its twenty-five rooms were arranged in a *U* shape around a small grassy inner court in which, thirty years ago, the original owner had had the foresight to plant some trees. In the summer it was probably a pleasant little oasis from the stark, treeless landscape surrounding Arco, but to Nichols, it was nothing more than a dive—the third such place he'd been forced to climb from the warmth of the Suburban to check out.

A *Vacancy* sign flashed in the window of the small office as Nichols pushed open the heavy glass door and walked inside. Stomping his feet on a rubber welcome mat, he looked up to see a twenty-something girl with long blonde hair and lustrous white teeth grinning at him. She was sitting at a desk behind a counter, wearing a deep-red turtleneck sweater and gloves.

"Cold?" Nichols asked, reaching inside his coat pocket.

"Freezing," the woman replied, rising from her chair and walking to the counter opposite Nichols.

Nichols pulled out his leather identification wallet and flipped it open to reveal his picture ID. Holding them up so the girl could easily read it, he said, "FBI Special Agent Larry Nichols. I'd like to ask you a couple of questions."

"Jessica Slater," she said as she looked at the credentials. Then she said, "Well, we haven't had any bank robberies lately, so what could possibly bring a good-looking FBI agent to tiny Arco?"

Nichols was taken slightly aback. He had received a far different, more submissive reaction at the two places he'd stopped earlier.

"Does Arco even have a bank?" Nichols asked.

"Nope," Jessica answered. "No bank, movie theatre, or night club." Then, with a wink she, said, "But we do have three farm-implement dealers, a huge grain elevator, and two veterinarians."

"I'm impressed," Nichols said, nodding his head.

"You ought to be," Jessica replied. "But you still haven't answered my question." Leaning forward and putting her elbows on the counter, she added, "What brings you to Arco?"

The woman was obviously flirting, and Nichols decided to play along. "Oh, you know, your common, everyday drug runner, terrorist, and anarchist."

"Finally!" Jessica said, holding out her hands in mock exasperation. "We've been trying to get the FBI here for ages. We have hundreds of those types; they're running loose on the streets."

Nichols replied, "Well, there's me and two other agents in the car outside. We can each handle a hundred or two, so you won't have any more worries. We'll clean up this town, missy," he said, doing a poor imitation of John Wayne.

Jessica drew back slightly and said, "Don't give up your day job, Agent Nichols, because you'll never make it as John Wayne."

Nichols returned his ID to his pocket and turned serious. "We're looking for two Asian men—Korean, specifically—driving a green Ford Taurus. Probably came into town last night late. Have you seen 'em?"

Jessica shrugged slightly. "Maybe. An Asian guy came in last night—short guy, stout. His head was all bandaged up, and he had some plastic bubble-looking thing over one eye."

"Is he still here?" Nichols asked.

Jessica shook her head. "Nope," she said. "He left earlier this morning. When he came in last night, he said he needed a room for only one night and he would be leaving early. He paid in cash. He looked like he was in pain and needed some sleep."

"Did he say why he was here or where he was going? Did he ask for directions or information about the area?"

"He didn't say anything other than he wanted a room. He was a little upset when I insisted he write down the license plate number on his car though."

"Do you have his registration card?"

"Sure; it's here somewhere," Jessica replied, opening a gray plastic filing box. "Ah, this is it," she said as she extracted the card and looked at it. "Funny," she said, handing the card to Nichols. "He didn't look much like a John Smith." Then, with a wink, she added, "I've had the occasional John Doe in here with some bimbo hanging on him, but this was the first Asian John Smith I've ever had."

Nichols took the card and examined it. Amazingly, Li had written down the correct license plate number, but the address was *111 Anystreet, New York, New York*, and the zip code was 00001. Nichols shook his head. "Do you ever question someone when they put down bogus information like this?"

Jessica cocked her head slightly and raised an eyebrow. "You're kidding, right? Some Asian guy shows up in a rental car, tells me his name is John Smith, and whips out a fat roll of cash to pay. Do you really think he's going to answer any question I ask with the truth?"

Nichols felt his cheeks flush slightly at his own naivety and managed a slight nod.

"He was going west," Jessica said, straightening up and putting some strands of long blonde hair behind her ear.

"Excuse me?" Nichols said.

"He was going west."

"How do you know?" Nichols asked, leaning slightly forward and sliding the registration card across the counter toward Jessica.

"Because he asked if I knew what the road conditions were like going out to Sunset, and he wanted to know if the highway department kept the roads plowed. He wouldn't have asked about the roads if he didn't want to travel on them," Jessica said.

"What's near Sunset Road?" Nichols asked with more urgency than he'd meant to show.

"Nothing," Jessica replied.

"Nothing?"

"Lots and lots of nothing."

Nichols pulled a business card out of his shirt pocket and handed it to Jessica. "You've been helpful. If you think of anything else—anything—please call the number on the card."

Jessica accepted the card, looked it over, and replied, "Of course, Special Agent Larry Nichols."

Nichols pushed open the glass door and was greeted with an icy blast of wind in his face. Ignoring the cold, he raced to the Suburban and yanked open the door. Jumping inside and slamming the door, he said, "Bingo. Li stayed here last night."

After a quick rehash of his conversation with Jessica, he said, "I think we should talk to the sheriff and see what he can tell us about what's near Sunset Road."

Hovey nodded his head slightly at Nichols. Then he looked at Pulsipher and said, "Drive to the sheriff's office."

CHAPTER FORTY-FIVE

Vaughn was bent over, just ready to push the blood-stained straw aside, when a voice called out from below, "Vaughn! Scott Vaughn, where are you?"

Startled by the voice, Vaughn rose up and turned from the bloody straw. Quietly, he eased forward just enough to see down to the barn's doorway.

Standing in the middle of the doorway was a lone figure, his head wrapped in a bandage and a plastic bubble over one eye. "Scott Vaughn," the man called out, his hands cupped around his mouth to amplify his voice. "Where are you?"

Vaughn stepped to the edge of the loft and called out, "I'm here."

The bubble-faced man looked up to where Vaughn was standing and shouted, "Why the shooting? What is wrong?"

Vaughn shook his head. "Nothing's wrong. I just had a little unfinished business to attend to."

"Come down here!"

Vaughn looked back at the growing red stain on the pile of straw and then at the man in the doorway. "Give me a minute; I want to check something," he said and took a step toward the straw.

"No, Mr. Vaughn," Li commanded. "Now! You are very late, and we must hurry."

Vaughn didn't move. "Who are you?"

Li took two steps forward so he was better illuminated. "It is me, Li."

Vaughn studied Li for a second then pointed at his head. "That thing over your eye makes you a little difficult to recognize." Then he looked back at the straw, trying to decide which way to go. "I'll be back, Mrs. Walker."

Shifting his gaze back to Li, he slipped his gun into his pocket and said, "All right, I'm coming down."

Vaughn descended the ladder, and Li angled deeper into the barn to escape the whirlwind of blowing snow that pelted him. Enough dull gray daylight filtered through the open doors to create a small halo immediately in front of the opening but left the sides of the barn in almost total darkness. Li walked to the edge of the light and waited.

Vaughn stopped ten feet from Li and slipped his hand inside his coat pocket, wrapping it around his pistol. "Okay," he said, "I'm here. Now what?"

"Do you have the suitcase?" Li asked brusquely.

"Of course."

"Where is it?"

"Safe. In the SUV I came in."

"You're very late. Why?"

Vaughn replied sarcastically, "Have you been outside lately?"

"Indeed I have, Mr. Vaughn," Li replied with a straight face. "But, you see, we had a time schedule, which you agreed to keep."

"Yeah, well, you forgot to tell Mother Nature about the schedule. She hasn't cooperated for the last couple of days."

As the two men stood facing each other, Li looked over Vaughn's shoulder. Shifting his gaze back to Vaughn, Li said, "You should have called."

"Who? Your buddies in Korea? Can they control the weather?"

"They could have devised an alternative plan." As he spoke, Li's unprotected eye shifted to something behind Vaughn and his eyes widened.

Seeing the facial expression, Vaughn instinctively spun around to see an Asian man creeping forward while racking the slide on his pistol. In a fluid motion, Vaughn pulled the pistol from his pocket, aimed, and pulled the trigger twice. The first bullet went flying harmlessly through the darkness and blew a small chunk of wood from a piece of weathered wall. The second found its mark in another man's chest. Although the man was technically still alive when he crumpled to his knees, by the time he fell forward onto his face, Vaughn knew he was dead.

Vaughn shot twice more, and Li cursed. Vaughn spun back around to him. Li had stupidly kept his hands in the open, where Vaughn could see them, instead of gripping his own pistol. Vaughn pulled the trigger without aiming. The bullet punched a neat hole in Li's right sleeve and tore into his bicep, spinning him around and sending him into the darkness onto his back. Leaping forward, Vaughn straddled the downed man. "Don't move," he screamed, aiming his gun at Li's face. "You move, you die."

***

Marena Walker silently rose from her crouched position in the dark corner of the barn. Her hands gripped the worn handle of a pitchfork so tightly her knuckles were white. Trembling with fright, her vision blurred with tears, she lunged forward on adrenaline-charged legs like a horseless knight with a lance. Her first three steps in the soft brown dirt on the floor were almost in total silence. Her fourth was not.

The noise from her foot crunching a broken glass jar caused Vaughn to spiral around on his already damaged knee. Whether at the pain caused by his sudden movement or the shock of seeing Marena alive, he hesitated. The slight pause was all Marena needed. Screaming, she lunged the last two steps.

There were four rusty tines on the pitchfork. All four pierced Scott Vaughn's coat then his shirt. The lowest one entered his body just below his sterling-silver belt buckle. The second went directly into his navel, the third two inches above that, and the fourth just below his sternum.

Vaughn's eyes flashed wide. He dropped the gun and reached up with both hands to pull the pitchfork from his stomach, but he was no match for the fear and anger charging Marena's arms. With another scream, she drove the pitchfork deeper into Vaughn's body. Letting go of the handle, she cupped her hands to her mouth and stared at Vaughn's pain-saturated face. A fraction of a second later, a gunshot sounded, and Vaughn crumpled to the ground as it hit him in the head. Screaming at the noise and the shower of blood, Marena looked down to see the man called Li still lying on his back, holding a pistol in his left hand.

Marena slid to her knees and began sobbing. The adrenaline that had fueled her was gone; her arms now hung limply at her sides.

Li got to his feet, and Marena peered up at him as he looked down at her quivering form. He trained the pistol at her head, and Marena bowed her head and closed her tear-filled eyes. Putting the pistol into his pocket, Li trotted to where Hwan was lying facedown in the dirt and scooped him up, putting the lifeless body over his shoulder. Without saying a word, he walked past Marena and trudged out into the raging snowstorm.

Marena sank deeper onto her haunches in the dirt, her shoulders shaking as she sobbed. After a moment, she wiped tears from her eyes and hesitantly looked at Vaughn's lifeless body. Almost instantly, she retched, spewing bile onto his legs. Gritting her teeth to keep from vomiting again, she twisted around and crawled as fast as she could to the barn door. Scooping up a handful of snow, she put it in her mouth, let it melt slightly, and spat. Then, with both hands, she scooped up more snow and washed blood from her face. With a fresh stream of tears gushing from her eyes, she struggled to her feet and began running, falling, and running again to where Greg's body lay in the snow.

CHAPTER FORTY-SIX

Li carried Hwan's limp body over his shoulder to the Tahoe and dropped him into the snow by the rear door. Struggling forward to the driver-side door, he breathed a sigh of relief as he leaned in and saw the keys in the ignition and the metal suitcase laying securely on the back seat. Hurrying to the back of the Tahoe, he opened the door and yanked bags of groceries from the cargo area. Then he picked up Hwan's body and flopped it into the SUV. Pausing only long enough to catch his breath, he started the Tahoe, drove it up beside the green Taurus, and jumped out. Opening the trunk, he grabbed Seok's frozen body, and like a slaughterhouse worker hauling a carcass, Li hefted him out and carried him to the back of the Tahoe. With a loud grunt, he managed to half-toss, half-shove the frozen body on top of Hwan's lifeless form.

Clutching his bullet-punctured arm, he hurried through the snow and into the house. Descending the stairs to the basement two at a time, he gathered maps, diagrams, and photographs that were scattered on a table and bounded back up the stairs and into the Tahoe. Breathing a sigh of relief, he started the vehicle and shifted it into gear. As he drove away from the abandoned farm, he glanced in the rearview mirror to see the woman drop to her knees beside a man's snow-covered body.

Li cursed the snow, his bleeding arm, and his sightless eye as he maneuvered the vehicle onto Sunset Road and headed toward Arco. Glancing down at the instrument panel, his shoulders sank when he saw the gas gauge showing empty and the little yellow warning light glowing brightly.

Looking up, a fresh wave of anxiety swept the problem of the empty fuel tank aside. The pale white lights of an oncoming vehicle glowed dimly through the onslaught of snowflakes. Li shook his head. He was taking his half of the road out of the middle, and the oncoming vehicle meant he would have to ease over onto his side of the road.

Li let off the gas pedal, lightly tapped the brakes, and gingerly eased the wheel to the right to make room for the approaching vehicle. Gripping the wheel tightly with both hands, he tensed, expecting the two vehicles to sideswipe each other. As the Tahoe passed the big black Suburban, only the thickness of a piece of paper separated their two side mirrors.

Ten minutes later Li guided the Tahoe under the awning of Arco's only gas station and shut off the engine. Climbing out of the SUV, he walked to the station's front door and pushed it open only far enough to poke his head inside. "I'd like to fill my vehicle with gasoline," he said.

A boy who couldn't have been older than eighteen, with purple and red hair almost to his shoulders, looked up from his comic book and said, "Ya gonna pay with a credit card or cash?"

"Cash," Li replied.

"Give me fifty bucks, and you can fill it up. If it takes more than that, you can come in afterward and pay me. If it's less, I'll refund the difference."

Li pulled his head out and let the door close. Reaching into his pocket, he pulled two fifty-dollar bills from his money clip and opened the door again. Placing the money on top of a bubblegum-vending machine by the door, he said, "There's one hundred dollars. You can keep whatever is left over," and he shut the door and turned back to the Tahoe.

Ten minutes later and with a full tank of gas, Li drove out from under the gas station's awning to an unoccupied corner of the lot and parked. Reaching inside his coat, he extracted the small satellite phone and punched in a series of numbers. A minute later, General Jung's voice filled his ear. "Yes?"

Li took a breath and let it out. Glancing over his should to the back seat, he said, "I have recovered the suitcase."

"Good," Jung replied.

"There were casualties," Li blurted.

"Yes?" Jung replied. "Explain."

"Hwan and Seok are both dead; I have a bullet wound in my arm."

"Their bodies?" Jung asked, ignoring the issue of Li's bullet wound.

"I have them in a vehicle with me."

"Can you dispose of them in a way that they will not be found?" Jung asked, his tone urgent.

Li thought for a moment. "It will be difficult," he replied, not knowing what else to say.

There was silence on the phone for a long minute. Then Jung said, "Find a place you can stay for tonight. We will contact you tomorrow with instructions. Do you understand?"

"Here? You want me to stay in Arco?"

More silence. Finally, "Are you able to drive?"

Li looked down at his aching arm, felt the strain of the bandage and the plastic bubble over his eye, and looked out at the near-whiteout driving conditions. "It would be difficult," he repeated his earlier answer in an understatement.

Li could hear only bits and pieces of the muffled conversation taking place on the other end of the phone. Jung finally came back on and said, "Stay in Arco. We will send someone to assist you by this time tomorrow," and then the connection was severed.

Li retracted the antenna, put the phone into his pocket, shifted the Tahoe into gear, and slowly eased onto the road.

Turning into the M-M Motel's small parking lot, he looked down at his arm. The blood that had soaked the sleeve of his coat gave the material a slightly darker tint than the wetness of the thousands of snowflakes that had landed on him but not so much that it was noticeable. Holding his arm to his side, he slid out of the Tahoe and walked into the motel office's small lobby.

***

Jessica Slater looked up from the cookbook she was reading as the door pushed open. In her friendly, lighthearted voice, she said, "You enjoyed your stay so much you decided to come back for another night!" It wasn't a question.

Li gave a weak smile and said, "The weather. I can't travel to my destination."

Pulling out a new registration card and sliding it across the counter, she asked nonchalantly, "Where you headed?"

Li hesitated for too long. "I was going to Seattle, but the weather has turned me back," he said, avoiding the question. "Do I really need to fill out another card?" he asked, and Jessica saw him glance down at his right arm.

She shrugged. "No, I guess not," she replied. "Will the same room be okay?"

"It will be fine," Li answered. "Thank you." He reached into his pocket and pulled out his money clip. Peeling off three twenty-dollar bills, he said, "I appreciate your help," and placed the money on the counter beside Agent Larry Nichols's business card. "Keep the difference for yourself."

Jessica scooped up the money and the business card in a single quick motion. "Thank you. That's very generous of you. I hope you have a pleasant afternoon and night," she said as she handed Li his room key.

She watched Li get into the Tahoe and drive to room thirteen. After he was inside the room, she pulled Larry Nichols's business card out from under the cash, picked up the phone, and dialed. When a voice answered, all she said was, "Guess who just checked back into room thirteen?"

Fifty-three minutes after Li checked into the M-M Motel, Hovey, Nichols, and Pulsipher plus Sheriff Clark, two deputy sheriffs, a Bureau of Land Management enforcement officer, and an Idaho brand inspector all converged on room thirteen. To Jessica's knowledge, it represented the single largest gathering of law-enforcement personnel ever to congregate in one place in Arco.

***

An hour later, an ambulance arrived at the decrepit old house, and three EMTs from Arco's volunteer fire department quickly began working to bring Greg Walker back from his dance on the cusp of death. At the same time, inside the barn, a sheriff's deputy was swallowing repeatedly to keep from vomiting as he snapped pictures of the grisly body of Scott Vaughn.

EPILOGUE

A LIGHT RAP ON THE door of hospital room 214 was followed by Wayne Hovey gently pushing the heavy wooden door open just far enough to stick his head inside, and Marena looked up from the Sudoku puzzle she was wrestling with. She smiled. Setting her pen and puzzle beside her on the couch, she motioned for Hovey to enter the room.

Two plastic bags hung from a metal stand. One contained clear liquid, the other dark-red blood. Both had long plastic tubes running from the bottom of the bag to a slightly hairy forearm.

"How's he doing?" Hovey asked softly as Marena rose to meet him at the foot of the bed.

"Good," Marena replied in not much more than a whisper. "Really good, when you consider what happened to him."

Hovey smiled and looked over at Greg. "I just talked with the surgeon who worked on him; he said he'll be out of here in a couple of days and good as new in a few weeks."

From the bed, Greg mumbled, "Is it going to take me that long?"

"Sorry, honey," Marena said, turning to look at her husband. "We didn't mean to wake you."

"You didn't," Greg said, opening his eyes slightly and running his tongue over his dry lips. "I've been lying here trying to replay the last few days, but my rewind mechanism isn't working very well."

Hovey chuckled. "It's the drugs. Once they wear off, it'll all come back—along with the pain."

"I'll take the memories but pass on the pain," Greg replied, licking his lips again.

"Your wife's quite the hero," Hovey said, moving to the side of the bed. "She took out one of the worst guys I've ever had to deal with."

"Vaughn?" Greg replied heavily. He looked like he was doing his best to fight a drug-induced desire to sleep.

Hovey nodded.

Marena quickly interjected. "I don't want to talk about it," she said. "I'm trying to erase it from my memory."

Hovey pulled his lips back in a tight, understanding smile and nodded. "I've been where you are right now. It's not a pleasant place. Time helps, but it never goes away." Then, changing the subject, he said, "But there's one thing I don't understand: How did you come to be hiding in the side of the barn in the dark while Vaughn thought you were up in the loft?"

Marena wrapped her arms around her body as if giving herself a hug and shivered slightly. Swallowing, she said, "When I ran into the barn, I was panicked, I didn't know what to do. I knew I needed to hide, but I was confused. When I looked around the barn, it was like I could see everything, but at the same time, I couldn't see anything. My mind was going a thousand different directions at the same time. For some reason, when I saw that rickety old ladder, it just seemed like the right thing to do. On impulse I ran to it and started climbing. When I got to the top, I saw the pile of straw and thought it was the perfect hiding place. I literally ran onto the pile to where there was the most straw, to where it was the deepest, and frantically started moving straw to make a place big enough to hide in." Then she paused to take a breath. "But I had to stop."

"Why?" Hovey asked.

"Because of a cat."

"Cat?" Greg asked groggily, drifting in and out of sleep. "You hate cats. You're allergic to cats."

Marena nodded. "While moving the straw, I uncovered a huge orange-and-white-striped cat. I don't know if that's where it lived or if was up there seeking shelter and warmth from the storm, but the thing hissed and snarled at me."

"What did you do?" Hovey asked.

"I tried to scare it away, but it wouldn't go. Something was wrong with its front leg; it may have been broken."

"Then what?"

"With my allergy, I knew if I couldn't scare the cat away, there was no way I could hide by it—being that close, I'd start sneezing within a minute or two."

"So you climbed back down the ladder?" Hovey guessed.

Marena nodded. "I hurriedly threw some straw back over the cat, walked off the pile, and brushed off my pants and boots." Marena chuckled. "You're going to think I'm crazy when I tell you this, but I brushed off my pants and boots because I was afraid that somehow I had stepped or walked where that cat had been and I would have cat hair on me that would make me start sneezing."

"That may have saved your life," Hovey interjected solemnly.

Marena gave him a questioning look.

"I've been out to the barn. Everyone who went in there left a perfect trail of snow wherever they went. I'm sure Vaughn knew you went up the ladder, but because you didn't leave a trail when you came down, he had no idea where you were."

"Then what'd ya do?" Greg managed to ask.

"As I bent over to brush off my pants, I saw the . . ." Marena hesitated slightly before saying the word. "I saw the pitchfork, or at least part of it. The handle was buried beneath the straw, but two of the tines were sticking out just enough for me to see them. I pulled it from the straw and tossed it down to the ground. Then I climbed down."

"What made you decide to hide where you did?" Hovey asked, shifting his weight slightly.

"The darkness. It's funny, but the darkest place in the barn was in the front corner beside the door. The daylight shone in through the door, but I guess light can't turn corners," she said, shrugging her shoulders.

"So you hid in the corner?" Hovey asked.

Marena nodded. "I crouched down and made myself as small as I could, holding the pitchfork across my lap. I was hoping Vaughn would go deeper inside the barn, and then I could sneak out."

"He went up into the loft; why didn't you run then?" Hovey asked.

Marena rolled her eyes. "Charley horse. When I saw him climb up the ladder, I stood up, but my legs suddenly cramped so badly I couldn't move. Just as I got my legs so they would move, that other guy—Li—walked into the doorway. I had no idea who he was or what he wanted, so I didn't dare move."

Hovey smiled slightly and nodded. "Okay, now I understand."

Marena let her arms drop to her sides. "So what about this Li guy? What's his role in all this? And what was in that suitcase?"

Hovey's smile widened, and he leaned against Greg's hospital bed. "Last question first." Waving his hand back and forth between Greg and Marena, he said, "You've spent the last few days driving around with one pound of octanitrocubane in your car."

"Umm, what's . . . ?" Greg mumbled as his eyelids slowly clamped down tight. Sleep had won out; he was gone.

"Octagern . . . octani . . ." Marena said, trying to get her tongue around the string of vowels and consonants.

"Octanitrocubane," Hovey said easily. "It's an explosive."

"Like dynamite?" Marena said, sickened at the thought that they'd been in a car with it for so long.

"Well, they both go *boom*, but that's about the only similarity. Octanitrocubane is probably the most powerful non-nuclear explosive known. Four ounces would obliterate an airliner. A full pound of the stuff would have—well, let's just say it would have caused quite an explosion."

"But what were they going to do with it?" Marena asked.

"We don't know all of that yet," Hovey said, "Mr. Li hasn't been very willing to share information. We think they intended to place the stuff inside one of the buildings at INL where some weapons-grade nuclear material is stored."

"To create a nuclear explosion?"

"Not exactly. The octanitrocubane wouldn't cause a nuclear explosion, but the blast would release huge amounts of radioactive material into the atmosphere. The experts tell me the prevailing winds would spread it both east and south, causing radiation poisoning over much of southern Idaho and northern Utah. It could potentially have affected almost two million people."

"But why not set off the bomb in New York or Los Angeles, where millions more could be poisoned?"

"There are only twenty nuclear power plants in the U.S., none of which are in major cities. And even if they blew up all of them simultaneously, it wouldn't release as much material as one building at INL. They chose the ideal facility to get the most bang for their buck," Hovey answered with a grin.

Marena shook her head at the thought. After a moment, she asked, "What happens to Li?"

"The North Korean government is screaming he is a diplomat and entitled to diplomatic immunity."

"Is he?"

Hovey frowned. "Let's put it this way. He's listed as a military attaché with the North Korean embassy in New York, so technically, yes. But that's just another way of saying he's a spy."

"So what will happen to him?" Marena pressed.

Hovey shrugged. "Not sure yet. In the end he'll probably be given to the North Koreans, but it's a little complicated because he had two dead companions stuffed in the back of your Tahoe. I'm sure there's going to be lots of haggling over this for a while."

"But you caught the guy with explosives, intending to blow something up, and like you said, there are two dead men. Certainly you can't let him go free."

Hovey held out his arms and shrugged. "Whatever happens will be decided way above my pay grade. And while I'm glad, really glad, we stopped him, if he goes back to North Korea, I can live with that. But between us, I truly wanted to get Vaughn."

"Which you did," Marena said.

"Which *you* did," Hovey replied with a smile, waving his hand back and forth between Greg and Marena. "We couldn't have done it without your help. Thanks."

Marena smiled warmly and reached out to pat a soundly sleeping Greg on his toes. "You're welcome." Then, as Hovey opened the door to leave, she said, "Mr. Hovey, may I ask you something?"

"Sure."

"From the first time we met yesterday, I keep thinking I'd seen you somewhere before. Have we ever met?"

Hovey wrinkled his brow as if in deep thought. "You know, you look sort of familiar to me as well, but unless you've been to Miami, I don't think so."

Marena shook her head. "We passed through there a few days ago on our way back from the Dominican Republic, but that's it."

Hovey smiled and said, "Well, I guess not, then." As he closed the door, he winked and said, "But you do have a very common name."

AUTHOR'S NOTE

Every novel, usually somewhere in the fine print on the first page or two, has some lawyerly language stating that the book is a work of fiction and any similarities between the events and/or characters portrayed within its pages to any actual events or real people are purely coincidental. With this novel, there is a small caveat. While it is fiction, some of the events depicted herein actually occurred, although, to protect the innocent, I have altered some of the circumstances. The same is true of the characters. While most are fictitious, some are not. So, in keeping with literary protocol, let me say that any similarity to any person, living or dead, is purely coincidental and unintentional—or nearly so.

ABOUT THE AUTHOR

MUCH TO HIS DISLIKE, E. James Harrison is not a *New York Times* best-selling author. However, he is the author of three other novels, all of which his wife and mother really like.

Born in Salt Lake City, he learned to type in the seventh grade on an old Smith–Corona manual typewriter and has been pecking out words ever since. He somehow managed to graduate from college with degrees emphasizing public relations and creative writing and has spent most of his professional life writing magazine articles about such gripping subjects as Internet technology or has kept veterinarians on the edges of their seats with articles about the latest advances in goat, rabbit, and hamster medicine. Those thrilling achievements pale in comparison to the radio advertisements and TV commercials he has written encouraging people to upgrade to the latest mobile phone or calling plan.

When he isn't putting words on paper for himself or others, he can be found boating and waterskiing with his family, working on the family ranch, flying an airplane, or traveling to see new things and meet new people.

He and his wife, Deborah, have two amazing daughters and an awesome son-in-law and are the proud grandparents of the four best grandkids in the world. He is not prone to hyperbole.

ENJOY THIS EXCERPT FROM CLAIR M. POULSON'S

WATCH YOUR BACK

"My boyfriend was just shot!" the frantic voice said.

"Where is the victim?" the dispatcher asked.

"He's with me," the caller answered, her voice shaking as she hurriedly gave the address. "He's dying! I don't know what to do for him. Please hurry."

"Officers and an ambulance are on the way. Is the shooter still there?" the dispatcher asked.

"No, he shot him and sped away," the woman said. "I thought he was going to shoot me too."

"What was he driving when he left?" the dispatcher asked.

"A dark-blue Cadillac Seville."

The dispatcher quickly put the information out to officers to be on the lookout for the Seville, surprised the woman's description of the car was so specific. Then she asked, "What's your name?"

The caller was breathing heavily and sobbing intermittently. "Brea Burr."

"And what is the victim's name?"

"Duane Trahan. He's bleeding badly. I need help now!"

"Help is on the way. Be calm and try to stop the bleeding."

"I'm trying, but it's gushing out."

The dispatcher spoke calmly, professionally, but Brea was getting increasingly upset. "Do you know who the shooter was?" she asked.

"It was that radio guy Bronson Melville. He's my ex. He was jealous of Duane."

That explained why Miss Burr was so sure of the vehicle.

Only when an officer arrived at the location did the dispatcher allow the call to be disconnected. She then placed a call to the police chief, who listened to what she had to say and then told her to send a detective to the scene.

***

Detective Gage Tipton arrived at the scene, and Detective Sergeant Jon Hanks responded a few minutes after him. Gage was the younger of the two, but he was assigned as lead investigator.

Gage found the victim deceased and Miss Brea Burr hysterical when he arrived.

That evening, after completing the crime-scene investigation, Gage went to the alleged killer's home. Melville's car wasn't present, and no one answered the door. No one had seen the man or his car during the first few hours following the murder, but shortly after leaving Melville's home in the Bloomington area, Gage passed a car going the other direction. It was not the blue Cadillac, but knowing what Melville looked like and thinking it could be him, Gage turned his Explorer and caught up with the vehicle.

He followed it for a moment, and then he hit him with his red light. The car, a light-green Toyota, sped up. Gage stayed right on its tail as he called for backup. To his surprise, the car screeched to a stop against the curb at Melville's home. The driver jumped from the vehicle and ran for his front door. Gage leaped from his own vehicle and ran hard after the man he was now positive was Bronson Melville. Gage was younger than Melville and in much better shape—Melville was somewhat overweight and ran slowly—and had him by the collar as the fugitive attempted to unlock his front door while at the same time attempting to pull a pistol from a shoulder holster.

Gage slammed him against the door and slapped cuffs on his thick wrists. The suspect's Glock fell to the ground, and Gage kicked the gun out of the way. Then he spun Melville around and informed him he was under arrest for the murder of Duane Trahan. But before Gage even had a chance to inform the suspect of his Miranda rights, he blurted, "Duane had it coming. He stole my girlfriend from me." No sooner had the words left his mouth than he apparently came to his senses and said, "You can't use that against me. You didn't inform me of my rights."

"You didn't give me time," Gage responded, pretty sure that what Melville had said would be admissible in court as a spontaneous utterance. He read him his rights at that point, and Melville continued to insist Gage couldn't use the earlier admission against him. By then a patrol unit had arrived at the address, and two uniformed officers joined Gage and his prisoner on the front porch. "He has blood splatter on his jacket," Gage told them. He glanced down and added, "And on his pants and his shoes. Take him to jail and hold him until I get there. I need to have his car towed, and then I'll come in to interview him."

Two neighbors approached Gage and told him if he needed them to testify, they would. Both claimed they had heard Melville say the victim "had it coming," an admission of sorts, so Gage took their names and phone numbers and asked them to make written statements and give them to him before he left Melville's home.

After he had received the statements, he spoke to several other neighbors. One of them claimed that just the previous evening Melville had threatened to "take care of Duane Trahan." A couple of others had heard the same thing. They all spoke of Melville as a loud, dishonest man most of them didn't like, despite his popularity with his radio audience. They made it clear to Gage that Melville's radio fans didn't know him like they did. They also mentioned Bronson had a brother, a shady ex-con who often came around, frequently with some rough-looking friends. They knew only two names: the brother was Alvin, and there was another guy they knew only as Dwight. They also mentioned that once in a while a guy in a loud, fancy silver pickup truck was there.

At the jail, the accused killer was placed in prisoner clothing, and his clothes and shoes were confiscated as evidence, along with the pistol that had been taken from where he'd dropped it at the arrest scene.

Before the defendant was locked up, Gage, assisted by Detective Lieutenant Bill Dollison and Detective Sergeant Jon Hanks, ushered him into an interview room for questioning. Melville declared his innocence loudly but refused to answer questions. He was allowed to call an attorney, and a few minutes later JC Hass, Attorney at Law, strode in and informed the officers that the interview was over. Gage groaned. *Anybody but Hass,* he thought.

The lawyer was allowed a few minutes alone with his client, and then Melville was taken back to a cell, continuing to loudly assert his innocence.

The officers conferred for a few minutes and then returned to the police department, where the lieutenant and the police chief joined them. The captain missed that meeting, as he was overseas on vacation.

Gage explained to the others how the arrest went down and reviewed the evidence he had collected. He mentioned the confession, the spontaneous utterance, Melville had shouted before he'd been informed of his rights. He then produced the signed statements of the man and woman who had heard him say it from the yard next door. He also showed his superiors the statements of those who had heard the accused say he was going to take care of Duane Trahan.

"I never did like the guy," Lieutenant Dollison said. "And it sounds like, from what you gathered from his neighbors, they don't like him either. Apparently he doesn't have very classy friends. It looks like we have a solid case against him. Good work, Gage."

That night, on radio and television newscasts, Attorney JC Hass stated that Melville was innocent and that the arresting officer was jumping to clearly erroneous conclusions when he'd made the arrest.

"The inexperienced young detective is trying to make a name for himself," Hass said. "He just returned yesterday from a three-day scuba-diving venture at Lake Powell. He should have kept diving for another day; maybe then an experienced officer would have handled the case, one who isn't so gullible. Detective Tipton actually believed the lies of a very shady woman by the name of Brea Burr who was angry at Melville for ending their relationship and accused him falsely in retaliation. I will prove Melville is innocent. Tipton has no credible evidence. Bronson Melville will soon be free and back on his very popular radio program."

No mention was made of the other witnesses, but JC Hass most likely didn't know about the statements Bronson's neighbors had made.

Contrary to what Hass had declared, however, Melville was soon charged with murder and held without bond in the county jail.

CHAPTER ONE

Three weeks later

It was an ordinary Monday evening in late May and an extraordinary first kiss on the doorstep. I'd been dating Denadene Stegner for several weeks, and I probably should have kissed her before tonight, but I didn't get to be twenty-eight and still single by being overaggressive. I'd dated a fair number of ladies over the years, but until I met Denadene at a regional young single adult activity in St. George, I simply had never felt the buzz.

Old habits are hard to break. I was in no hurry and had no intention of pushing the relationship. I liked her a lot, but I was not in love with her—not yet, at least—and maybe I never would be. Denadene seemed patient enough. She still dated other guys. I knew about her dates because she'd mentioned them to me. She'd even named one of them: Isaac Sparks. She'd actually mentioned him three or four times. Seemed to think he was a pretty good guy.

Like Denadene, I'd been on a date with someone else too since our first one. But for the past few weeks, I hadn't asked anyone else out. I told myself it was just because I hadn't really had the opportunity to date others, but I had to admit I enjoyed her company a lot.

I figured I had time to find out for myself if she was *the one* and to move the relationship forward if that's what I wanted to do. That first kiss had me thinking maybe I *should* move it forward. It really was nice. I supposed taking my time would also give her time to decide if I might be a mistake in her life or if Isaac Sparks or the other guy she'd dated might be a better prospect than me or if she was even interested in a serious relationship with anyone. She was twenty-four and had been through a very bad, childless marriage that had ended two years ago. She had told me a couple of times she didn't intend to ever make the same mistake again. So even though deep down I thought I wanted to, I didn't push her. That first kiss had been a big step for me. I had never been the kissing kind. That kiss had surprised me. I wondered, though, if she kissed the other guys she dated like she had kissed me. But I didn't think I really wanted to know.

We'd been to dinner and a movie and talked about taking an overnight trip to Zion National Park the following Friday and Saturday—I had those days off work—but Denadene wasn't sure if she had to work on Friday or not. She told me she wanted to go, although I wasn't sure she meant it. I hoped an overnight date (I was more than happy to pay for two rooms) wasn't pushing too much. She'd spoken to her boss, attorney JC Hass, that morning about getting the day off, but he'd told her to check with him in a day or two, as he might need her for some work on a high-profile case in which he was defending a local radio personality, Bronson Melville, charged with murder.

Melville was popular with some of the local folks, and his arrest had stirred a lot of gossip and even anger among his fans. His neighbors and a lot of other people were glad he was in jail. They were not fans. But the general public had no idea how solid the evidence we had collected against Melville was. So as not to stir things up further, we kept that information quiet, as did the prosecutor's office. Attorney Hass denied we had any credible evidence against his client and claimed I had fabricated it or, in the alternative, that I believed a witness Hass said was lying. We didn't care what Hass thought. What mattered was what we could prove in court, and we had what we needed and more to convict his client of first-degree murder.

Denadene and I had both tried not to let it happen, but the murder case was a bit of a thorn between us. She was a legal secretary and was loyal to her boss, whom I considered to be a first-class jerk. I had trodden lightly with her about my feelings for the guy. Hass and I had tangled in court before. Like the public, Denadene didn't know how much solid evidence we had against her boss's client. I discussed none of the particulars with her. All I could tell her was that I was confident we would get a conviction. On the other hand, JC Hass repeatedly told Denadene it had been a very bad arrest and kept insisting the *supposed* witness, Brea Burr, was a known liar who had it in for his client and would be destroyed in court if she was foolish enough to testify. He also told her the arresting officer was trying to make a name for himself.

Of course, I was the officer Denadene's boss repeatedly tried to tear down, and she knew it. I had arrested Bronson Melville, and I had no doubt about his guilt. Melville was a very bad man, one who had pulled the shades over the eyes of much of the public. As JC Hass spread his lies, I, with the help of some of my colleagues, continued to build on the already-solid case.

But Hass didn't know I was the man his legal secretary was dating quite regularly and for whom she wanted the day off. At least, that's what Denadene had told me, and I had no reason not to believe her. She had expressed no desire to tell her boss, which was fine with me. He was a competent attorney but was blatantly dishonest, and he had an extremely overinflated ego. If he'd known Denadene's date was to be with the arresting officer on his high-profile case, he would have, I was certain, told her she had to work on Friday.

"I'll call you," she told me shortly after that sweet kiss on her doorstep.

"When?" I asked.

"I should know by Wednesday," she said, smiling at me. "I made JC promise to let me know by then."

"That'll work," I said. Then I grinned at her. "Bat those pretty baby-blue eyes of yours, and he'll be sure to let you have the day off."

She punched me lightly on the shoulder. "You know I have no intention of encouraging him."

Hass was also a divorcé, except he'd been through three marriages. The man was more than twenty years older than Denadene, but that hadn't stopped him from asking her out several times. She told me she kept their relationship strictly professional, but I knew he'd take her out if she showed the least amount of interest.

"I know," I said. "I was just kidding. I'd better go. I have to interview a couple of people tomorrow about the Melville case. One of them is expecting me early in the morning."

She smiled. "Okay. It's been a wonderful evening, Gage. I promise I'll call," she reiterated. "I think I will be able to persuade JC to give me the day off. I really do want to go with you."

"I'll be anxiously awaiting your call," I replied. I thought about kissing her one more time, but that would be pushing it, and I was not a pusher in the romantic arena. So I simply waited until she had gone inside and shut the door to her apartment and then headed back to my blue Ford pickup.

Denadene did not call me on Wednesday, nor did she call me on Thursday. I was anxious to know if she could go with me, and I was already feeling disappointment. Maybe she didn't want to go after all. But I tried her cell phone a half dozen times anyway. It went to voicemail each time. I had optimistically booked a couple of rooms and needed to cancel them soon if we were not going. I was feeling desperate, so I called the JC Hass Law Office early on Thursday afternoon.

I didn't recognize the voice of the woman who answered. After telling her I needed to talk to Denadene, she said, "Ms. Stegner did not come to work yesterday, so Mr. Hass asked me to come in and help out."

"And you are?" I asked.

"My name is Lily Kwick," she said. "I've covered for Ms. Stegner a number of times before."

"She didn't come in? That makes no sense," I said anxiously. "She promised she would call me either yesterday or today and she hasn't."

"I'm sorry, but I didn't catch your name," the temp said.

"I'm Detective Gage Tipton," I said reluctantly. I hadn't wanted to identify myself to that particular law office.

"Oh," Lily said in a tone that indicated my name was an unsavory combination of nasty words. "Mr. Hass would not want her to speak with you, Detective Tipton. Any communications he has about the Melville matter will be with the prosecutor in the case. But I'll tell him you called."

"No, that's okay," I said. "Please don't bother. I can speak with the prosecutor as well." I added that last bit because I didn't want to let her know my interest in speaking with Denadene was personal and had nothing to do with the murder case. Mrs. Kwick could think what she wanted. "Thanks for your time, Mrs. Kwick."

"*Ms.* Kwick," she said with a bit of a growl and ended the call before I could apologize for my blunder.

I stared at my phone for a moment, my mind in a whirl. I wondered if I'd been mistaken to think Denadene enjoyed my company and wanted to continue to date me. But I also wondered if Hass had discovered *who* Denadene wanted to go with on Friday, and if he had dismissed her from his one-man law firm because of his intense dislike of me.

But that didn't make a lot of sense. I mean, if he had fired her, she would still have called me. I believed her to be a woman of her word. The worry that had been eating at me became a distinct discomfort in my stomach. I put my phone in my pocket, walked out of the police station, and drove directly to Denadene's apartment in my official, unmarked, tan Ford Explorer. Her dark-blue Volkswagen Jetta was not in her assigned parking space.

I parked my car in her designated spot and ran up the stairs to her apartment. I stood where we had shared our first kiss on Monday night and rang the doorbell. I waited, wondering if I cared for her more than I had let myself believe. Maybe she was giving up on me and didn't want to talk to me. I thrust that uncomfortable thought aside and rapped on the door with my knuckles. There was no answer.

I finally gave up and walked back down the stairs to my Explorer. I had met Denadene's parents and felt comfortable with them, even though they knew that at that point Denadene and I were just good friends who were dating and nothing more. She'd grown up in Cedar City, and her parents still lived there. I sat in the driver's seat and found their home phone number and called. Her mother answered, and I said, "Hi, Mrs. Garford. This is Gage Tipton."

"Hello, Gage. I'm glad you called," she said. "Perhaps you can tell me what's going on with our daughter. We can't get her to answer her cell. It's not like her."

That statement did not relieve my angst in the least. "I'm sorry," I said. "That was why I was calling you. I can't seem to reach her either. I haven't spoken with her since Monday. She was going to call me about a trip we had planned for the weekend, but I haven't heard from her."

"She told me about the trip," her mother said. "She was very excited. Her father and I thought maybe you two had decided to leave early. I even tried to reach her at the law office yesterday, but some other woman answered the phone. She was quite rude to me."

"I got the same treatment," I said. "She told me Denadene had failed to come to work yesterday morning and she was filling in for her."

"She told you that?" Mrs. Garford asked. "She told me Denadene had quit and she had taken her place." Mrs. Garford was starting to sound frantic. "I've been trying to reach her since I spoke with that woman yesterday afternoon. I know Denadene is uncomfortable with her boss, but she is loyal to him. She would never just quit and leave him hanging unless she felt threatened in some way, and I don't believe she has."

As she spoke, I found myself wondering why Ms. Kwick would tell me one thing but Denadene's mother another. Which of the two versions was the truth? Or were they both lies? I also wondered why Denadene had never told me about her discomfort around Hass. She had only told me he'd asked her out and she had declined. As far as I knew, that was the end of it.

"Would you mind going by her apartment to make sure she's okay? Maybe she's sick and her cell phone is dead," Mrs. Garford said.

"I'm actually here now. Her car is gone, and she didn't answer her door," I said.

There was a long silence, and Mrs. Garford was breathing heavily into the phone. "Gage, I'm really worried. I'm afraid something has happened to her. I don't know what to do." I could hear soft sobbing.

"It's been more than twenty-four hours since anyone has seen her, so I can list her as missing. We'll find her."

The first thing I did after getting back to the office was put an attempt to locate (ATL) out on Denadene and her blue Volkswagen Jetta. Just in case, I called the Dixie Regional Medical Center. I had to identify myself as an officer before anyone would tell me she was not a patient there. I officially filed a missing person report with my department. Finally, despite knowing I would not be well received, I headed for the law office of JC Hass.

A short, plump lady in her mid-fifties, whom I assumed must be Ms. Lily Kwick, said with a smile as I stepped in, "Good afternoon, sir. Are you in need of the legal services of Mr. Hass?"

"Just answers from him will do fine," I said as I pulled out my ID and showed it to her. "I'll need a few minutes of his time."

The woman let her smile slip. She straightened her short grayish-brown hair with a quick snap of her wrist. "Detective, Mr. Hass has no desire to speak with you. I thought I made that clear when you called. It would be highly improper since he is defending the man he told me you falsely arrested."

I stepped close to her desk—Denadene's desk, actually—and leaned toward her. "Ms. Kwick, you seem like a very nice woman, but you are wrong on two counts. First, Mr. Melville is guilty of murder, and we will prove it. Second, I don't want to talk to Mr. Hass about his client's case. I want to speak to him about Ms. Stegner. Now, you can either buzz his office and tell him I'm coming back to speak with him, or I will announce myself when I go back."

"Don't you dare! That is not allowed," she said testily.

"This is only your second day, Ms. Kwick, and you are temporary, so I don't think it's up to you to decide if I speak to Mr. Hass or not," I said, trying hard to restrain my growing anger. "Either buzz his office and tell him I'm here to see him, or I will go back there unannounced."

I stared at her, and she stared back, stubbornly shaking her head but not allowing her eyes to meet mine. Finally she said, "He's not in, Detective."

I didn't believe her. Surely she would have told me that right away if it were true. I straightened up, turned, and walked past her desk toward the office with the brass nameplate that read *JC Hass*.

"You can't do that," she shouted after me.

I did not reply—simply knocked on the door. "Who is it?" a male voice called from inside.

I grabbed the doorknob, turned it, and stepped inside. As I suspected, Ms. Kwick had been covering for Hass. "I'm sorry to bother you, sir," I said as Hass pushed his chair back from his desk and frowned. I wasn't sorry in the least.

"Who are you, and what do you want? You have no business barging in here like this. I told Ms. Kwick I was not to be disturbed," he said angrily as he rose to his feet and pointed a finger at me. "If you need an appointment, schedule it with her."

So he didn't even recognize me. That actually made me angrier than I already had been at the guy. "I am not here seeking legal advice, Mr. Hass. If I needed legal advice, you are the last person I would come to. No, I'm the officer you've been so busily maligning," I said. "I'm Detective Gage Tipton. But I'm not here to discuss the Melville case. I'd like to know why Denadene quit her job with you."

A puzzled look came over his face, and he plopped back into his chair. "What are you talking about? She didn't quit. She didn't show up for work yesterday morning, which is very uncharacteristic. I'm worried about her. She's not answering her phone. She would have given me appropriate notice if she were going to quit, but she likes working here. She likes *me*. What makes you think she quit?"

"That's what Ms. Kwick told Denadene's mother," I answered, jerking a thumb toward the front office. "Either way, Denadene is missing, and I am trying to locate her."

"Missing?" Hass said as he leaned forward in his chair. "I figured she was home with the flu or something."

I nodded. "A formal report has been filed." I didn't think he needed to know I had filed the report myself. "Her car is gone too. Her parents are distraught. They were particularly upset when your temp told them she had quit her job. Denadene hadn't mentioned she'd intended to quit."

"Lily said that?" Hass asked. He was staring past me, but he jerked his eyes back and said, "Denadene did not quit; that I can assure you. She's a good friend and an excellent legal secretary—the best I've ever had. I'll straighten out the misunderstanding with Lily."

"That's between you and Ms. Kwick. I'm concerned about locating Ms. Stegner. When did you last see her?"

"That would be Tuesday at about six when we closed the office for the evening. I walked with her out to her car. She seemed just fine. She gave no indication she might not be in the next day."

"I'm told she was planning to call a friend about whether you were giving her the day off on Friday," I said. "They had plans to go out of town."

"Do you know that for a fact?" Hass asked.

"Yes, I do. I'm taking her disappearance very seriously, speaking to people who might be able to help me, people she knew."

"I'm surprised she didn't call her friend." He hesitated, as if thinking about what he wanted to say next. Finally he went on. "I told her she could have Friday off, and she thanked me. When she didn't come in yesterday, I tried reaching her two or three times and finally phoned the temp agency and asked them to arrange for Ms. Kwick to cover for her."

My stomach roiled, and I felt chills on my arms. Something was very wrong.

I had never been invited to sit, so I turned toward the door. Then I stopped and turned back. "Please call me if you hear from her, Mr. Hass." I pulled a card from my pocket and dropped it onto his desk.

I was halfway out the door when Hass said, "You believed the lies of a scorned and unsavory woman and arrested an innocent man, Detective. You need to wise up and arrest the right person, if you're smart enough to figure out who that might be."

I did not turn around. "We'll see who needs to wise up," I said over my shoulder. I stopped a moment later at Denadene's desk, where Ms. Kwick was squirming uncomfortably. "In the future, don't lie to me," I growled. "And don't lie to Denadene's parents."

I left her red-faced and stammering as I went out the door and slammed it behind me.